MICHAEL MCGILLICUDDY AND THE MOST AMAZING RACE

A NOVEL BY

TREVOR A. DUTCHER

Michael McGillicuddy and the Most Amazing Race

ISBN: 978-1-7330990-1-1

Contact the author at:

trevor@trevordutcher.com

http://www.trevordutcher.com

For My Family.
Without your undying support and encouragement, this never would have happened.

You know all those things you've always wanted to go do? You should go do them.

— E J Lamprey

1

AT THE HOMESTEAD

Outskirts of London, 1880.

Young Michael McGillicuddy sat in the workshop across from his father, Seamus, at an old wooden table, aged just eleven. It was Michael's eleventh birthday, no less. They had just returned to the workshop from gathering some wood to feed a small pot belly stove in the corner, its meager flames providing a bit of warmth, and a touch of extra light. Seamus sat on his stool, hunched over, with his elbows on the table and his teacup set to the side. He was focused on his work, staring through thick magnifying goggles, like watchmakers use, fitted with magnifying lenses that flip down over the eye, each lens providing greater magnification than the last. The goggles enabled him to work on the tiniest of gears, with the best visibility into the delicate clockwork machinery he was handling. He held a device in his left hand and turned a screwdriver with his right. Michael sat with eager anticipation, watching his father intently.

He was a precocious child, to say the least. And although wise, capable and mature beyond his years, he was still gangly, with scrawny arms and legs which he struggled to control gracefully.

With his tousled brown hair and a light dusting of freckles across his nose, he was just an average eleven-year-old boy by most appearances, and just awkward enough to be teased pretty regularly at school.

They were building a mechanical device together. It was roughly a foot tall, and person-shaped in the most basic possible sense. It had a metal, heavy-framed torso, a head and metal arms and legs that moved independent of each other. The table was crowded with jars of rivets and screws, and other spare parts, and the tools were all neatly sorted. Michael had pulled them from Seamus' tool chest and held them at the ready, in case his father needed help. They had spent endless hours here, sorting, tinkering and pulling things in and out of that old chest. Although Michael didn't realize it yet, Seamus planned to give the chest to his son. It would be his birthday gift, tonight, just after supper was finished.

While he waited to help, Michael organized the parts into proper jars and groupings. If parts didn't already have their own jar, he sorted them into neatly stacked piles, first by type, then by shape, then by size. Washers with washers. Nuts with nuts. Bolts with bolts. All arranged in symmetrical stacks. From a very early age, Michael craved order, neatness and symmetry. This wasn't Seamus' teaching, but Michael's own compulsion. He couldn't help himself.

The family was of modest means, and like their home, the workshop was simple. Its walls were lined with wood cabinets and black countertops. The cabinets were filled with tools, spare parts and other items of varying utility that Seamus had collected over the years. They had been working on this project for months and Michael was eager for the payoff.

"Can I close him up now?" Michael asked.

"It's ready. Go ahead, son."

"What are they called again?"

"Automaton, it's a small machine that moves on its own, and in some ways acts like a person," Seamus said. "Some are small and simple, like this one. Others are big and more complex. Some are the same size as me, if you can believe that. "

"Au-TOM-a-ton." Michael repeated, nodding in agreement.

Michael smiled. His gaze went soft, and he found himself stuck in a distant stare. His imagination had run off without him again, considering all the things he could build, but after a moment, his attention snapped back to the workshop with a jolt. It was time. He could barely contain his excitement. He held the figurine in his hand and studied its makeup. Inside the torso of the small automaton, he could see all the rockers, springs and gears. It looked like the inside of a clock, but far more complicated. It was a beautiful piece of machinery, the most amazing thing Michael had ever seen. It was so intricate, so fine and so unbelievably complicated for something that he could hold in his hand. The idea, the automaton's design, was actually his own. Seamus had simply helped build it. Michael picked up the chest plate from the table and screwed it shut, covering up all of its delicate inner mechanics.

"This is our best one yet," Michael said.

"I think you're right," Seamus said. "You thought up a good one, son. I'm very impressed. Now go on, wind it up."

Seamus couldn't decide who was more excited; him or Michael. He handed over a key, like the ones used to wind music boxes, and Michael pushed the key into its lower back. He wound its springs tight and set it on the table top. As he pressed a button in the back, just between the shoulders, the automaton set in motion. It walked smoothly across the table, feet stepping and arms rocking in offsetting rhythm to keep balance. Michael stared in amazement with his mouth hanging open. Seamus stared at his son, beaming with pride.

"It's amazing," Michael whispered.

"You're really going to be something," Seamus said.

"Yeah. Something."

Michael was preoccupied by its hypnotic movement.

"Can we add the piston spear on its arm tomorrow?" he asked.

"The piston spear is the best weapon there is, hard to beat in competition."

"Of course we can," Seamus said with a smile. "You have a very real gift, Michael. You know that right?"

"You mean my birthday gift?"

"No, son. Not your birthday gift. I'm talking about your vision. Your ability to imagine things out of thin air, and then build them. Your ability to see things, patterns and solutions, things that other people don't see. It's extraordinary. What do you plan to do with it?"

Michael wiped his nose with the back of his wrist and sniffed.

"Well, I don't know. I guess I can help you. Maybe someday I can be in your crew, for one of your races. I can help you with the engines, and fix things if they break. Like you do at the factory."

"Maybe you could, son. I would like that very much. And that day may not be far off. I'm preparing for a race right now, you know. I have a lot of work to do to get my vehicles in shape, and I could certainly use an extra set of hands. They're beat up rather badly from the last one."

Michael smiled and nodded, wiping his nose again.

"Ok, Poppa. I can help you. We can be partners."

Seamus rustled the hair on top of Michael's head with his hand. He smiled down adoringly at his son and nodded toward the house.

"Mum called us in for supper some time ago. It's never wise to keep her waiting," he said. "So, in you go."

Michael grumbled. Not ready to leave the workshop yet, he searched for a way to stretch their time together. His eyes dashed left and right. He had it.

"Tell me again about the time you beat the Baron, Poppa!"

Seamus's belly shook as he laughed.

"That was a long time ago, Michael, but alright."

Seamus pretended it was a chore. But in truth, he never grew tired of telling it, not to Michael or anyone else for that matter. But he especially liked telling Michael.

"We were near the end," he started, "I was in my dirigible, and the Baron was in his. It was just me against him! There was no one else in sight."

Seamus paused for dramatic effect and finished his tea, gulping it down slowly, staring at Michael as he drank. Michael stared on with wide-eyed anticipation, desperately waiting for the next little morsel. Seamus set his teacup down and continued.

"We'd been through all manner of peril. Storms. Fires. Sabotage."

"Don't forget the sea creatures!" Michael shouted, wagging his finger at Seamus.

"Yes, even horrible sea creatures!" Seamus roared.

He held his hands up with his fingers curled like large, foreboding hooks.

"With hooks for hands! Hooks I tell you! We were tattered and torn, exhausted from our journey."

"Yes!" Michael nodded. "And then…"

"The Baron and I were flying neck-and-neck. He was pulling away from me, just as we approached the finish line. He extended his lead, and he was starting to move out of reach."

"And then…?"

"And then, on the brink of loss, ready to embrace my own defeat, I had an idea. A brilliant idea it was. I went to the engine compartment. I ripped off the cover. I opened the baffle to its widest possible setting. It was pure insanity, something the average man would never dare try. It would give me the extra bit of speed I needed to win, but the cost would be high. The engine would run hot, and maybe even blow. It was a risk like none I'd ever taken!"

"And then…?"

The anticipation was killing him. Seamus leaned back on the counter.

"And then I waited to see if it worked."

"But what then, Poppa? Say the next part."

"Then my dirigible picked up speed, then a little more, and

more still. The engine hummed. The rotors whirred, and pushed me through the air. The engine glowed red. I didn't know if it would last!"

"And then…?"

"I was gaining on the Baron, inching closer and closer. Finally, in the last hundred feet or so, I barely passed him. I won the race by a hair. Maybe two hairs, but not much more! As I crossed the finish line, the seals on the engine blew. Steam shot everywhere. My craft slowed, and the engine was ruined. But not before I had reached out and snatched a victory straight from the Baron's own two hands! I took it right from him."

"Yes, and then…?"

The pitch in Michael's voice rose. His eyes widened, and his face beamed with joy. His fists were clenched, pumping up and down. This was his favorite part.

"Keep going, Poppa. Then what?"

"I anchored my dirigible, and I slid down a rope to the cheering masses. I was crowned the winner and awarded my prize! I was hoisted up on the shoulders of all, and I was celebrated for a most amazing victory!"

As Seamus went on, he stepped around the table and hoisted Michael up on his big, burly shoulder and pranced around the table, bouncing him up and down as if Michael himself had won. Michael laughed out loud with the pure and uninhibited joy that only a child can experience.

"Go around again, Poppa!"

Seamus pranced around the table again, bouncing up and down.

"Sea-mus! Sea-mus! Sea-mus!" he chanted. "They cheered my name!"

Michael grinned as he hugged his father's head. He pranced another lap, and Soairse yelled from the house again.

"Seamus, get in here and eat right now, or you'll be sleeping with the horses!"

Hearing her call, he took a final victory lap around the table. Then he slowed and lowered Michael to the ground gently. He stared down at his son, with doting eyes.

"We'd really better get in there, son," he said with a huff. "It's time."

He was short of breath.

"Yeah. I guess."

Michael's words hung heavy with disappointment. As he walked to the workshop door to head back to the house, he had one last idea. He stared up the muddy path that led back to the house.

"I'll race you to the porch, Poppa!"

Michael turned and looked back at Seamus with his bright-eyed look, ready to run. But as he turned, his face went blank.

"Just give me a second, Michael."

"Are you alright?" he asked.

Seamus was leaning over, with one hand on the workshop table bracing himself. His other hand was on his chest.

"I may have overdone it, Michael, with all that bouncing..."

Seamus paused.

"Just give me a second, then we'll run up."

Fear shone through in his eyes and resounded in his voice. His breath was labored.

"Alright, Poppa."

"Yes, just. Another second."

Seamus winced and clutched his chest. With a long groan, he collapsed to the floor. Michael ran to his side, terrified. His eyes welled up. Tears streamed down his cheeks.

"I'm sorry, Poppa," he uttered meekly.

Tears continued to stream.

"Please wake up. I'm sorry! I won't ask you bounce me anymore!"

Seamus didn't respond.

"Poppa?"

2

JOHN MEETS CYRIL

Paris, 1895. Fifteen Years Later

John Ramshorn sat on the balcony of his two-story Paris flat, enjoying his typical breakfast of Earl Grey tea and a toasted English muffin with strawberry jam. It was the perfect kind of morning, one where the warm spring sun pressed through the cool, moist air warming the body inside and out. Birds chirped softly in the background, and the smell of fresh-baked pastries from the nearby *boulangerie* wafted through the air. In the distance, John caught a glimpse of the newly erected Eiffel Tower, built for the most recent World's Fair, set against the background of the Seine. A British expatriate, he had moved to Paris ten years prior, originally for work, as a lecturer teaching mechanical engineering at the university. But he stayed for his love of the city.

In the streets below, the city was coming to life. Merchants propped up wooden window coverings and opened the doors to their shops. The morning sun hung low in the sky and glistened off the moist cobblestones of the *Rue de l'Universite*, creating just a silhouette of Leo, the local vegetable monger, setting out his crates of onions, beets and carrots.

"Good morning, Leo!" John shouted down.

"Morning, John."

"Today is going to be an amazing day, Leo."

"You say that every day, John."

"And every day I turn out to be right!" John yelled back, with a big jolly laugh.

The approaching sound of clopping hooves pulling carriage wheels over cobblestones meant the newspapers would be dropped off at the corner soon, and John could get started on his day. He inhaled deeply, enjoying the morning air and all that it had to offer. Then he exhaled in a long, relaxed sigh. As he finished his last sip of tea and stood to clear his dishes, he heard a knock at the front door.

Surprised, John shuffled through his living space as briskly as he could, in from the balcony and through the kitchen, down the stairs, in between the sofa and the large chest that sat the front room, and finally over to the door. On the way, he pulled his robe tight and used his fingernail to scrape off a bit of dried food. It hardly made a difference. John's appearance was as slovenly and disheveled as it ever was. He used his hands to push his long, black, unkempt hair out of his face and smooth his gnarly beard. As he did, he wiped away a stray dab of strawberry jam, and more than a couple of crumbs.

When he opened the door, he saw a tall, slender, middle-aged man standing on his stoop, sharply dressed in a smart grey suit and derby hat, with a watch chain hanging from the pocket of his vest. He cut an impressive figure, both in appearance and in stature, wearing wire-framed spectacles with round lenses, a perfect push-broom mustache, and spit-shined shoes with spats. His appearance was flawless. John looked him up and down with a *humph*, aware of the contrast.

The man held a walking cane topped with the silver head of a bulldog in his right hand. His left hand hung at his side, gripping a metallic device. It was a brass tube, roughly a foot long and two inches wide, with copper and bronze adornment. The tube was capped at each end by bronze fittings affixed with semi-spherical clear gems set in the ends.

"John Ramshorn?" the man asked.

He spoke in a brusque manner, with a classic English accent.

"Yes," John replied, unimpressed.

"My name is Cyril Hastings, and I have something for you. It is very important. May I come in?"

John glanced down at the brass apparatus knowingly.

"Yes. *Absolutely.*"

He stepped to the side and waved the man in.

3

MICHAEL MEETS CYRIL

Michael's Homestead, Outskirts of London
Four days later

Michael McGillicuddy, a handsome young man, now aged twenty-six, sat at the table in his workshop tinkering with his latest project. He had been awake since well before dawn, enthralled with a new idea that came to him in his sleep. It wasn't the first time, not even close. It wasn't perfect yet, but he was working on a prototype.

As he had been for the duration of his entire childhood, Michael remained a relentless gadgeteer, an eternal tinkerer, and an inventor of at least local renown. It was his gift and his passion, but it was also a distraction. A constant distraction, and today was no different. He gasped, and reached for his pocket watch.

"Oh, no, I'm late again," he said.

He grabbed his coat and satchel from the counter and rushed toward the door, deep in thought. As he left the workshop, he collided with a man standing in the doorway.

"Oh, I'm terribly sorry. I didn't even see you there."

"Clearly," the man said. "It seems you were focused on something other than successful navigation around human beings. Perhaps you could put your gadgets away, and focus on walking."

The man dusted himself off.

"Michael McGillicuddy, I presume?"

"Yes," Michael said, a little confused. "But I really need to go, I need to get to the factory, and in a hurry. How may I help you?"

"My name is Cyril Hastings, and I have something for you. It's very important. May I come in?"

"What is this about?"

"Some people call me the Messenger."

"Who calls you that?"

"That is neither here, nor there. I have an extraordinary opportunity for you. It is not for the faint of heart, weak of mind or those lacking intestinal fortitude. You have been personally selected, invited, one might even say *challenged*, to participate in a most difficult, but rewarding endeavor."

"Selected? By whom?"

The Messenger stared back in silence.

The hair on the back of Michael's neck stood on end. His skin tingled, and his eyes opened wide.

"May-I-come-in?" the Messenger repeated impatiently, through clenched teeth.

"I know what this is about. You want me to be in the race."

"I am sure I have no idea what you're talking about. Be that as it may, shall I leave this Chrysalis with you?"

The Messenger extended his arm toward Michael and offered him a tubular brass apparatus. As he offered it to Michael, arm outstretched, he cocked his head and raised one eyebrow. He stared at Michael, considering his worthiness to receive it.

Michael reached out to grab the Chrysalis, remembering once again that he had to go to work. He gave it a quick tug, but the Messenger didn't let it go.

"May I?" Michael asked impatiently.

The Messenger held it tight in his iron grip.

"Do not take this lightly, young McGillicuddy. Far greater men than you have perished in such pursuits."

"My father was a multi-winner. I know plenty, he told me all about it."

"Yes, very well then," the Messenger said with an air of contempt. "Far be it from me to stand between you and something you understand so well; something you believe you're so well prepared for. Godspeed, young McGillicuddy. Godspeed."

He released the Chrysalis to Michael and tipped his cap. Michael thrust the Chrysalis into his satchel and rushed past in a hurry to get to work. The Messenger watched as Michael trotted to his buggy, and drove off toward town.

"You have no idea what you're getting yourself into, McGillicuddy," he mumbled. "None whatsoever."

4

MICHAEL RUSHES TO WORK

Michael ran through the back door at work, hoping to enter unnoticed.

"McGillicuddy!" the voice belted out.

"Bang to rights," he mumbled to himself.

"Sorry I'm late, Mr. Wentworth."

"Don't you mean late *again*?"

"Yes, right. Sorry I'm late again, Mr. Wentworth. I had a very strange visit from someone, and got delayed. It won't happen again."

"You were visiting for an hour? On my time? Not good, McGillicuddy," he said, tapping his watch, "not good at all. I'm trying to run a business here. One of my lines shut down while you were out visiting, and now I'm losing money because I'm not making any product. If you weren't so good, I'd fire you right here on the spot. Fix it, McGillicuddy. Now!"

"Yes, of course, which machine is it? I'll get right on it, Mr. Wentworth."

"The Whistling Gypsy."

"Whistling Gypsy. Right, I'm on it."

Mr. Wentworth had his own names for the machines, based on

the noises they made, or things they reminded him of. The Whistling Gypsy was one. The 'Wheezing Geezer' and 'Tommy Tip-Tap' were two others. The factory was a massive facility, one that could employ the better part of a small town. There were machines everywhere, all of which Michael, or his father, or even his grandfather before him, had built or repaired at one time or another. Boilers poured out steam, release valves whistled, conveyor belts moved boxes down the lines, and the sounds of all the machines combined into a soothing hum that Michael found relaxing. He was prone to daydreams and distraction, but on the factory floor, the hum of all the machines helped him find a peaceful focus. After a long walk across the production floor, he arrived at the Whistling Gypsy where he was met by Colin, the line-worker assigned to work the machine.

"Wentworth is pretty steamed, Michael. Where the hell were you?" Colin said in his deep, gravely voice.

"It's not important where I was, Colin, I'm here now. What's going on?"

"Same as always, mate. It was running just fine. And then it stopped running."

"Useful."

"Yeah, well if I knew what was wrong with it, then I could fix it myself now, couldn't I? And then we wouldn't really need you here. Fancy that."

"Did you check to make sure the clutch is engaged?"

"It's engaged," Colin said.

Michael checked the clutch anyway.

"Ok, the clutch is engaged."

"I told you it was engaged. You didn't believe me?"

"What about the back bushings, did you check the bushings? Did they slip out of place again?"

"Nope, they're perfect," Colin said, annoyed.

Michael checked the bushings.

"Ok. The bushings look good. Let's see what we have here."

Michael pressed the button to start the machine back up. It rattled, roared and shimmied back to life, but only for a second. As it ground back to a halt, there was a high-pitched squeal of metal grinding on metal. Then it fell silent.

"You didn't fill the oil reservoir today, did you, Colin?"

"Um, yeah, I'm sure I must have. Right? I mean yeah, I always fill the oil reservoir. Standard procedure, mate. Step one."

Michael peeked into the reservoir.

"It's bone dry, Colin! You've cooked it. This could take a whole day to fix. I need my tools."

As he turned, Colin grabbed his arm.

"So listen, Michael. If Wentworth finds out about this, it's my neck."

Michael understood that as well as anybody.

"Yeah," Michael said. "I'm not sure how they packed so much anger into that tiny little man, but somehow they did. Stunning achievement."

"Seriously, mate. He'll show me the door. Are you, you know, are you sure it's not something else? I suggest that maybe you can check again, to make sure that that's really what the problem is, and, you know, not something else. Do you follow me?"

Michael sighed.

"Follow you? Good lord, I'm about three days ahead of you, Colin. Look, I can try to take care of this. But you need to start paying attention to these things. Ok?"

"Last time, Michael. Never happen again, mate. I swear."

Colin held his hand up with his palm out toward Michael.

"On my honor."

"I've heard that before, and I can't protect you forever. It's going to catch up to you at some point. Why don't you just fess up to Wentworth? Tell him what happened. Be honest."

"McGillicuddy!"

Mr. Wentworth came storming toward them, shouting as he approached.

"I need this machine running McGillicuddy. I need it running now!" he screamed as he banged on it with the bottom of his fist.

"Cut the chit-chat get a move on, son! What's the issue here? Why are you just standing there doing nothing? I don't pay you to stand around talking, do I? Did you find the problem yet?"

His tone cut like a knife, and his chiding words stung like the crack of a whip on bare skin.

Pearls of sweat beaded up on Colin's forehead. Colin looked at Michael, hopeful, but resigned. Michael looked at Colin, conflicted but undecided.

"Well? Did you find the problem?"

"Look, Mr. Wentworth," Michael said. "I hate to say this, I really do. But the issue here is really, well, it's really quite simple."

Colin cringed like he was about to get smacked in the head with a board.

"The issue, simply put is…"

"Is what?" Wentworth screamed back.

"The issue is, well, it's really just - simple wear and tear."

"Wear and tear?"

"Yes. The gearbox has a lot of hours on it, and these things don't last forever. I may need to take the line down for the rest of the day, but I can change everything that needs changing. I have all the parts I need in the maintenance room. It will be as good as new, but it will take some time."

Colin relaxed his shoulders and breathed a sigh of relief. Wentworth clinched his fists in anger. The veins in his forehead bulged, and his face invented a new shade of red.

"Rest of the day? Unacceptable! I need it running now, McGillicuddy! You have one hour, the same as your meeting this morning!"

As he shouted, he poked Michael in the chest with a stiff index finger.

"One. Hour."

Then he turned and stomped off, just as abruptly as he had arrived.

"God, what a wanker," Colin said.

"Which one of you?" Michael mumbled.

Colin missed the jab. Michael studied the damage, and left to get his tools and some parts. Colin found a chair and sat down, elbows on knees and chin in hand, to wait. He didn't know what else to do. Michael returned a few minutes later carrying a tote full of parts under his arm, and an old wooden toolbox in his other hand.

He wasted no time getting to work. Colin sat watching, impressed. He worked quickly and precisely, in such synchrony and with such focus that Colin wondered if Michael might be a machine himself. Michael would pull out a part, replace a gear, turn a screw, cut some pipe, adjust a spring – and step by step he ran through the repair job, never pausing, never showing any doubt, never wondering what to do next. He'd reach for a part without looking, and it would just be there where he reached. No matter what he needed or where he had set it down previously, when he reached for it, it was there. Michael moved true as clock-work, and in less than an hour the machine was up and running. He even added a self-oiling pump, a preventative measure designed to protect Colin from himself.

Michael closed the cover and pressed the button to start the machine. It jolted back to life, shook a little, and then settled into a nice smooth rhythm. He stood there, beaming, watching it run. Then he turned to Colin. He smiled even wider, and nodded. Colin tried to resist, but he couldn't help but smile back. There was something endearing about that silly grin, contagious even.

"Good as new," Michael said. "It's an older machine, so I split the oil line off of that one there, and I ran some pipe over here. Your machine has its own oil pump now. It will keep itself oiled, so you don't need to check the reservoir anymore, it will just take care of itself. The gearbox is new, so there shouldn't be any issues until well after you retire."

"How do you know how to do that?" Colin asked.

"I don't know. I can just see it. I look at the problem, and I can see what I need to do. Then I do it. Easy."

"You figure it out as you go?"

"No, it's not like I guess my way through. I can just see the correct path from start to finish, like a map that someone drew for me. It's all right there from the very beginning, in my head."

"You're an odd duck, mate."

"Perhaps. But my father always said we should appreciate all gifts, no matter how big or small they are, or what form they take. That's pretty good advice, wouldn't you say?"

"Seamus was a wise man, and I liked him a great deal. Thank you, Michael. I appreciate what you've done for me here."

Michael shrugged.

"I'm just doing my job."

"You went beyond. I hope you don't get too much grief from Wentworth because of this."

"Me too."

"Why do you let him treat you like that, anyway? You're a smart one, mate. You don't need to stay here and take that kind of abuse from him. I don't have a choice, I mean, what else am I gonna do? I've been sitting here running this tin can most of my life. And I still can't seem to get it right. But you. You could do anything."

Michael shrugged again and wiped his nose with the back of his wrist.

"I don't know. I just don't let him get to me. I'm just here to do a job. The thing that matters most is that I can keep these beauties running. That's what my father did, and now it's what I do. Wentworth is just noise."

And then he heard it.

"McGillicuddy!" shouted Mr. Wentworth. He was stomping back toward them.

"Your hour is up McGillicuddy, and that machine had damn well better be purring like a cat."

Michael pulled a rag from his back pocket and wiped the top of the machine, and stuffed the rag back in his pocket.

"Purring away, Mr. Wentworth. Belly full of milk, napping on a warm carpet."

"I'll be the judge of that!" Wentworth growled.

He shoved his way past the men to inspect his machine. He leaned in, squinted and looked it over - as if he had any idea what he was looking for. He nodded knowingly, and grunted a lot, as he ran his eyes over its many complicated parts. Michael looked at Colin with eyebrows raised, and Colin just shrugged back. Neither of them had any idea what he could possibly be looking for. The machine was running, and that should be good enough. After a few more grunts, he gave up. He turned his hostile gaze to Michael and Colin.

"Hmmph. Why are you two buffoons just standing there? Get back to work! I've got a business to run!"

He huffed and wagged his finger at both of them to shoo them away. And with that, he stomped off, just as abruptly as he had arrived once again.

"You're welcome," Michael mumbled under his breath.

He stood watching Mr. Wentworth stomp down a long aisle of machines back toward his office, grumbling at anyone he saw along the way. In the distance, a door slammed. Michael could return to his regular work now.

5

MICHAEL OPENS THE CHRYSALIS

After a long and exhausting day at work, Michael finally made his way back to the house. It was late in the evening, well past meal time. He and his mother had continued living at their homestead long after Seamus had passed, and Soairse never remarried. It was not for lack of suitors, but Seamus had been her one and only true love. The life they lived together, abbreviated as it was, was part of the life she lived now. She wouldn't have it any other way.

"Mum, I'm home," Michael said as he walked through the door toward the kitchen.

"Glad to hear it, Michael, how was your day, dear?" she said from the back room.

"It was fine, the usual."

"I already ate, Michael, but I made you a plate. It's on the counter; you go ahead and eat."

He had already started, and he finished quickly.

"Thank you for supper. What are you doing back there?"

"I'm just putting a few things away, Michael, I'm fine."

He dashed down the hall to the back bedroom to see what she

was doing. She was putting some hat boxes up on the shelf in the closet.

"Mum, stop! Just leave it. I'll take care of it!"

He snatched the box out of her hands.

"They're not even heavy, Michael, I'm fine! Honestly."

"I'll do it, really. Are these all you have?"

"Yes, that's the last of it. You don't have to do that, you know."

"It's fine. I'm happy to do it. But I have to run out to the workshop for a minute to try something. You call me if you need anything else put up, ok?"

"Go ahead, dear, head on out. I'm fine. I'm sure I'll be sleeping long before you make your way back into the house. So, goodnight."

"Goodnight, Mum."

Michael sped out of the room, through the front room, out to the porch, and down the worn mud path leading from the house back to his workshop. It was his refuge - his home away from home. As he entered, he tossed his coat and satchel back onto the counter. When they landed, he heard an unfamiliar thud. He looked at the satchel and recalled the morning's visit from the Messenger. He had been so wrapped up in the day's work that he completely forgot about the Chrysalis. He walked over to the satchel, reached inside and felt around until he found it. He stared at it silently. He was awestruck by its workmanship, and confused by its significance.

"What in the world do I do with this, Poppa?"

He was pretty certain it related to the race. He remembered his father mentioning something similar many years ago. But now that he held it in his hand, its purpose was none too clear. As he looked it up and down, he noticed his name was engraved into the side of the tube in fancy calligraphic text: "M. McGillicuddy." Michael rolled the tube in his hand to look at the other side. He noticed a raised plate on the back side. It was rectangular in shape, an inch wide by two inches in length, and it stood about a quarter inch high off the surface of the tube, with an oval indentation in its surface. There was some brass gear work under the plate that stuck out from underneath on either side.

"That's odd. Must be a switch or button of some kind," he mumbled to himself.

He tried to slide the plate up with his thumb. Nothing.

He tried to slide it down, and then side to side. Nothing. It held firmly in place and didn't budge in the least.

Failing at that, he tried to twist one of the caps off, but to no avail.

Michael set the Chrysalis on the table and just stared at it for a moment, pondering it. Frustrated, he picked it back up and pressed the plate with all his might. It still didn't move. Feeling defeated, he relaxed his grip. As he relaxed, his thumb settled into the center of the oval indentation, and he felt something happening, a vibrating sensation under his thumb. He looked at the plate more closely. The gears began to turn, one gear slowly turning the other. Michael stood in suspense, waiting to see what would happen.

After a few revolutions of the gears, the Chrysalis clicked loudly and torqued a little bit in his hand, like something inside had just popped or released. *Did it just self-destruct?* He wasn't sure. He noticed one of the end caps had come loose. He grasped the cap between his thumb and forefinger and, with a careful tug, the cap detached from the end with a small puff. As Michael held the cap in one hand, and the Chrysalis in the other, he peeked inside with one eye.

"It's always so dark in here," he said to himself as he looked around.

He glanced toward the gas lights, wishing they were brighter, just as his mother walked in.

"Michael," she said.

He flinched.

"You startled me."

"I'm sorry dear, I didn't mean to scare you."

"I thought you went to bed."

"I was about to, but I thought I should let you know something. The tax collector came again today."

"Why didn't you tell me earlier?"

"I didn't want to trouble you. But you should know, he's become very firm now. They've raised the taxes on our land again. He said there are no more extensions he can give after this one. It's our last one."

"Why do they keep raising our taxes when we can barely pay them to begin with?"

"I'm not sure, Michael. But he was very clear this time. If we don't pay what is due by the end of summer, then they are going to take our land. They'll sell it to get the money owed, and turn the rest over to us. If there is any."

"They can do that?"

"They can."

"How much is it this time?"

"Just under ten thousand quid."

He gulped.

"That much? We don't have anything near that amount, it's outrageous."

"I know," she said.

She hunched, and wept into her hands.

"We'll figure it out," she said. "We always have. It will be more difficult this time, but we… You've always managed somehow."

"I can pick up more hours at work," he said, "and take some projects on the side."

"I'm sorry, Michael. I shouldn't have even brought it up, or put this kind of pressure on you. But I don't know what to do."

"It's alright," he said. "We'll figure something out."

"I need to get some rest," she said. "But I wanted to be sure you knew. Don't stay up too late. I will see you in the morning, dear."

"Goodnight, Mum."

She left to go back to the house, and Michael turned his attention back to the Chrysalis. Unable to see inside the tube, he tipped the opening down toward the tabletop. Something metallic came gliding down from inside, and then it fell onto the table with a metallic clang.

"A bloody key? What in the world for?" he exclaimed.

It was no ordinary key. It looked more like the work of an artisan than a locksmith. The intricately designed skeleton key was copper-gold in color, probably a rare alloy. The teeth of the key were complicated, much more so than any skeleton key he had ever seen before. Unique in its design, however, it had two distinct sets of teeth, one set of teeth at the end, like a normal skeleton key, and a second, separate set of teeth placed mid-shaft. The shaft of the key was long and slender and its surface was decorated with fine scrollwork. The head of the key was shaped like a dragon, with its head was turned to the side and its mouth opened, exposing its sharp teeth. Its wings were outstretched and delicately scaled in texture. Its tail curled downward in a tight spiral around the shaft, and its clawed feet gripped a spherical, opalescent gemstone where the head connected to the shaft. The dragon's eyes were set with ruby colored stones.

"It's gorgeous," he mumbled to himself. "But, seriously, what am I supposed to do with this?"

He tipped the tube further and a thick token slid down and plopped out onto the table with a solid thud. The token was the thickness of four coins stacked on top of each other. When he picked it up, it felt heavy and solid in his hand. The edge around its circumference was smooth and polished, a flawless shiny silver. The face of the token also bore the image of a dramatically carved dragon, inset with ruby eyes. It shone with the beauty of a newly minted coin. He turned the coin so he could see its edge. It was stamped with letters around the outside.

"Admission," Michael read aloud to himself, as he rolled it in his fingers. "This must be my ticket in," he said. "But where?"

With his interest piqued, he poked his finger down inside to feel around. The inside felt like it was lined with paper, so he pressed his finger against the inside edge and pulled it slowly upward. He unfurled the parchment on the tabletop and anxiously pressed it flat. His eyes were wide and he breathed heavily. His tongue stuck out a little while he worked, like it often did when he concentrated. With the parchment flattened, he studied the words written in fancy script.

Congratulations on your selection and we proudly welcome you in as a member of this most highly-revered assemblage of scholars, thinkers, inventors, adventurers, mathematicians, scientists, strategists and students of life that history has ever known. Be warned, though. Our ranks also include some scalawags and saboteurs. Knowing the difference will be the key to your success in this year's race. In the course of your journey, consider the following:

1. An emu cannot fly, but an ostrich has four toes.

2. Find the Magic Square. 9 steps right, 40 steps up, 8 steps left, and 49 steps down. The constant is your key.

3. Solitude is your enemy.

4. View the world through another man's lens. You can learn a lot if you study it closely.

With all that said, be advised that this year, the race will consist of three legs. One will be traveled by land, one by sea and one by air. Any method of transport is permitted. However, the mode of transport must be respected: the land leg must be traveled by land, the sea leg must be traveled by sea, and the air leg must be traveled by air. A map of the first leg, the land leg, is enclosed with this letter. As always, the race will begin promptly at 8:00 a.m. on July 8 departing from the Gatling Meadows, near Cavenshire. The sea leg will depart from the port near Gillingham, and the air leg will depart from Rouen. Make due preparation. You are properly warned now not to cheat the rules, lest you risk being "disqualified."

Along the way, you must collect a set of specified milestone tokens, all bearing the same designation. The first to collect all of the required tokens, each with proper designation, and arrive at the designated finishing point will be named this year's winner. Good luck, and Godspeed.

"Land, sea, air. Point to point to point. Grab some things along the way. Seems pretty simple," Michael mumbled. "But why was I invited?"

He leaned on the workbench with both hands, and stared out the door of the workshop into the distance.

"And how did he get my thumbprint? I need to go see John."

6

INSIDE VIXEN'S LAB

Utrecht, the Netherlands

"Do you really intend to go?" Wim asked of Vixen.

"Of course I do," she replied. "And why wouldn't I?"

Wim van Buren and his wife Mirta stood at a workstation in a large laboratory situated in downtown Utrecht, the Netherlands. They were having a lively conversation with their daughter, Vixen, as they so often did. An open Chrysalis sat on the table, next to an unfurled sheet of parchment held flat by a key, and a token resting on top. The key on the parchment was solid silver, its shaft simple, the length of a finger. They key's head was delicately carved in the shape of a butterfly sitting on a flower, passable as jewelry, like a brooch or large pendant. The face of the token bore the same butterfly design.

"Is there anything I can say or do to change your mind?" he asked. "You know the risks. We've been over this."

Mirta, Vixen's mother, interrupted.

"Wim, how long have you known her? When she sets her mind

to do something, have you ever been able to change it? Ever? Really, now."

"No, not really."

There was a quiet pause as they stood in the expansive laboratory, an impressive facility, standing two stories tall with one wall along its length composed entirely of floor-to-ceiling glass, facing Utrecht's centrum. Iron spiral staircases led up to second-story catwalks and more workstations. The lab was well-equipped, with the best of everything money could buy, a fortunate consequence of her government's interest in her work. It was a very high honor, recognition of her advanced work in the fields of alchemy, advanced modern chemistry and the ethereal sciences, and allowed her the happy freedom to focus on her work without concern for financial limitations. But it also came with strings attached. As part of their arrangement, the government reserved its right to access Vixen's research, and the right to send her 'directed research' projects, which it exercised often.

"How can you just go, Vixen? What about your work?" Wim asked.

"Truth be told, father, it's actually a good time to break. Most of my projects are finishing. And frankly, I could use a holiday before I start something new. I think I've earned that."

"Holiday? It will be no holiday. I assure you of that! And what have you finished?"

"First phase of my Alchemy Orbs, for one thing. Come, I'll show you."

Vixen walked her parents over to one of the lab's many work stations. Two small wooden chests, each the size of a toolbox, sat on the counter of a now-defunct work station. Between the two chests, there was a large hole, more than a foot across, burned right through the chemical-resistant counter.

"Alchemy Orbs?" Mirta asked.

"Yes. You might recall the ancient alchemy of the medieval period. It was rightly focused on the transformation of matter, a worthwhile endeavor for its time. But the science was horribly misguided, both in approach and in purpose.

"You mean like when the royals tried to transform lead into gold?" Mirta asked.

"Yes, precisely. The methods used at the time were as archaic as they were incompetent and unenlightened."

Vixen flipped open one of the boxes.

"But I've solved for all their shortcomings."

Wim and Mirta peered inside. Eight shiny glass spheres were carefully arranged in two rows of four, nestled in a blue satin enclosure, like large royal easter eggs, in a large royal egg crate. Each sphere measured the size of a fist and would fit nicely in the palm of an adult hand. She lifted the tray of orbs out of the box to reveal a second tray containing eight more, directly underneath. She plucked a red one from the tray and held it up proudly. The pearlescent liquid inside swirled in a mesmerizing fashion. Other orbs were colored blue, green and even yellow.

"Now," she continued, "through extensive experimentation and the development and application of some novel reactionary science, I've created the alchemical elixirs contained in these orbs. Everything I have done here builds upon the work of those who went before me, but I have raised that science to an entirely new level."

"Do they actually work?" Wim asked.

"Functionally speaking, yes, they do work. But they are not yet perfected, not to my liking anyway. Some preparations are more stable than others. But correcting for that will be a simple exercise in fine-tuning the formulations and reactive processes used to create them. The lion's share of the work is finished. I have copious notes and instructions logged, a student from the university could probably finish it, assuming, of course, that I would ever let one touch my work. Which I wouldn't."

"I'm intrigued," Wim said. "What do they actually do?"

"Different elixirs have different properties, but most deal directly in the alchemical transformation of matter."

She thrust her hand forward.

"This one transforms water into stone. Its efficacy is quite ephemeral though. So far I've only been able to maintain a stable transformation for about thirty seconds in some batches, and as high as thirty minutes for others. After that, the stone turns back to water. Stabilization, timing control and controlled reversal will all come in due course, and I have a good idea of what needs to be done."

Wim nodded his head, his interest growing deeper.

"Alright," he said. "What else."

"This one transforms most stone into air, but it's even less stable. My most stable transformation held for nearly a full minute, but it's often much shorter. Sometimes it only lasts a few seconds. I need to analyze it further, but my working hypothesis is that the amount of calcium in the stone is an important factor. I have some thoughts on how to correct for that, which I can work on when I get back."

"That doesn't seem very useful," Wim said. "Stone into air? Why would you need to turn stone to air?"

"Don't be so short-sighted, father. It's easy to pick it apart now, in its infancy, but this capability will be revolutionary, mark my words. The most important part for right now is establishing a sound, repeatable basis for the science, and getting it to work at all. That's the hardest part, and I've completed that. The next step is to modify the elixirs for stability, then adapt their chemistry to other useful, practical applications in industry. The possibilities are virtually limitless."

Mirta interrupted.

"Don't be so negative, Wim. She's done some exceptional work here."

She turned to Vixen and took on the tone of a doting mother.

"I'm proud of you, Vixen. We are both very, very proud of you. Aren't we, Wim?"

Wim grunted.

"Yes, very impressive. Important work to be sure, but it's not complete. She should stay and finish up her research while it's still fresh, and get things into a more stable state. Avoid unnecessary distractions, Vixen, and focus on your work."

Vixen shot a stern look at him.

"I see what you're doing, father. Just stop."

Then she smiled and carried on.

"This green one is a photo-luminescent elixir. It glows in the dark, and it lasts about a day. One of my lab assistants got some on his hand the first time we tested it. He didn't sleep that night, his hand lit up his room up as bright as day."

She giggled at his misfortune.

"This one alters the density of matter and can actually make wood, stone or metal lighter than air, without changing its form or its size. The stability is much better on this one, it lasts 30 minutes most of the time."

"You can do that?" Wim gasped.

"Yes, child's play."

"Now that is impressive."

"Yes. I know."

"But why don't the elixirs affect the glass orbs?" Mirta asked.

"Excellent question. There's a specially-designed neutral, non-reactive coating on the inside. It took time to figure that part out, and we did have a minor setback - do you see that hole in the countertop?"

Wim and Mirta looked and nodded.

"Imagine our surprise when the disintegration elixir actually worked for the very first time. When we tried to fill the orb, not only did it disintegrate the orb, but also the countertop, and poor Baxter to boot. God rest his soul."

Mirta and Wim blessed themselves and looked at each other with somber faces, politely mourning the loss of poor Baxter.

"Oh God, I'm kidding, nobody died! Not lately, anyway."

She chuckled again to herself.

"I've also been asked to do some work on aether fuels. And a dream distiller. The work is very preliminary. Just basic concepts for now, hardly even worth mentioning. That work will come later. I can finish some things up while preparations are being made for the race. You'll barely even notice I'm gone."

"We'll notice, Vixen. I really wish you would reconsider," he said. "I've been through it first-hand, it's not an appropriate endeavor for you. They're ruthless. You've always done as you please, though, so I don't suppose this time will be any different."

"You're a very wise man, father. And this will be no different."

7

MICHAEL MEETS WITH JOHN

After spending most of the day traveling by train to visit John, Michael arrived at *Gare du Nord*, the train station in northern Paris. He spent the trip jotting notes and pondering the cryptic note he received from the Messenger. Lost in thought, he was startled by the ticket inspector.

"*Bonsoir Monsieur. Paris Nord. Je crois que ceci est votre arrêt.*"

"Paris Nord already?" he said. "*Merci Beaucoup.*"

Michael stowed his sketch pad and pencil into his satchel, each in its proper place, and headed for the door. As he scurried down the aisle, he realized he was the last one off the train. Again.

"*Bonne Nuit, Monsieur.*"

"*Bonne Nuit.*"

Michael made his way through the terminal and stepped out into a warm Paris evening to hail a ride on a horse-drawn tram to take him to John's flat. Along the way, he considered what he might say, questions he would ask John and what he was getting himself into by participating in the race. The ride through the city was quiet. It was supper hour. Most of the merchants had closed up their shops for the day, and locals were returning to their flats for the evening.

Michael shared the tram with a handful of other riders. A young couple that couldn't take their eyes off each other, sitting close, and speaking softly to each other in French, and an older man sitting by himself reading a newspaper. The man folded his paper, struck a match to light his pipe and tossed the match out of the tram. Michael watched as the match flew through the air. It landed on the stoop of a small shop, *Rousseau's Apothecary.* The name was painted across the front window in gold and black lettering. The window was filled with medicine bottles, elixirs and jars of herbs, all neatly labeled and arranged in perfect order. The tram continued past the shop to the sound of clopping hooves, wheels running over cobblestones and the young couple's whispers. At the intersection of *Rue de l'Universite* and *Avenue Bosquet*, Michael paid the driver a few francs for his trouble and walked the final block to John's flat.

When Michael arrived, he stood in front of the door and paused. He took a deep breath, sighed and pulled the lapels of his jacket straight. John was an accomplished adventurer and he could be self-aggrandizing at times. He usually came across as charming, but sometimes he just seemed obnoxious and full of himself. His pursuits were legendary, but nobody held John in higher regard than he held himself. Michael knew this well, and prepared himself. He took another deep breath, then knocked.

Thirty seconds passed with no answer. He stepped back from the door and looked up to the second story, checking for lights shining through the windows. He began to worry that John might not be there, when he heard the door's heavy metal lock disengage. John flung the door open with the flair of a bullfighter. When he saw who was standing before him, he stepped out and welcomed Michael with a big bear hug and a hearty pat on the back.

"Michael McGillicuddy, good to see you, boy! To what do I owe this honor?"

His voice was big and confident.

"It's been a long time, John, I thought it would be good to catch up," Michael said, flashing a charismatic smile. "I hope you've been well and I'm not interrupting anything. Is this a good time for you?"

"Come in, boy. Come in," he said, John shut the heavy door and set the lock back in place with a loud clank.

"Much obliged, and thank you for seeing me."

"No bother! No bother at all. Come in, boy, let me put a kettle on for some tea. Please, have a seat," John said.

John barreled his bulky frame up the stairs toward the kitchen, smoothing his gnarly beard with his hands. Michael hadn't been there in years, but as he stepped inside, a familiar and comfortable feeling washed over him, like wrapping himself in a warm blanket on a cold day. Maybe it was John's own confidence that rubbed off on him, he wasn't sure, but it always felt good to be there, to be around John.

While the water was heating, Michael looked around, reflecting on memories of times past that he had spent there. It was still a simple room with tall bookshelves covering the walls, just like he remembered. The shelves were packed with assorted leather bound books - academic titles, map books and atlases. As Michael pored over the shelves, he saw reference books including '*Sprockets, Springs and Gears - Animation Systems For Watches or Warfare*'; '*Seafaring: Navigation by Compass or Star*'; '*Lighter than Air Craft: Launching, Landing and Maintaining Flight*', '*Languages and Customs of Modern European Nations*', and '*Steam Power, Part I*'. Literary titles ranged from classic selections - Shakespeare, Voltaire and Montesquieu - to some lesser-known selections such as Constantinescu's *Beguiling Arcana - Volumes I, II and III* and Scheherazade's *Tome of Infinite Legends*. To Michael's dismay, some of the volumes were out of order, so he fixed them. The thickest volume, by far, was the '*Anthology of Modern Transport: Designs and Methods for Building Self-Propelled Vehicles.*'

On the opposite wall, an antiqued map of the world hung in a heavy brown frame hung over the fireplace. Michael approached the map and studied it, and all the scores of pins stuck into it, presumably to mark all the places John had been. There must have been a hundred or more, spread across the entire globe. As Michael glanced around the room, his eyes fixed on the large cargo chest near the couch. He couldn't even begin to imagine what treasures it held from John's many ventures. He walked over, about to open it for a peek inside, but got distracted by something else. There was a lone bronze picture frame on one of the shelves, set slightly askew. Michael went to straighten it, but as he got closer noticed the old sepia tone photograph inside. It was a picture of John and Michael's father, Seamus, standing arm-in-arm in front of an anchored dirigible. The looks on their faces suggested they had just achieved something remarkable together. Michael looked around the dusty old room but didn't see any other photographs. Not one.

"This water's going to take a few minutes," John shouted from upstairs. "Come on up here, talk to me boy, what brings you to my doorstep?"

"Well, you know I trust you, John. After my father passed, you looked after Mum and me," Michael said, walking up the stairs to the kitchen.

"Aye. It was the least I could do. How is your mother these days?"

"She's fine, just getting older, as well all are. She's still as fierce as she ever was. Just a little bit older, and moving a little slower."

"She always was a feisty one. The fire burns hot in that heart of hers - that's for certain," John said with a hearty laugh.

"Yes, well, I suppose that's true, John. But more to the point, the reason for my visit is that I wanted to let you know I've been invited to participate in the race this year. I was hoping to get some advice from you."

"Is that so? Look at you, little Michael McGillicuddy! Invited to play with the grown-ups. It's a damn shame that I will have to beat you so soundly, boy. I am none too keen on crushing the souls of the people I'm so fond of. But all is fair in love and war, and in this race. I believe you know my history."

Michael smiled.

"Yes, I've heard all about it. Many, many, many times. Nevertheless, I'm in this for the win. It simply can't go any other way."

"Ha! Everybody plans to win it, boy! But only one vehicle will, and it certainly won't be yours."

He shook with a big belly laugh, his tone indignant.

"That much I can say for sure."

Michael slunk down in his chair, blushing slightly at the idea that his ambition would seem so ridiculous to a past participant; someone of John's stature, someone Michael respected so greatly. Recognizing this, John tried to soften his tone. But softness wasn't John's strong suit.

"Look, Michael, it's a man's game, and you need to appreciate that. It's not for, you know, little gear-monkey farm-boys," he said with a wave of his hand. "No offense."

"What? Man's game? I am a man, John. I'm not the little boy you used to look after anymore, and I'm not some little gear-monkey. It's been a long time. Look at me."

He was in fact grown. Now aged in his mid-twenties, he stood with average height and above-average muscularity, his biceps and pectoral muscles showing through his shirt. He was a fully grown, handsome young man with simple good looks and a boyish charm. John stared at him for a second, looking him up and down, and realized that Michael had a point. But he wasn't about to admit it.

"A man? Alright then, *man*. Tell me the name of your woman."

"John! Honestly."

They were interrupted by the whistle of the tea kettle. John shuffled over to get some teacups.

"Can we talk about this or not, John?"

"What do you want to talk about?" John said as he poured the tea.

"The race."

"The race? There's not much to tell. It's an annual event, something we do as members of the Order of the Blue Cloak. The Order is a closed and rather secretive society. Each year one of our members designs a new competition, and from time to time, new members are invited in, just as you have been. So there you have it."

"I know there's more to it than that, John. I had a visit from the Messenger. I received a key and a token and some notes, so I sort of understand all that. But I was hoping you could give me some advice on what to expect, as a participant. It's my first time, and I can't ask my father, so…"

Hearing this, John leaned in. He looked him straight in the eye and spoke in a stern, matter-of-fact tone.

"You want my advice? OK. Here's my advice to you, Michael. Toss the key. Throw away the token. Burn the parchment. Get back to work at the factory and go take care of your mother."

"I won't shy from this John. I'll go, with or without your blessing," he said.

Then his tone softened, bordering on desperate.

"I just thought I could count on you for a little help."

"I am trying to help you, boy. Aren't you listening? I've always looked after your best interest, as well as I could, anyway. This is dangerous business you're playing with. I'm impressed, and I'm happy for you that you were invited. It means they have already evaluated you, assessed your ability and deemed you worthy. The invitation itself a very high honor, make no mistake about that. But I'm also concerned for you. You're a smart lad, but you've lived a sheltered life. What do you really know about the world, besides that factory you work at, your mother's land and the road that connects the two?"

"I know enough John. I'm a legatee. My father won, and so can I."

"What do you really know about people, Michael? This race, you need to understand - It's just a game for some. For others, it's serious business. And for others, well, there are no higher stakes. It's the other participants that should trouble you the most, and that's what you need to be aware of. If you insist on going, then by all means, go. But watch your back and be careful who you trust, boy. That's the best advice I can give you. It's very simple."

John clanked his cup of tea down on the counter without ever having sipped it.

"Now you've got me all riled up. Let's go down and grab a scotch, what do you say? Care for a dram? A little nectar of the gods?"

"I thought you'd never ask, I'd love a spot."

"Then what are we waiting for?"

John motioned toward the steps.

Michael had enjoyed a few fine scotches in his time, but for some reason it always tasted better with John. Scotch was scotch, but a scotch with John was an experience. As they reached the foot of the stairs, John reached for a couple of glasses on a side table, where he kept a bottle of his very favorite nectar. As he did, Michael spoke.

"I'm very sorry, John. I didn't realize you had company."

"What?" John replied. "I don't…"

He turned to look over his shoulder, then he bristled.

"What are you doing here?" he demanded.

"Ouch," the woman said, in her soft, sultry tone. "I thought you'd be happier to see me, pumpkin. Is that any way to treat a guest?"

"You're no guest."

"Really, John. You're hurting my feelings."

"Impossible. The devil has no feelings."

The confident-looking woman sat on the couch, in the same

spot where Michael had sat before he went up to get his tea. She was visibly his senior, but not by much, aged in her early thirties. She wore a black and white striped leather corset over a flowing white blouse. Her sleeves flowed loosely, and flared ends covered her hands. A necklace with several small glass vials hung from her neck, and her black and white striped leather pants hugged her supple, yet slender, frame in a most complimentary way.

She wore black, round-framed glasses with darkened lenses, a black leather top hat, and a thick belt with cylindrical flasks and a dangling leather pouch. Her jet black hair was bone-straight, pulled back into a shiny ponytail that reached halfway down her back. A tuft of thin braids intertwined with a thin purple ribbon hung down from underneath her top hat, just past her temples to her jawline. Her face was pale, and her ruby red lips popped in sharp contrast to her alabaster skin. Michael stared, entranced. She showed no emotion, but was hauntingly beautiful, frighteningly serious and alluringly seductive, all at once. She placed her hand on her chest, and spoke with a pouty tone and an English accent.

"I see that I've come at an inopportune time, love. Shame on me. We can chat later, John, or maybe you can just talk with Mech. That's really up to you. But I best be going now, gents. Toodles."

She stood and strutted toward the door, slow and confident, one foot in front of the other. She dripped with sass and sensuality, from the wag of her hips to the flick of her hair. From the pout of her lips to the tone of her condescension. She unlocked the door, gave it a shove and stepped outside. But on her way out, she stopped abruptly as if something had just occurred to her. She looked back over her shoulder, her gaze locked on Michael, and a coy grin surfacing on her face.

"Have we met, darling?"

She flipped up her darkened lenses to reveal steely silver-grey eyes, tinted with a subtle tinge of blue. Michael stared in awe.

"Oh, I don't think so," he said. "I would have remembered that."

"Oh, let there be no mistake about that," she said. "You would have."

"I'm Michael McGillicuddy."

"Of course you are."

She winked, and held her hand out in front of her face. Her hand was clad with rings made of silver, pewter and bronze, a different design on each finger. She kissed her fingertips and blew a kiss toward him with a long, slow exhale. The intensity of her stare made Michael uncomfortable.

"*Bonne nuit,*" she said in her sweetest voice. Then she strutted off into the darkness, hips wagging, without a care in the world.

"Those eyes," Michael said with a shudder, "My god, it's like she looked right through me. They're piercing."

"Oh, she can see right through you, boy. And so can I. I tell you what, you just forget about her, OK? Trust me on this one!"

"That's not what I meant, John. I just - Stop it, would you? Who was that? How did she get in here?"

John took on his darkest, most serious tone.

"You don't worry about who that was. Do you understand me? That was not anyone you ever need to associate with. Full stop."

Michael was disappointed and put off. Judging from John's abrupt change of tone, he understood their conversation was likely over.

"Yes. Very well then. I'm sorry to have interrupted your evening, John. It was truly wonderful to see you, but I should probably be on my way. Thank you for your hospitality. I will see you out there."

"I guess you will," John said with a nod. "Good luck, boy, please take care of yourself. And remember what I told you."

"Yes. You too, John."

"Your father would have taken my side on this one, Michael. I hope you understand that."

"I don't think he would have, John. He would have wanted me to do this. I owe it to him to notch a win. Good luck to you."

With that, Michael made his way back toward the train station, disappointed that his meeting was not more productive. Deep down, he had hoped that John would invite him to team up, act as a mentor, and perhaps even stand in for his father, as he had done so many times before. But not on this occasion. Once he was back on the train, Michael reflected back on childhood memories of his father, and wished he could be here to help. He wished they could do this together. That was supposed to be the plan.

8

UNDER THE CIRCUS TENT

1895 - Performance of the Black Steam Circus - London

"And with the strength of five men - nay - ten men! Watch him bend iron bars with his bare hands! Please welcome MECK-a-NICK-u-lees!" The Ringmaster's big, booming voice filled the big top. Circus music piped out of a steam calliope, and the smell of popcorn hung in the air as the audience *oohed*, delighted by his inhuman feats of strength.

Mechanicules bent the iron bars with ease, tore apart heavy chains like cotton candy, and lifted giant iron slabs that, when he dropped them, shook the ground so violently that their impact was felt through the grandstands.

The Ringmaster stood in the center ring donning a traditional red jacket and pants, replete with tails, black lapels and gold braided strands adorning his coat. He adjusted the black bowtie around the neck of his tuxedo shirt, removed the black top hat from his bald head and bowed to an adoring crowd. He stood back upright, placed his hat on his head and straightened his perfectly-waxed, van dyke-style mustache and beard between this thumb and forefinger. He smiled at the crowd, with his arms stretched wide, and turned side-to-side, to give them one last moment to fully appreciate his singular magnificence. He nodded politely and continued with his narrative.

"Ladies and gentlemen, please put your hands together now, and show your greatest appreciation, for Mechanicules - the strong man with no equal, the beast without a rival, the strongest man in the world!"

The crowd roared.

Mechanicules, the 'mechanical Hercules,' was so named for the combination of his mechanical right arm and his Herculean strength. He stood tall and proud in the center ring, striking a pose. Dressed in a burgundy colored military jacket with copious gold strapping across the chest, his uniform conjured an image of the coats worn by Napoleonic hussars. He stood panting, and short of breath. He was way above average height, broad across the shoulders, and his physique left no question about his strength. His face was painted with white circus makeup, and black accents above and around his icy-blue eyes, giving him a gothic, vampiric look. He stared silently into the crowd. His longish black hair was rough cut, framing his face as it hung down.

His hussar's jacket had no right sleeve, and this was by design. His mechanical arm was on full display, clad in dark brown leather and antiqued brass machinations, with heavy-duty gear-work in the shoulder, elbow and wrist. A pneumatic piston adjoined the upper and lower arm, which drove the bending motion at the elbow and added extra strength. The Ringmaster continued on, giving Mech a chance to catch his breath. Calliope music continued to pipe out in the background, and the smaller acts went on in the other two rings.

In one ring, a tightrope walker balanced precariously, thirty feet off the ground with no net. She wobbled a little. First left, then right, and recovered her balance. She squatted, did a flip and landed perfectly on the rope with both feet, which drew more *oohs* out of the crowd. In the third ring, an eclectic group of torch jugglers, fire eaters and acrobatic contortionists - the Hellfire Troupe - mesmerized the crowd with their flame-handling skills. Members of the Troupe juggled flaming objects and tossed them back and forth. Some of the members lit torches and extinguished them in their mouth, others filled their mouths with flammable liquid from flasks on their belts, and blew the liquid across the torches, to create dazzling fireballs in the air. The crowd roared, feeling the heat on their faces, and demanding more. Four clowns and a mime ran from ring to ring, and provided some comic relief during the short breaks in the action. It was a well-run show, where no mistakes or sloppiness were permitted. No lulls. No downtime. The entire operation was a master class in showmanship.

"And now ladies and gentlemen," the Ringmaster's voice bellowed, "please cast your eyes upon the center ring for this evening's grand finale - Mechanicules will now perform his most impressive feat of strength."

Mechanicules approached a metal bar propped across two heavy metal poles standing upright out of the ground. The pole crossed chest-high as Mech stood in front of it, and its ends extended past the upright supports on either side. As he stood in front of the bar, taking deep breaths and focusing his strength, one circus performer after another walked over, wrapped their hands around the pole and hung down from it like a weight. All of the clowns, the Hellfire Troupe, the mime, the tightrope walker, the knife thrower, the magician and the rest of the performers took their spots. Mechanicules stepped under the pole in a squat. He gripped the pole in his mechanical right hand and grimaced as he pressed up with his legs and right arm to lift it, with all the members hanging from it. Slowly and gradually, to the delight of a mesmerized crowd, Mech pressed the bar up over his head and stood upright, with the entire cast hanging from it. The audience roared, with wild applause and raucous cheers. His strength was unmatched in any corner of the world.

"Ladies and gentlemen, for one last time this evening, please show your appreciation for Mechanicules and the crew of the Black Steam Circus!"

The crowd obliged, and the calliope music played them out as the cast bowed and left the tent one by one. As the audience filed out, the Ringmaster and Mechanicules left the center ring. They walked out the back of the big top, where a small tent city housed the show's performers in the rear. As the cast of the performers dispersed, some would make their way out back to quarters, sleeping tents. Others would wander into town to partake in local beverages, flophouses, gambling, or some simple time alone. These tents were where they lived. It's where they slept and dreamed. Where they dressed, ate and socialized. It was their home. They were a family. A rag-tag, hodgepodge of a family composed of discarded odds and ends, perhaps. But a family, nonetheless. It was the only family most of them knew, and the Ringmaster stood as their *de facto* patriarch.

The Ringmaster and Mech went to the Ringmaster's personal tent. It was, of course, larger than the rest. Rank had its privilege. As they approached the entrance, the Ringmaster put his hands together and shoved them through the slit in the curtain that covered the door. He threw his hands apart and tossed the curtains aside as he walked in, only to be startled by the woman sitting at the communal table. She sat leaning back, with her arm slung over the back of the chair, wearing dark glasses and a black top hat, eating a plate of fruit from a prepared buffet that included an assortment of meats, fruits, cheeses and bread. The performers were always invited to the Ringmaster's tent after an evening's performance for a communal meal - a family dinner of sorts. Some came, some did not. Each day was different. He was happy to provide it though, as it helped keep them loyal. But more important, it helped keep them close, where he could keep a watchful eye.

"Belladonna, you're back," the Ringmaster said. "I wasn't expecting you."

"Nobody ever does, love," she said in her deadpan tone. "Hello, Mech."

Mech acknowledged her with a nod. The Ringmaster sat in a chair opposite Belladonna. He grabbed a short glass and flipped it in the air, end-over-end. He caught it midair, never breaking eye contact, and slammed it down on the table to pour himself a drink. Belladonna popped a grape in her mouth and bit down, hard enough that her teeth clapped together. She wasn't impressed. Mech stood behind the Ringmaster with his arms crossed.

"So what's the good word, lass?" the Ringmaster inquired.

"I paid a visit to John Ramshorn, as you asked. It sounds like he's participating again this year."

"Hardly a surprise to me. He's a perennial invitee, and always a serious contender. And the status of his debt?"

"We didn't discuss business. He had a visitor, Michael McGillicuddy."

"Seamus' son?"

"Yes, now that you mention it. I think that's right."

The Ringmaster stared distantly, but didn't respond.

"McGillicuddy was invited as well," she continued. "It sounded like he was asking for guidance from John."

The Ringmaster was troubled by the prospect of Michael's participation.

"I can't be bothered to worry about McGillicuddy right now. But I do need Ramshorn to make good on his debt. It's been a long time coming. Many years in fact. I'm gravely disappointed, Belladonna, that this isn't resolved yet. I'm disappointed in him, and I'm disappointed in you, quite frankly."

"It wasn't the proper time to discuss it," she said.

The Ringmaster slammed his fist on the table. His drink jumped and splashed out of its glass.

"I'm not concerned with propriety, Belladonna. I'm concerned with getting what's owed to me; getting what's rightfully mine!"

She stared back through her dark glasses, leaning back in her chair. She was unfazed and defiant. She cocked her head to the side, popped another grape in her mouth, mashed it between her teeth, and slowly began to chew. But she didn't say a word.

"There is a simple way to resolve this. Mech, I need you to take a message to John Ramshorn. Let him know that if he can ensure that McGillicuddy never makes it to the finish line, his debt will be extinguished. I don't care how he does it. We will kill two birds with one stone - and a McGillicuddy along the way, if that's what it takes. This is my year to win. I will move the sun and the moon to do it, and damned be *anybody* who gets in my way."

Mechanicules acknowledged his orders with a nod and bolted out of the tent. As Mech walked out, Phillippe Toussaint, the Magician, walked in.

"Relax everybod-ee, I am 'ere now."

He spoke with a heavy French accent, laughing out loud as he entered. He held his arms outstretched, hands open, palms up, nodding confidently to present himself. He dropped his hands down to his side and quickly lifted them back up, gracefully fanning out a full deck of cards in each hand. He closed the fanned cards down and stuffed the squared-up decks in the pocket on the inside breast of his shiny plum-colored magician's jacket. Phillippe's conceit was outsized, fueled by devilish good looks and a well-established history of romantic success. He was strikingly handsome, as he would so often tell people, with his tan skin, shiny white teeth and jet black van dyke. He wore thick hoop earrings, one in each ear, and black eyeliner to accentuate his glimmering hazel eyes. On stage or off, Phillippe loved to make a grand entrance.

He walked around the table behind Belladonna. As he moved, he set his tophat down on the buffet. He placed his left hand on the back of Belladonna's neck. As she reeled around to see what he was doing, he reached around with his other hand, and snatched some grapes from her plate. He tossed the grapes in his mouth and mashed the juicy bits between his teeth.

"*Voila*! Ha-ha-ha!" he said, with a mouth full of fruit.

He slurped loudly and breathed audibly through his nose.

"Jesus, you're obnoxious," Belladonna said.

"Come on. You 'ave to admit; it's a good trick, yes?"

"It's not even a trick, Phillippe, you just stole some grapes off my plate."

She was indignant.

"Yes, of course. The grapes, wa-la-la. Tell me then, Belladonna, *pret-tee woo-man*, what do you think of this?"

He raised his hand slowly, his fist clenched. He brought his arm up to the side and held it straight out, pausing for dramatic effect. With his other hand, he extended his index finger and pointed to the clenched fist. He glanced at Belladonna, flashed a sinister smile, and raised an eyebrow. She sat and watched as he slowly relaxed his fingers. His thumb and forefinger stayed pinched together, but the rest of his fingers slowly unfurled, little by little. Belladonna stared on, confused. His grip opened up a little more, and then she saw it drop down from his hand. It was just dangling there, between his pinched fingers; swinging slowly, back and forth like a pendulum.

"My necklace!"

He had snatched it from her neck while she was distracted by the grape theft. She shrieked, in a rare show of genuine emotion. Her voice was shrill, projecting equal parts panic and anger. In a single, continuous motion, she leaped from her chair, snatched the necklace with one hand, and slapped him across the face with the other. She moved with the blinding speed and unrelenting ferocity of a cobra striking its prey. Caught off guard, Phillippe stumbled back into a chair and fell to a sitting position. Belladonna stood over him pointing an accusatory finger. She recovered control of her emotions, and spoke in her droll, deadpan tone, struggling to calm her breath.

"You would be well-advised, Phillippe, never to touch me, or any of my belongings, again. If you do, you will most certainly pay a steep price. Do we have a proper understanding, dear?"

"Ok, Ok," Phillippe said.

His hands were raised in sarcastic surrender.

"You win. I am all done with the touching of you. And your... trash."

He waved his hand to shoo her away, and touched his cheek with his finger. There was a small cut on his cheekbone where one of her rings and split his skin, and a dab of blood had formed. He put his finger in his mouth and sucked the blood off.

The Ringmaster had watched patiently, but he grew frustrated by their childish antics.

"Alright. That's enough out of you two lovebirds" he said in his booming voice. "Stop it this instant. Look, we are coming up on an important event. We will finish our last few performances, then we need to turn our energy and attention to the race, as we've been planning all year. This one belongs to *me*. I won't lose again. Not to Ramshorn, not to another McGillicuddy, not to anyone."

Then he turned to Belladonna.

"And speaking of losing - I am losing my patience with you, lass."

He refilled his glass, and turned to put the empty bottle back on the buffet. He turned back to Belladonna to continue his lecture.

"Oh my god, I'm so tired of hearing you," she said.

Her tone was morose.

"You'd be wise to shut it," she said. "Or I'll give you the belch voice."

He sipped his drink and chided her further, wagging his finger as he spoke.

"Youuuu. Wouuuuldn't. Daaaare."

But instead of his ordinarily booming voice, his words were voiced in a thunderous belching sound. He was surprised.

Belladonna held her hand out. He could see that one of her rings was flipped open, it's compartment now empty. She had deposited the fine powder into his drink when he turned to stow the bottle.

She pushed out her bottom lip to make a pout, and batted her eyelashes.

"It looks like I already did. So sorry, sweetness, I guess you have to keep a closer eye on me. I'm such a naughty, naughty girl."

"Bellll-aaaa-dooon-naaaa!" he blasted.

Every syllable was a loud, protracted belch.

"Can't understand a word you're saying, love. I guess I best be going."

But then her tone hardened.

"Be glad I only gave you the belch voice. It could have been the fever and boils; or worse. So you best watch your tone with me."

She sneered, gave a condescending curtsey, and strutted out of the tent.

9

BELLADONNA'S SECRET GARDEN

Belladonna strode into her tent and flung open the curtain covering the door. She felt no need to socialize and was happy to get away from the Ringmaster. Besides, her plants needed tending.

"Hello, my little darlings," she said with a sweet tone.

She pranced around with extra bounce in her step, dangerously close to something resembling happy.

The plants traveled everywhere she did; each pot was labeled with a stake in its soil. There was woody-stemmed Oleander, with stiff green leaves and pink blossoms, set next to the Monkshood with its long stems, velvety leaves and enticing purple flowers. Another pot held White Snakeroot, with delicate, lacy white flowers, and some of the larger pots held rosary pea. A pot with Dumbcane sat near the entrance, with wide feather shaped yellow-green leaves, right next to a Mandrake with its small purple flowers. Some of the plants stood over eight feet tall, including a Manchineel, some Angel's Trumpet and even a *Cerebra Odollam.*

She tended to the plants in a motherly way, pinching off some dead leaves and watering the soil with a tin pitcher. She lifted the lid from a wooden crate and peeked inside. The compost was moist, and the mushrooms were growing well. The delicate looking fungus stood up out of the compost on slug-colored stems, just a few inches tall. Their caps were pale grey, with iridescent green and blue spots that glowed softly, casting an enchanting aura across her pale skin.

"You look beautiful," she said, talking to the mushrooms.

Satisfied with their development, she closed the lid and turned to the last plant.

"*Bonjour mon homonyme,*" she said sweetly. The plant stood as tall as she did, lush with purple blossoms, its branches weighed down by deep-purple pods. Some refer to the plant as Deadly Nightshade. Others call it Belladonna. It was her name-sake. She pinched another dead leaf, just as the Ringmaster burst in.

"That was completely unacceptable, Belladonna!"

His voice had returned to normal, and he sounded angry.

"I only used a little," she said.

She spoke with a dulcet tone, shrugged her shoulders and batted her eyes.

"You're fine," she said. "Your voice already is back to normal. Relax, love."

"I'm not fine, and I won't tolerate your insolence any longer. You may not have noticed, but we have a hierarchy here, a pecking order, and I sit at the top of the heap. I'm the top dog. I'm the boss here. I make the rules. I won't let you break that down. This is my show, my program. So you can either get with the program, or you can get out."

"Please. You can't be serious."

"Oh, I'm deadly serious."

"If I leave, who would do your dirty work? You certainly won't."

"Where do you think Mechanicules is right now?" he said. "He's cleaning up your mess, doing your job for you, delivering a very clear message to Ramshorn. You've nearly outlived your usefulness to me, Belladonna. So fall into line or just move along. It's really quite as simple as that."

Her tone grew more aggressive.

"Is that supposed to scare me? Do you think I *like* it here? Do you think I wouldn't love to leave, and never come back?"

She got louder.

"You think I like being part of this freakshow?"

Her words were strained, ripped through gritted teeth.

"I was born into this hell-hole of a life and I have loathed every single moment of it. My parents brought me in and then they died, leaving me with you, these sideshow freaks, and this dreadful mess of a life. I didn't seek this out. It was put upon me. I did your bidding as a child, just so I could eat. Now I'm stuck here, doing more of the same, ashamed of my past and fearful for my future."

He stared back with raised eyebrows, letting her get it out of her system. She took one final shot.

"I do the things you can't bring yourself to do on your own, because you don't have the courage for it. You need me."

Infuriated as he was, he calmed himself. He spoke with a metered and unemotional tone.

"Do I? Do I really need you? Nobody is keeping you here, Belladonna. You know where the door is. Here, let me step out of the way. You're free to go any time you choose. Shall I hold the curtain for you? Because I will."

"You say that so easily, but where am I supposed to go? You know as well as I do that I can't. People stare, they judge, they conspire against me. They cross the street to avoid coming near me. When I go into town, they see me coming and close their shop doors. No matter where we stop, it's always the same. It might take a few days, but word travels fast, and it's the same every time!"

"Well, consider this. Maybe they have good reason to be concerned. Maybe they are right to be afraid of you. Maybe that will never change, no matter where you go."

She pondered the notion.

"Besides," she said. "I could never leave Mech behind. He needs me here. You know that, and you use it against me."

"You have a safe place here. We can have a cooperative relationship, and provide for each other's needs. But there has to be some give and take, and you will show me some respect. This will be the last time we have this conversation. Do *we* have a proper understanding?"

Belladonna sat quiet, defiant. She offered no response. Just a cold stare.

"I'll take that as a yes," he said.

The Ringmaster left, mumbling under his breath, but she didn't hear what he said. She clenched her fists, flung her head back and let out a throat-inflaming scream. Then she plopped onto her cot, in a defeated huff.

As she sat staring upward, Beatrix Delacroix, the tightrope walker, burst into the tent with her tiny five-foot body, wearing a puffy chiffon skirt that came down to her knees. She donned a tan leather corset, pressing up her ample busts over a pink lacy top, and wore pink satin fingerless gloves that ran up to her elbow. Her skin was fair, a perfect match to her golden-blonde hair which was pulled back into a tousled bun, with a few stray wisps that hung down in her face. Her legs were clad in white thigh-high stockings that ran down into silky pink ballet slippers. She was excited, invigorated. She was the newest member of the Black Steam Circus. Having joined recently, she was still learning about its members, getting to know people. She had decided today was a good day to get to know Belladonna.

"That was brilliant back there, the way you dispatched Phillippe! "Whack!" she said with her squeaky voice, as she swiped her hand through the air with a gleeful laugh.

Belladonna stared back, quietly stunned and wholly unmoved.

"I've been waiting for someone to do that," Beatrix went on. "I bet it's been a long time coming."

"Phillippe is a horse's ass," Belladonna said, emotionless.

Belladonna sat there, stone still, tracking Beatrix' movement with her eyes as she paced back and forth around the tent. The energy she had was unnerving.

"I know! He thinks he's so handsome, so charismatic. Ooh-la-la, look at me, I'm Phillippe!" Beatrix said, bouncing and waving her arms.

"Crackers, he makes me crazy."

She was happy all the time, a person who could find the good in the worst of situations. She even sounded happy complaining about Phillippe. Then she glanced around the tent, and realized she had never been inside before. There had never been any occasion. Belladonna kept to herself most of the time, and nobody complained. Most who knew her were quietly grateful. Beatrix pointed a finger around the tent's interior.

"So. What's with all the plants?"

Still feeling vulnerable, Belladonna indulged.

"I use them."

"For what?"

"A lot of things," she said. "This is a Barking Tree. Its bark contains an oil that affects the vocal cords. It's what I used to give the Ringmaster the Belch Voice."

"The bark of the barking tree made him bark?"

"Yes, that's right."

Beatrix laughed a squeaky laugh.

"Oh, that's hilarious! I love it!"

Belladonna stared back coldly, her face devoid of emotion.

"And this is Dumbcane. When you eat it, it makes your mouth, tongue and throat swell up, followed by facial numbness, swelling and drooling. And I mean severe drooling. Just a spot of its extract can make you look pretty foolish. Moderate doses are debilitating, but usually temporary. A large enough dose could prove fatal."

"So… why would you eat it?"

"You wouldn't."

"I don't understand."

"Not on purpose anyway. But if a little bit accidentally fell into your food…"

Belladonna shrugged and looked away.

"Right," she said slowly, starting to understand.

Her happy edge wore dull. She stood dumbfounded, slightly fearful.

"That's…weird."

"This is a manchineel tree. Some call it the *manzanilla de la muerte*. If you don't already know, that's Spanish for little apple of death. When it's milky resin touches your skin, it causes severe fever and large painful boils. It is a dreadful experience, incredibly potent. Horrible to look at."

Her tone grew sensual.

"And the fruit? Devastatingly toxic."

"Uh. And what, exactly, do you use them for?"

Beatrix found herself feeling withdrawn and uncomfortable; not her perky self at all. The transformation had only taken a second in Belladonna's presence. Others had experienced the same discomfort. She was unsure of what to say next. The emotion drained from Belladonna's face, and she resumed her deadpan tone. Beatrix was quietly judging her, and Belladonna could see it.

"You're asking a lot of questions."

"What?" Beatrix said nervously.

"You're asking. A lot. Of questions."

Her tone was terse, and her stare chilling. She shifted back to her more mocking tone.

"Why so curious, cupcake? What are you after?"

Her lips pressed into a pout, and she batted her eyelashes, waiting for a response.

"Well? What is it?" she pressed.

Her fleeting moment of vulnerability had passed, and the window for Beatrix make any sort of meaningful connection had shut tight.

"I don't understand. I was just being friendly…"

Beatrix stopped herself.

"I think I should go."

Belladonna flipped up her lenses and leaned in nose-to-nose. Beatrix could feel Belladonna's warm, moist breath on her face. Her eyes were piercing and unrelenting. She whispered her response slowly.

"I think that's a good idea."

Beatrix turned on a heel and rushed out of the tent without another word, which left Belladonna and her plants all alone, just as they had been so many times before. And that suited Belladonna just fine.

10

INSIDE THE BIG BARN

During the long train ride back from John's flat, Michael reflected on the events of the last few days. He was intrigued, but nervous, and he doubted his readiness. There were so many emotions to process, so much information to digest, and so much preparation required. John's admonishment had weakened his fragile determination and the magnitude of what lay ahead weighed heavily on him. When he arrived back home, he stood in the yard of his homestead, and looked up toward the heavens. In the middle of the night, under dark skies, lit by a sliver of a moon, and surrounded by a symphony of crickets, Michael stood once again in the worn mud path that ran from the workshop to the house, pondering what to do. He looked over to a larger barn, across the property, where the grass in between was tall and undisturbed.

Maybe John was right. Maybe he should toss the key and forget about it. The homestead was familiar. Work was easy. Life was predictable. But should he just carry on with his day-to-day routine? Or should he follow in his father's footsteps, honor his legacy and seize the opportunity he had dreamed of so wildly since his childhood?

He looked at the house and thought of his mother. He hated the idea of leaving her alone for any length of time, and if he went, he could be gone for days or weeks. She was mostly self-sufficient, but she liked the help and the company Michael provided. He tried to convince himself that she needed him to stay. But deep down, he knew what he truly feared was that she might do something to over-exert herself in his absence. Right or wrong, Michael still carried a great deal of guilt from his father's death, and, as a result, he watched over his mother like a hawk. Would she be ok without him? What if something happened while he was gone?

He would also need to miss work, and Mr. Wentworth would not like that; not one bit. He might never hear the end of it. And Colin. Colin would almost certainly lose his job without someone there to fix his daily disasters. Nobody else could do it, he told himself. He had so many projects going on in the workshop, so many new ideas to explore, three new ones just from the train ride. It would be so easy to just forget about the race, to just walk back into the workshop and disappear into his work. Just like every other day. This was his dream, though. His destiny. It would make his father so proud, if he could just see Michael competing, let alone winning. With a final glance around, he decided, he knew what he needed to do. He took a deep breath, then he strode right off that beaten mud path. He marched through the tall grass, and over to the large barn, with a new-found determination.

He stood in front of its doors, appreciating their grand scale. When both were open, the entrance was nearly fifteen feet across. But on this night, the doors were chained shut, as they had been for years. He reached into his pocket and pulled out his keychain, spinning the keys to precisely the right one. As he opened the lock and dropped the chains to the ground, he leaned into the heavy wooden door and gave it a shove. He walked into the pitch black interior, pulled a pack of matches from his other pocket and lit an oil lamp. Once the first was lit, he walked it around the interior to light the next, and then the next. One after the other, he gradually lit up the whole of the barn's enormous interior.

After he placed the lamp back in its mount, he took a deep breath, turned around and looked to the center of the barn's open space. There they sat: Seamus' dirigible, his steam-powered side-wheel paddle boat and his racing buggy. The dirigible was in a serious state of disrepair. It was larger than Michael had remembered, with a gondola big enough to seat a pilot, plus five or six others. Its last voyage was brutal. The steamer was outdated, and its buoyancy was suspect. The racing buggy, while faster than what Michael ordinarily drove, was old and slow by current standards. Michael ran his fingers through his hair and down the back of his neck. He shook his head.

"It looks like I've got my work cut out for me," he mumbled to himself. "Wish me luck, Poppa."

11

CHECK-IN AT THE RACE

Three Months Later
7:00 am - July 8, 1895 - Gatling Meadows

It was race day. One by one, the participants checked in at Gatling Meadows, the designated starting point for this year's race. The morning air was cold and wet, and the meadows were still lush and green, still unfazed by early summer's heat. They had come together in the geological bowl known as Gatling Meadows, a vast expanse of flat earth surrounded by hills in a near-perfect circle. There were only two ways to get in to or out of Gatling Meadows. Possum Pass to the north, or Giblet Gulch to the south.

As the participants got organized and prepared their vehicles, the sun beamed down through broken clouds as thin spears of light kissed the meadow floor and warmed the ground. Plumes of steam rose from the grass and drifted with the slight breeze. The participants had spent months making preparations to stow their sea and air vehicles at appropriate waypoints marking the starts of the second and third legs. One of the biggest challenges participants faced each year was to find a way to move a vehicle into place securely, to store them at the ready for the second and third legs without detection by other participants, or people acting on their behalf. A vehicle stored in the open, unattended, was susceptible to theft or sabotage. While the rules surmise the race will be conducted in a sportsmanlike manner, history has shown that's not always the case.

Hundreds of spectators descended upon the meadow to witness the start, filing into makeshift grandstands. The scene at check-in bordered on chaotic. Michael was among the mass of people, and he politely shoved his way through the crowd. When he found the check-in, he approached the table and introduced himself to the attendant.

"Michael McGillicuddy, um, checking in?"

The attendant looked up and eyed Michael for a second.

"Michael McGillicuddy" he repeated. "Checking in?"

"Yes. I heard you. Are you asking me a question, young man?"

"No, I'm telling you I would like to check in."

The attendant glared at him for a few seconds, and then he closed one eye. He squinted with the other eye, and held a ledger up to his face, nearly touching his nose."

"Yes, McGillicuddy, of course. You must be Seamus' boy."

"Yes, that's right."

"Mmm hmm. Token, please."

"Token?"

"You do have an admission token, don't you?"

"Oh. Yes, of course."

Michael shoved his hand down into the pocket of his trousers and felt around, but found nothing. He gulped a little, embarrassed, and reached into his other pocket.

"Ah. Here you go."

He pulled the heavy, polished token from his pocket and held it out proudly.

"Ruby-eyed dragon?" The attendant said. "Very good. May I?"

Michael nodded, and the attendant swiped the token from his

hand. He pulled a device out from under the table and placed it on the table in front of him. It looked like a coin sorter, with a tall metal back forming a flat vertical surface. It had tracks and grooves and levers connected to wheels for the token could travel across, back and forth. The slots, tracks, wheels and levers tested the token's weight, height and thickness to a very specific degree, in an effort to detect fakes. The bottom of the sorter had two metal wells that tokens would be sorted into. One well was stamped *Authentic*, and the other *Counterfeit*.

"I'll just need to validate your token," the attendant said.

Michael felt anxious, even though he had no reason to. He hadn't done anything dishonest, but he still worried that the token might fall into the counterfeit well. For no reason at all, he found himself feeling as though he was about to be caught for wrong-doing when none had occurred.

"Why the self-doubt?" he thought to himself.

The attendant dropped the token in the slot at the top of the validator. As it dropped in, it rolled toward the right and up onto a rocker mechanism. The token rolled most of the way to the end of the curved rocker. But the rocker didn't drop, and the token rolled back left. As the token came back across the rocker, it fell through a slot, down to the next level. On a slight decline to the left, the token passed through several gates that measured its precise thickness and height. When it reached the rocker at the other end, it rolled past and dropped down another level, then back right. As it passed through the final gates, it dropped into one of the wells with a dull metallic clank.

The attendant leaned in to see which it had fallen into and turned toward Michael with a look of surprise. He dabbed the point of his pencil on his tongue and placed the ledger down on the table top. He leaned his face down toward the paper, nose nearly touching it, and scribbled something down.

"McGillicuddy. Pull your vehicle up to the starting line. Stall ten. And Mr. McGillicuddy…"

"Yes?"

"For what it's worth, young man, I knew your father, and I was quite fond of him. The man had a heart of gold. He helped me more than once though difficult situations, and he expected nothing in return. The lord did us all a great disservice in taking him so early."

Michael nodded.

"Thank you for saying so. I appreciate it."

"I wish you luck, young man. Please tell your mother Soairse I said hello."

"And who might you be?"

"Barnaby Higginbottam," he said. "The third."

Michael nodded, and stepped away to find his vehicle. With so many people, it was hard to tell which direction the starting line was.

"Are you lost?" he heard.

Surprised, Michael turned to see a woman staring back at him. She offered a handshake.

"Scarlet Sinclair. MI-4, British Intelligence, at her Majesty's service," she said.

She sounded so elegant and sophisticated, with the face of a porcelain doll and shoulder-length red hair that dangled in loose ringlets from under her derby cap. She wore a grey woolen dress, split up the side, brown leather boots laced to mid-shin and a handbag slung across her chest. Her eyes sparkled and her handshake was confident. She immediately struck Michael as extraordinary, as few others had.

"Michael McGillicuddy," he replied. "I guess I'm a mechanic. I was just…looking for the…starting line. I need to move my buggy."

"Yes, Michael, I know. Charmed," she said with a curtsey. "I haven't seen you here before. Do you know these blokes?"

"I only know one of them, it's my first time participating," he said as he looked around, distracted.

"First time. Lucky you. What do you think so far?"

"It's all very new, and a bit overwhelming if I'm being honest. But it's also quite exciting."

His eyes darted around. He seldom made eye contact with her. She kept trying to talk with him, but his mind was elsewhere, and he was notoriously bad at chit chat. While they talked, a short, stocky man, aged in his mid-thirties, strolled up to the check-in table. He smiled a confident, easy smile, as if all was right in his world. He walked with a smooth but purposeful gait, and his arms swung back and forth pumping up and down across his chest with each step. He had a big barrel chest and tree-trunk-sized arms and legs; thick, but not chiseled and he carried a heavy smithing hammer in his right hand. He was dressed in a dark short-sleeved shirt under a grey vest, and a black kilt with grey and silver plaid accents. His hulking biceps tested the limits of the shirt sleeves, and his barrel chest tested the buttons of his vest. His hair was shiny orange in color, his beard was thick and wiry, and thick, curly hair stood up off of his arms, like a sweater worn ragged. He stepped up to the table.

"The name's Copper," he said.

He doffed his cap, and spoke with a heavy Scottish brogue.

"Last name?"

"Nah. Sorry, laddie. People just call me Copper. And you can too, if ya like."

Copper gently pointed a thick finger at the attendant as he spoke with a smooth and easy diction, flashing a confident and charismatic smile. He pulled his token from the inside pocket of his vest, and flipped it with his thumb into the air toward the attendant. The attendant caught the token on the fly and dropped it into the validator.

"OK, Mr. Copper. You're all checked in. Pull your vehicle to the starting line, please, stall twelve."

"It's just Copper," he said, as he walked away.

It was a nickname he received when he was a young boy, and it stuck through adulthood. The name referred to the color of his hair; not strawberry blond, not orange, not a classic redhead color at all. His hair was unique, quite literally the color, sheen and texture of thin strands of copper wire. Scarlet watched him walk away, then went back to talking to Michael.

"He's been through this several times before," she said, referring to Copper. "He's never actually won, and he's usually just here for the fun of it. He never takes it too seriously, despite tremendous potential. But it's also not surprising. From what I understand, that's his approach to everything in life. He's immensely capable, strikingly intelligent, but he takes it easy. He does what he likes, and never gets too worked up over the details. As a result, he's never terribly competitive. I'm not too worried about him."

"That's a shame," Michael said.

"Not really, he doesn't need to work hard. His family is wealthy. They make and sell the vast majority of the metal tooling, pliers and hammers and such, all across Europe. It's family money that makes this possible for him. He has nothing of his own at stake. When this is done, he'll probably just go back to swinging a hammer; working in the family business as a blacksmith. And I gather he'll be just fine with that. Win or lose, I don't think this will change a thing for him."

She paused.

"Now. The man over there, on the other hand, in the red coat. That's a whole different story. That's the Ringmaster. A perennial contender, but he's never won, despite his greatest efforts. The best he's ever finished is second place. Three times, in fact."

"That sounds pretty good to me," Michael said.

"It depends on your perspective. For many here, second place is the same as last. If you're not winning, you're losing. There is no middle ground. The Ringmaster happens to be someone who feels that way; and quite strongly I might add."

"Is that so?"

"It is. He has been terribly frustrated of late, and has resolved to win this year. Keep a watchful eye with him, just to be safe. He has a big crew he runs with. And they all play for keeps."

"Crew?" Michael asked.

"Yes. Crew."

"Right. That makes perfect sense."

Michael drifted away, lost in thought, wondering if he should have a crew of his own. Had he made a mistake coming alone? Who would he have brought, and what would they be responsible for, he wondered. Then he remembered what John had said about trust, and questioned Scarlet.

"Why are you being so helpful?" he asked.

"Am I helping? I thought I was just making conversation. Glad to have helped in any event."

He caught himself. In a moment they would be competitors, but in the meantime, he might as well take what information he could. In the distance, the Ringmaster stood some thirty yards away, talking with distinguished-looking man, perhaps a military man or high ranking noble, judging from his clothing. He wore a patch on one eye, and tall chimney-stack top hat. The men were having an animated conversation that involved a lot of pointing and arm waving.

"Who is the Ringmaster talking to over there?" Michael asked.

"That's Baron Kamper von Braun. He's a multi-winner, the winningest ever, in fact."

"Oh, bloody hell!" Michael said. "The Baron is here?"

"Yes, of course he is. It's hard to imagine he wouldn't be."

A lump formed Michael's throat. The Baron had been successfully competing since Michael was soiling his knickers. One thought led to another, until he found himself reimagining the day his father died, replaying every moment of the story of Seamus' victory over the Baron, right up to the point of his collapse. Michael had always drawn upon his father's stories for strength and inspiration. That usually brought him comfort. But here, today, he only felt anxious.

"Michael?"

The sound of Scarlet's voice jolted him out of his daydream.

"Sorry, what?"

"I thought I lost you there for a moment. I said the Baron has won four times, in fact. I expect he will be among the favorites here."

"Favorites?"

"Yes, for the oddsmakers."

"Oddsmakers? What do you mean oddsmakers?"

"Oh, you have so much to learn, Michael!"

She sounded disappointed.

"As for the Baron, he's accomplished and very well-funded. His grandfather was a Luxembourg banking magnate who married the daughter of a Noble. Relying on family contacts, they started a business and built out much of Europe's current rail system. And the rest, as they say, is history. Family money all the way down. And lots of it."

"So, the Baron is Luxembourgish royalty?"

"Nobility, yes. And he will be very well equipped, formidable."

"He's not invincible, you know," Michael said. "My father beat him."

"Yes. I'm aware."

Michael looked back surprised.

"How does she know so much?" he thought.

He tried to convince himself of the Baron's weaknesses, but the pit in his stomach remained. As Scarlet finished, a woman to their side started speaking. Her words came quick and crisp, as she scurried up to the table.

"Vixen van Buren. I would like to check in, please."

Michael and Scarlet looked over. Vixen waited patiently while the attendant checked her in. She stood with perfect posture, chin up and out, shoulders back and hands crossed in front of her. She looked smart and stately in her full-length maroon dress trimmed with a bustle and bow.

"Now she's an interesting addition," Scarlet said with a huff. "You don't see many women, here. It's usually just me, in fact. Unless, of course, you count the Ringmaster's creepy sidekick, Belladonna Atropa. I don't know much about this Vixen woman yet; I know she's an alchemist, and I know she does some work for her government and private industry. Very bright, and apparently she's developed an impressive portfolio of inventions, but I haven't had the chance to dig very deep."

"So, you check out everyone here?"

"Yes, of course. It is what I do, after all."

She spoke with a healthy dose of self-satisfaction.

"Even me?"

"Even you. Can't wait to see what you've got, Michael, I expect to be impressed. You're not going to let me down now, are you?"

She spoke with a flirtatious purr.

"Well, I'm not totally sure what expectations you've set for me," he said. "So at this point it's rather hard for me to answer that question."

He had missed the flirtation in her voice. The attendant finished checking Vixen in.

"You're all set, Mrs. van Buren. Pull your vehicle to the starting line, stall eight."

"Miss."

"Pardon me?"

"You said Mrs. van Buren. It's Miss. Miss van Buren."

"Right, my apologies. Good luck Miss van Buren. Stall eight. Off you go, now."

She glanced at Michael and Scarlet while she slipped on her driving gloves and pulled them up to her elbows. Recognizing they were probably competitors, she offered a gesture of sportsmanship.

"Good luck to the both of you," she said, followed by a nod and a delicate curtsey.

She spoke with a genuinely pleasant tone, honestly well-wishing, devoid of any pretense.

"Good luck to you as well, Miss van Buren."

His words came more comfortably than usual, and when his eyes met Vixen's, he found a certain comfort in her soft gaze. Normally, he would look away, or stutter. Or fumble with something to distract himself with anything but the conversation at hand. But she was easy to look at, easy to engage with, and the words just came.

"Safe travels," he continued.

"Thank you. And you as well."

She wound her hair up into a bun and staked it with a wooden rod as she scurried off to her vehicle.

"She seems nice enough," Scarlet said. "But that doesn't mean much to me. You never really know until you know. Do you know what I mean?"

"What?"

Michael had drifted off again, as he was prone to do.

Scarlet smiled knowingly.

"What were you just thinking about?"

"What? Nothing."

"Right, of course not," she said. "Nothing at all, I'm sure. Anyway, that big hairy mess over there, that's John Ramshorn; but you've already met, haven't you?"

Michael nodded. John looked more disheveled than usual. His ill-fitting clothes were soiled with food and grime, his hair a mess. Michael waved to get his attention, but John was distracted and looked away.

"We've met, yes. But you're really making me uncomfortable knowing so much," Michael said. "I'm not sure whether to keep you close where I can see you, or put as much distance between us as possible."

"Given what I've already told you," she said. "How would a perception of distance make you feel any better?"

"Touché," he said. "But that's really not helping. Just stay where I can see you, ok?"

Scarlet turned serious and gave Michael a quick warning.

"Don't look over. But Dorado Eschevarria is walking this way."

"Dorado what?"

"Things just got interesting. He is crafty bounty hunter, and as tough as they come. Guns are really his first choice - powerful guns, mind you. But he's also tricky, very sharp and wily. I can't wait to see how he does."

Despite her warning not to look, Michael looked anyway. Dorado was walking directly at him, wearing a black leather trench coat and a tattered gambler-style hat. Under the dirty, crumpled trench coat, Dorado wore a dusty pinstripe suit, and weathered leather boots. His pants were held up by a heavy leather belt packed full of gadgets. Among them were two pairs of Darby Cuffs that clanked together as he walked, and leather holsters on each hip holding six-barrel gatling pistols. A rifle in a holster hung across his back.

The years had not been kind to Dorado. His deeply creased, tobacco-brown skin told the tale of a man who spent a lifetime outdoors. An ever-present toothpick stuck out from the corner of his weathered lips, and he wore the brim of his hat down low, covering his eyes. He gave Michael a stiff shoulder bump as he passed by on his way to the check-in. As Dorado reached the table, he cast a shadow over the attendant. He spoke quietly, in a soft but raspy voice with an elegant Spanish accent, as cool as ice.

"Good day to you. My name is Dorado Eschevarria. I am here to crush my competition with merciless fury. May God take pity upon any man who dares to stand in my way."

He pounded his admission token down on the table.

"Yes, well, aren't you an ambitious one, Mr. Eschevarria!" the attendant said as he validated the token. "All set now! Stall eleven please!"

He held his hand out, waving Dorado away. Dorado glared back at him, pondering whether to bother with a response. Without a word, he tipped his hat, smacked his toothpick, and turned to walk away. Michael dusted himself off after being bumped. He straightened his vest and hoisted his satchel back up on his shoulder.

"That was incredibly rude," Michael said. "Wholly undignified."

"You need to thicken that delicate skin of yours," Scarlet said.

She grabbed both of his hands and turned them upward, to peek at his palms.

"Callouses! I certainly didn't expect that. You know, from looking at you and all."

"I work with my hands."

"Yes, I know. And fine hands they are. I just didn't expect it. You're just… a little too handsome and wholesome to have callouses. That's all."

She giggled, and placed her hand over her mouth. Oblivious once again to the attention he was getting, Michael kept talking.

"Yeah, I suppose. Anyway, I've spent a lot of time working on my vehicles to get them ready for this, so I hope they are up to the task. You know, up to the same level as some of the others here."

He rubbed the back of his neck and looked around to see what he was up against.

"Your vehicles?" she said with a smirk.

"Yes, my vehicles. Now what?"

"If you think a swift buggy is all you need to get you through this competition, then you've got another thing coming. I can't wait to see the look on your face."

"What is that supposed to mean? It's a race, is it not?"

"It is…more or less. Simply put, it means this won't be like driving to the factory for work and back. It's so much more involved."

"Involved? How so?"

"Oh, Michael. I wouldn't want to spoil the experience for you. Just be careful."

"Careful?"

"Michael, look around you. There are what I would guess to be a record number of new entrants here this year. You know what that means, right?"

"No, not really."

She sighed.

"Let me make it easy for you. There are twenty spots open each year. The fact that we have so many new entrants this year suggests many of last year's participants, you know, either refused to show up this year, or, well, couldn't."

"Couldn't make it?"

"They're no longer available to compete. At *anything*. I certainly hope this year is less dangerous."

She leaned in and patted him gently on the chest with her open palm.

"Be safe out there, Michael, and be smart. I have faith in you, but I won't let up. And neither will anyone else."

Michael stared into the distance, and tried to process her words. Perhaps he should have taken John's advice after all. Perhaps he should have stayed home.

AT THE OPPOSITE END OF THE CHECK-IN, TWO PITHY YOUNG MEN walked up to register their attendance.

"Henry Wilfork, checking in," one said.

"With William Wilfork," the other said.

"Be a lamb, would you, and speed this along," Henry said. "We have a race to win."

"Token please," the attendant said.

Henry threw his token down on the table and adjusted his trousers.

"Serious pops, let's move it along. We really need to go."

The twin brothers stood in front of the attendant with forced smiles, maintaining unwilling patience with the man and his ridiculous rules. The attendant eyed them and looked down at his ledger.

"You young bucks would be well-served to learn some manners," he said. "Not to mention, some respect for your elders."

The brothers stood tall and proud, chest out, hands on lapels. Their square jaws bore handsome smiles with perfectly straight, if not slightly oversized, pearly-white teeth. Henry took off his wide-brimmed hat and ran his fingers through his wavy blonde hair.

"Let's go, old man. We don't have all day."

The attendant made a sour face and shook his head at Henry's abrasive tone. He dropped the token into the validator and let it run its course. It fell into the metal well marked *Authentic*, with a heavy clank.

"Shame," the man said as he looked down at it. "Stall five. Good luck, gentlemen. And I use that term in the most generous possible way. I really do."

Henry flashed an obscene gesture at the attendant and slapped Will on the back.

"Let's go, brother."

As they shoved their way through the crowd, they came upon the Baron.

"Hey. You're Baron Kamper von Braun," Will said.

The Baron perked up at hearing this. He postured up and looked down his nose at them.

"That's what they tell me," the Baron said with confidence.

Will pointed at the Baron's chest.

"Arrogance! I like that. Listen, we hear you're pretty good."

"I've heard that as well," the Baron said. "In fact, I've won this event five times, more than any other participant. It sounds as though you have some well-informed sources."

"That's great. I'm glad to hear it. So here's the thing, we could really use someone like you. So if you'd like to pack gear for the winners, grab your things and meet us at stall five. We could use an extra set of hands to carry our bags."

"Yeah," Henry added. "We might even let you try the cloak on at the finish line."

The brothers laughed out loud, and exchanged congratulatory pats on the back. And with that, Henry and William set off meandering through the crowd, ably offending anyone within earshot. As they walked through, Vixen caught Henry's eye, and he stopped.

Henry jabbed William with his elbow and nodded in Vixen's direction.

"Whoa, get a load of this one, Will."

"Dibs," Will said.

"No chance, man," Henry replied, "She's got my name written all over her. And before this race is over, she'll have my scent all over her, too."

He chuckled to himself and approached her. He came up from behind, and gave her a firm smack on the backside. Startled, she spun around with a look of surprise.

"Hey there, beautiful. Why don't you meet me at the finish. It shouldn't be hard to find me. I'll be the handsome one standing on the winner's podium."

He stood in a cocky stance. He held his chest out, and raised his square jaw high, with a big toothy smile, nodding confidently. But his peacockish display only roused her anger. She stiffened up, spoke with her hands on her hips, and occasionally wagged an angry finger in his face.

"First of all," she said, "never touch me again. Second, I am an intelligent, educated woman with dignity, class and grace. That said, I do as I please and I take what I want, when I want it. If I had even the slightest bit of interest in the likes of you, young man, I would have let you know already."

Henry reeled back, but Vixen wasn't finished with him.

"And make no mistake," she said, "I will never, ever play doting female prey, waiting around for a swift smack on the bottom, giggle and throw myself into your arms, powerless to resist your Neanderthal advances. Do you know anything about me?"

Henry's cheeks began to burn as Vixens voice grew louder and drew more attention. People were watching, and he was growing more uncomfortable.

"Third, there won't be any room on the podium for you, Mr. Teeth, as it will be fully occupied by me, and my newly inflated ego. Fourth, don't ever touch me again. Fifth…"

"Never touch you again," Will said, interrupting. "He's got it, ok? I beg your forgiveness of my bother, ma'am, he's a bit of a horse's arse. You shouldn't waste your time dignifying his crass behavior. I suspect you have too much class to stoop to such a level."

"Well, thank you. So nice to see a little respect, finally."

"Of course," he said, tipping his cap. "Instead, you should spend some time with a real man, someone like me. Somebody who…"

"Oh my God, you're unbelievable."

"What?" he said, with hands out.

As Vixen stomped off in disgust, another participant arrived to check in. She brushed by him on her way past.

"Reginald McHedgie," he said. "Checking in."

Away from the check-in tables, near the starting line, the Ringmaster cinched the leather straps down on the cargo bag, securing it to the back of his vehicle.

"Mechanicules," he said. "Do the others know what they need to do to set up our forward camp? Once we get to the first stop, I don't want any slack. The tents should be arranged ahead of time. Equipment and rations should be ready upon our arrival. There can be no delays."

Mechanicules nodded.

"Superb, everything has to run like a well-oiled machine. Too much preparation has gone into this to allow any mistakes."

He turned to Belladonna.

"I trust your preparations are complete?"

"Relax, cookie. I know what I'm doing. It's all under control."

"Excellent."

KAMAL KHAN WAS A LATE ARRIVAL INTO THE MEADOW, RECENTLY arrived from South Asia. He stepped out of his vehicle and walked, or rather flowed, through the crowd. Some people move with a bounce in their step. But Kamal glided. He nearly floated across the ground with a smooth and regal gait. His look was confident. His stare was unflinching. Every movement he made was slow and smooth, deliberate and purposeful. His clothing was notable, dressed head to toe in fine black fabric. His pants were tight around the waist, but free-flowing and loose through the legs. They fell into pleats and tapered at the ankle. His top was woven from the same fine fabric, all black, flowing and loose, cinched tight around his waist by a black fabric sash tied in a knot by hand. A black turban covered his hair. His expression was blank. His complexion was deep olive with dark rings under his eyes. An astrolabe, a navigational device, hung from his sash on one side. A small dagger and sheath were tucked into the sash, right next to it.

As he presented his token for validation, the attendant noticed the palm of Kamal's hand. It had strange, squiggly lines drawn on it, that ran out from under his sleeve, over the palm and all the way down to his fingertips. It wasn't the attendant's place to ask, so he minded his business and assigned Kamal his stall.

After he checked in, Kamal walked back through the crowd again, slowly and methodically, carefully evaluating his competition. He moved in the direction of Henry and William Wilfork. They saw him coming and chattered among themselves.

"Hey Will, look there."

"Who is that?"

"Kamal Khan, I'm pretty sure," Henry said. "I've heard some things. You know what they say about him? They say he has some sort of magical powers or something. Look at him, what do you think?"

"Magical powers? I call phooey, brother. What's he gonna do, turn me into a lizard or something?"

"I dunno, I'm just telling you what they say. Look at that outfit, whatever it is," Henry said. "I mean, just look at him. There has to be something going on there. You can tell just by looking at him. Something smells rotten. I don't like the guy."

As Kamal got closer, Henry stepped into his path, which brought Kamal to an abrupt stop.

"Hey pal," Henry said. "Kamal Khan, right?"

"I am Kamal Khan. Yes."

With the back of his hand, Henry whacked Will in the chest.

"See, I told you it was him."

Will was surprised at this. He didn't recall a disagreement, but Henry continued.

"My brother Will here, he says you know some dark magic or something. Can you do magic?"

Will was indignant.

"I didn't say that. I never said that, Henry."

"Sure you did," Henry said with a wink. "Will here, he told me all about you. He says you can do all sorts of magic."

Henry wiggled his fingers in the air while he talked.

"So come on now. Show us what you can do real quick. Whatcha got?"

Kamal stood tall and stared down his nose at Henry. Henry was acting like a schoolboy egging on a fight.

"One who deals in gossip betrays a confidence," Kamal said, "but one who is of a trustworthy spirit is one who keeps a secret."

"What did you just say to me?" Henry asked.

Kamal nodded and walked toward the starting line, gliding away gracefully. Henry turned to Will and smacked him in the chest with the back of his hand again.

"That guy is a freak. A real clown, I tell you. Let's go, brother. And keep a close eye on him."

12

RECITATION OF THE RULES

As the participants finished their check-ins, spectators were guided into the wooden grandstands. A band played nearby, all ten of its members decked out in their finest uniforms. As the band played, a black sedan pulled in to the center of Gatling Meadows. It stopped near the grandstands, and the driver stepped out and opened the back door for his passenger. The man who stepped out was moderate in size, but dignified in appearance. He stepped out, walking past the grandstands and up the stairs to his speaking platform. He rested his hands on the rails and leaned forward staring out at the crowd. Dressed in a smart suit, he tipped his head back to peek out from under his derby hat, which he wore pulled down around his eyes, nearly touching the bridge of his nose. A bushy mustache covered most of his mouth, like the bristles of a brush, and they moved visibly at the slightest motion of his lips. The blended hum of voices in the audience faded, as the crowd took notice of his presence. He picked up a megaphone and addressed the participants directly, reading from a sheet of paper on which he had prepared the morning's remarks.

"Thank you for your courtesy, and thank you all for joining us today for what should prove to be a most entertaining venture. We are pleased to see such a robust turnout. Now, you must already have some sense of our purpose here today, or you would not have come here, of all places, now would you? So I will dispense with the formalities and get to the business at hand. Listen closely, for the words I speak may differ from your past experience, or current expectations. Nevertheless, these words shall be the rules of the race and for our purposes here should be treated as law. For those of you who have been indoctrinated in the Order of the Blue Cloak, you know that our membership is significant, and our reach is broad. We have placed designated 'officiants' across all potential routes and waypoints of this year's race. In all likelihood, you will not know who they are; but rest assured - they most certainly will know who you are. Ignore the rules at your own peril. If you fail to comply you will be, hmmm, *disqualified.*"

He paused for dramatic effect, consulted his notes and continued his address.

"Each vehicle may start with one or more persons in it. Teams will be allowed this year. Regardless of how you start, you are permitted to join a team, to leave a team or to change teams at any time you so choose. If you choose to stay solo throughout, that is also acceptable."

He paused and referred to his notes again.

Michael felt suddenly awkward, like a child on the playground not wanting to be the last one picked for a team.

"Teams?" he thought.

He felt sudden pressure to find a teammate. John would be a natural choice, but there was no line of sight to make eye contact with him, so, he turned and looked toward Scarlet in the next stall. She was one of the few participants he had spoken with, and probably the only other person here who would consider pairing up with him. She saw him look over, but she just looked back, raised her eyebrows and shrugged. She understood the unspoken question, but declined to give an answer. As Michael's focus moved past Scarlet, he saw Vixen in the background. She peeked back over at him with what seemed to be a hopeful look. But when their eyes met, she quickly scrunched her nose and looked away, staring straight ahead, concentrating. He wasn't sure what to make of it.

The emcee continued.

"Each of you has been assigned to stop at designated waypoints, these waypoints are set forth in the papers delivered with your Chrysalis, and you may find additional information along the way, if you're sufficiently clever. The path you take from one waypoint to another is completely up to you, but the successful participant, or team as the case may be, will stop at a series of waypoints, collect the designated tokens, and will be the first to arrive at the finish line with a complete and matching set. Along the way, your own path may cross with the paths of the others, but the journey will not necessarily be the same for any of you. In fact, some paths will be far more difficult than average, and some far less so. Such is life, and you will need to adapt. There will be stops, there will be tests and there will be tokens to be collected."

"Tests?" Michael mumbled to himself. "What does that even mean?"

"Like life itself, this event won't always be easy, and it won't always be fair," he said. "In order to succeed you will need to apply mental and physical dexterity. You will combine acquired knowledge with raw intelligence, common sense with intuition, and, of course, no small amount of logic will be needed. A small dose of luck will also serve you well, but only if you believe in that sort of thing. As you make your way along your assigned route, you will be tested at certain milestones. If you successfully pass the test, you will collect the token bearing your marking. Milestone tokens will bear the same designations as your keys and your admission tokens. If you decide to combine into a team with other participants, you may not mix and match tokens of varying designations at the finish. The milestone tokens presented at the finish line must be one complete set, bearing one designation, and one designation only. Anything less is incomplete, and thus a failure."

Michael took a deep breath. He wasn't sure he understood anything the man just said. Milestone tokens? Designations? Tests? His stomach sank again. He felt lost and ill-prepared. What had he gotten himself into? This was something he had wanted to do since early childhood, a lifelong dream. Yet, here he was, about to start, and he couldn't help but feel he had made a horrible mistake by coming. How could he not know more about the rules? It was a secretive society and a secretive process, draped in ambiguity. Details were shrouded. He knew that. But how could he allow himself to arrive here today with so little information, so little knowledge? Then again, how could he not?

The emcee carried on.

"The race will have three legs this year – the first is a land leg, which you will begin momentarily. At the end of the land leg, you can rest overnight in Gillingham, if you so choose, before beginning a short sea leg. The sea leg will be followed by the air leg, departing from Rouen, just to round things out. Your method of travel is of no consequence, be it blimp, bi-plane, split-tail or hang glider, so long as you fly when you are meant to fly. But the mode of travel must be respected: the sea leg must be traveled by water vessel, on or under the water. The air leg must be traveled by air, and the land portion, of course, must be traveled by land. Heed this warning: do not attempt to vary any of the modes of travel, for example, by flying across the sea leg or driving a buggy across the air leg. As I mentioned earlier, we have officiants posted along the course. They will see you, they will know, and they will take action to swiftly *disqualify* the unscrupulous rule-breakers among you. This completes the recitation of rules. Rules not mentioned simply do not exist."

He paused momentarily, to let it all sink in.

"Now, before we begin, let's review one of this year's available advantages."

"Advantages?" Michael mumbled to himself as he rubbed his hands together. "Finally. Some good news."

The emcee continued.

"In recognition of past achievements, and to provide an incentive for the future, all prior winners have once again received one advantage token. To the extent that you earned any advantage tokens for this year's event, they would have been provided to you when you received your Chrysalis.

Michael's shoulders sank. He received none.

"As always," the emcee continued, "you can redeem the tokens to purchase advantages throughout the race. There will be a specific number of designated redemption points along the route. It will be up to you to find them, though. They are not marked on your maps. Token Traders and Trading Posts can be identified by their symbol. Different Traders can provide different advantages. As with everything else, their markings will be subtle. But if you know what to look for, you will find them just fine. One token will get you one advantage. But choose wisely, because not all advantages are created equal."

The emcee snickered to himself and took a moment before he continued.

"The first available advantage is a thirty-minute head start. I can offer this singular advantage to you right now. The rest will be up to you to find on your own. If you choose to redeem this advantage, you will be allowed to leave thirty minutes earlier than everyone else. If you would like to redeem your token for this advantage, please raise your hand and come forward."

The Baron casually raised his finger in the air.

"Baron Kamper von Braun, please step forward to redeem your token. Is there anyone else?"

The Baron was the only taker.

"Very good," the emcee said. "With that out of the way, let us now address one final issue: The Prize. With this year's race being so cerebral in nature, it is only fitting that our winner should be anointed a full-fledged Fellow in the Order of the Blue Cloak, replete with all of the honors, privileges and distinctions attendant thereto. The winner, or winners, will also receive a cash prize of fifty thousand quid. Now, there is only one cash award, winner takes all, and multiple members of a winning team will need to split it among themselves as they see fit. And, last, but definitely not least, there is the greatest prize of all: bragging rights, and the honor of planning our next event. Now. If you haven't already done so, man your vehicles."

The participants gathered their belongings and rushed toward the starting line.

13

LINING UP THE VEHICLES

The participants readied themselves, and their vehicles of various forms. Some drove traditional buggies, with flared fenders and wire wheels. Vixen was among them, with her silver box-topped buggy and windows all around. Copper's vehicle, on the other hand, was anything but traditional. The whole thing was composed of a single wheel, taller than he was. It stood almost upright, leaning slightly to the side, held up by a retractable metal peg at the bottom.

"That's an odd looking vehicle," Michael said.

"It's a monocycle," Scarlet replied. "It only has the one giant wheel. The tire spins around the outside of that huge circular frame. He'll sit inside, in the middle, on the seat in the inner part of the frame. The tire rotates around the outside to propel him forward. Very spiffy."

As she finished, Copper seated himself into the monocycle and harnessed himself in, locking heavy buckles in place.

"It's fast and maneuverable, but not terribly comfortable," she said.

"How do you turn a vehicle that only has one wheel?" Michael said.

"You just hold on and lean to the side. The bars are more for brake and throttle than they are to turn the wheel," she said.

"Fascinating."

THE WILFORK BOTHERS, HENRY AND WILLIAM, SETTLED INTO their steam-powered motorcycle. Henry drove, Will rode in the sidecar. Once they settled in, they each put on their leather aviator caps and bronze aviator goggles. Then, over the cap and goggles, they each strapped on a bronze face guard that covered the lower portions of their faces, just below the goggles.

Reginald McHedgie was sitting in the stall next to them. He leaned over and spoke.

"What are you doing with those crazy masks?" he said with a chuckle. "We already know who you are."

Henry leaned toward him and explained.

"Not that I need to justify anything to you, pal, but you can see we have no windshield."

"Yes, I can see that."

"We can't leave anything to chance. Can't take a rock in the teeth or bug in the eye. We need to take care of these gorgeous faces of ours. But look, in reality," he said with a sarcastic tone. "It's not about us. We do it for the ladies. Lots of broken hearts, if we scarred these faces up. Uproar if I lost a tooth or an eye. Come on now! We do it for the ladies, man!"

"Yes, of course, and I'm sure the ladies appreciate it. Are you gents going to ride together like that?"

"Of course we are. We do everything together."

They looked at each other nodded.

"Are you ready brother?" Henry said.

"Oh, I'm ready, brother."

Will looked back at Reggie and adjusted his goggles one last time, before wishing him well.

"Good luck, jerk."

THE RINGMASTER CLIMBED UP INTO THE SEAT OF HIS VEHICLE. IT was taller than most with an open-top and tall wheels. Each of its four wheels was as tall as Copper's monocycle. The open-top cruiser had four metal seats, two in front, two in back, that sat on springs to cushion the roughness of the road. The springs squeaked loudly as they compressed under his weight as he sat.

"Mech, Belladonna. Let's go." Mechanicules climbed the side ladder to get up in the raised seating area and offered a hand to pull Belladonna up. One seat sat empty.

"I trust everything is in order?" the Ringmaster asked.

"I already told you. It's all set, cupcake. Relax for once, will you."

MICHAEL STEPPED OUT AND WALKED AROUND TO THE BACK OF HIS open top buggy. He had made a few modifications to the buggy, upgrades if you will. One such modification was to add a rack to the back, specifically designed to hold the chest from his father's workshop. Michael cinched the leather straps down. He checked the lid, just to be sure it was closed, and locked it. He rubbed the side of the chest with his hand.

"Here we go, Poppa. I hope I can make you proud."

He stared at the chest, deep in thought, before he was interrupted.

"What do you have there, Michael?" Scarlet said.

"Sorry, what?"

"What do you have there? The chest."

"Oh. It was my father's. It held his tools."

"I see."

"It's very dear to me, my most cherished possession, perhaps. I mean sure, it holds a bunch of tools and whatnot, but it also holds some of my fondest memories."

"What do you mean?"

"We spent a lot of time together in his workshop, when I was young. He taught me to think about new ways of solving problems, designing things. Building, working with tools. A lot of the projects we did together were done with the tools in this chest. On my eleventh birthday, he was going to give it to me. As my birthday gift."

"Well, it looks like he followed through. You have it now, right?"

"No, not exactly. He never got the chance to give it to me. He died that night."

"Oh, Michael, I'm so sorry to hear that."

"It's really fine," he said.

But it really wasn't. Michael had never fully recovered.

"Shortly after he passed, my mother let me know he had wanted me to have it; that it was meant to be my gift that night. It's been a treasure to me ever since. I figured I might as well bring it along, you know, to carry some tools, supplies and a few other things I might need along the way."

He rubbed the chest again.

"I'm hoping there is also a little luck inside. Like the emcee said, it certainly can't hurt. I could use some."

He dropped the satchel off his shoulder and placed it in the passenger seat. The satchel was heavier than usual; he usually just carried papers and notes that he had made, or sketches and designs for things he wanted to build. But today it carried more. Michael settled into the driver's seat with a huff. He reached into his satchel and pulled out an old sepia photograph of himself as a young boy, sitting in his father's lap. He wedged it into the trim on the buggy's dashboard, and prepared to start the race.

14

THE RACE BEGINS

The emcee cleared his throat and raised his megaphone.

"With everyone checked in, we are now in a position to begin this year's race. Heed the rules you've been given. Good luck to you all, and Godspeed. Baron Kamper von Braun, you have chosen to redeem your token for a sizable time advantage. Your time begins now."

He fired a pistol in the air, and the Baron sped off, alone. Michael gulped.

"That's it?" he mumbled to himself.

The pistol report brought a hollow feeling to Michael's stomach. There was no turning back now. The race had started. The lack of pretense was unsettling to him, like being shoved unceremoniously off an emotional ledge. The Baron sped away from the starting line toward the horizon, gradually shrinking out of sight as the others waited for their time to go.

CYRIL HASTINGS SAT PATIENTLY IN HIS OFFICE AS A TELEGRAPH came in.

"The race has begun," it read.

He leaned back in his chair and placed his hands together, fingertip to fingertip, and took a deep breath.

"Put the officiants on notice, the race is now in progress," he said.

The woman he spoke to tapped out a hasty telegraph, alerting the officiants. When she finished, she closed the case on her telegraph machine and quietly left his office, closing the door behind her.

MICHAEL'S MOTHER SOAIRSE SAT AT HER KITCHEN TABLE TALKING with her good friend Emilie. The smell of coffee wafted through the air, as she peered through fogged up windows into the yard.

"How are you doing dear, with Michael being away and all?" Emilie asked.

"Oh, I'm fine. I do miss him, but I trust that he'll be home safe soon enough."

"Are you worried about him?" Emilie asked.

"Of course I am. He's my little Michael."

"He'll be fine, dear."

"I guess I just have to trust that he will," Soairse said.

Her tone betrayed a lack of conviction. Emilie put her hand on Soairse's.

"Did he talk to you about going, before he left?"

"We had a long conversation. Several, in fact. To be honest with you, I really didn't want him to go. I remember the stories that Seamus used to tell me. So much danger out there. But it's been his dream to follow in his father's footsteps. He spent his childhood talking about it. When Seamus passed, it fell by the wayside. But once he got his invitation, I just couldn't imagine him not going. I couldn't possibly ask him not to. So after several emotional talks, we agreed he would go, with my full blessing and support."

"I understand. It couldn't have been easy for you."

"It most certainly wasn't. He was so insistent that I take things easy, that I not over-exert myself while he was gone, he's always so concerned about me lifting or moving anything. He even went to the market and stocked the house full. Everything down low where I could reach it. The top shelves emptied and neatly placed in boxes on the countertop. Honestly, sometimes he treats me like I'm an invalid."

"He's very thoughtful," Emilie said.

"He built a giant feed bin for the animals out back so I wouldn't need to load hay or seed while he was gone. I found it very sweet, but I can handle myself. Honestly, I've done just fine up to now, haven't I? Am I really such a burden on him? I thought I would have shown him differently by now. I hope he doesn't see me that way."

"I don't think he does. You did such a wonderful job raising that young man, without Seamus there. It couldn't have been easy for you, to get by for all those years. I know John helped for a while, but you really did it on your own. You're a strong woman, and you should be very proud of what your son has become."

"He is a very special young man, Emilie. I just wish it could have been different for him. I feel like he was robbed of something. John did help while he was around, but it was Michael who carried us through after John moved to Paris. You know, this is the first time Michael has ever spent an extended time away. It's so odd to think about it, but for the first time ever, in twenty-six some odd years, he's off on his own today. I mean, really on his own."

BACK AT THE FACTORY, COLIN SAT IN FRONT OF HIS MACHINE. THE self-lubricating oil reservoir was working just fine, and parts were running through the machine on their own. There was little else for Colin to do, so he just sat there watching quietly from his stool, resting his chin on his hand. Colin was having a good day, for once.

~

WIM AND MIRTA VAN BUREN LOOKED ACROSS THE TABLE AT EACH other. They had just finished breakfast and were sitting in anxious silence. Wim checked his pocket watch.

"They should be starting soon," Wim said.

He snapped his watch shut.

"Yes, I know," Mirta replied. "She's going to be ok, isn't she?"

"I think so."

"God, I hope so."

~

THE EMCEE FLIPPED HIS POCKET WATCH OPEN TO CHECK THE TIME.

"One minute," he announced. "Prepare yourselves."

Michael looked to his right. Kamal Khan stared back at him. Uncomfortable, Michael turned away. He looked left, and saw Scarlet. She smiled ever so slightly and nodded politely, but the competition was about to begin. Vixen was visible just behind her, and his eyes met hers. She gave him another look, but he still wasn't sure what it was. Arrogance? Interest? Indifference? He was awful at reading people. He preferred straight talk, and was oblivious to pretense or innuendo. As he waited, he glanced further down the line to see John, and beyond John, he saw the Ringmaster sitting up high in his large-wheeled vehicle. He was accompanied by Mechanicules and Belladonna, who he recognized as the haunting woman with the dark glasses from John's flat.

"That's odd." He mumbled to himself. "What is she doing here?"

He could see they were having stern words with John. John looked uncomfortable. As Michael looked ahead into the distance, soothing steam plumes swirled from the meadow floor. Without a word, the emcee raised his pistol in the air, and cracked another shot. The crowds roared from the grandstands as the participants sped away from the starting line and across the meadow.

Panicked, Michael mashed his accelerator. But the Ringmaster was quick to leave the starting line, securing an early lead. So were the Wilfork brothers in their lightweight motorcycle, followed closely by Copper in his monocycle. As they sped across the meadow, the racers jockeyed for position, and bumping ensued. As they made their way to Possum Pass and departed the meadow, the road split in two, one fork leading northeast, the other leading southeast. One group, which included the Ringmaster, Kamal and John among them, headed northeast, while another cluster including Michael, Scarlet, Vixen, Copper veered southeast.

Michael was disappointed to see John go in the opposite direction. But the race was on. He looked at the photograph on his dash, gripped the wheel tightly and raced down the dusty road toward whatever it was that might lie ahead.

15

ARRIVAL AT ADDER ROCK

The Ringmaster sped away from the meadow down a barren stretch of dirt toward Adder Rock, followed closely by Kamal Khan, Dorado Eschevarria and several others, kicking up trails of dust as they went.

"Adder Rock is at least a couple hour's drive from the floor of Gatling Meadows," the Ringmaster said. "It's an isolated area, not surrounded by much of anything."

"Sounds charming," Belladonna said sarcastically. "Can't wait to see it."

Backed by rough, rocky hills, like those surrounding Gatling Meadows, the town's name was derived from a single geographic feature - at the highest point, on the tallest peak of the rocky backdrop, a large chunk of rock protruded out from the hillside. The silhouette of this protrusion was shaped like the head of a snake, an indigenous Adder, posed with its mouth open and stalactite fangs hanging down. Its shape at sunset was striking. Adder Rock had been a bustling mining town at one time, but no longer. Its coal was largely depleted, and what little remained was hardly worthy of commercial pursuit. And when the coal ran out, so did the jobs. Workers and businessmen alike moved on to more fruitful endeavors, leaving a small contingent behind who settled permanently. Those who remained were mostly derelicts and roughnecks who couldn't do better elsewhere. And with as remote as Adder Rock was, any person passing through was fair game.

Just a few miles outside of town, the racers jockeyed for position, swerving back and forth, trying to steal an opportunity to pass on the long, narrow road. The town began to take shape at the horizon. Belladonna glanced down at the papers in her lap.

"We need to find an entrance to the mine, near the center of town," she said.

The road cut right through the middle of Adder Rock. The town was lined with old wooden buildings on either side, their paint chipped and peeled from years of neglect. What remained were mostly commercial buildings, left from days past when the town had thrived; storefronts for the now-defunct *Hotel Devernany*, *Skully's Grocer* and *Heftworth & Gripstrong's Blacksmith Shop* were the least dilapidated, while the *Thornichrift Pharmacy* barely stood erect. With its windows shattered and its shelves bare, it sat next to *Griswold's Tasty Tavern*, now just a burned out shell. The road through the center of town let out periodically to side streets, and down these side streets is where the residential areas could be found. The town was quiet, and mostly barren. As they approached the center, Mechanicules pointed at a vehicle parked in the distance. They were the first of their group to enter, but the others were close behind.

"That looks like the Baron's vehicle, love," Belladonna said. "I bet we'll find the entrance to the mine close by."

Just as they pulled up close, the Baron emerged from the mine shaft and trotted out with something in his hand. He hardly even acknowledged their presence, then he hopped into his vehicle and sped off. Kamal and Dorado pulled up just as the Baron was leaving. Seeing this, they realized that for whatever delays the Baron experienced here, they had closed their lead on him and would need to move quickly to keep it closed. After a glance at their papers, Kamal glided back toward the *Thornicrift Pharmacy.* Dorado calmly strode toward *Atwater's House of Pleasure.*

"Off you go, love," Belladonna said. "Chop chop."

The Ringmaster stepped out and pondered going down into the mine shaft alone. He stood at its doorway, staring into the darkness. The entrance looked fragile, propped up with a rudimentary frame built of wooden timbers used to prop up the rocks that might otherwise collapse in the absence of such support. A moaning sound echoed as the wind blew into the shaft. He glanced at Mech and Belladonna, reviewed his papers and tucked them into the inside pocket of his coat. He pulled an oil lamp from the back of his vehicle.

"Mech, you come with me, and bring the piston hammer. You may need to bust up some rock down there. Better safe than sorry."

Mechanicules nodded, and retrieved the piston hammer attachment for his mechanical arm from a case stowed in the rear. With his left hand, he pulled a lever that disengaged his mechanical forearm. With a twist and a click, the mechanism slid off, just below the elbow. He slid on the piston-hammer attachment and locked it in place with a satisfying click. The piston hammer was heavier than the mechanical hand he normally wore. The reciprocating hammer device was powered by a metal coil spring attached to a series of heavy metal gears and a reciprocating arm. As the spring unwound and the gears turned, the heavy metal head pulsed back and forth like a jackhammer. He wound the spring tight with a crank inserted into the forearm and tucked the crank into his coat. The Ringmaster smiled pleasantly.

"Are you ready?"

Mech raised the piston hammer upright and test fired it. *Shoomp, shoomp, shoomp, shoomp.* The hammer quickly fired back and forth in rapid succession. Its recoil shook Mech from head to toe. Despite his tremendous strength, not even Mechanicules could hold himself still against its brute force.

AROUND THE CORNER FROM THE CENTER OF TOWN, IN ONE OF THE houses, a shanty really, some local roughnecks sat at a table playing cards. Their game was interrupted by the metallic clang of Mech's piston hammer.

"Bloody hell, what was that?" one of the men growled, looking up from his cards.

Another man responded in a raspy voice.

"Sounds like we have some guests, mates. Grab some iron, let's give 'em a proper greeting."

"ALRIGHT, COME WITH ME, MECH," THE RINGMASTER SAID. "Belladonna, you stay here and keep an eye on our things. Watch the others, no funny business."

Belladonna sneered and flipped her hair back.

"Yes, love. As you wish."

The Ringmaster lit his lantern and headed in. As he and Mechanicules strode into the shaft, they slowly disappeared from sight, leaving the residual light of the lantern, and their long shadows cast on the walls, as the only indication of their movement. As they walked deeper inside, the light in the shaft faded, and the entrance fell as dark as night again.

16

APPROACHING THE FORK

Down the southeast path, the other cluster of drivers made their way out of Gatling Meadows, and continued down the dirt road in a tight group. Michael remembered from looking at the map that there would be a three-way fork in the road several miles out, and he wanted to be ready. The Wilfork brothers, donning their goggles and face masks, sped down the road with ease and found themselves at the front of the pack. Michael was next, with Vixen, Copper and Scarlet behind him.

"Will," Henry shouted. "Did you say we should take the left fork or the right?"

"Go to the left," Will said.

"Are you sure? My gut says to go to the right."

"I'm sure. I have it right here. Go to the left. I think it's the fastest."

"Alright, brother, left it is."

No more than three seconds passed.

"Are you sure it's left?" Henry asked again.

"Positive," Will replied, "without a doubt, it's not too far out, brother. Be ready."

With no notice, the brothers turned hard and cut across the road, taking the left side of the fork. Their abrupt maneuver forced the others to react, swerving unexpectedly, trying to avoid collisions among themselves. The vehicles swerved left and right, trying to regain control as they approached the fork. But Scarlet and Copper were forced to the middle prong. Michael and Vixen each recovered just in time, but were forced to the right.

17

IN THE MINESHAFT

Having found his bounty down in the shaft, the Ringmaster strode back up the tunnel toward the mine entrance, with Mech right in front of him. Daylight grew brighter as they approached the mouth. The Ringmaster could see Belladonna's silhouette standing outside the shaft as he got closer. The sun was bright, and he squinted.

"Success!" he shouted.

He held up the shiny token retrieved from below.

"And not for nothing," he said. "Mech was nearly killed by not one, but two separate traps down there. Falling rocks, and a pit that opened up! The floor fell right out from under him. I grabbed him by the coat before he went in. He's lucky I was there!"

He shoved the token back into his pocket, and, as he got closer, the silhouette of a large man stepped into the doorway. Backlit by the sun, the Ringmaster couldn't see who it was.

"Who goes there?" the Ringmaster demanded.

"Oh, there you are," the man said. "So kind of you to join us."

He raised his arms and brought a sledgehammer down. With a dull thud, it dislodged the timbers supporting the doorway. The doorway collapsed. The Ringmaster and Mech were trapped inside.

"What the devil is going on?" the Ringmaster asked Mech. "Who was that man?"

He could faintly hear people talking outside, but the sound of the voices was muffled by the fallen rock. It was a voice he didn't recognize.

Outside the shaft, in the light of day, the man with the sledge-hammer addressed the others."Welcome to Adder Rock, I don't recall inviting you, and it's quite rude of you all to show up unannounced. But now that you're here, please, make yourselves comfortable," he said with a laugh. "We're so happy to have you."

Inside the shaft, thin spears of light poked through the crevices in the fallen rock, setting the dusty air alight. The Ringmaster put his cheek to the rock, and peeked through a crevice. The man with the sledgehammer was still there.

"I see two men with him," he said. "There might be others."

One captor held Belladonna firmly by her arm, to keep her from running. The Ringmaster looked closely. She looked more annoyed than distressed. In this, he took comfort. *Annoyed* was how she always looked. She feared no imminent harm.

"Belladonna is fine," he said. "Not sure what's going on with the others."

He put his cheek to the rock again, peeking through. Belladonna looked at the man holding her, and she smirked. With her free hand, she flipped up her glasses and stared at him with crystalline eyes.

"What are you looking at?" he said.

"A dead man," came her reply. "He just doesn't realize it yet."

With her free hand, she touched her fingers to her lips, and blew him a long kiss.

"Knock it off and stand still," he said.

He squeezed her arm tighter and gave her a good shake, to let her know he meant business.

"Oh, I wish you hadn't done that, love."

"You're going to wish for a lot more if you don't quiet down."

She shrugged.

"Have it your way, then."

Another man dug through the racers' vehicles in search of any valuables. Another stood at a distance, pointing a pistol toward Dorado and Kamal. Kamal sat peacefully on the ground with his legs crossed. His head was bowed and his hands were folded. He was mumbling something quietly. Dorado couldn't tell what he was saying, the words were indecipherable. Dorado, on the other hand, stood still. Quiet but agitated, he smacked his toothpick, eyeing the man pointing the gun at him.

"Don't get any ideas," the man said.

Inside the shaft, the Ringmaster peeked out again. They were stealing from him, and he was quickly losing patience. Mech glanced at the Ringmaster and held the piston hammer upright. The Ringmaster nodded.

"No point in standing here wasting time. Hit it."

The Ringmaster stepped back and covered his ears as Mechanicules braced himself. He pressed the head of the piston hammer against the fallen rock, near a spot where some light shone through. He leaned into the wall and let the piston hammer loose. *Shunk, shunk, shunk, shunk, shunk.* The clanging of the metal head pounding against the fallen stone was deafening. His face grimaced and his body shook with every blow. The piston hammer worked its way through the fallen debris. The men outside froze, surprised, while bits of rock shot toward them and skittered across their shoes. With each thrust, the hole grew bigger. As the dust settled, Mech and the Ringmaster emerged from the tunnel into the daylight. Their captors stood rapt, in surprised disbelief.

Seeing the opportunity and seizing on the distraction, Dorado drew both six-shot gatling pistols and emptied one gun into the man with the sledgehammer and the other into the man pointing the gun at him, six rounds each in less than a second. His draw was fast and they never stood a chance. One of the remaining men, the one holding Belladonna, was startled by the gunshots. He flinched at the sound, and in doing so, he let go of her arm. She side-stepped, and quickly slipped behind him, wrapping her arm under his chin and around his neck. With her other hand, she jabbed him in the back. The man gasped. His arms stiffened and shot outward, but she held on tight. He winced in pain at first, then his expression washed over with a look of surprise. Surprise was followed by horror. His back arched and his head tipped back. His mouth hung open as he groaned. The groan became more desperate, as his stiff-ened arms quivered spastically. She held her arm firmly around his neck, with her body pressed tight into his back, and her cheek pressed tight against his.

"What the hell is she doing?" the Ringmaster muttered. Mechanicules just watched. He already knew.

As Belladonna held the man tight, leaving no room to move, his face paled and his skin shriveled. His cheeks pulled in against the shape of his cheekbones, and his eyes sunk into his head. His lips dried and cracked, pulling back over his teeth and gums. He wailed, with his arms and legs flailing. His back arched more aggressively. His skin faded to a dull, pale grey as his arms and legs thinned and shriveled, and his knuckles became more pronounced and the bones in his wrist showed under his skin. Belladonna dropped him to the ground and stood over him, her glasses tipped up. She stared down where he lay, face-to-face. Eye to lifeless eye.

"You shouldn't have been so rough on my arm, love," she said, unapologetically. "You left a lady no choice but to defend herself. Let this be a lesson to you, and anyone like you."

She batted her eyelashes and pouted her lips at him, then flipped her glasses down and strutted back toward the Ringmaster. One foot stepped directly in front of the other, hips wagging, as if nothing had happened. The man on the ground passed a final, wheezy breath, and then he gave in.

"What in God's name did you just do?" the Ringmaster asked.

"You've never cared before, pumpkin. Why now? Your first time isn't so easy, is it?"

Her tone was cavalier. She licked her thumb, and smudged away some dirt from the Ringmaster's face. She gave off airs of indifference. In truth, she was deeply affected, but she refused to show it. To talk about it would be to acknowledge it, and she wasn't in the mood to do either.

"He… He looks like a mummy," the Ringmaster said.

It was a disturbing sight, but he couldn't look away, no matter how hard he tried. Belladonna spoke as she walked back to their vehicle.

"For all intents and purposes, darling, he is a mummy. A dried out husk of his former self. But I think we should probably be going now, is that right? Things to do? Places to be? Races to win? Where's that well-oiled machine you're so fond of? *Tout de suite.*"

18

YOU'RE A VERY ODD FELLOW, YOU KNOW THAT RIGHT?

Michael and Vixen sped through the open fields of the countryside. Vixen led, and Michael followed. Both moved at a good pace, jostling in their seats with each bump in the road. Vixen looked back, then ahead again. Michael adjusted his goggles and leaned forward, keeping a firm grip on the wheel. Vixen looked back over her shoulder again, then slowed and pulled to the side and stopped. She was lost and needed to check the map. Much to her surprise, Michael stopped behind her. She stepped out of her vehicle and spread her map across the hood, largely ignoring him. He flipped his goggles up on top of his head and watched. She glanced over with a furrowed brow.

"Can I help you with something?" she said.

"No, I'm fine," Michael said. "Are you lost?"

"No, I'm not lost. I just need a moment to gather my bearing. But don't let me keep you, I'll be just fine. You should feel free to move along, Mr…"

A long pause followed.

"Mr…"

"Oh. Right. McGillicuddy," he said. "Michael McGillicuddy. But please, just call me Michael."

"I'm Vixen van Buren, pleasure," she said with a hurried curtsey. "And if it's all the same to you, I'll stick with Mr. McGillicuddy. I'm a lady after all, and a lady shouldn't be too familiar."

"Very well then, *Miss* van Buren."

He smiled, and just stared at her awkwardly. He was out of clever things to say. His repertoire was admittedly sparse.

"Oh right," she said. "You're the young man from the check-in. I saw you there, didn't I?"

"Yep."

He smiled, and continued to stare.

"So," she paused. "Do you need something?"

"Nope."

He kept smiling.

Vixen looked around, then back at him. He was a bit odd, a touch eccentric, and his social skills lacked a certain polish. Nevertheless, she found him strangely charming, with his boyish face and wavy brown hair. His smile drew her in, in a comforting, disarming kind of way.

"Alright, then, Mr. McGillicuddy."

She looked down at her map, feigning intense concentration, hoping he would leave. She glanced back up, just to check. He was still staring at her, with that silly grin on his face.

"Very well, then," he said with a nod.

She looked back at the map. She ran her finger along the lines on the paper, trying to plot a course. She looked back up. He was still staring at her with that eager grin, like he wanted to say something, so she finally gave in.

"Oh God, what is it? Just say it."

"Nothing. It's just, you know, it's down and to the left."

"What is?"

"The road you need. It's down that way, about six miles out, you'll want to turn left."

"Is that so?"

"Yes. Absolutely."

He nodded with confidence.

"To get to Coddington?"

"Yes, that's right."

"You're going to Coddington also?"

"I am, yes," he said.

She looked around the expansive countryside. Roads were neither named nor marked. She looked at the map and made her best guess of where she was. Then she ran her finger along a line, from that point, over to a point that would be six miles out. There was an intersection where her finger stopped. A place to turn left. She looked up and smiled, impressed. She turned her attention back to the map.

"That's a fine start, Mr. McGillicuddy, but we're pretty far off from where we're supposed to be. The road you want to turn on, it runs into a web of other roads, with lots of dead ends. I hate to backtrack, so it looks like we'll need to navigate the mess ahead."

"Indeed, we will," he said, still smiling.

"It's a mess."

"For some, perhaps. But it's actually pretty easy, if you know the right way."

"Easy, you say?"

"Yes, easy. You just head out about six miles to the intersection I mentioned. After you turn left, follow that road until you reach the fork. When you reach the fork, go right. Follow that through the old town, no need to stop, just pass on through."

"That's it?"

"No, not exactly. On the back side of the town, there is another intersection, where you can turn left or right. Turn left. If you turn right, you'll be headed toward Whistle Rock Point. You don't want to go there."

"Ok. Got it."

"Keep going until the road splits again. Take the right side of the fork. When it splits again, take the right fork again. Continue down the road through a heavily wooded area, until the road bends to the right. The road will wrap to the right for a long stretch and then back left.

"Hold on," she said.

She tried to interrupt him, but Michael kept going.

"When the road comes back left there will be another intersection.

"So I go right again?"

"No. Left this time. Before long, you will merge back onto the main road where we would have been to start with; you know, if we hadn't come this way in the first place."

"I see."

"At that point, you'll be in fine shape. Just dandy. Trust me. But don't take a wrong turn. You could end up hopelessly lost. You may never find your way out."

"Wait. What?"

"Yeah, it's all pretty straightforward," he said, still smiling. "Just do what I told you, and you'll be fine."

"Right."

She stared curiously, her eyes squinted.

"So, you must be a local, I take it?"

"Oh heavens, no," Michael said. "I live on the outskirts of London."

"Then how do you know the route so well from here?"

"Oh, right. That. I read the map before we left."

He grinned wider, proud of himself. His smile was contagious, and she couldn't help but smile back.

"That's it? You read the map?"

"Yes."

"And now you've memorized it?"

"I suppose I have, yes."

"You're a very odd fellow, you know that right?"

"I have to be honest. You're not the first to point that out."

She shook her head in disbelief and walked around the rear of her buggy. She stepped with prim and proper posture. She was precise in her movement as she folded her map and walked back to her seat.

"We have precious little time," Michael said. "The others are on a more direct route. Would you like to follow me out, or just take your chances?"

"Thank you for the gesture, chivalrous indeed. But I think I'll keep my options open for now, Mr. McGillicuddy. You follow your path, I'll follow mine."

"As you wish, Miss van Buren."

He started his buggy, pulled out ahead of her and sped away. She started her buggy and pulled out quickly behind him. She turned left where he turned left, right where he turned right. After several twists, she called out to him.

"You need to understand something. Just because I'm behind you, Michael, that doesn't mean I'm following you! I could get through this just fine without you. I just want to be clear about that."

He looked back over his shoulder and smiled.

"She called me Michael," he mumbled to himself. "I wonder what happened to *Mr. McGillicuddy*?"

SCARLET AND COPPER DASHED DOWN A DIRT ROAD, NEARLY NECK-and-neck. Copper enjoyed a small lead as he casually motored down the road. The monocycle was fast; far better than average. Although his teeth clapped together with each bump, he was not dissuaded. He pressed on, as fast as he could go and, unafraid to swerve where necessary to avoid being passed. Scarlet followed closely in her buggy, her hair pulled back, driving gloves pulled up to her elbows and her goggles down in place. Wavy tufts of her strawberry blonde locks fluttered from beneath her goggle straps. She leaned forward and pressed against the steering wheel, willing the buggy to go faster. Neither was certain where the other was going, but for now they were both just racing as fast as they could toward Arch Rock Castle. Neither of them wanted to let the other arrive first.

The Wilfork brothers, Henry and William, were on the most direct route to Arch Rock Castle. Henry raced the motorcycle as fast as he could. The wind whistled over his ears, and Will hunched down in the sidecar, holding on tight.

"We should be getting close," Will shouted over the road noise.

"What?" Henry shouted back.

"I think we're getting close, brother. It's not far from here."

Henry flashed a thumbs up, and they continued down the road. Before long they arrived in an old downtown and made their way to Arch Rock Castle. They pulled up in front, near a spot that looked like an entrance.

"It's quite a castle," Henry said.

"I've seen nicer," Will said, "but I could get by if I had to live here."

Arch Rock Castle was, in fact, a lesser castle at one time, once inhabited by a lower duke, and named for its architectural style. But it was no longer inhabited, judging from its appearance. Nothing in the town seemed to be. It looked deserted.

He looked over at William.

"You ready, brother?"

"I'm ready, brother."

Will grabbed a leather pack from the sidecar and hoisted it over his shoulder and they strode up the steps with bold, confident strides.

Michael zoomed through the maze of dirt roads, and Vixen trailed just a few lengths behind. He handled all the twists and turns with such ease and confidence, it looked like he'd driven it a hundred times before. Her map sat on her passenger seat, fluttering softly with the breeze. She glanced at it periodically, convincing herself she knew where she was going, and considering breaking off on her own.

"What if he doesn't remember as well as he thought?" she thought to herself. "What if he is going the wrong way and taking me with him? What if I can get there faster on my own?"

She dismissed the notion, though, recognizing how much slower it would be to have to read and drive. It wasn't practical at all. As badly as she wanted to maintain her own independence and confirm her own ability - two things she valued deeply - this was not a time to cut and run.

"I don't actually need his help," she told herself. "But I can still take full advantage of what he is willing to give. I lose nothing by following him, and I only stand to gain. So long as he is going the right direction. So really, I'm just taking advantage. I'd be foolish not to, right?"

Vixen took comfort in the notion that she was the one who was actually in control, that *she* was merely allowing him to serve a purpose. Her reliance on his guidance was not an issue of weakness, but one of convenience. With comfort newly found, a satisfied smirk appeared on her face.

"The company could be much worse, I suppose."

Copper pressed his throttle forward and pulled away from Scarlet as he neared an intersection. He checked over his shoulder to measure his lead. When he turned back, Michael, and then Vixen, merged into the road ahead of him, their two roads now merging back into one. To avoid a collision, he pulled the throttle back and veered onto the rough shoulder. Michael and Vixen motored ahead, barely noticing, and Scarlet sped right past him. She gave a salute as she passed him, finger to forehead, with a quick swipe, and squeezed the bulb on her air horn to honk as she passed.

Ooga.

Copper gritted his teeth, and his biceps bulged, as he pushed the throttle back to full, chasing after them on the way to Arch Rock Castle at the highest possible speed. They entered the former township of Coddington, where they hoped to find Arch Rock Castle. The whole area appeared abandoned, defunct, as they arrived at a large stone building at the town center. The former Citadel, now referred to as Arch Rock Castle, was modest by castle standards, but still impressive to the average person. Constructed from blocks of granite, its architecture relied heavily on the use of arches. Right angles were nearly impossible to find there, hence its new name.

"It doesn't look like anyone else is here now, but the tracks in the dirt suggest someone was here pretty recently," Michael said. "I don't plan to waste any time."

"It's a long journey, laddie," Copper said with an easy smile. "I'm not too worried where anyone else is. Ahead, behind, don't really care."

Michael felt hesitant as he looked up the steps toward the entrance.

"Anyone know what to expect inside?"

"I expect we'll find a token inside, or perhaps a trap," Scarlet said. "Or both. Whatever we do, we should be careful."

Michael sighed, shouldered his satchel and started up the steps. Not to allow too much of a lead, the others followed him up as another buggy pulled up. It was Nigel Teague, the spoiled and obnoxious son of Maximillian Teague, pulling in behind them. He was a plain looking fellow; skinny, long and angular, but otherwise unremarkable, other than his thick black-framed glasses and crooked teeth. Phinneas Mann pulled up shortly after. Phinneas parked as Nigel walked up to Copper.

"Well, well, look what the cat dragged in," Copper said.

"It's good to see you too, Copper," Nigel said.

Nigel's voice was nasal, and pitched higher than most. He sniffed a lot when he talked, and he made an awkward face, with his upper lip curled, exposing his teeth.

"I never said it was good," Copper said.

"Charming, as always," Nigel said with a sniff. "I don't know why you always have to act this way toward me. So uncivilized. Grudges are a waste of time and energy, so why spend the effort? That's what I've always wondered about you. So much effort, so much waste. You could put that energy into something more productive, do something with yourself. It's like your parents have always said, so much promise, yet so little delivered. Just let it go, would you."

Copper huffed.

"Sorry lad, I've got the Scots blood in me. Grudges don't just pass like a fart on a windy day. And don't you go talking my ear off about this. I don't have the patience for your yammering today. So button your lip if you know what's good."

Nigel was visibly offended, but Copper was moving on. He had no interest in standing around, or in giving Nigel time to start talking again. He reached into the compartment in his monocycle to grab his heavy smithing hammer, and he made his way up the steps.

19

BENEATH THE CITADEL

Michael led the others up the stairs toward the entrance.

"Not many people realize this," Nigel said as they walked, "but this castle, this place now referred to as Arch Rock Castle, it used to have a different name. It used to be called the Coddington Citadel. Arch Rock Castle is a nickname, for the architectural style used in its construction. You may have noticed this outside, you wouldn't have seen a lot of right angles, or square corners or straight edges. Pillars and arches, just pillars and arches, everywhere. Arched windows, arched doorways, even arched ceilings in the halls. If I'm right, most of the rooms here won't have flat ceilings. Instead, the four walls will probably arch upward and taper into a single apex where they all meet in the middle. Insets into the walls? Arches. Bookshelves? Arches. It's odd, don't you think? Why so many arches?"

"Nigel, don't start," Copper said. "Just walk."

"Well, I'm just saying. I thought you'd be interested to know. Terribly sorry. And even if you're not interested, maybe someone else is. Did you ever stop to consider that? Some people have a genuine interest in these sorts of things. History, architecture, culture. Don't deprive them, just because you're not interested."

Nigel paused as he awaited a response, and Copper was thankful for the moment of silence. But Nigel started again.

"In any event, as I was saying, the reason they call it Arch Rock Castle now, and not Coddington Citadel, is, well, because there is no more town of Coddington. Look around, everyone is gone. Sure the buildings are here, but it's a burned out corpse of a city, ruined, destroyed, kablooey, kaput, no more. The Citadel was the military stronghold of the township of Coddington, the source of all governing power and the center of defense of the city. When the city went bust and corruption spread, people left here in droves. They scattered into the countryside to form little fiefs. Little towns all over the place. They popped up everywhere, joined by a web of narrow roads from fief to fief. A few stayed behind, but it's nothing like it used to be."

Michael looked at Scarlet and rolled his eyes.

Scarlet shrugged.

"He is right, you know."

Michael shrugged back.

"I didn't really ask. Nobody did."

Nigel continued while they walked up the stairs to the entrance.

"Nobody really knows what went wrong," he said, "what set Coddington on the way to its eventual demise, but its decline was swift."

Michael pushed the door of the entrance open.

"This whole town," Nigel continued "now largely abandoned, was once a center of industry, a hub of business, a busy waypoint between the coastal ports and heavily populated inland destinations. The carriages that hauled goods across land from Gilberg to Swiftshire needed a place to stop for food, for sleep, you name it. All right here. The result? This sleepy little town quickly boomed into what you see here now. Except with people in it."

"Nigel, honestly," Copper said. "Clamp it."

"Right, sorry."

As they walked through the entrance, the entry looked like a place where a royal ball might be held, or where jesters might gather to entertain a royal court; Large, spacious, with intricate carving and open space. Nigel looked up and pointed.

"See? No flat ceilings, just like I said. I did say that. Do you see how they just taper up to a single apex in the center? That's not easy to build. Look at it. Think about that. Do you know how they make these arches work?"

"Nigel. For the love of all things holy, just stop talking!" Copper said. "I implore you."

Nigel looked hurt.

"Sorry," he said again.

Vixen pointed to a hallway.

"I think we should go that way."

She glanced at her papers.

"We need to go down several floors, to a room downstairs. Well, I do, anyway. I'm not sure about the rest of you."

"I'm going there as well," Michael said. "Let's go."

"Aye, same," Copper said.

"Downstairs? You know, the man who lived here at one point," Nigel said. "I've heard stories. This was his castle. There is a lower basement. Strange things going on down there, that's what they say. Very strange indeed."

Nigel kept talking, all the way to the point they arrived at a heavy arched door at the end of a hallway, built from thick wood and clad with iron straps. Michael studied the door.

"Thoughts anyone?" he said.

"Yes. I have a thought," Vixen said. "This place is supposed to be empty, if we listen to Nigel. Abandoned. Nobody lives here. But the gas lights are all lit. Why?"

They all looked around at each other.

"There are tire marks outside," Michael said. "Maybe the people who came ahead of us lit them."

"That doesn't make any sense. Look around. Every one of them is lit. If I came through here, just to get in and to get out, as

I'm doing right now, I wouldn't bother to light every blasted lamp in the place."

"What are you afraid of, Miss? The bogeyman?" Copper asked. "Krampus?"

"I'm just asking the question," Vixen said. "Logically speaking, there is no reason for all these lamps to be lit. Think about it. It just strikes me as odd, that's all I'm saying. Am I the only one?"

"It is peculiar," Michael said, "but I'm not sure it's cause for fear."

"Honestly, what do you think is behind that door?" Copper asked.

"Why are you so eager for us to go?" Vixen said.

"Why are you so hesitant? Step aside, will you? I haven't got all day."

"Wait," Scarlet said. "I'd like to check something before I go. If you don't mind."

She reached into her handbag and pulled out a small leather case. She unsnapped it, flipped the lid open and pulled out a brass device, shaped like the eyepiece of a telescope.

"What is that?" Michael asked.

"It's my looking glass."

She placed one end of the looking glass against the door, and moved her face toward it. She placed her eye to the eyecup and stared through it.

"Looks clear," she said, "just a stairwell leading down to another floor."

Vixen shoved herself between Michael and Scarlet, which made for cramped quarters in a narrow doorway.

"Hold on just one minute," Vixen said. "Are you trying to tell me you just looked through to the other side of that door with your looking glass? Impossible. It's solid wood."

"Open the door and see for yourself," Scarlet said.

"Yes, open it," Copper said. "Please, God, just open the blasted door."

"May I see that looking glass, please?"

Vixen held her hand out expectantly, ready to receive it. As a woman of science who lives for mathematical proof and empirical evidence, she was understandably skeptical. But Scarlet was in no mood to share.

"Sorry, I'm afraid I can't do that - Vixen, is it?

"Yes, that's right, Vixen van Buren. Pleasure."

"Yes, pleasure. Well, it's government issued, Vixen. I'm afraid I can't let it out of my possession. Terribly sorry. Rules and all, you know how it goes."

Vixen snorted in frustration.

"Hold it up to the door, then. I'll just have a peek through. You don't even have to let it out of your possession. I just want to see."

"I'm sorry. I just can't do that."

"Well, come on. Why not?"

"Like I said. Rules."

"Pssssh," Vixen huffed.

"Ladies, if we may?" Michael said. He placed his hands gently on Vixen's shoulders to steer her out of the way of the door.

"We'll solve nothing by standing here bickering."

He placed his hands on Scarlet's shoulders and steered her out the way in the same manner.

"Let's just have an actual look, shall we?"

He reached down and put his hand on the doorknob. His words sounded confident, but his movement showed a lack of conviction. He hesitated, then turned the doorknob slowly. He pulled the door open, slowly and carefully, and as he looked through, he saw it.

"It's a stairwell," he said.

"Of course it's a bloody stairwell," Scarlet shouted. "Who knew there would be stairwell there? Oh, right. Me. I think I already said as much."

Vixen sneered and turned away.

"Well, I'm going in." Copper said.

He tried to shove his way past.

"You all can stand here and talk about…whatever."

But Michael started down ahead of him. It was a long way down a dimly lit stairway with an arched ceiling and rough stone walls. The soft glow of the lamps near the top lit the way, but the light dimmed with each step down. Soft light was visible at the end, but it grew dim and dark in between. As they reached the bottom, there was a landing at the end of the stairs. The landing was a small room in its own right, also dark, except for a bit of residual light that shone in from the larger room on the right.

"What is this place?" Copper asked, looking over.

"It's enormous," Michael said. "Like a wing of the British Museum."

It was cold and damp inside. The air was musty and moist. The larger room was lit by gas lamps mounted to the walls, and chandeliers hanging from the ceiling. Michael stepped out of the landing and found himself face to face with a life-size statue, a soldier, fitted with armor and a broadsword. It was exquisitely carved of fine white marble, with beautifully smoothed surfaces and exceptional detail. Scarlet marveled at its artistic quality.

"It's stunning. Some of the finest carving I've ever seen," she said.

The statue stood on a square pedestal, which bore a simple inscription: *The Sentry*. Michael stared back, awestruck by its lifelike appearance. The Sentry's expression was eerily human, his motion perfectly frozen in time, his determination perfectly captured. He stood with a sword raised in one hand, his other arm outstretched, pointing an index finger back at Michael. It was so lifelike, in fact, that Michael felt unsettled.

"It's not polite to point," he mumbled.

Michael looked around the rest of the room. He noticed that there were a number of other statues scattered about, and their chaotic arrangement bothered him momentarily.

"They just stick them anywhere?" he thought.

But as he studied the statues a little closer, searching for some order in their arrangement, he found a common characteristic. Not counting the Sentry statue near the landing, every other statue was arranged in one of two outer perimeters, concentric rings. The statues all faced inward toward the center.

He and the others walked around quietly, uncertain, examining the stone carvings. Nobody really talked. Not even Nigel. They spread out, and Phinneas moving the farthest away. The statues, as indicated by the labels on their respective pedestals, included Archers, several Infantrymen and a host of well-armored Cavalrymen. The Cavalrymen sat on beautifully-carved, armor-clad horses. Each Cavalryman held a jousting lance tucked into his armpit, or a heavy mace in a raised hand, ready to strike.

Michael scanned the room with his eyes, studying the others' expressions, wondering what to do, seeking some kind of insight. Copper looked indifferent, as usual, and Nigel looked paranoid. Vixen's face was awash with fascination. Phinneas drifted aimlessly, while Scarlet walked toward the center of the room, confident and focused. He followed her, to see what had grabbed her attention so. He noticed the center of the room had a cluster of square pedestals rising from the floor, forty or perhaps even fifty, in total. The pedestals were evenly-spread, spaced with two or three feet between them in any direction. The arrangement of the pedestals was concentrated in a large circular area at the center of the room, surrounded by the concentric rings of statues, arranged facing inward at the pedestals.

Each pedestal had a locked box mounted on its top. Shaped like large jewelry boxes, or small treasure chests, each box was unique. Some were surfaced with wood and brass, others with leather and bronze, still others in shiny gold, encrusted with gemstones.

"What is the meaning of all of this?" Scarlet murmured.

The others slowly gravitated toward her, unsure what to think. Vixen's eyes fixed upon the ornately decorated keyhole on one of the chests. Shiny silver, smooth and beautifully carved. Drawn to its beauty, she stepped toward it. But as she did, she tripped over something. She let out a shriek when she looked down.

"Oh my god, there's a dead body!"

Michael rushed over, Scarlet and Copper followed. They all moved cautiously, keeping aware of their surroundings. None were keen to meet a similar fate.

"Good Lord," Michael said. "Someone made a pin cushion of him."

The man's body lay on the ground, face down, with several arrows protruding from his back.

"Tight pattern," Copper said. "Excellent marksmanship."

His words were met with blank stares.

"What?" he said with a shrug. "I'm just saying, I know quality when I see it."

"I heard there were some ruthless types in this race," Michael said. "But honestly, this is ridiculous. Safe to say I have no plans to harm any of you, at least not intentionally. I hope I can expect the same in return. Can I get your words on that?"

Copper smiled innocently and shrugged again, offering little comfort. Nigel remained speechless.

"Is it one of the other participants?" Copper said. "My guess is that it will be. Competition can be right fierce."

"I don't think this is foul play," Scarlet said.

"Of course it is," Michael said. "The man's been shot to death with a half dozen arrows. What are you suggesting? That he somehow shot himself in the back?"

Vixen was pale from the shock of seeing the body. Still weak in the knees, she leaned on a pillar for support.

"If it was foul play," Scarlet said, "He would have been picked clean. Anything of value, any potential advantage, would be taken from him."

"How do we even know he's even one of us?" Vixen asked. "You know, a participant worth pilfering."

Michael crouched down. He rolled the man to his side, exposing his face. As he did, there was a collective gasp.

"It's Henry Wilfork," Copper said. "Egad, his brother must have grown tired of him. Can't say I blame him, obnoxious turd that he was."

"Honestly, I don't believe that's what happened," Scarlet said.

"And why not?"

Scarlet pointed to the box on top of the pedestal, right in front of where Henry lay. Nigel stepped around the other side of the box, to the opposite side from where Henry's body was. He peeked over to the front, and looked down to see a key inserted into the lock. Its head was still protruding. The head of the key was shaped like a polished silver frog.

"Scarlet's right," he said.

"Henry's key is still in the keyhole, and his box isn't even opened," Scarlet said.

"It's an interesting point," Michael added, "but why shoot the man full of arrows and then just leave his key here?"

"Precisely!" Scarlet said. "If you were going murder the man, you would also take his key, or at least empty his box. Otherwise, why bother? You'd take whatever you could get."

"Not if you're a marble archer," Nigel said.

"What nonsense are you babbling about now?" Copper asked.

Nigel pointed back at one of the marble statues. It was an Archer. The sculpture stood with its bow drawn. Its arrow was nocked, the string was drawn tight and aimed right back at Nigel.

"Nonsense," Michael said. "It's a stone carving."

Nigel looked down toward the floor where Henry lay, then back up at the Archer.

"It's a perfect line. Just look at it."

Nigel gulped and stepped to the side slowly and carefully.

"It's like he's guarding this box; and those three boxes there. They are all lined up on the same perfect line. Take a look, see for yourself."

"Rubbish" Vixen said. "Statues don't kill people."

"Well then, you explain what happened to him," Nigel said. "I'm telling you, there's something very odd about this place. I told you that upstairs, and now you see for yourself."

Nigel looked around, scanning the other boxes. Michael could see that he was anxious.

"I have a bad feeling," Nigel said.

"Relax," Vixen said. "We're underground, in an old and largely abandoned citadel, filled with strange statues that serve no apparent purpose. It's quiet. There's nobody else around, other than a dead body full of arrows. What could possibly go wrong?"

She cracked a grin. She was having fun at his expense, but he wasn't amused.

"We could all end up like Henry, that's what could go wrong."

"Oh, please," Vixen said.

Nigel snorted back.

"Rubbish," Phinneas said as he walked back toward them. "Absolute rubbish."

Nigel walked around inspecting some of the boxes, with a look of consternation on his face. He dragged his hand gently across the top of each box as he passed by, and fingered the key in his pocket. Michael had the same idea. As cold as it seemed, Henry wasn't their responsibility. Michael scanned the locks with his eyes as he moved from pedestal to pedestal. There was a solid iron box, its keyhole decorated with a black iron scarab. The next was made of dark brown wood and iron straps. The emblem on the keyhole was an octopus, with twirling tentacles.

The next looked familiar, a wooden box, chestnut brown and fortified with heavy iron strips, with a heavy iron lock securing the lid. Just below the keyhole there was another emblem. It was a pewter dragon, with ruby eyes and a spiral tail. Michael tried to pick the box up off the pedestal, but he couldn't. He tried to slide it, but it wouldn't move.

Nigel inspected the boxes around him, just a few steps away.

"I can tell you this much," Nigel said, "I won't be choosing a box that sits on a line covered by an archer. No chance."

"Sage advice," Phinneas said, as he inspected some boxes on his own.

Then he stopped. Phinneas had found one he liked. He stepped toward the pedestal and heard a heavy metal click. He froze in his tracks. He stepped back and heard the click again. He looked down and saw a square inset in the floor, like a large wooden tile several feet across, just in front of the pedestal. He stepped on the inset again and heard the click. But this time he realized that the noise was coming from the chest. He stepped off the wooden inset, then on, and then off again. *Click. Click. Click.*

"Hey!" Phinneas shouted. "This pedestal has a switch in the front. It's the wooden plate in the floor. It's sensitive to weight. You have to stand on it to open a shutter on the keyhole. The key won't go in otherwise."

He stepped back onto the wooden inset, and the shutter on the lock clicked open, ready to receive his key. The lock was marked with a sunburst. He pulled the key from his pocket excitedly. It had two sets of teeth, and its head was shaped like the sunburst on the chest.

"Sunburst," he said. "A perfect match!"

He looked around, paranoid.

"And no Archers. That's good."

He slid the key into the lock, and it glided in smoothly.

"It's a perfect fit," he thought to himself.

Scarlet still felt uneasy. She looked down at Henry's body, then back at his box. His key, with its frog-shaped head, was still set in the lock. The emblem on the box was a polished silver frog.

"Something isn't right," she said.

Michael slid the teeth of his key into a lock decorated with the ruby-eyed dragon. It slid in smoothly as well, another perfect fit. Scarlet pulled her key from her handbag. She studied it closely.

She held it up and ran her fingers over the key's two distinct sets of teeth.

"Too easy," she mumbled.

She paused, thinking for another second. Michael gripped his key, ready to turn it.

"Stop!" she shouted.

Michael froze, and looked up with surprise. Phinneas, however, knew better than to let a competitor distract him. He glared at Scarlet, smug like a stubborn child, and turned his key defiantly. At a quarter turn, the lock clicked, and he smiled wider. The wooden inset beneath his feet fell open. With a gasp, he fell through the floor and disappeared into darkness. Relieved of his body weight, the spring-loaded door snapped back up and locked itself shut.

Vixen screamed. Michael froze.

"Michael, whatever you do, do not turn that key," Scarlet warned.

"What's the problem?" he asked. "The box matches my key perfectly."

"Pull the key out Michael. It's not right."

She walked over to the box Phinneas was trying to open and looked closely.

"See? Henry tried to use a frog key in a box with a frog emblem. Phinneas had a sunburst key in a box marked with a sunburst. You see how it turned out for them. I don't think we want to follow in their footsteps. Literally or figuratively."

"Bugger," Copper said. "Then what do you suggest we do, lass?"

Scarlet held her key up and pointed at its teeth.

"The two sets of teeth on the keys are separate, different. It's not a typical design at all. Have you ever seen a key like this, Michael?

"No, I suppose not."

"I think the two sets of teeth serve distinct purposes, I've seen something like this once before. If I'm right, the locks have two separate sets of tumblers. The first is a security feature. If you have the wrong key and the teeth don't clear the first set of tumblers, it will trip a mechanism inside the lock and set off a trap. You could end up falling through the floor like poor Phinneas, and ending up God knows where. If you clear the first set, then as you keep turning, the second set of teeth will engage with a second set of tumblers. If you have the correct key in the correct box, then the box will open. But if you don't, well, you saw what happens."

"But if we're not meant to match key-to-emblem," Michael said, "then how are we supposed to know which box our key opens?"

Vixen interjected.

"Even if you're right," she said. "How do you explain Henry? I still don't believe that was a booby trap."

"Do you believe that Henry is, at the present time, dead?" Scarlet asked.

"It's hard to argue with that," Vixen said.

"Well, then. Something we agree upon."

Scarlet swept a wisp of hair out of her face with a flick of her fingers and let the point linger, staring silently.

"You still haven't explained how he died," Vixen said. "Who put the arrows in his back?"

While they argued, Michael knelt down on a knee and set his satchel on the ground. He pulled out his invitation and unfurled it on the floor, studying with hurried eyes.

"There's nothing here," he mumbled.

He scratched his head and stared at the paper, hoping something would suddenly make sense. But nothing did.

When the ladies' argument had exhausted itself, all eyes turned to Michael.

"Michael, what are you doing?" Vixen asked.

"I don't know. I'm looking for something. I'm just not sure what. I feel like there is something here, something I'm missing."

Vixen reviewed her own.

"I may have something here," Vixen said.

"What is it?" Michael asked.

She knelt down next to him and pointed to some text on her parchment.

"A clue, possibly. Look here: '*The sentry keeps a watchful eye, and guards well all the things that matter.*'"

"The sentry? Like the Sentry statue by the stairs?"

"I don't know. Maybe."

"Follow me," he said.

The group walked to the statue that greeted them at the end of the stairs and studied it carefully, hoping to find some meaning in the clue. They walked around it in a slow circle, and scrubbed it with their eyes, looking for something, anything.

"So what are we looking for?" Copper asked.

"I'm not sure," Vixen said. "A symbol? An etching? Anything that might be something."

"Useful," Copper said. "Very useful."

Michael pointed.

"The pedestal says '*The Sentry*.' But if this is the sentry your notes refer to, what is he *guarding well*? The stairs?"

"Look at his hand," Vixen said. "He's pointing. Is he looking at something?"

"He's pointing back into the stairwell," Scarlet replied.

"He's keeping a watchful eye on the landing. Guarding something well," Vixen said.

"Like what?" Copper asked. "A secret passage?"

"I don't know," Vixen said. "But I can just feel it. I know I'm right about this."

Michael stepped into the dimly lit landing and could barely see his hand in front of his face. He felt along the wall for something, but didn't know what to expect. Maybe a lever or a switch. Anything other than plain rough stone.

"What is it lad, do you feel anything?" Copper said.

"There is a rough spot - like a carving or something. It's really hard to tell. It's too dark. I can't make it out. Does anyone have a lantern or candle to shine a little light?"

Nobody did. The gas lights on the wall were immovable.

"I have something," Vixen said. "Step aside, please."

Michael stepped out of the landing to let her in. She rummaged through her handbag and pulled out a wadded up ball of cloth. She unraveled it, revealing a glass ball, an alchemy orb. It contained an opalescent greenish liquid that swirled around inside, glowing ever so slightly. She removed the cap and dribbled some of its thick contents on the wall where Michael had been feeling around. A warm greenish glow lit the dim landing, its light growing brighter as the elixir mixed with the air.

"Is that better?"

"Yes, much better. Thank you. But what exactly is that?" he asked.

"Too much trouble to explain right now. Just don't get any on you," she said with a wink.

"Right," he said. "Noted."

Michael went back to where he had felt the roughness. He saw some engravings on the wall. Characters of some sort scrawled into the stone. The markings were odd and unfamiliar. But their arrangement was pleasing. Perfectly symmetrical columns and rows; three columns by forty or fifty rows. The space they covered was as tall as Michael as he stood next to it. The first two characters in each row looked like characters of a foreign, non-Roman alphabet. The last character in each row was more familiar; a star, a frog or a gear, to name a few.

Scarlet shoved her way into the landing to look for herself. Her body rubbed warmly and softly against Michael's, and it was not an accident. He felt her pleasant warmth through their clothes, and gave her a sideways glance, to let her know he noticed. But he didn't say a word. She nodded without saying anything either, before raising her eyebrows and looking back to the wall. She studied the columns and rows, up and down, as she held her key in her palm.

"Bizarre," she said. "I recognize the owl from my key, and the frog from Henry's. But what about the first two columns?"

Michael chuckled to himself.

"I have it," Michael said. "I can't believe I didn't see it sooner."

He held his key up to the wall.

"It's a simple cryptogram. See here? The first two characters in each row are the shapes of the teeth on a key. The third is the emblem. The key with teeth that match these two patterns will probably open the box with this emblem," he said, pointing.

He ran his key down the column in search of a match.

"See right here? Never mind that the head of my key bears a ruby-eyed dragon. That's not relevant. According to this chart, my key, with these teeth, will open a box marked with a king's crown. I think."

"But that would be counter to everything we know so far," Vixen said, "It's totally illogical. My Chrysalis was inscribed with a butterfly. The head of my key? A butterfly. The symbol on my admission token? A butterfly. The marking on the tokens that I am meant to collect? Certain to be a butterfly. Now, you're saying that despite all of that, and despite the fact that I saw a lock marked with a butterfly - it's literally right over there - my key will *not* open that box? That I should open a *different* box? At least two of us have already perished here. I've no plans to be a third."

"Then go open your butterfly box," Scarlet said. "Please."

"Vixen has a point," Michael said. "It doesn't really fit the patterns we've seen. But it has to be right. What else could it be?"

He walked away to find a box marked with a king's crown. As he left, the most competitive instincts in his competitors kicked in all at once, and they all smashed into the landing at the same time to line their keys up against the cryptogram. Copper shoved to the front, found his match first, and he trotted back to the columns.

Vixen found her match and dashed off, Nigel too. That gave Scarlet room to slide in. When she turned around, she could see that Copper had already found his box. He looked down at the floor and saw a wooden inset, right in front of the column where his box sat.

"Oh, no, I don't think so," he said. "Not today."

He looked for something heavy to place on the plate, but the statues were too heavy to move. So he settled for Henry. Michael watched uncomfortably as Copper dragged the man's body unapologetically across the floor and placed Henry's full weight on the wooden inset. As Copper let Henry's weight down, the shutter on the keyhole clicked open. Copper stood back upright and dusted off his hands with a big smile. He was as proud of his problem-solving skill as he was unfazed by the nature of his ballast. When Copper looked up, he saw them staring back with judging faces, mouths agape.

"What?" Copper said, with a shrug. "It's not like he has any other plans."

"Horrible," Vixen said. "Just horrible."

"Utterly barbaric," Scarlet added.

Michael shook his head and walked between columns, searching for a box marked with a king's crown. When he found it, he looked across the room and saw an Archer statue turned directly at him. The archer's bow was drawn, his arrow nocked. Michael drew the key from his pocket, studied its dragon marking, and looked at the king's crown emblem on the box. With a sigh, he inserted the key into the keyhole, and swallowed uncomfortably.

"It's just a statue," he told himself.

His hand trembled. But why? The cryptogram showed a clear match. He checked it twice, three times in fact. It was the right box. But what if he was wrong about the cryptogram?

He started to turn the key and heard a click. He looked up to see that Copper had already opened his box. Nigel had as well. Seconds later, Scarlet and Vixen opened theirs. Michael turned his key, little by little, gently and carefully. He passed the quarter turn mark, hopeful the first set of teeth would clear the tumblers. Slow and steady, he proceeded. His jaw clenched. He could feel the prickling sensation of beads of sweat forming on his temples. Self-doubt filled his head. He stopped and took a breath, looked around, and turned the key past the half-revolution mark. As he did, he felt some resistance in the lock. He prayed in his head that he was disengaging the lock and not unleashing something terrible.

A little more, and the lock clicked and the lid released. He sighed in relief, and could breathe again. But when he lifted the lid, he was confused. The box was shallow, much more so than he expected. It contained just a small glass vial with four metal pins. The vial was sealed with a cork, secured by thin copper wire. He looked closely at the pins and rattled them around in the vial, not sure of their purpose. Four simple pins, each an inch long, as thick as a pencil lead. There was also a slip of parchment with a hand-written note.

First north, then east, the wind doth blow
South, then west, will let it go
Box in building, shape of a block
Pins like wind can crack the lock

"That's it? Crack what lock?" he grumbled.

But he would have to figure it out later. He thrust the vial and parchment into his satchel, ready to rush to his buggy. But he paused at the steps and went back to the box, just to double-check that he hadn't missed anything. When he did, he noticed a small ribbon poking up from the back of the box. He pulled on the ribbon. It lifted an inset tray part of the way up, like the top tray of a jewelry box. He pulled the tray all the way out. And there it was. It was gleaming, and beautiful. The most beautiful token imaginable, a milestone token, concealed in a hidden compartment beneath the tray, glistening like hidden treasure. He had nearly missed it. Thick and heavy in the palm of his hand, the token's detail was flawless, beautifully polished with a raised ruby-eyed dragon on its face. He marveled at its quality, then realized Copper and Nigel had already run back up the stairs. Loathe to waste any more time, he rushed to catch up. It had been a long day. Tomorrow promised to be even longer. He would need time to prepare.

"Good luck to you ladies," Michael said as he ran into the landing.

"Right behind you," Scarlet shouted.

20

SEVEN LITTLE AFFLICTIONS

More than an hour had passed since they drove out of Adder Rock. The Ringmaster, Belladonna and Mech sat in uncomfortable silence. Nobody had spoken a word since they left. The sun ducked below the horizon as the Ringmaster drove toward the next stop. Belladonna rode in the passenger seat, Mech was in the back. He sat upright and alert. He never tired, his endurance was unparalleled. Belladonna leaned back in her seat and fixed a distant gaze on the horizon. She was exhausted from a long day, and emotionally drained from the confrontation at Adder Rock. She stared at nothing in particular, with eyebrows raised, silently waiting, expecting, perhaps even daring, the Ringmaster to say something. He knew the wiser course was not to ask. Ignorance was bliss, after all, and the approach that had served him well up to now. But tonight, his curiosity got the best of him.

"That was really something back there," he said.

She grinned.

"That was nothing."

"I disagree. That was definitely something. What did you do to that man?"

"I did what needed to be done. Don't act like you didn't expect it."

"But what did you do?" he said. "I've never seen anything like it."

"That's by design, love. It's really quite simple, though. I used my talon."

Her tone suggested he should have known. Her index finger was still encapsulated in a full metal sheath, like a suit of polished armor for her finger, hinged appropriately at each knuckle, so she could bend her finger. A long metal point protruded from the fingertip, slightly curved, like the sharpened talon of an eagle. She held her hand up into the orange light of the sunset, and its warm glow danced off the shiny silver full-finger ring. She could see the Ringmaster's reflection on its shiny surface, distorted as it was, and the shimmer brought her great satisfaction.

"I've seen what you can do with the powder in those rings," he said. "First hand, in fact."

"That you have," she said.

"But that was very different. You seemed like a completely different person back there. Not the person I know."

He was visibly uncomfortable.

"Know? What do you really *know* about me? The rings are just for fun."

She spoke with a sultry, haunting manner.

"This is for when I really mean business."

She looked at her hands.

"Seven little rings," she said.

She held her hands up and twiddled her fingers in a rolling motion.

"These seven little rings can wreak havoc. This one gives the belch voice. But you know all about that already. Amusing, but mostly harmless and quite temporary."

"Amusing is a matter of opinion, and we may not agree on that."

"Everyone has an opinion, love. Some are just more correct than others. This though, the content of this ring is far more interesting; it causes severe hallucination. A concentrated extract from hallucinogenic mushrooms. It takes a while, but once it kicks in, the hallucinations are powerful, and the effect can last for hours. Slow, boring, but effective. I can do the same with Monkshood. But when I mix the two, it's much faster. And violently potent."

"Monkshood?" he asked.

"Yes, Monkshood. Wolfsbane. Either way."

"Wolfsbane. Of course. Where do you come up all this?"

"I have a lot of spare time, love, between tending to your errands. Too much time, perhaps. I read, I experiment. Idle hands are the devil's playground. Is that how the saying goes? Something like that, I think."

He shifted in his seat. He recalled in his own head several occasions where circus animals had suddenly died under suspicious circumstances. He wasn't about to question her about it though. Not now. No chance.

"This one makes you sleep, mostly extracts of opium poppies, and a few other things. Useful, but also entirely boring."

She feigned a yawn and placed her hand over her mouth.

"Sleep. Whatever."

She stared at her hands, contemplating the other rings, and she cracked a devilish smile.

"Now this one is far more interesting. I call it the Berserker. It's the extract of the Angel's Trumpet. The toxin is highly potent, strong enough to kill a man with ease."

"Angel's Trumpet?"

"Yes - eat the flower, and you hear the angel's trumpet. Is that clear enough for you, love? A large enough dose is easily fatal, but in a smaller dose it can drive a man stark, raving mad. And I do mean *raving* mad."

She stared at the rings reflectively, as if recalling a time that she may have used it. The Ringmaster shifted in his seat again, and looked at her crosswise. He was growing more uncomfortable.

"You are enjoying this far too much for my liking," he said. "This Berserker - it's also temporary, I presume?"

"No, not really. That one tends to be pretty permanent. Sorry, pumpkin, but there's no going back on that one."

"Hmm," he grumbled.

"This one gives The Fever and Boils, it's immensely violent, in fact. The oil from the leaves of the manchineel tree raises blisters on the skin, producing boils of biblical proportion!"

"And these last two - this is acts as a truth serum, short-acting, and only effective for a few hours. But the victim can't help but tell the truth during that time. Any truth. And of course, some powdered Dumbcane. It numbs the mouth, causes severe swelling and drooling."

He was at a loss for words.

"Seven little rings. Seven little afflictions," she said, breathing out a relaxed sigh.

"So what does any of that have to do with the talon? And the man back there?"

"Oh, my talon is different," she said with a smirk. "That one really sends a message."

"A message?"

"Yes, loud and clear, love. I think you saw that back at Adder Rock."

"The talon? It did that to that man?"

"That's right. These rings are child's play. The contents of these vials I keep on my belt, though, they're administered with the talon. Just a dip and a poke are all it takes. That man back there, he got off easy. The mummification toxin is fast-acting. His suffering was much shorter than it could have been. I could have given him the Wheezing Suffocation just as easily. That one takes much longer to run its course, several minutes even in the fastest case. It would've felt like an eternity to him, though. And this last one. I just call it *fireball*. No explanation needed."

"But why the difference in how you administer them? I mean, not that I care, but it is a strange distinction."

"Not that I expect you to understand," she said, "but the powders in the rings create, for the most part, inconvenience. Annoyance. Irritation. Some are worse than others, but inconvenient nonetheless. Sometimes I need more powerful means to accomplish my end. Well, actually, it's *your* end, if I'm being honest."

She smiled and watched his reaction. He shook his head slowly, disavowing any responsibility for her actions.

"You make your own decisions, Belladonna."

"Yes, freely. For sure, love. No duress. Ever."

He swallowed loudly.

"But why the need for the talon? Just drop it in a drink. Like you did to me, with that awful belch voice. Preserve your anonymity, you know? Same result, yes?"

"I've tried that before. It's just not right," she said. "What you're suggesting, it's just not sporting."

"Sporting?"

"If I set out to take something from somebody, something so precious as a life, and to do it so intentionally, don't you think I owe them the decency to stand with them, face to face, to let them see their assailant? Maybe even offer an explanation? Should I not be honest and forthright in my intentions? Should I not look them in the eye as they slip away into the darkness? It seems only fair, really. I even give a fair warning. Anything less feels cowardly."

"Warning?"

"Yes, when my mind is made up, I blow my victim a kiss, to say goodbye. I let them know I'm coming for them. It may take time, but I'm coming nonetheless."

He shivered as he struggled to absorb what she said. Belladonna had been a faithful servant, but he never considered any of the details. He never had to, and he preferred it that way. Goosebumps rose on his arms, and the hair on the back of his neck stood on end, as a chill ran down his back.

"To be so close, to feel their muscles clench; at first it's just a reaction to the talon going in, as its sharp tip pierces soft flesh; but soon I can hear their breathing change as the poison courses through their veins and starts to take its effect. Their breath becomes labored. Their body tenses up as the toxin sets in and wreaks its true havoc. Being so close makes it a far more intimate experience, much more so than just sprinkling poison into someone's food and walking away. So impersonal. Not fair."

"Intimate?"

She paused and inhaled deeply through her nose. Then she sighed slowly and turned toward him.

"High risk, high reward, love."

"Reward?"

"You wouldn't understand."

He was at a loss for words again. He glanced at her and back to the road as he drove. She could feel him silently judging her.

"Don't look at me like that," she said. "I told you, you wouldn't understand. You never do anything for yourself. You don't have the stomach. You're so much happier to just snap your fingers and have things go away when they become inconvenient for you. Perhaps one day it will be me who disappears, and that much I understand. But you never have to worry about them, you never even have to think about them again. It's so easy to be you. But don't you dare try to understand me."

He'd struck a nerve, and her otherwise impenetrable facade had crumbled.

"Come now, Belladonna. Relax."

"No, don't you start with that. You *made* me what I am, but you will *never* understand me. I do terrible things for you and in order to get through it, I have to find something acceptable in the process, something to convince myself what I am doing is ok. I have to make it a game in my head. Once a decision is made, once I've marked someone, I let them know, subtly. And once I blow that long, soft kiss; once I've put them on notice, the game is on. Sometimes the game is short, like today. Sometimes it goes on longer, like a cat toying with a mouse. But here's the thing about that mouse; it is bloody doomed, there's no question about that. What matters is how long the cat takes to get bored, and end the game. Have no doubt about this: I am one very bad pussycat, and the things I have done for you haunt my dreams."

She stared at him, eye to eye.

"And make no mistake. I hate you for that," she said.

Her teeth were clenched, and she spoke with a growl in her voice.

"I hate you to my very core."

The Ringmaster sighed and shook his head, clearly refusing any responsibility.

"Everything that's happened, it was always necessary, Belladonna. Always necessary. We never had a choice."

It was a lousy attempt to soothe her; more dismissive than reassuring. The conversation would go nowhere, and she knew as much. She flipped her lenses down to cover her eyes. She pulled her knees up into her chest, wrapped her arms around, and set her chin on top. She stared out the side, into the distance, quiet once again. A tear streamed down her cheek and fell into her lap. She turned away so he wouldn't see, and refused to wipe it away, lest he become aware of her vulnerability. She could never allow it. He had to see her as unbreakable, so she refused to let on, ever.

Not another word was spoken the rest of the way. Silhouettes of hills passed by as they drove, and the Ringmaster steered his vehicle down the moonlit road into the night, toward the town of Gillingham.

21

THE GAME PARLOR

Tired and weary, Michael finally arrived in Gillingham, exhausted. Not just from the time spent, but all the talking, arguing and debating. He found it utterly draining. He just wanted to get to his room, close the door and enjoy some closed, quiet space before collapsing into bed. He stood outside for the moment, beside his buggy, basking in a symphony of light and sound; the glow of the moon, the rhythmic chirp of crickets and frogs croaking at the edge of the creek behind the hotel. Nobody was out at this hour, and the sounds reminded him of home. He breathed deep and took a moment to appreciate it, then he grabbed his satchel and garment bag, double-checked the lock on the chest, and went inside. He was greeted by a friendly clerk, a well-dressed older man with a white beard trimmed short and tight. He seemed eerily familiar to Michael, but he wasn't sure why. He had never been to Gillingham before.

"Good evening, sir, welcome to the Coxswain Inn. How may I assist you tonight?"

The clerk was upbeat and strikingly lucid for his age and the hour of day. He spoke with a confidence and sharpness that made him sound like a man of high intelligence, someone who ought to be much more than a simple innkeeper.

"Michael McGillicuddy. I would like a room for the evening, if I may. Departing early morning, thank you."

"Wonderful Mr. McGillicuddy. Here's your key. Room 369, sir. Third floor."

"Thank you."

"You're welcome, Mr. McGillicuddy. If you're interested, sir, some of the other members of your party have convened in the game parlor. In case you wish to join them, sir."

"My party?"

"Yes, sir. In the game parlor. At your leisure, sir."

He held an open hand out toward a room connected to the lobby.

"That sounds enchanting. But I'm exhausted."

The clerk nodded.

"Very well, Mr. McGillicuddy. Have a wonderful evening, sir."

"Thank you very much, and you as well."

Michael slung his satchel over this shoulder and knelt down to grab his garment bag. When he stood up he found himself face-to-face with Scarlet.

"Scarlet. Hello."

"Hello to you, Michael," she said with a bounce, leaning in close.

"Why don't you come join us in the game parlor. It's been a long day, come let off some steam."

She put her arm through the crook of his, crossing at the elbows, and gave him a gentle tug toward the parlor. Without hesitation, the clerk offered his assistance.

"May I hold your garment bag for you, here at the desk, Mr. McGillicuddy?"

Michael sighed.

"Yes, if you could. But I'll only be a minute. Keep it close by, please. Thank you."

"Of course, Mr. McGillcuddy. As you wish, sir."

"Excellent!" Scarlet squeaked. "Come along, now!"

She tugged his arm again, more assertively this time, urging him toward the parlor. As they approached, a burly attendant opened the sliding door and allowed them to pass. When they walked through the entrance Michael was overwhelmed by the size of the room, its decor and the sheer number of people and tables inside. It looked exhausting. Filled with gambling tables and parlor games, the room was alive, and worthy of a spot in Monte Carlo. People milled around, talking, drinking, playing and laughing. The ambient hum of blended voices was accentuated by the occasional clinking of glasses, as cheers rang out for a winner in the distance.

"So what do you think so far," Scarlet asked. "Has the experience been all you had hoped for?"

"It's so much more involved than I had imagined," he said, "but it's fine. My father was a past participant, a multi-winner, mind you. He talked about it a lot when I was growing up, but I don't remember it sounding so complicated."

"Yes, of course, he was probably light on the details. We, or rather they, like to keep things under wraps, for a variety of reasons. I'm sure he had his own. These events have evolved over the years as well, so I imagine this is all very different from what he would have described. And mind you, every year is different, no two are ever the same. Next year may be completely different still."

"Of course," he said. "It's exhilarating, but if I'm being honest, it's overwhelming. I do have a few ideas for my own, though in case I win the design rights for a future event."

"Yes, well, baby steps, Michael. Do you have any predictions yet?"

"For what?"

"For who will actually win this year," she said.

Michael inhaled and stuck his chest out. He spoke with exaggerated self-confidence.

"As I said, I'd like to think it will be me."

She smirked and nodded at his naiveté.

"Yes, don't we all. And how many tokens have you collected so far?"

"I'm not at liberty to say," he said. "Why do you need to know?"

"Relax, Michael. I'm just curious."

"Right, sorry. I'm just really tired, and I get short when I'm tired."

He was about to tell her he had only one, when she abruptly changed the subject. She stared into the distance at someone across the room.

"What is he doing here? I'm sorry to interrupt Michael, but I need to check something. I'll be right back."

She dashed off in the direction she had been staring. She started out with a strident and purposeful gait, but as she got further away, she regained her composure. Her stride relaxed, her shoulders lowered and her expression calmed. She greeted the man happily and they exchanged apparent pleasantries. She nodded down a hallway, suggesting they move the conversation to a quiet spot before they disappeared from sight. Alone again, Michael strolled around, watching people play at various tables. He didn't mind being around people, he just preferred to watch from a distance and avoid the idle chit-chat where possible. So that's what he did.

DORADO ESCHEVARRIA, THE BOUNTY HUNTER, STOOD SILENTLY leaning against the wall in a quiet corner of the parlor with the brim of his hat pulled down low. He watched intently, with arms crossed. The corner was a comfortable place to stand for a man who put so little trust in other people, particularly his own adversaries. From here, he could see all comers, and no one could approach from behind. He smacked on his toothpick, moving it with his tongue from one corner of his mouth to the other, quietly surveying the room. He watched how people interacted with each other. A bluff at a card table, a raised eyebrow, a hand placed softly on a shoulder, a wink and a smile, a stern look or a pointed finger. A lot was happening all at once. People falling out, new bonds forming, and even some overt alliances were starting to show. Dorado had a gift for understanding people, their instincts and predispositions. He could see through false facades, read between the lines, hear the unspoken word, and infer significance and meaning from subtle and even involuntary gestures in body language. He stood alone, watching everyone, talking to no one. He wasn't there to socialize, and he certainly hadn't come to play parlor games. Of course he enjoyed a good game of poker, but only at the right time and for the right stakes. Neither was present here. For the time being, he had only one purpose, to analyze the competition and form a strategy for the rest of his journey.

VIXEN SIPPED A DRINK AND STROLLED DOWN AN AISLE, WATCHING the gameplay with interest. Out of her element, this was all new and exciting. On any other day, this type of free time would be spent in her lab, or with her face buried in a book. The excitement of the race and the adrenaline of the day put her on a euphoric high though. That made her feel uncharacteristically social, and a little extra-outgoing. Of course she wouldn't gamble, she knew the mathematical odds were stacked heavily against her, and that, statistically speaking, she may as well just leave her money at the door and save the time for something else. The lavish decorations in the place hadn't come for free. The patrons had all paid, and continued to do so with their losses.

Vixen was far more drawn to games of skill. Chess, Go and Mancala piqued her interest, far more than roulette or blackjack.

Games of skill gave her a level of control. And why leave anything to chance? Feeling energized from the day's action, she pondered whether to play game or strike up a conversation. She saw Michael standing at a chess table, just a few steps away. He was obviously lost in thought, but she approached him anyway.

"Good evening, Mr. McGillicuddy."

Startled, he turned and looked.

"Oh. Good evening. So we're back to Mr. McGillicuddy, now?" he said.

She smiled politely.

"Yes, that's right. A lady shouldn't be too forward. I'm a little surprised to see you down here. This doesn't seem like your cup of tea."

"It really isn't. And the thought of retiring to my room is more than appealing. I had been on my way, in fact, but Scarlet found me in the lobby and dragged me in here."

"Scarlet? She *dragged* you? Is that so?"

"It is, yes."

"She must be much stronger than she looks."

Michael chuckled.

"Why so concerned?"

Vixen paused.

"No reason really. I'm just trying to figure you out, wondering where your focus is."

"What do you mean by that?"

"Well, it is a competition, after all."

He grinned.

"Are you referring to the race? Or to something else?"

Vixen blushed and looked away.

"I'm talking about the race, of course."

"Yes, the race," he said. "I'm aware of the competition. About that; do you plan to win?"

His grin turned into a full-fledged smile.

"I most certainly do," she said.

Michael just kept smiling and staring at her uncomfortably, nodding his head. He had again run out of things to say. She still found him to be a touch odd. Not in an off-putting way. More of an awkward, but endearing, way. He was there, talking, but not really saying anything at all. His inaccessibility made him seem mysterious, and that intrigued her. She stared into his eyes, wondering what was going on inside his head, trying to catch a glimpse; but she found no success. Michael was often guarded and inwardly focused. His spoken word was often the only information people knew of him, and they were left to guess at the rest. She stared for another second, also stumped for what to say next. This was a puzzle she wouldn't solve right now. So she raised her glass and said the only thing she could think of.

"Cheers."

IN AN OPEN SECTION OF THE PARLOR, JUST ACROSS THE FLOOR, A crowd formed. The Ringmaster, Belladonna, Mechanicules and Beatrix, the tightrope walker, sat at a table having a conversation. Beatrix had traveled ahead with Phillippe and other members of the Black Steam Circus to establish a forward camp in Gillingham. The conversation was lively and animated, but Phillippe had stepped away, in his self-absorbed style, to put on a show.

He started with something easy, but flashy enough to draw attention to himself, juggling four clear glass balls, then twirling them in a circular flow in one hand. A couple stopped to watch him, and then a few more. He pocketed the glass balls and he regaled them with stories of his magical prowess, as his hands gestured wildly. After some over-the-top hand waving, he threw a small ball of fire into the air from his fingertips, a simple effect achieved with common flash paper.

As far as stage magic went, it was nothing special. All of it was novice material, in fact, but it served his purpose. The fiery bursts were met with an audible reaction from a pair of onlookers, as the glow of the flames washed across their faces and reflected off the gloss of their eyes. Their reactions drew in more onlookers, and before long he had groomed himself a decent crowd of at least twenty people. Satisfied with his draw, he studied his choices carefully, and walked among them, speaking of his worldly travels and mystical acquaintances. He shook a hand, patted a back, leaned in close to talk or whisper, and moved on to the next. He chose a woman from the crowd to help with a card trick, and after some friendly goading, she agreed to go along.

Her selection as his mark was no mistake. She was older than the rest, and wobbly on her feet, but clearly a woman of means. Judging by her stuffy demeanor, fine jewelry and expensive clothing, she was a member of the local aristocracy. Phillippe led her by the wrist as he paraded her around in front of the small crowd and explained the card trick he was about to perform. In the process, he lifted an expensive gem-laden bracelet from her wrist and put it in his pocket. He kept her distracted with questions to answer, and directions to move here, and then there. She never noticed the lift.

He reached inside the breast of his coat and drew out a deck of cards. He showed the deck, front and back to anyone who wanted to see it before spinning the cards into a perfect fan. He invited her to pick one, and she obliged. His audience looked on with eager anticipation and they made their own guesses of the outcome, as if any of it mattered at all. It didn't. It was all diversion. All of it. When he finished his trick, he tipped his top hat to some happy applause, bowed out gracefully and sent her on her way. He thanked the crowd one last time for their attention, and his audience dispersed as he walked back to the Ringmaster's table.

Phillippe was especially pleased with the evening's performance. As he approached the table, Belladonna stared off in the distance. She was still, like a cat ready to pounce on a bird, and as Phillippe sat down, Belladonna left.

"I like this place," Phillippe said, as he took his seat, "I like these people. Good people here. My kind of people."

The Ringmaster looked back at him with a cold stare. Phillippe raised an eyebrow.

"Do we have a problem?"

"No, Phillippe. We don't have a problem. Not yet, anyway. But that bracelet you lifted off the old woman, that's house money. So just hand it over, and I'll see to it that you get your usual cut. Just like always, you know the rules."

Phillippe sighed and leaned back in his chair, disappointed at being caught. He reached into his pocket, grabbed the bracelet and slid it across the table.

The Ringmaster cleared his throat, staring Phillippe down. They weren't finished yet.

"Wow. Ok, fine. And I am very impressed with you. You are a very shrewd man, do you know this?" he said, wagging a finger.

"You have a much better eye than you used to. Kudos to you *monsieur*. You win this round!"

He reached into his other pocket. He pulled out two gold cuff-links and tossed them across the table like dice. They skittered across the table and came to rest right in front of the Ringmaster. With that, Phillippe looked up at the Ringmaster reluctantly, hoping they were finished.

"The billfold, Phillippe. Hand it over."

Phillippe shrugged, as if he was ignorant. The Ringmaster nodded to Mech, who leaned forward with a menacing look. He turned his head to crack his neck, and glared at Phillippe. Phillippe tried to resist, but caved under the pressure.

"*Vous êtes terrible*!" Phillippe yelled. "That was some of my best work. How did you see that?"

Phillippe's face turned sour. He slid a fat billfold across the table, bursting with paper notes. He spat on the floor to show his disgust.

"Take it easy, Phillippe, you'll get your fair share, just like always. Don't you worry about that."

Phillippe stood up without saying another word, slammed the chair back into its place and stormed off.

MICHAEL CLEARED HIS THROAT AWKWARDLY.

"I could use a glass of water," he said to Vixen. "Can I bring something back for you?"

"I'm quite alright, Mr. McGillicuddy. Thank you for the offer, but nothing for me."

She stood proud, with her chin up and out. She put on a strong front, and looked off into the distance. But as he turned away, she glanced over to look and their eyes met. She softened and smiled again, blushing slightly. She realized she'd been caught looking.

"Very well," he said. "I'll be back in a minute."

He left for the bar to get some water.

"I'll be right here," she said.

She turned to watch another table, and was jarred by collision with Belladonna.

"Oh my," Vixen exclaimed. "Please excuse me."

"I can try, love, but no promises, now. You're the chemist, am I right?"

She placed her hand gently on her chest as she spoke, and looked Vixen up and down, from her high collared shirt to her velvet coat to her long ruffled dress. It was a slow study, from top to bottom. Vixen ignored the intrusive stares as she responded.

"Alchemist, chemist, scientist. Yes, any of those would be correct."

"Right. So you must be pretty smart then. Have you figured it out yet?"

She walked slow circles around Vixen while she talked.

"Figured what out?"

"Have you figured out that you don't belong here, and that you have no real chance of winning this thing. I mean, honestly. Look at you, so soft. So pretty. So delicate and inexperienced. You don't stand a chance out there with these people. They're vicious animals. You know that right?"

"I think I'll be just fine, if it's all the same to you. Is that why you came over here? To try and intimidate me? If that's why you're here, then just scurry back under the rock from whence you came. I don't scare easily."

"No, my sweet rose petal. That's not why I came. That was just an ice breaker. What I really wanted to tell you is that you're wasting your time chasing after that Michael fellow."

Vixen bristled at her presumptuousness.

"I'm not chasing after anything. Other than victory in this race, and the right to say I told you so."

Belladonna wouldn't be convinced.

"You're surprised, and you're blushing," Belladonna said. "You blush so easily. What got you? The fact that I can see through you, or the fact that, deep down, you know I'm right? I've been watching you. Watching from a distance, but watching no less. Anyway, I suppose it's really none of my business now, is it?"

Belladonna circled again, but Vixen stood firm. As Belladonna rounded behind her, she stopped. She leaned in close and whispered in Vixen's ear from behind.

"Look out, princess, and watch your back, because, well - I bite."

She chomped her teeth together next to Vixen's ear and chuckled to herself as she strutted back the table with her usual swagger. When she returned, she was met with immediate questions. The Ringmaster seemed more anxious than usual, and that was saying a lot.

"Who were you talking to?" he demanded.

"Vixen Van Buren. She's nothing. Relax, love."

"What were you talking about?"

"Nothing, really. I was bored sitting here, listening to you droning on about what a genius you are, how you're going to win, how it's your destiny and all that. A girl can only handle so much. I thought I'd go for a stroll, play a little game, just to get in her head. Is that alright with you, love?"

"Enough with the games, Belladonna."

He addressed the whole table generally.

"Our most serious work starts tonight. Do you understand your assignments? Tonight is a pivotal night. There can be no mistakes; execution has to be perfect, and I will accept nothing less. Are you all clear on what needs to be done?"

They nodded.

"Belladonna, go inform the Hellfire Troupe."

"Yes, right away love. We'll all do our parts. And, just so we're clear, what will you be doing?"

He leaned back in his chair and folded his hands across his belly and rested his boot-clad feet on the table.

"I'll be running the show. Just like I always do. Now get to work."

MICHAEL RETURNED WITH HIS GLASS OF WATER.

"What did that woman want?" he asked.

"I'm not sure. I've seen her around, and I know she's in the race. She's quite rude, I can tell you that much. No air of dignity whatsoever. She came over here uninvited and said the most obnoxious things to me, to try and intimidate me."

"What did she say?"

"It's not important, really, but I don't like her. Something about her makes my skin crawl, she makes me feel very uneasy. I can't put my finger on it, but she gives me a very bad feeling."

"Yes, I met her once on a visit with John. There is definitely something strange about her."

"Indeed. So, tell me, Mr. McGillicuddy, what did you find in your box?"

Michael was surprised at her forthrightness. Although it was supposed to be a friendly competition, they were still competing, after all.

"Back at the Citadel," she prompted. "You did get your box open, didn't you?"

"Yes, I got it open. I'm not really sure what was in it, though."

"You didn't check?"

"Oh, I checked, and I took its contents. I'm just not sure what I got. It's just a short note, and a glass vial containing some metal pins.

"Metal pins?"

She chuckled at how silly that sounded.

"Yes, that's right, I found some metal pins. How about you, what did you find in yours?"

She slumped her head before answering, realizing the irony of mocking his pins.

"I got a sprocket," she said.

"A sprocket?"

She burst out laughing.

"Yes, a bloody sprocket, just a thumb's length across. After all of that, after all of the trouble we went to, I really expected something exceptional, you know? Maybe a sapphire crested tiara, or perhaps a big pile of shiny gold coins."

Her eyes lit up and her hands motioned an outline of how big the pile of gold would have been.

"I don't know. Something extraordinary. Certainly something better than a rusty metal sprocket. Honestly."

"Did you find a token?" Michael asked.

"Maybe. How about you?"

"Maybe," he replied.

They strolled around, enjoying each other's company as they walked through the parlor when they came across a table that caught Vixen's eye. Two men were setting up a fresh game board, one she hadn't seen before. It was a large wooden cube. The cube had an eight-by-eight grid of squares as its playing surface, like a checkerboard, but the squares were all the same color. The box had a bronze crank attached to a large bronze gear affixed to one side. A wagering table sat off to the side. It held a hefty pile of banknotes, where anxious observers stood. They must have had a significant stake in the outcome, and the bank notes on the table were likely theirs.

"What an interesting game. What is this?"

"Cubetta," Michael said." "You've never played?"

"No, I've never even seen it before."

"It's pretty complicated, much more so than it looks. It combines equal parts strategy, skill and luck; but it's a lot more difficult than you might think."

"Is that so?"

"It is."

"I don't mind difficult. Keep going."

"The game shares some characteristics of chess or checkers, but differs in many important ways. Not the least of which being that the game is actually played on a three-dimensional playing surface. Rather than a flat board on a table top, the game is played on the top of the battle cube."

"Like checkers, you say? It's so much larger than a checkerboard. The cube must be three feet across. And the squares are so much larger."

"A keen observation," he said. "The larger squares are necessary to accommodate the larger game pieces. Do you see the large crank on the side of the cube, connected to the large gear?"

"How could I miss it? It's almost the size of the side of the cube."

"Right. Well, the board starts out flat. But the individual squares on the game board, you see, each square is actually the end of a wooden column, and each column stands up vertically inside cube. When you turn the crank, gears inside the cube move the wooden columns up and down. Each column moves independently, and randomly."

"So, each square can end up at a different height?"

"Precisely, that's what gives the board it's three-dimensional look. When it's your turn, you turn the crank one full revolution. The squares of the board move up and down at random intervals to create an ever-changing playing surface. The game pieces sit at one of four possible levels –the original flat position, raised one cube high, two cubes high or three cubes high. The levels are referred to as 'Zaelyx,' 'Unyx,', 'Deuryx,' or 'Thaelyx,' respectively."

"So how do you play?" she asked.

"Just watch for a second, they're about to start."

The players sat across from each other on stools, arranging their pieces in the back two rows. Instead of wooden chess pieces, or simple wooden checkers, each man loaded his side of the board with hand-made pieces, automatons that each had built. Nevermind skill or chance, Cubetta is a game of pride. The success or failure of any particular piece depends on its maker. Differing views abound about what makes a good playing piece - it might be a piston hammer, a torch, a scissor clamp or any of the other bludgeoning, piercing or striking weapons. The genius of a winning strategy lies partly in the gameplay itself. But it mostly lies in the design of the pieces. Luck helps, but design is where bragging rights are won and lost.

Each man's set of sixteen pieces was distinctive. Each set is representative of its maker, and his pieces bear his signature in their design, and duplicates could be found where the design of a strong piece had proven successful in prior matches. Some pieces stand ten to twelve inches tall, others are short and squat. Some are wholly offensive in nature, relying on delivering a strong attack, while others are fortified to withstand them and counterstrike. But they dish out only moderate attacks of their own. When each man finished arranging his pieces, they shook hands.

"Good luck to you, Neville."

"You as well, Jonah."

Neville pulled a gold coin from his pocket and rolled up his sleeves.

"Call it," he said, as he flipped the coin in the air.

"Tails," Jonah said.

"Ha! It's heads, I've got the billet."

"That means Neville moves first," Michael told Vixen.

She nodded.

"You see, having the billet, that's a reference to vintage Cubetta boards. Some older boards actually have a billet attached to the side opposite the crank - it's an indicator that flips back and forth to point at the player whose turn it is. Variations are numerous, some are automatic and move when the crank turns, others are manual. It really just depends on the board maker's style."

"You're quite the Cubetta expert, aren't you?"

"You could say that. I've been playing since I was a child. My father and I used to build our own pieces together. Those are some of my fondest memories."

To start the game, Neville moved a piece forward, and Jonah turned the crank. The metal gears inside the box ground together and the squares on the board moved up and down in beautiful disharmony. Some squares raised up a little, some raised up a lot, and some raised up to their apex and headed back down before finding their level. With the levels of the board reset, Jonah made his move. The two men went back and forth for eleven or twelve rounds, over the course of several minutes. On his next move, Jonah turned the crank to set the board, and moved a piece backward, retreating from a mounting threat. If the board were to set in an unfortunate manner on a later turn, his piece would be vastly outnumbered in a battle, and he could see it.

"He can go backward?" Vixen asked.

"Yes, he can move any piece one space in any direction. The space you move to has to be connected to your current square.

Forward, back, sideways or diagonal moves are all acceptable." Michael explained.

"And what about that spot there, couldn't he just escape up to the next level?" Vixen asked.

"No, you can't change levels. Same level only. No up or down."

"Got it."

"It's the same with attacks. Attacks can only be mounted on pieces sitting on adjoining squares at the same level. Watch here, they're getting close."

Neville turned the crank and set the board for his next move. One of his pieces came to rest at Deuryx, beside Jonah's piece, also at Deuryx. He seized the opportunity, and called out the coordinates for his attack.

"E4 at Deuryx engages F4 at Deuryx."

Michael perked up at this call. Some of the onlookers gasped.

"I like that call," Michael said. "Now watch, it's going to get good!"

He was visibly excited, a break from his usual calm and reserved demeanor. There was excitement in his voice, and his hands were more animated than usual.

"That was actually a bold move, but I like it," Michael added. "The head-to-head battle seems well-matched. But suppose for a moment that he wins the square. Look at the surrounding squares. His piece will be surrounded by four opposing pieces. Granted, they are all at different levels now, but one turn of the crank can change everything. That's what makes this game so interesting."

Vixen nodded her understanding.

"On the following move, that same piece could be subject to an attack by a four-on-one matchup, depending on how the levels set. You always have to look several steps ahead."

"Like chess," she said.

"Yes, in a way."

The players activated their automatons on the squares at E4 and

F4, respectively. It was a good matchup, pitting Neville's reciprocating piston spear against Jonah's swinging hammerdasher. The automatons moved toward each other to engage with rarely seen precision and fluidity. The pieces were of very high-quality, the players were established veterans. The piston spear stood vertically and walked on two legs. It had two moving arms, but in the place of its hands, it had clockwork reciprocating spear tips, thick metal lances that surged in and out, back and forth, like giant sewing machine needles, each one six inches long. The opposing automaton also stood vertically and walked on two legs. One arm ended in a heavy hammerdasher, an oversized sledgehammer-type weapon that can be wielded with ferocity.

It was a classic matchup of speed and precision against brute force. The automaton with the swinging hammerdasher struck first. It slammed its heavy weapon down hard and fast, but it landed only a glancing blow on its opponent. Its weapon crashed down into the board with a loud bang. The piston spear was rocked off balance by the aggressive strike, ready to tip over, and the audience let out a disappointed sigh at what seemed to be an easy and anticlimactic defeat. But just before it tipped, the piston spear managed to right itself. It stood back upright and lunged forward, thrusting a reciprocating spear tip at the opposing piece. The spear found its target with ease, and surged back and forth in rapid succession. In less than a second, the spear pierced seven holes through its opponent's torso. Each thrust of the spear tip sounded like a knife jabbing into a tin can. The spear pierced right through the hammerdasher's inner mechanical workings and came out through the back. Metal bits flew all over the game board, and the hammerdasher, thoroughly perforated, collapsed on the board in defeat.

"Success!" Neville shouted.

He removed the defeated piece from the board and started a *bone pile* off to the side. He won the battle, and therefore won the piece. It was his to keep and his victory was two-fold: on the one hand, he had earned an advantage on the board; and on the other hand, he won the physical piece and everything in it. To be sure, it was severely damaged, but he could salvage some of its parts. And given that weapons were often modular, he could attach the hammerdasher weapon to any piece he built in the future.

"It's just one battle," Jonah said. "Don't get too excited, you're a long way off from winning the war."

It was Jonah's turn now. He turned the crank to set the board, and he did so with exciting results. Of his four pieces that sat on the columns surrounding to the piston spear, three came to rest at Unyx: one to the front, one to the back and one set on a diagonal. The piston spear also set at Unyx.

"See there?" Michael said. "That's exactly what I was talking about. Do you see how his three pieces are all surrounding the piston spear, all at the same level?

"Yes, I see it," Vixen said, "So he has a choice of which piece to attack with, is that right? So he will attack with the strongest one?"

"No, that was my point earlier. The three pieces can all combine their strength to attack the one, and there's no limit either. With proper strategy and a fortunate turn of the crank, you could actually produce an eight-on-one matchup. It's exceedingly rare, but entirely possible."

"What a fascinating game," she said, "I hope to play sometime. I love a good game of strategy, but I must admit that I wouldn't even know where to begin with making those pieces."

"That's quite alright. This is Cubetta at its highest level, and in its purest form. There are plenty of other variations that don't require players to build their own automatons. I could show you some time, you know, under proper circumstances."

"Very well. It's a plan then, Mr. McGillicuddy."

She smiled, offered her hand, and they shook on it to secure the deal. With the board set in place, Jonah glared over the top of his glasses and smiled indulgently as he called his next move.

"F5, F3 and G3. All engage F4 at Deuryx. Three-on-one attack."

~

ACROSS THE ROOM, NEAR WHERE THE RINGMASTER WAS SITTING, A commotion began to brew. A man appeared to be in distress. He stood up from the table, and looked around frantically. His face was swelling badly. His upper lip puffed up to the point that it touched the tip of his nose, and his bottom lip hung down off his face like a slab of raw liver. He tried to talk but he couldn't form his words properly. He drooled profusely, and he placed his hands on his face touching and poking all over, to test whether he could feel anything.

"I cahn fee my fay," he blubbered.

His tongue swelled up so big it protruded from his mouth. His eyes widened in fear, as he looked around for help.

"I cahn fee my fay," he repeated, louder and more panicked this time.

He pawed at his own face with desperate hands.

"What is wrong with your face?" one of the women at the table asked. "You can't feel it?"

He nodded.

"I cahn fee my fay!"

Strings of drool swung from his chin. Clear fluid dripped out of his mouth and off his bottom lip.

The people at his table stood and moved backward, staring on, terrified by his facial misfortune.

He wailed with a bubbly moan and ran out of the parlor in a panic.

Seeing this, the Ringmaster looked at Belladonna. She sat quiet, looking innocent and uninformed, and fiddled with her fingernails, pretending she hadn't even noticed.

"Is this your handiwork, Belladonna?" he asked.

She didn't look up, but just stared at her nails.

"Belladonna?"

"He was rude to me," she said with a pout.

"Was it the Dumbcane?" he asked.

"Yes. That's right."

She nodded. But she still didn't look up from her nails.

The Ringmaster shook his head.

"I wish you would stop doing things like that."

KAMAL SAT QUIETLY AT A GAMING TABLE, MINDING HIS OWN business, enjoying a game of Mancala. It was a simple way to unwind after the stresses of Adder Rock. He enjoyed the game itself, but he appreciated the cool, smooth feel of the stones in his hand. He was particularly fond of the sound the stones made when he scooped them from the board and jiggled them in his palm. He was playing with a new-found acquaintance with whom he shared a common interest in the game. They exchanged few words, other than to offer and accept the challenge of the match. Kamal and his opponent sat focused, with silent and fixed determination. As Kamal considered his next move, someone slammed a drink down on the table next to him. When he looked up, he saw it was William Wilfork. William was belligerent, and had probably consumed a little too much of the local grog. Perhaps it was an effort to numb the pain from the loss of his brother.

"You," Will said.

He spoke with righteous indignation, and a bit of a slur.

"I know all about you."

He poked Kamal in the chest with his finger.

"I beg your pardon?" Kamal replied.

"My brother, he said you know magic. You do strange magic, that's what he told me."

He swayed as he stood in place.

"I bet it's that same magic that killed my brother. I saw what happened back there. At the Citadel. I see you, and I don't trust you, magic man."

"I know nothing of your brother's demise. And I can assure you that I played no part in it," Kamal said. "But I am sorry for your loss, and you have my sympathy."

"Come on, magic man! Do something. Show me what you can do! I know you've got it in you."

"If I am not mistaken, Mr. Wilfork, I believe that we were on completely separate paths for the entirety of the day, and I do not recall seeing you, or your brother, at any point along the way; but once again, I am sorry to hear of your loss."

Kamal spoke in a controlled and metered tone. William leaned in close and poked Kamal in the chest again. It was an obvious effort to provoke him into something.

"Show me."

"Alright then, Mr. Wilfork, if you insist."

Kamal stood up from his seat. Smooth and fluid, he rose in an uninterrupted glide. Standing fully erect, he towered over William by a full head, and then some.

Kamal picked up William's drink from the table, and gulped it down. He set the glass back down on the table and fluttered his fingers in front of his face.

"Avada Kadabra," Kamal said. "That was two tricks."

"It was?"

"Yes. First, I undermined your beliefs and convictions. I made you question your ability to provoke me, and in so doing, I made you question the rest of your abilities as well."

William was slow to process the jab. He wasn't sure how to respond, so he took the easy route.

"Yeah, well that's only one. So what was the other?"

Kamal shook his head.

"Were you not watching? I just made your drink disappear. Have a pleasant evening Mr. Wilfork."

He turned to his Mancala opponent and graciously apologized for the intrusion.

"I regret that our game has been interrupted in this manner. You were a worthy opponent and I respect your ability. I'm sorry that I am not able to finish our match, but I must now retire for the evening. Please accept my apology."

His opponent acknowledged him. Kamal offered a shallow bow, turned and walked with his regal gait, nearly floating across the floor toward the lobby.

22

THE CHESS MATCH

Vixen and Michael watched with palpable excitement as Jonah initiated his three-on-one attack against Neville's lone piece. The pieces, two scissor-claws and a piston hammer, made short work of Neville's piston spear. The piece lay motionless on the board, reduced to a pile of shards. But it was an isolated battle. He'd lost just one piece, and the game would go on. Jonah turned the crank to reset the board as Michael pulled the watch from his pocket to check the time. But as he pulled his hand out to withdraw the watch, his milestone token came out with it. The token fell to the ground and rolled across the floor. Michael gasped as it rolled away. The token rolled down an aisle, past some tables, and between the feet of passers-by, almost out of sight. Michael gave chase, and the token eventually fell flat in the middle of an aisle. He walked over to the token and knelt down, but before he could pick it up, somebody walking by kicked it. The token slid across the floor and hit a man sitting at a chess table, right in the foot. The man looked down at his shoe and leaned down to grab the token. He studied its glistening finish as Michael approached, pleased by its beauty.

"Sorry to bother you," Michael said, "but that token actually belongs to me, I really just dropped it a moment ago. Sorry to have disturbed you. So, if I may? The token?"

Michael held his hand out ready to receive it, as Vixen caught up to him.

"Did you find it?" she asked.

As she caught her breath, she noticed the man at the table fondling the token with his thumb. He glared at her with a suggestive look.

"Oh. Hello," Vixen said. "Michael, what's happening here?"

"I was just asking this gentleman to return my token."

"I'll tell you what," the man said.

He spoke with a rough and raspy voice as he puffed his cigar.

"I'll give you a chance to win this token back. Beat me in a game of chess and you can have it. If you lose, I keep the token, and the lass here stays with me, too."

"I beg your pardon," Vixen said. "How dare you. I'll not be table stakes, or some prize to be won! Show some respect!"

"Now hold on!" Michael added, "the token isn't yours to wager. That token belongs to me, I just dropped it. So if you could just return it please, I'll be on my way."

He held out his hand again.

"Oh, I don't think so," the man said. "You must be mistaken. You see, this token belongs to me. But like I said, I'll give you chance to win it, since you seem so infatuated with it."

He took another puff of his cigar.

Vixen spoke softly to Michael.

"He's not going to budge, is he?"

"No. I don't expect he will," Michael said.

Michael tried to swallow but his throat was dry. Chess was not his game. He knew his limits, but he had to get the token back. Then something popped into his head, something his father used to say: *When times are tough, stick with what you know*. So he did.

"I'm not much of a chess player," he said nervously as he cleared his throat. "Would you fancy a game of Cubetta instead?"

The man put the token in his pocket.

"I think we're done here," he said. "Be on your way."

"Hold on a minute," Vixen said. "You wanted us to play a game of chess for something we wanted - the token - is that correct?"

"Aye," he said.

"Well, fair is fair. And since you're so keen on me, why not try and beat me? I will play the game in Michael's stead."

"So you prefer to play for your own honor, do you? A fine gentleman you're traveling with here."

Michael shrugged as the man leaned in toward Vixen.

"So all I have to do is beat you at a game of chess?" she asked.

"That's right. If you think you can."

"It's really not important what I think. So do we have a deal? I beat you, and we walk out of here with that token in hand?"

He took another puff of his cigar and leaned back in his chair. His pudgy cheeks were covered with grey mutton chop sideburns. He used his foot to shove the opposite chair out from under the table, and nodded for Vixen to sit.

"My word is my bond," he said.

He puckered his lips as he exhaled, and his cheeks filled and bulged outward. He blew smoke up into the gas light that hung above the table. A circle of people was gathering around the table as word of the challenge spread, and Copper was among them. One of the local residents, anxious to gossip, whispered to Copper.

"This will be a short game. That's Gideon Quinn, he is one of the best chess players in the country. He lives here in Gillingham, but he tours the continent playing in tournaments. When he's in town, he spends a lot of time at this table. People come from all around, just to play against him. Some just for the experience, to say they tried. Others play for stakes. But none of them ever wins. He's a crusty old bird, too, real chip on his shoulder. "

"Is that so?" Copper asked.

"You saw he was just sitting there alone, right? All by himself? There's good reason for that."

Vixen took her seat.

"Alright then," she said, as she studied the board.

She set some pieces into place, looked across at Gideon and pointed.

"Pass the castle, please."

"It's called a rook," he said.

He flicked it at her with his finger, and it fell into her lap.

She picked the piece up, and placed it on the board without reacting.

"Do you even know how to play?"

"I've played before, yes," she said. "And since you seem so keen on wagers, shall we raise the stakes?"

"Suit yourself. How much more do you want to lose?"

Michael nearly died.

"What is she doing? Is she crazy?" he thought to himself.

His pulse raced. He just needed the token back. Now was not the time for heroics.

"How about this. You win," she said, "and you keep the token, and my buggy."

She placed her keys on the board.

"If I win, we get the token back. Plus an advantage token."

"What makes you think I have an advantage token?"

"The pin on your lapel," she said. "You're a token trader, am I right?"

He grumbled.

"I'm here for participants to redeem tokens. Not to hand them out to the likes of you."

"Right. So do we have a deal, or do we not?"

He squinted, and nodded slowly.

"I keep the token, the buggy and *you*. Yes, we have a deal."

"Very well, then," she said. "Please present your wager."

He reached into the inside of his coat and drew out an advantage token. He slammed it on the table, next to her keys, which she met with a smile.

"Superb. And the other token?"

Gideon placed Michael's lost milestone token on the edge of the table, next to the keys and the advantage token. The table stakes were properly presented, and the game was ready to start.

"Ladies go first, is that correct?"

"Switch your king and queen," he said. "For crying out loud, queen goes on her color. Do you want to just forfeit now and be done?"

"I'd really rather not, if it's all the same to you. But thank you."

"Have it your way then. This is my table. You're playing black, white goes first. I'll start."

A knot formed in Michaels' throat. First move seemed to give him an advantage.

Gideon made his first move. Pawn to e4, a strong opening, offering many variations of play.

Vixen stared at the board for a moment, unimpressed. Wisps of hair hung down around her face, having come loose from the hustle of the day. She pulled the stake from her bun, rewound her hair nice and tight, and pushed the stake back through. With pursed lips and squinted eyes, the look on her face said she was ready for business. She made her move: pawn to c5.

"Playing the Sicilian Defense," he said. "Do you know how to play it all the way through?"

It was a strong opening for black, and one that suited Vixen's personality well. Some might opt for a strong defensive posture relying on counter-attacks, but the Sicilian defense is a particularly aggressive opening. She would seek to establish a strong offensive posture early in the game.

Vixen raised an eyebrow.

"Do you want to play, or do you want to talk?"

He slammed his knight onto the square at c3.

"Grand Prix Attack, a classic," she said, smiling. "It looks like we have ourselves a game. Don't blink, now."

From that point on they moved their pieces in rapid-fire succession, one player responding to the other; instantly and reflexively. Move after move, they looked like they had rehearsed this game a thousand times prior. With openings completed, they moved into their mid-game at lightning speed. When one player advanced, the other attacked, each attack was met with a swift counter. Pieces fell one after the other. The crowd grew larger as word traveled of such a worthy matchup. A buzz filled the room as the onlookers whispered to each other. Each player had demonstrated expert knowledge of the game, anticipating all possible combinations, evaluating relative strength in a fraction of a second, and responding to changes in momentum instantaneously as the exchanges continued. It was a marvel to watch.

Vixen left a bishop unprotected, and Gideon took the bait. She smirked the slightest smirk, and the stage was set for a new flurry to come. She was setting her end-game up with expert precision. Rook takes pawn, knight takes rook, and so the battle ensued. The trades were quick, and the pieces continued to fall like soldiers at war. Her plan was working flawlessly so far.

"Check your king," she said.

He moved to protect his king, pounding another piece into position to block check.

"Check!" he said.

The crowd gasped. She had a strong position, her pieces were well-coordinated. But Gideon was a true master. She felt near victory, despite him being a far better player than she had anticipated. The end seemed near. Michael was nervous, but cautiously optimistic. Gideon remained determined.

He moved to block her check, and she took his queen.

Michael pumped his fist in the air.

"She got his queen!," he thought to himself. "That's it, victory is ours! We're on our way!"

Gideon moved, and took Vixen's queen in response. The hum of the onlookers grew louder as speculation brewed. For those who knew and had watched Gideon for any amount of time, this was unlike anything they had ever seen.

"Damn it, Vixen!" Michael said. "Protect yourself!"

She looked up at him reassuringly. The trade was intentional, she had done it on purpose.

Gideon slid his knight over slowly to check Vixen's king.

"Check," he said.

She hadn't expected this particular line of attack though; she had recognized the possibility but dismissed it as a weaker branch of play. He was demanding a response nonetheless. She looked him in the eye. Her face cycled through emotions – surprise, distrust, disbelief, worry and confusion. What was she missing? She pulled herself back together, determined and focused once again. It was not the move she would have played, certainly not one she would recommend, and it seemed like a low percentage gamble in her calculation. He played it nonetheless, and she was on the defensive. She moved to protect her king. He pushed a rook into the back row.

"Check."

Michael cringed and his eyes opened wide.

She studied the board intently. With her brows furrowed and her lips pressed tightly together, she looked as determined as ever. The winning combination was there. She knew it, she could feel it. She just had to find it for herself. Suddenly she relaxed her squint and the wrinkles in her forehead smoothed over - she saw a path to victory. Gideon would have to cooperate, but the path was there if he took the bait.

After a few more exchanges, she pushed a piece forward.

"Check," she said.

Gideon was surprised by her move. He found her to be the most worthy of opponents. He knew it, and he didn't like it. He adjusted his hat, glared back at Vixen, and leaned forward. His elbows rested on the table, his eyes tracked back and forth. He traced out every possible option that remained. After a long draw on his cigar, he looked up at her.

"You're not as good as you think you are," he grumbled.

As he spoke the words, his smoke-laden breath wafted into her face. A potent mixture of anger and smoke turned his voice especially raspy. Vixen's expression was resolute, her posture tall and strong. He tossed the last of his cigar onto the wooden floor and stomped it out with the heel of his boot.

Michael watched with his fists clenched.

"Better lucky than good," Michael mumbled to himself. "That's what my father always said."

Gideon ran his hands over his mutton-chop sideburns. He looked troubled. He studied the board a moment longer, then he made this next move. He took a risk, and Vixen pounced.

"Worst possible choice," she said.

She slid a piece over in calm response, and four moves later she made a declaration.

"Check, and mate."

The crowd gasped in unison, then fell eerily silent. Copper looked over at the local who had been bragging about Gideon's mastery of the game. He just chuckled to himself and shook his head slowly. Michael was so excited, he pumped his fist and jumped in the air a little, standing out awkwardly against the backdrop of a stunned and motionless crowd.

Vixen stood up from her seat and politely offered her opponent a handshake.

"No hard feelings?" she said.

He stared back into her eyes he but he didn't move. The silence was painful for everyone watching. What would he do? Vixen pushed her hand closer, insisting on the gesture of sportsmanship. But Gideon just stared.

"Very well, then," she said. "I guess we'll just be taking these and going on our way."

She reached for her keys, Michael's milestone token and Gideon's advantage token. They were hers to take, she had won fair and square. But as she leaned in to collect her prize, Gideon reached over and grabbed her wrist.

"Being the gentleman that I am," he said, "I'll let you take your keys and your token. But the advantage token stays with me. I can only redeem, I'm not authorized to gamble them away."

"Rubbish! Why did you offer it then?"

"I never thought you stood a chance, frankly."

"Well that's hardly sporting," she said. "Total bollocks! We had a proper wager."

"Did we? Well, I will tell you what you have now. You have ten seconds to get out of my sight."

He stood abruptly, and shoved his chair backward with the backs of his knees as he rose. He put his hands on the table, and leaned over with an ill-intended glare.

"One second longer and the two of you will regret ever walking in here. I don't take kindly to hustlers."

He pulled his jacket back to reveal a holstered pistol.

Michael nodded at Vixen.

"Vixen, it's time to go."

Grudgingly, she conceded the advantage token. She grabbed her keys and Michael's token, and they left the parlor in a rush, hoping to get out of harm's way before things escalated.

23

ENTER THE HELLFIRE TROUPE

It was getting late. Most of Gillingham's residents had retired for the night, as had most of the guests of the Coxswain Inn. The streets were still, and the cold of night had silenced the crickets and frogs. The only light on the streets was the iridescence of the moon and stars, and a soft yellow glow that leaked out from a few scattered windows. It was a perfectly tranquil evening. That is, of course, until the tranquility was disrupted by the Hellfire Troupe.

They emerged around a corner, from a side street leading out of town. They marched brazenly down the middle of the main street, right through the center of Gillingham to the hotel. The whole of the Hellfire Troupe were there, a dozen of them, men and women alike. They juggled lit torches and tossed them back and forth as they walked. The more acrobatically-inclined carried torches in their hands while doing cartwheels, round-offs and long sequences of backflips all strung together. Others drew flammable fluid into their mouths from the flasks on their belts, and they blew the liquid across lit torch flames to create fireballs that burst through the air.

As casually as they moved, an uninformed observer might assume they were just practicing. But their intentions were far less honorable. Each member was clad in black from head to toe - pants, shirts, kerchiefs over their mouths, and leather boots. Exposed portions of their faces were smudged with coal dust. They moved slowly and deliberately, doing little to conceal their presence.

As they continued to march and flip and cartwheel their way down the street, they stopped in front of the hotel. A pair of members drew from their flasks and blew out two large fireballs. Instead of blowing them into the air, they blew the flames directly into a pair of vehicles parked in the front of the hotel. Copper's monocycle was the first to go. After a few more incendiary puffs, it was fully engulfed in flames. They continued their purposeful march past the hotel, setting more vehicles ablaze as they went. The Troupe continued their slow and steady parade toward the water's edge and disappeared around a bend without ever saying a word or breaking their stride. As they marched into the darkness, the vehicles burned, unabated.

24

WHAT HAPPENED TO NOT BEING FAMILIAR?

Powered by a rush of adrenaline from the chess match, Michael and Vixen rushed through the hallway, and up the stairs to the third floor. Michael led Vixen by the hand to keep her close. He stopped at room 369, withdrew his key and unlocked the door. He threw the door open, and pulled her through into the center of the room, then shut the door, locked it quickly and leaned up against it with a sigh.

"*That* was inspirational," he said. "You were absolutely amazing down there. Where did you learn to play chess like that?"

"My parents are academics. Both are university professors, and they value the exercise of the mind as well as the body. They taught me to play at age four. We played a lot in my early childhood, but by the age of nine, neither of them could properly challenge me. And, mind you, they were each quite good in their own right. We lived in England at the time, but we moved back to the Netherlands when I was eleven, to be closer to family. I was homeschooled from that point on, and they arranged for me to study chess under the tutelage of Sir Lawrence Alma-Tadema. He was a brilliant chess master, and an extraordinary mentor.

Michael nodded.

"I know the name."

"Oh, he is very well-known. With his training, I played, and won, several championships up to the time when I started university. It's worth mentioning that many tournaments didn't allow girls to play. At one point I actually cut my hair short and competed as Victor Van Buren, but that only lasts for so long, you know.

"Do you still compete?"

"No, not anymore. Once I entered university, I quit playing competitively to focus on my studies. I've had my own lab to fill my time ever since then. But I do still play occasionally with friends and colleagues, to keep sharp."

"It looked like he had you in trouble at the end, but you made that one move and everything changed."

"He caused the change. I simply gave him the opportunity," she said. "It was a calculated risk. I had no choice but to take a chance, and hope it worked out for the best. And I most certainly would have lost if I hadn't."

Michael stood there, smitten, taking in her words.

"Fascinating," he said. "And for what it's worth, I think it was terribly unsportsmanlike of him to take the advantage token back. A deal is a deal. A man should stand by his word. Always."

"Men have been shot for less," she said.

Michael stared back, eyes wide.

"So I've heard, anyway," she said with a shrug.

"I can't believe the way you took it to him. That was just brilliant. Did you see his face? He was livid."

"I saw it," she said. "I don't think he's accustomed to losing, and certainly not to a woman."

She spoke with an air of conceit as she tucked a lock of hair behind her ear.

"You are truly amazing," he said.

Caught up in the excitement of the moment, he burst forward and swept her up in a celebratory embrace. He lifted her clean off the floor. Her feet dangled, relaxed, and she wrapped her arms softly around the back of his neck in a delicate embrace, their foreheads touching. She let out a giggle and threw her head back, basking in the glow of her own victory, and when she looked back down, their eyes locked for a fleeting moment. In that one electric second, the world stopped turning, and everything moved in slow motion. Neither of them could hear another sound, just the beating of their own hearts and the deafening sounds of their own breath. Michael stared into her wide, inviting eyes, and she swallowed uncomfortably. He realized he was still holding her up off the floor, and he set her back down gently.

"I'm sorry to have gotten so carried away," he said. "Brilliant chess play today. Very well done."

Vixen had fully blushed by now. She looked at the floor and nervously tucked a wisp of hair back behind her ear again. Her posture went soft, and she gazed off to the side, looking almost timid. It was a new look for her, as Vixen rarely shied from anything.

"Thank you," she said politely, "and you… drove your buggy very well today. Masterful navigation."

She stared at the wall, trying to look as though she was concentrating on something else. She tried to pretend that the moment had passed; but she knew it hadn't.

Michael was eager to change the subject. He tugged on his bow tie.

"It's been a long day," he said. "This thing is strangling me."

He sat down at the vanity and looked in the mirror, trying to loosen the knot, but he struggled to get it undone.

"Do you need a hand with that?" Vixen teased.

She had recomposed herself, and was wearing a new-found, confident smile.

"I suppose I could use a hand, it's knotted pretty tight."

"Here, let me see what I can do."

She approached him slowly. As she walked behind, she ran an

extended index finger lightly across his shoulders, down his arm, and over the back of his hand. She stood beside him, studied the tie and looked back into his eyes. She reached down slowly, and pulled her dress up to her knee, just high enough to give her the freedom to move her leg. She stepped over his knees, and lowered herself gently into his lap, and sat face-to-face, straddling him. Her warmth was welcome. Vixen swallowed audibly again.

"That's quite a knot," she said.

"In your throat?" he said with a wink.

"I was talking about your tie, Michael. Now let me loosen it."

She leaned in closer. As she worked on the knot, his hands came to rest in the crooks of her hips. She didn't move them away.

"Did you call me Michael?"

"I believe I did."

"What happened to not being familiar?"

She shrugged. Her lips curled into a coy smile. Her eyes conveyed a greater goal, something more than loosing his tie.

"I think we're past that, are we not?"

The warmth from her face radiated onto his, and her hair smelled clean and floral, as she worked the tie loose and stared into his eyes. She unfurled the last loop of the knot and slowly slid the tie out from under his collar, and the collar to fell open. Neither of them spoke. She dropped the tie to the floor and placed her hand on his cheek. Their eyes never strayed, and their hearts raced amid the silence. Vixen curled her lips, ready to say something when somebody banged on the door. They quickly rose, and Michael rushed to the door. Someone was shouting from the other side.

"Michael, you need to come downstairs right now!"

He recognized the voice, and opened the door to see Scarlet standing there.

"What is it?" he said.

"Terribly sorry to bother you, but somebody has set fire to some of our vehicles, I thought the two of you would want to know. Your buggies could be at risk."

He was confused to see her standing there.

"I appreciate the concern. Very much so, in fact. But how did you even know I was in here? That we were in here?" he asked.

Scarlet didn't say anything. She just held out her hand and raised an eyebrow. Michael looked down to see the looking glass in her palm.

"I see."

"No, Michael," Scarlet said. "*I* see."

As Michael looked back at Scarlet, something clicked for him. It was in that moment that Michael finally realized something. Something of tremendous importance. How did it take so long for him to realize?

"Oh my god," he gasped. "My chest!"

He grabbed his key as he rushed through the doorway, pushing past Scarlet as he charged to the stairs.

25

KAMAL'S RITUAL

Before he retired to his room, Kamal stopped at the hotel restaurant for a light dinner of whitefish and steamed vegetables. He was particularly fond of the carrots, which were difficult to find at home. When he finished, he politely thanked his server, paid for his meal and retired to his room for the night. When he arrived, he closed and locked the door behind him. He emptied his pockets and placed the contents on his vanity, including a bronze double-toothed skeleton key. The head of the key was decorated with three feathers. The feathers were intricately carved, with every rib of every feather finely detailed. The feathers spread outward from a large opal at the base of the shaft. A shiny gold token bearing the three-feathered emblem on its face also sat on the vanity, next the key. The key and token lay on top of a parchment map, hand drawn with a fountain pen. It was his map for the sea leg. He studied it briefly, just long enough to see that he was meant to leave from the port of Gillingham, and sail east through the English Channel. He would make his first stop at an island in the open sea.

He sat down in the middle of the floor, crossed his legs and prepared to meditate. While seated, he removed his shirt to expose an intensely muscular upper body. Kamal was a strong man to be sure, not hulking or massive, but chiseled and well-defined, with finely drawn tattoos that covered most of his upper body.

Tattoos of a cloud and lightning bolt appeared on the inside portion of each forearm. The artwork was stunning; thick, rolling, frothy thunderclouds with rich texture and shading. Bolts of lightning discharged down his forearm from each cloud. Not simple bolts either, these were the most powerful kind of lightning, the kind one would see in massive electrical storms; the kind that spreads out with dozens of branches that, in turn, split off from each other into dozens more. The tattoos ran from the crook of his elbow down across his wrist, over his palms, and all the way to the tips of his fingers.

His back was covered across the shoulders by the outstretched wings of a Coatl, a dragon-like serpent with the wings of an eagle. His right upper arm was decorated with a cobra that wound around his bicep in a long spiral. The ribs on his right side bore the image of a Cerberus, the mythological three-headed hell-hound that guards the entrance of Hades, and an image of two criss-crossed swords appeared on his lower back. Three separate eyes, just standalone eyes with lids and lashes arranged in the shape of a triangle, appeared on the outside part of his left shoulder, and two large fireballs were inked low on each side of his abdomen, which created the illusion of fire rising from the waistband of his pants.

He sat on the floor and unfurled a cloth roll. The roll-up case contained three lances, long needles the size of crochet hooks, and a small silver tray with some matches. He struck a match, and withdrew one of the lances from the cloth roll. He waved its sharp tip back and forth through the dancing flame to sterilize it. When he was done, he blew the match out and set it on the silver tray and set the lance down next to the match. He closed his eyes and took long, meditative breaths.

He bowed his head and chanted various incantations in his native tongue. With each incantation, a different tattoo animated on his skin. The lightning on his forearms flashed and dissipated, before the lightning bolts struck down to his fingertips once again, holding their place. The cobra slithered around his bicep in several rotations, and the eyes on his shoulder blinked and scanned around the room observantly. The Cerberus raised its head, howled and chomped the air with its sharp teeth, and the Coatl flapped its mighty wings to stretch. He continued reciting all the incantations until he had given life to every one of his tattoos. He folded his hands in his lap, said a short blessing, picked up the lance and held it to his fingertip just above the silver tray.

"I offer this gift of my blood to you, to give you life of your own, and in return I ask that you will answer my call in my own time of personal need."

He pressed the lance into the tip of his finger, and pierced his own flesh. A droplet of blood formed and dangled from his fingertip. He held it out as an offering to the Cerberus. The Cerberus turned a head upward, lapped at his fingertip, and drank the droplet in. He repeated the motion, giving each tattoo the sustenance it needed. This was a daily ritual, one he practiced every evening before he slept. When he was finished, he wiped the lance clean and re-rolled the case. Feeling drained, as he always did following his daily ritual, he blew out the lamps and retired to his bed for a deep sleep.

26

STARTING TO FEEL THE HEAT

9:47 p.m.

Michael and Vixen raced down the stairs to the ground floor, to the front of the hotel where their vehicles were parked, a crowd had formed to help. Copper stood over the remains of his monocycle. It was already burnt to the ground, tipped over on its side in an ashen pile.

"Ah, bugger," he said. "There's no salvaging it. It's totally roasted."

Michael dashed toward the flames as fast as he could. He knew he parked near where the fire was, and desperately hoped it was not his buggy, and therefore his chest, that was burning. Patrons of the hotel, and even residents of nearby homes, rushed out of their doorways with buckets and glasses, and even vases, full of water to help douse the flames. But the straw-filled seats, wooden buggy frames, and on-board coal fuel made for quick kindling. The vehicles burned hot and fast.

As he got closer he saw his buggy had not yet caught fire, but two others, one on each side, were engulfed in flames that threatened to leap to his. He slowed, squinting, holding a hand up to block the light and heat. His chest sat exposed, in the back of his buggy, dangerously close to ignition. This smell of wood smoke wafted through the air and Michael felt helpless. With nothing to douse the flames, the only thing he could do was move the chest to safety. Desperate, he grabbed the water containers from oncoming residents and doused his clothing, soaking wet, and jumped into the seat.

"Michael, don't be foolish!" Vixen yelled.

The buggy wouldn't start. He released the hand brake and ran around to the back to push. The heat was intense, and the buggy was heavy. He could feel his hands begin to burn, pushing against the hot surface.

"Come on, lad, you're going to get yourself killed," Copper shouted. "Just get out of there."

Michael kept pushing, inch by inch, straining against the weight of the buggy.

"Seriously, lad, get out!"

Michael kept pushing.

"I'm not joking, get out of there!" he yelled.

It was too much to bear, standing and watching, as Michael struggled. Against his better judgment, Copper rushed in to help him push. He ran in beside Michael and pressed his shoulder into the back of the buggy. Together, they were able to move the buggy, and its precious cargo, to safety. Exposed pieces of the wooden buggy frame had started burning with small lapping flames, but Michael removed his shoe and beat them out to smoldering plumes.

"Thank you," Michael said to Copper. "You quite honestly have no idea how much this means to me. I couldn't have saved it without your help."

Copper waved a hand.

"Don't mention it," he said with his smooth and breezy diction. "But don't go making a habit of doing stupid things like that in the future, lad. I can't promise to help you the next time. It's just a buggy, for Chrissakes. And not even a very good one."

Michael chuckled and shook his head.

"If I can ever repay your kindness, don't hesitate to let me know."

Michael held his hand out, offering to shake. Copper accepted, with a slap and a squeeze. A strong, jerking shake from Copper's leathery paw made him cringe in pain. He shook his hands out, both of them slightly burnt, stinging badly.

Scarlet was approaching from the distance, walking with a visible limp.

"Is everything alright?" she asked.

"I think it is now," Michael said. "Where are you coming from, I thought you were right behind us."

"I was, I'm sorry about that. I turned my ankle at the top of the stairs, in my foolish rush to follow you down. You had already run off with Vixen. Once I made my way down the steps, I must have taken a wrong turn and ended up in the back, on the wrong side of the building. But I found my way."

"Is your ankle alright?"

"It should be fine. It's sore, but I'll live. It looks like you and Vixen have things under control. So I think I'll just leave you to your business."

"Scarlet, are you upset about something?" Michael asked.

She paused, considering the question.

"There's really nothing for me to be upset about. Goodnight Michael, and good luck."

With that, she limped back toward her room. Volunteers worked to tamp out the remaining flames as the Ringmaster, Belladonna and Mechanicules arrived. They wandered in at the same time, but spread themselves out to mix with the crowd. They feigned concern and offered to help wherever they could, but in truth they were only there to quietly assess the Hellfire Troupe's handiwork. By the time the fires were extinguished, several competing vehicles had been destroyed. Speculation ran rampant among the participants about who the culprit might be.

Quietly, above the fray, Dorado sat in the sill of his open second-story window, with his back against the sill and one leg kicked up. He smacked on his toothpick, watching, listening. He snorted at the rubbish he heard below. The voices blended together, but he could pick up bits and pieces from where he was sitting, if he listened closely enough. There was plenty of blame to go around, some were even called out by name. Kamal was mentioned as a possible saboteur, and more than once. Someone else suggested Dorado was the perpetrator. On hearing such foolishness he grunted, removed his toothpick and spat in disgust. He put the toothpick back in his mouth, stood up out of the window sill and closed the window. He had heard enough.

Apart from Copper's monocycle, two other vehicles belonging to a pair of participants, Groot Niemand and Magna Vastum, were among those destroyed. Each had just arrived in Gillingham, and later than most. Neither had had the chance to unload their belongings before the fires. They were furious, and stood cursing their fates, as they were likely out of the race at this point, unable to continue. With the fires nearly extinguished, he buzz of the crowd faded and people retreated for the evening. As the crowd thinned, Vixen approached Michael.

"Are you alright? You could have been terribly hurt."

She grabbed his hand to look at it.

"I'm fine," he said.

"Michael, you're burned."

"It's not bad," he said with a wince.

"You need to take care of it, let's get you some ointment and a bandage."

"Maybe you can come give me some help," he said, "perhaps we could finish the conversation we started earlier?"

He grinned and winked, but she looked away.

"It's been a grueling day," she said. "We could both probably benefit from some rest. Back at it tomorrow?"

Michael paused, disappointed.

"I"m not sure I understand."

"A good night's rest is definitely in order," she said. "Sleep well, Mr. McGillicuddy."

She patted him lightly on the chest. Michael watched, at a loss for words, as Vixen walked off into the shadows and back to her room.

"I guess I'll go get some rest now myself," he mumbled.

27

A TRICKY BALANCING ACT

2:00 a.m.

Beatrix dashed through the shadows, avoiding detection, careful to stay clear of the moonlit open areas as she made her way down the street. She pranced about, fleet of foot, with Phillippe in lumbering tow. He carried a heavy canvas bag slung over the curve of his bony shoulder, and struggled to match her pace. They stopped and stood in the shadows of a three-story building, just across the street from the Coxswain Inn.

"I think that's it," Beatrix whispered, pointing to the upper corner.

"Yes. I believe it is. The first room on the end," Phillippe whispered.

"Ok," she whispered. "Tie it on."

Phillippe stood facing her, silent, less than enthused by his late-night assignment. He relaxed his shoulder and let it slump. The bag slid off and crashed to the ground with a clatter. He didn't care. It was late, and he was tired.

"Shhh. We can't screw this up," Beatrix said in a terse whisper.

"Yes, of course. We should not screw it up," Phillippe said. "So maybe then, *you* should carry the bag now."

"Knock it off, Phillippe, and just tie it on."

With a huff, he leaned down and pulled a rope from inside. He tied the rope around the handle of the bag and handed the other end to Beatrix. She tied it around her waist.

"I'll see you up there," she said.

Phillippe looked straight up, toward the third story balcony where they were headed.

"Yes, of course. I will see you up there."

She flashed an energetic smile and winked at Phillippe from behind a thin wisp of blond hair hanging down over her eye. She crossed her eyes to focus on the wisp, and blew it to the side with a puff. Then she shrugged, and smiled even wider, pointing upward.

"I'm going up."

"Yes," Phillipe said. "Off you go, little spider."

She spit in her hands and rubbed them together, looking for a good spot to start her climb up the balcony's support beam. She gripped the beam firmly, with her hands up high and pressed her foot into the beam. Then off she went. Without any hesitation, she scaled straight up the beam, hand over hand, and foot over foot, straight to the third-story balcony.

She hopped over the rail and looked back down at Phillippe, flashing a thumbs up gesture. He signaled back with the same, but his was more sarcastic. She untied the rope from her waist and reeled up the slack. Hand over hand, she pulled the rope up. When the slack ran out, she felt the full weight of the bag at the other end.

"Aw, crackers," she whispered. "It's really heavy!"

"Yes, this much I know. Good for you to figure it out on your own, though. Very nice job," he whispered back.

She dragged the bag up and over the rail, and it flopped onto the balcony with a thud.

"Shhh!" Phillippe hissed. "Someone could be in that room."

She waved him off, and opened the bag to get a rolled up rope ladder. She hooked its metal ends over the balcony rail and tossed it down for Phillippe to climb up. Even with as slender as Phillippe was, the wooden rail still creaked and rocked under his weight. Beatrix tried to hold the rail still, but she could only do so much.

"Shhh," she hissed back. She could hear the bed on the other side of the wall creaking. The room was occupied, and its occupant's sleep had been disturbed. Phillippe slowed his movement to control the noise, eventually joining her on the balcony. She knelt down to the bag and pulled out a crossbow. She cocked the bow, set it on the balcony floor, and reached into the bag for a metal grappling hook. She folded a towel nice and thick, tied it to the front of the grappling hook, to muffle its impact, and attached the hook to the end of a metal cable.

"Grab the harness and put it on," she said.

While Phillippe suited up in the harness, she changed her shoes to some thick leather-soled slippers. Phillippe hoisted a heavy metal device, a cable tensioner, out of the bag. He fitted the tensioner over the rail and secured it in place. Beatrix picked up the crossbow, loaded the grappling hook, and readied herself to shoot.

"Are you ready?" Phillippe asked.

"Ready as I'll ever be," she said with a nod.

Phillippe pulled a gold pocket watch from his vest. It was a beautiful piece, with elegant numbering. He stared at it fondly, running his thumb over the lid, which bore the monogram ARS. It was probably very expensive, but he had no way of knowing. It was the one spoil he managed to keep for himself, of all the things he lifted during his performance in the parlor. Despite the Ringmaster nearly confiscating his entire bounty, he had missed the pick of this watch. That made Phillippe proud. He was getting better. Even the man who knew exactly what to watch for had missed it. Phillippe flicked the cover of the watch open. It was now

2:20 a.m. He rolled his eyes. Exhausted, he shoved the watch into his pocket, aglow with a rare sense of genuine pride.

Beatrix eyed the gap across the road as she took her aim at the hotel across the street. She needed to drop the grappling hook into the balcony enclosure across the street. They couldn't climb up the other side. The balconies were cantilevered, and had no stilts. This was the only way in. The shot would require a precise arc. She put her cheek to the stock, closed one eye and raised the bow.

"Not so high," Phillippe whispered.

He put his hand near the end of the crossbow and pushed it down.

"Stop it," she whispered back.

She corrected her aim, pulled the trigger and sent the hook sailing. The cable whistled through the air as it uncoiled from the bag. It reached the apex of its arc and descended toward the balcony. Just a hair short. The hook slammed into the top of the rail of the opposite balcony, but fell into the balcony enclosure nonetheless. The towel dulled the sound of the impact.

"Right on the money," she said.

Phillippe turned his nose up and waved a dismissive hand.

"Too much height, too little distance. I tried to tell you this. But you did not listen," he said.

His tone was smug.

"A little lower, like I say, and you don't hit the rail. That would have been the perfect shot. If only you listen."

"Just hook it up, would you? Why do you have to be so obnoxious?"

"Don't you worry about why I do what I do, little spider. You just worry about yourself, and do your job. OK?"

Phillippe slid a crank arm into the tensioner and fed the cable between two fine-toothed gears. He flipped a lever into place and the gears bit down on the cable. He wound the crank and drew the slack in from the other side. The hook latched on the opposite rail and the cable pulled taut, stretched tight across two creaky wooden rails, three stories above the street.

"Do you think the rails are strong enough?" she asked.

"I do not know. But I hope that they are," he said.

"Ok, you know what to do," she said.

She handed him a bronze trolley, an encasement with three rollers in it. He snapped the trolley to his harness, and Beatrix grabbed a satchel and slung it over her shoulder. She patted the bag twice, and nodded at Phillippe before hopping up on the rail with perfect balance.

"See you on the other side," she said, pointing across.

The thin wisp of hair had fallen back down over her eye. She blew aside with another puff and took a deep breath, arms out to the side. On her first step, the cable dipped and the rail creaked. She rocked, but she recovered, throwing one leg out to the side. She continued across, one step after another, and with quiet precision, she made her way over. She hopped the rail, squatted down and looked around before waving Phillippe across. The coast was clear. He set the grooved wheels of the trolley on the cable, and snapped it shut.

He climbed over the rail to the outside of the creaky balcony, and squatted to test whether the trolley would hold his weight. Satisfied, he leaned back, let go of the rail and shoved off with both legs. Suspended in mid-air by the trolley, he glided across the street, dangling from the cable toward Beatrix. As he reached the middle, the rail pulled out. Then it creaked, and pulled out even more.

Beatrix gasped, hoping the rail would hold long enough for him to reach the other side, but when it slipped, it created slack in the line. The slack, in turn, created a low point in the cable. His momentum slowed as the cable drooped slightly. She waved her hands wildly.

"Come on, you can make it," she whisper-yelled. "Just a little farther."

Phillippe's approach slowed, and came to a complete stop, just a few feet short. As he was about to roll back toward the middle, he kicked his legs, spun and reached out with one hand. He leaned back with an outstretched arm and just barely hooked a fingernail into the splintered wooden rail to pull himself in. Always the showman, he hopped into the balcony with flair, and struck a smiling pose with his arms stretched outward, as if it say *Ta-da*. Beatrix rolled her eyes.

"Are you ready, now?" he whispered.

Beatrix smiled and nodded eagerly, eyes wide open.

"Let's do it," she said in her soft, squeaky voice.

Phillippe pulled a flat metal tool from his pocket, crouched down and slid it between the window frame and the bottom sill, next to the lock on the inside of the glass. As he slid to tool sideways, he could see the lock release through the glass.

28

AN UNEXPECTED PARTNERSHIP

Michael woke promptly at 5:40 am. It would be another long day, so he rose quickly to collect his belongings. As he did, he noticed his tie. It was still laying on the floor next to the chair in front of the vanity. He picked it up and smiled fondly. He checked and double-checked the drawers to make sure they were empty, which they were. Under the bed too. He doubly confirmed that the closet was empty, it was, as it should have been. And despite knowing for certain that he had placed his key, token, and parchments in his satchel the night before, he double-checked just in case, to be sure they were still there.

He found the key and maps inside, but the token was not. He thrust his hand down into the bag in a panic. He peered in closely, and dumped it on to the bed. The key, maps and all of his other personal belongings were there, but the token was nowhere to be found. He scrambled to check every possible place. He recalled the rules read aloud at Gatling Meadows. *The milestone tokens presented at the finish line must be one complete set, bearing one designation, and one designation only. Anything less is incomplete, and thus a failure.*

"This can't be happening," he said to himself. "Where could it be?"

His eyes dashed around the room when he noticed the balcony window was unlatched and slightly raised. He didn't remember leaving it open, but so much had happened. He scoured every square inch of the room, twice, and found nothing. A feeling of numbness set in as he stood in the middle of the room with his hands on his hips, unsure what to do next. It was gone.

"I've waited my whole life for this," he thought. "What am I supposed to do now?"

Perplexed and desperate, he shouldered his satchel and went downstairs to collect his garment bag from the front desk.

VIXEN ROSE AT AROUND 6:00 AM WITH A START. SHE SAT UP STIFF, overwhelmed by a strange feeling of anxiety. She had collapsed into bed the night before, exhausted, without taking stock of her room. But as she woke in the morning, something troubled her. She rubbed the sleep from her eyes and glanced around from her bed. The window was raised, and somebody had gone through her belongings. The clothes from her garment bag were strewn about, and the contents of her handbag were dumped on the floor. She stepped out of bed onto the cold wooden floor and knelt down to pick up her things.

"Somebody was here," she thought. "*While. I. Slept.*"

She shuddered at the thought. Fueled by anger, violation and vulnerability, she shrieked with fists clenched.

"Who would do such a thing?" she wondered aloud.

Resigned that the intrusion had already occurred, she gathered her things from the floor. The key she received in her Chrysalis, a reticule that held few quid worth of bills and coins, her token, a hairbrush, a kerchief, some silver framed lenses and her driving gloves. A feeling of helplessness and overwhelm set in when she realized her maps and other documents were missing from the dresser. Without them, she lacked the ability to continue the race. She wouldn't know where to go. Her mind raced. She could try to follow someone, but if their intended paths diverged, how would she ever know? She could end up in the wrong place, with no milestone token to find. She looked over at the vanity.

"Of all the unmitigated gall!" she shouted.

Vixen had brought two boxed sets of alchemy orbs with her. The boxes sat opened on her vanity, and an orb was missing from its compartment. She tried to contain her emotion. But she was going to be able to continue, she had some serious issues to resolve. Her run was likely over.

MICHAEL WALKED INTO THE HOTEL LOBBY AND WAS GREETED BY the clerk.

"Good morning, Mr. McGillicuddy. Shall I retrieve your garment bag for you?"

"Yes, if you would be so kind. Thank you."

"Did you have a pleasant evening, Mr. McGillicuddy?"

"Well, a lot happened, and not all of it was pleasant. I will say that."

"I'm very sorry to hear that," he said.

He set the garment bag on the counter.

"Is there anything I can be of assistance with?"

"Doubtful. I've lost something very important."

"Shall I check the lost and found for you?"

"No, I don't expect it would be there. But thank you."

Michael turned and walked to go outside.

"Safe travels, Mr. McGillicuddy," the clerk said.

Michael stepped out of the lobby and onto a sunny porch. He raised a hand without looking back, and gave a half-hearted wave as he left. He walked to where his buggy was. He threw his bags in the back seat, and sighed when he noticed Vixen. She was visibly upset, so he walked over to check on her.

"Are you alright?" he asked.

"No, I'm not alright. I was robbed last night, Michael. Bloody robbed. Someone came into my room while I slept, through the window, and ransacked my room."

"Did you wake up? Who was it?"

"No, I didn't wake up. I had no idea they were there. But someone was most definitely in there. My clothes were tossed about, my bag dumped out and my papers were taken, my map, everything. I think I'm done for in this race. I have no way to carry on now."

She clenched her fists, and her body shook.

"I'm just so angry right now!"

"That's very interesting," he said.

She bristled at his insensitivity, and he corrected his course.

"No, that's not what I meant. I mean it's horrible, but interesting, in the sense that I think the same thing happened to me. Through your window you say?"

"Yes, through the window. The door was bolted. I'm sure I latched the window, but when I woke up it was unlocked, slightly raised. My belongings were bloody tossed about. They also took something from the boxes I had on my vanity."

"What was taken?"

"Just some things I brought with me, it's not important."

"My window was also raised when I woke," he said. "I don't think it's a coincidence. I'm missing the token I found at the Citadel. I searched my room quite thoroughly. I thought I might have misplaced it, but now I am certain it was stolen. First the fires, and now this. Who would behave in such a way?"

At the edge of town, in the makeshift tent city, the crew

of the Black Steam Circus began to stir. Breakfast was being served in the meal tent; bread, cheese, boiled eggs and some fruit, served family style, as always. Inside the tent, the Ringmaster received a briefing from Phillippe.

"The shot was much too high," Phillippe said. "I tried to tell her. But she did not listen."

"Shut up, Phillippe, it was a perfectly good shot, it landed right in the balcony," she said.

"Enough, you two. I don't care about the shot, what I care about is results. How did we do?"

"The woman, Vixen," Phillippe said. "She has been, how do you say? Disabled."

"McGillicuddy as well," Beatrix added.

She tossed his ruby-eyed dragon token to the Ringmaster. It slammed into the table with a metallic clang. He was pleased with the outcome, but troubled that Michael still remained a factor at this stage.

"Why hasn't Ramshorn taken him completely out?"

Phillippe shook his head.

"I think you have to ask this to Mr. Ramshorn. I do not know the answer."

"So that's it? I'm disappointed in both of you. This borders on complete failure."

"No, That is not it." Phillippe added. "We also dispensed with the man in all black. Kamal. Scarlet and Copper too. It was a productive evening. The Troupe also made it down to the boat slips. We are in good shape now, we have good advantage."

"That sounds better. Everyone you named, they're all disabled?"

"Effectively, yes, I do not see how any can continue. Difficult to cross the sea leg without a boat. Or papers. Hard to finish with a missing token."

"Well done, for once. It's a good start, but we still have plenty more to deal with, not the least of which is the Baron. The remaining participants are very capable, but so far our plans are coming together nicely. And speaking of the Baron, what is his status?"

"We do not know. He's is very dodgy and hard to track. Our paths rarely converge and we've seen very little of him since the start."

"Fine, we can sort him out in due course. Let's prepare ourselves for the day. Go make sure the boat is ready."

MICHAEL AND VIXEN CONTINUED DISCUSSING THEIR UNLIKELY coincidence.

"I'm just saying. I think the odds are pretty low that this was a random event," she said. "I'm not sure what to do now."

"Agreed," Michael said. "Quitting isn't an option though. Not for me anyway. I have to find a way."

Vixen pondered her circumstance for a moment, then changed the subject.

"How are your hands feeling?"

"They're tender. But, I'm really fine."

"Good. I'll just be honest. I didn't like seeing you surrounded by those flames last night. I was genuinely worried for you. For your safety that is."

Michael smiled.

"I appreciate your concern. *Ms. Van Buren*."

She chuckled, and put her finger on his tie.

"I like your bow tie. *Mr. McGillicuddy*."

"Yes, thank you," he said.

Then he cleared his throat.

"I only hope that I haven't tied it too tightly. I have such issues."

He raised his eyebrows suggestively.

"Well if you ever need a hand, I'd be more than happy to help. You know, with your tie."

She let loose an innocent giggle, blushed and covered her mouth. He enjoyed the banter, and found her more than charming; quite lovely in fact. But he forced himself to set that aside for the time being. A lot was at stake. He needed to win the race, but he had no clear path to continue. His face became sullen, and his gaze grew distant.

"What's the matter?" she asked.

"It's just; Where do we go from here? I need to finish this race. I need to *win* this race. Far too much depends on it. I don't know about you, but I'm not ready to give up and leave."

Scarlet came stomping toward them from the distance, from the direction of the port. She did not look happy.

"We have some low-down, flea-bitten, dirty-dog, scurvy, slime-eating, rotten-tooth, rubbish-breath scalawags among us. That much I can tell you!"

"Scarlet, what happened?" Michael asked.

"Oh, well, thank you for asking. I could just spit. Matchups this year are tight, as you know. Competition being as stiff as it is, I tried to get an early start. To get out ahead of all of you. No offense."

"None taken."

"So I headed to the docks before dawn. I arrived to find my boat burned down to the water's edge. I'm not talking about some inconsequential damage. I mean quite literally burned down to the water. With everything on it. My supplies, my equipment, my emergency rations. Unbelievable. All my planning, up in literal flames and I have no way to get across. I could just murder somebody right now," she growled.

Michael took her anger in stride.

"Yes, well, as unfortunate as that may be for you personally, Scarlet, there appears to be a recurring theme. We've run into a patch of trouble ourselves. I believe my token was stolen from my room last night, as were Vixen's maps and documents. All while we slept. Somebody wants us out."

"My apologies for interrupting," Kamal said.

He appeared out of nowhere. Their heads reeled around as he spoke, softly and politely.

"Yes, hello. I am Kamal Khan. Please forgive my intrusion. I could not help but overhear. In my many years participating in this event, I have never seen such shameful acts of incivility. I, too, have been a victim of the despicable saboteur you speak of. My map, my token and my skeleton key. All taken from my sleeping quarters.

He looked defeated.

"I'm afraid I am unable to continue. Though I find such behavior reprehensible, I have found my inner peace with this and will be leaving soon. May I ask what you plan to do from here?"

"Not so fast," Michael said. "I don't know how you all feel about this, but we could still try to form a team. It's not too late, you know. The rules do allow it."

"And how would that work?" Scarlet asked. "Give up control of my pursuit? Split the prize?"

"Yes, that's certainly an option."

"I like doing things my own way, thank you. And I'm none too keen on sharing my prize, if I can help it."

"Well, the way I see it," Michael said, "I've lost my token and I can't finish on my own. I have no way to produce a complete set of tokens at the finish. I can't possibly win alone. If I heard correctly, Vixen has no map, so even with her token, she probably couldn't finish the course or find her tokens without a staggering dose of blind luck. I have a ship, and it's very well prepared for the channel. I know its history, and I've taken proper precautions."

He pointed at Scarlet.

"Scarlet managed to keep her token, maps and skeleton key, but she has no boat to sail out of here on the sea leg. Am I right?"

"Yes, that's right."

Then she patted the small bag hanging off her shoulder where she had stowed her key and token. She looked down with concern as she opened it to confirm its contents.

"Oh, you've got to be kidding me!" she said. "My key is gone!"

"So, there you have it. None of us can go on alone," Michael said. "The way I see it, we have two choices. We can quit now, or we can team up and share the spoils of victory. Sharing something is better than nothing at all."

Vixen nodded.

"I would be willing to join," she said.

"That's great," Michael said. "An no offense, Ms. van Buren, but I think we'll also need someone with a matching map and token; and probably a matching skeleton key for good measure. Scarlet is close, but if we need her key again later, it could be the end of the line if we don't have it."

Copper walked by as Michael was finishing, with his burly chest out, arms crossing back and forth with each stride. He had a leather bag in one hand and his smithing hammer in the other. He looked well-rested, with some extra bounce in his step.

"What are you all doing standing around wagging your jaws?" he said. "Shouldn't you be leaving?"

"Sabotage," Michael said, with a disappointed tone. "We're trying to sort it out, but it seems we may not be able to continue."

"Well. Sounds like you all are a right sorry lot, in a heap of trouble."

He doffed his cap.

"You were worthy competitors, and I enjoyed our time together, but I'll just be off to my ship now."

He slid his finger down the side of his nose, smooth and easy, and pointed outward at them and nodded as he turned away.

"Best wishes to you all, and better luck next year," he said with a chuckle.

"So you're heading to port now?" Scarlet asked.

"Aye."

"Which boat is yours?" she said. "Is it the one with the large timber hull. The one with the red and gold coat of arms hanging from the crow's nest, with a beautiful woman carved into its wooden bow, her arm outstretched and her finger pointing forward to lead the way?"

"Aye lass. That's her. The *Lady Davina Daracha.* A fine vessel she is."

"Very fine indeed, I saw her when I scouted the port a few weeks back. She looked like a very fast ship. Is she fast?"

"Aye, you can bet on it. She's right seaworthy, fast like the wind, strong like a mighty oak."

"She sounds amazing. Are you headed there now? To board your *Lady Davina Daracha*?"

"That I am, lass."

"Well I hate to tell you this, but you are going to be *right* disappointed when you get there. I know the *Lady Davina Daracha.* She was moored in the slip next to mine. Both were burned down last night. Complete losses. So yes, I suppose we are a pretty sorry lot. All of us, in fact. Aren't we now?"

"Bloody hell, are you serious?"

His shoulders hunched as he dropped his bag and hammer to the ground.

"Oh, I'm deadly serious," she said. "But you don't have to take my word for it. Go and see for yourself, we'll just stay here and sort out our sorry little issues while you're walking."

"Walk? Bugger! First my monocycle, now my *Lady.* This just ain't proper."

"So, like I was saying," Michael continued, "No one of us can go on alone, but as a team we could do it together."

He pulled out his invitation and separated it from his other papers.

"Do you see right here? In the clues on my invitation. *Solitude is your enemy.* Like it or not, I think I was meant to team up. We all were. It's fate. Copper, what do you say?"

"I'm listening," he said. "Keep talking, lad."

Scarlet interjected.

"I could be convinced," she said, "but I refuse to carry any dead weight. I'm not in this for the charity of it, and I won't take on any more mates than needed. More heads means a smaller piece of the prize. So who's got what to offer? Ante up, folks."

"I have a well-prepared boat," Michael said. "And I presume Copper has the matching map, key and token we need. Am I right about that Copper?"

"Aye," Copper said. "It sounds to me like we have the minimum necessary covered between the two of us. So let's go, lad, just you and me. No dead weight, like she said."

There was an awkward silence.

"What?" Copper asked with a shrug. "Oh, again with the faces now? What is it with you people?"

"It's a good start, you and I," Michael said. "But I like Vixen's orbs, they could prove useful."

Copper chuckled.

"He said he likes your orbs, lass."

"Right, anyway," Michael continued. "Scarlet's knowledge and experience, and, I assume, her network of contacts could prove invaluable if we ever need them, and Kamal's, well… About that. What can you offer this team?"

"I have abilities I believe will be of great usefulness to all of you."

He pointed to the astrolabe hanging from this belt.

"For one, I am an expert navigator of the seas. But I also have this."

He reached into his pants pocket and pulled out an advantage token. He held it out in his palm to show them. It was beautifully crafted; polished, thick, and as heavy as two pocket watches. The outer edge and rim of the token were shiny gold. Its inner face was polished silver, decorated with a calligraphic letter A, encrusted with gems.

"Where did you get that?" Copper asked.

"I won it from a man in the game parlor. If you agree I am worthy, I would be humbled and honored to join such an able-bodied team."

Michael did the math in his head. The prize of fifty thousand quid, split five ways, would leave him with ten thousand for himself, assuming they won. While it was not as good as having the full prize for himself, it was better than nothing, and sufficient to pay his taxes.

"So there you have it," he said. "A ship, orbs, maps, milestone tokens, advantage token, expertise," Michael said, pointing at each person around the circle as he stepped through the list.

"You really do catch the details, don't you?" Scarlet said.

"I may not talk much, but it doesn't mean I'm not paying attention."

"I see that now."

"So what do you all say? Do we have a team? Who's in?"

He put his hand out toward the middle of the circle. Vixen placed her hand on top of his.

"In," she said.

Copper put his hand on top of hers.

"Aye. Me too."

Kamal put his hand on top of the others.

"It would be my honor," he said.

Michael turned his eyes to Scarlet.

"Scarlet?" he asked. "What say you?"

She hesitated and huffed. But she slapped her hand on top. She looked him in the eye and smiled.

"You can count me in," she said.

He smiled back at her, just as somebody tossed a worn leather bag down at their feet. They all looked down at the bag, and a big, meaty hand plopped on top of the stack.

"That sounds like a grand plan, a very fine plan indeed," the voice said. "You can count me in as well."

"John!" Michael shouted. "What are you doing here?"

"I'm doing you all a big favor, that's what. Someone needs to keep you on the straight and narrow."

As John studied the group, his announcement was met with blank stares and emotionless blinking. Using his other hand, he gestured his thumb at Michael.

"Don't you all worry about a thing, Michael here will vouch for me."

John gave Michael a hearty pat on the back.

"Well, go on, boy. Tell them I'm in. After all, it is your boat, ain't it?"

In his gut, he knew John could improve their chances of winning. But one-sixth of the prize was not enough money.

"Michael, do you know this man?" Vixen asked.

"Yes, of course. I've known him my whole life."

Scarlet chimed in.

"And why should we split our prize with you?" she asked. "What's in it for us? Do you have any tokens or maps? Keys? Vessels?"

"I did yesterday," John said.

Then he held his hands out and shrugged.

"But no longer."

"Then I ask you again, what do you have to offer this team?" she pressed.

"What do I have? Ha, that's rich!" he said. "I should ask the same of you. To start with, I have more experience and know-how than the whole lot of you put together, and then doubled over one more time. I've been competing in this little boondoggle since you all were crying for a teat. And if, by chance, we end up anywhere near Paris, and I suspect we will, I know the city better than pretty much anybody. And I do mean *anybody*."

John paused to let that sink in.

"And better still, I know most of the other competitors, the serious ones, anyway. I know how they work, how they think, and I know how to beat them. All of them. Even the Baron. So, let's not be confused here. I'm the one doing you all the favor, by joining up with you. It's not the other way around. No, no."

He wagged his finger into the circle.

"Go on. Tell them, Michael."

Michael cleared his throat.

"John, can I speak to you for a moment? Over there?"

Michael pulled John aside for a private conversation.

"John, I'm a little embarrassed to bring this up, but I have a situation. You see, I've already agreed to team up with the four of them, with a five-way split of the prize. The problem is this. My mother and I, we have a large tax due on the homestead and I've been working to scrape together enough to pay it, but I simply don't have it. You know I'm in this to win, and I think you would help our chances of that. I'd love to have you join us. But one-fifth of the prize money is only ten thousand quid for my share. That will just barely pay the tax collector with a couple quid left over. One-sixth doesn't cover the bill. Even if we did win, which would be amazing in its own right, I couldn't pay. My mother and I, we'll lose our home."

"How much do you owe, boy?"

"Just under ten thousand. Ninety-eight hundred, or so."

"I see," John said, while he stroked his beard. "Well one sixth is roughly eighty-three hundred. It's still a lot, and it would go along way to get you there. It's better than nothing, am I right? What are you trying to tell me here, boy?"

"What I'm trying to say, John, is that time is short. I won't be able to earn the extra money elsewhere. If I don't win it here, then that's it. They'll foreclose on the homestead. We'll lose our home. Mom will have nothing."

"Soairse," John mumbled with a distant whisper.

"Yes. Exactly. So the way I see it, John, I've already committed to the four of them. I've given them my word, and my word is my bond. You know that. Like my father always said, if you don't have your honor, then what do you really have?"

John nodded.

"So I can't go back on them. But I also need to pay the taxes due, and with only a sixth of the prize, I won't be able to do that. Do you follow?"

"Go on."

"Now here you are. You don't have any way forward. For all intents and purposes, you're finished. With all due respect, John, I'd like to propose a deal to you. I'll vouch for you to the group. If they agree, you can join us. And if we win, everybody gets their one-sixth share. But in exchange for my voucher, if we win, you commit to me now that you'll make me whole on what I need to cover the tax. From your one-sixth share, you'll give me fifteen hundred or so, to cover my remainder. That way, you can stay in the race and I can still win enough to pay my taxes, you keep what's left. What do you say to that?"

John stood with a stern look, stroking his beard. He stared into the distance and nodded slowly, his brow furrowed, thinking through Michael's proposal. His eyes tracked back and forth as he worked through something in his head. He cocked his head to the side, measuring Michael up. It should have been an easy decision. If John didn't agree, he might as well go home, he had no other way out of Gillingham. So why hesitate? What else was he considering?

"What say you, John? Do we have a deal?"

John looked past Michael, at his potential teammates, checking them up and down. They all stared back, some with icy glares and tapping toes. They were anxious, and rightfully so. Time was wasting, their competition was already pushing out to sea. John stared at them as he ran his hand over his beard to smooth it down one more time. After a few more seconds, John looked back at Michael and his face perked up.

"Fine. You've got a deal, boy."

The way John spoke, his tone suggested he was the one giving something up; that he was the one doing Michael the favor. It was a style of communicating that John had mastered ages ago.

"If we win this together," he said, "I will allow you to take whatever you need from my share. I will do you that favor, but just this once. You have my absolute word on that. Now don't let me down, boy. Let's go win this thing."

Michael smiled with boyish excitement as John slapped him on the back.

"We can beat them all," Michael said. "Even the Baron."

John held his hand out, and they shook on it. It was official.

29

HIDDEN IN PLAIN SIGHT

Michael and John rejoined the rest of the group, where plenty of questions were thrown about.

"What would keep Kamal from leaving with the advantage token? He could take it anywhere, and switch to any other team."

"How do we know Copper won't skip out with the everything that we need and leave us high and dry?"

"Why do we need to split the prize so many ways?"

"Why do we need John at all?"

"What guarantee is there that one of us isn't the saboteur, just waiting to strike again?"

The evening's buggy fires, the ensuing burglaries and subsequent boat fires set everyone on edge, and understandably so. Trust now came at a premium.

"People. Honestly, let's be rational," Michael said.

"Why should we let Kamal in at all? Didn't he just spend the entire land leg traveling with another group? Maybe he's a plant, maybe he's still playing for a different team. How would we ever know?" Copper said.

"He knows the sea," Vixen said, "and we could use his advantage token at some point."

"I can hear you talking," Kamal said. "I'm standing right here."

"So, John just shows up out of nowhere," Scarlet said. "Empty-handed, and we're just going to let him in, and share our purse with him?"

"Hey, I'm also standing right here," John said.

"He's very capable," Michael said. "He can help us."

Questions continued and Michael grew impatient.

"Look, everyone. We need to move on here if we are going to compete. We could spend all day going round like this, but it's not productive. I have a plan. Look around. Of the people in this group, think of the one person you believe is most trustworthy. On the count of three, point to that person. Are you ready? One. Two. Three."

Everyone pointed at Michael.

"Oh," he said.

He bowed his head humbly and smiled.

"This is so unexpected. Well, thank you, I suppose. I'm not sure what to say, really."

"Oye. Tick-tock," Copper said, tapping his naked wrist.

"Right, sorry, so here's the idea. To address the trust concerns that everyone seems to have with regard to Kamal's advantage token, and since all fingers pointed at me, I will carry it. Copper, give your skeleton key to Vixen and your token to Kamal so they're split up and you don't control them all. We can rip Copper's map into six pieces and each of us will take one piece. That way we all become dependent upon each other. There's no concentration of strength in any one person, and no one person can run off without the rest of us. We will either win this as a team, or we will lose this as a team, plain and simple. Is everyone comfortable with that?"

One by one, some more grudgingly than others, they all agreed. Copper was the last to give in.

"I worked really hard to get all of this," he said, "and I don't fancy the idea of handing it over to someone else."

"Do you have a working ship to carry you across this leg?" Michael asked.

"No, I reckon not."

"Then you have no choice, as I see it."

"Aye," Copper said. "Count me in."

"Then that's what we'll do," Michael said.

He held out his hand.

"Copper, let's have that map."

THE RINGMASTER LOOKED THROUGH A BRASS TELESCOPE TOWARD the horizon. The bow of his boat gently rocked with the soft swells of the sea. He lowered his telescope and breathed a generous gulp of salty sea air.

"The skies are clear and the wind is good," he said. "If we maintain a pace of twenty knots, we should reach Ring Island in less than three hours. Mech, hold us steady at twenty knots or better, and set a course for east by southeast when we exit the port."

Mechanicules turned the large wooden wheel to set their course.

WITH THE TEAM AGREED AND THE VEHICLES LOADED, MICHAEL and his crew drove to port. When they arrived, they parked in front of an old building. The building sat on piers at water's edge, extending out over the water. The sign in front read *J. Smithson, Stone Mill*. Years of exposure to salty air had its way with the wooden structure. It looked dilapidated, but the water wheel still turned, driven by the runoff from the creek behind the Coxswain Inn. Two tall smokestacks rose from the roof.

"We're here," Michael said.

"Where?" Vixen asked.

"At my ship," he said.

He motioned toward the mill.

"Holy hell," John said, "Can I still change teams? I'm sorry, boy, but that's not a boat at all. That's a bloody stone mill. And if you don't know the difference, then we're in a heap of trouble."

"Sorry, John," Michael said, "but it's you who can't tell the difference. And I'll take that as a compliment. Thank you very much."

He grabbed a pry bar from his chest, and walked down to the mill. Standing on the pier that ran alongside the water wheel, he ran his fingers along a long blue trim board running down the side of the building, from the axle of the water wheel to the back edge of the mill furthest from the shore. He found his spot and jammed the pry bar behind the trim board. With a good tug on the pry bar, the nails came loose and the board fell down into the water. When it fell, it uncovered a wide open gap, a groove that ran from the axle of the water wheel to the back of the building.

"Michael, what on earth are you doing?" Vixen shouted.

"Funny thing about this stone mill," he said. "It's got this great water wheel, this very powerful water wheel."

"Yes, I see that," she said.

Michael paused for effect, and pointed at the roof.

"So, what do you suppose those smokestacks are for?"

"I haven't the faintest idea," she said. "What is this about?"

He just smiled and continued working.

He jammed the pry bar into the vertical edge of the back wall of the mill, like he was trying to open a giant packing crate. He shimmied the bar downward and continued to pry, and before long, the whole back wall of the mill opened from the top, and fell down into the water with a splash.

"The lad's gone mad," Copper said. "What in the world is he doing?"

John smiled, and smoothed his beard.

"I know exactly what he's doing."

Michael disappeared around the corner inside the building. Moments later, a loud rattle boomed from inside, and the smokestacks started billowing black smoke. The water wheel reversed its rotation. The wheel traveled down the open groove toward the back of the mill, where the bow of a steamship appeared. Michael was piloting Seamus' side-wheel steamboat, the *SS Soairse,* updated with a few improvements, of course.

"It was a bloody boat shed. That's brilliant," Copper said.

Michael tugged a cord with boyish excitement and sounded the steam horn. He steered the boat around to the opposite side of the pier and the others loaded their belongings. He ran back to his buggy and shouted at Copper.

"Can you give me a hand here? It's really heavy, and I could use the help."

While they unloaded the chest to move it on to the boat, two men pulled up next to them in a powerful steam-powered coupe, towing a trailer with a small one-man blimp. The airship's gas bag was inflated and ready to fly, and the airship was tethered to the trailer by cables. The gondola was barely large enough to carry a single grown man.

The men jumped out of the coupe and dashed to the airship. One of the men, the taller of the two, had a gangly build and a thin face. He opened the door of the gondola to climb in. Scarlet recognized him immediately. She remembered his distinctive, pointy features, his overly-pronounced Adam's apple, and his scruffy chin-beard.

"That's Ratface Reggie," she mumbled.

Michael heard her.

"Did you just call that man Ratface Reggie?

"I did. Hold on, I'll be right back."

She walked over to the man, interrupting him.

"Pardon me, but aren't you Reginald McHedgie? We met in Gatling Meadows. Stall nineteen, if I'm not mistaken."

He was distracted, obviously in a hurry, but he indulged her.

"That's right, what do you need? I'm trying to do something here, in case you couldn't tell."

"I can see you doing something. But I'm left wondering what exactly you're trying to do."

"What does it look like I'm doing? Scum-buckets destroyed my boat, so I'm going to fly across this channel in my cousin's airship. Not that it's any business of yours."

"It's most certainly isn't. But do you think that's wise?"

"No choice. Got to do it."

"I believe you're aware of the rules, are you not? The sea leg is meant to be traveled by sea craft. And this, my good man, this is no sea craft. You'll be subject to disqualification," she said.

She wagged a motherly finger as she spoke.

He looked at her dismissively.

"You're actually in the race? Yes, of course, I remember you now. You're the annoying know-it-all. Look, I'll take my chances, but thanks for your concern. You just worry about you. And keep your beak shut about what I'm doing. OK?"

She wasn't sure which was more offensive, his crass words, or the ease with which he was willing to cheat. It was his business though, so she shrugged and walked away.

"Suit yourself, then. Good luck, Mr. McHedgie."

He put on a leather aviator cap and pulled a pair of goggles down over his eyes. He climbed into the gondola and shut the door, signaling his cousin with a thumbs up to let loose the final cable. The airship lifted off the trailer. It rose ever so slightly, and hung in the air just above the trailer. While he adjusted the levers inside the gondola, his airship turned with the breeze like a fluffy dandelion seed. He pedaled the foot pedals from inside the gondola like one would pedal a bicycle. The pedals, in turn, drove a propeller at the rear. He pulled a lever to adjust his rudders and pedaled even faster. With the rudders tilted and the propeller whirring, the tiny airship gained altitude and glided out over the water. When he achieved an altitude of fifty feet or so, he set the rudders even, leveled his path and continued pedaling his way over the watery expanse.

Scarlet walked back over to Michael.

"Why did you call him Ratface Reggie?" Michael asked.

"It's a mnemonic device I use to help me remember people's names. Look at his face, he looks like a rat."

"I see," Michael said. "Should I ask what device you used to remember my name?"

She looked away.

"I'd really rather not say," she said.

"Well now you have to tell me. What is it?"

"I think it's better if I don't."

"Just say it."

"Fine. Michael Milk Toast. Are you happy now?"

Copper and Vixen enjoyed a good laugh.

"Milk Toast?" Michael asked.

"That's right, you know, sort of soggy and bland. Boring," she said.

Michael didn't say anything.

"Oh come on now. I meant no offense by it, it's just a device. Based on first impressions. It doesn't mean anything. After we talked, I knew somewhat better, sort of."

"Milk Toast…" he mumbled. "Fascinating."

FROM THE TALLEST BUILDING OVERLOOKING THE PORT, AN ELDERLY man sat quietly on a stool with his elbows on the table, struggling to stay awake. The table was empty, other than a simple hand mirror and a paper with some scribbled drawings. Dutifully, he stared out the window and down to the beach. After what had been an otherwise unremarkable morning, he saw what looked like a small airship slowly lifting off from the shoreline in the distance. He stepped off the stool and shuffled across the floor, and scooted a tripod-mounted telescope closer to the window to get a better look. The end of the telescope was fitted with six different lenses arranged on spindle, like glass petals on a flower, each one progressively stronger than the last. He put his eye to the eyecup and peered through while he rotated the lenses in succession. At first, just the general shape of a lighter-than-air craft cruising past a steamboat was visible. He rotated to the next lens, which zoomed in closer, so that an airship filled the view through the eyepiece. On the next rotation, it zoomed in tighter on the gondola. The gondola was small, with one person packed tight inside, taking up every available inch, and its pilot was pedaling furiously. On the next turn of the lens, he zoomed right in on the gaunt, bony face of Reggie McHedgie. Reggie was looking around cautiously through his goggles. He seemed concerned, almost paranoid, as he pedaled like mad through the air.

"Son of a gun! McHedgie is going for it," he said.

He flinched at the realization, remembering his job, and he stutter-stepped in place for a moment. At long last, he was finally going to see some action.

"Sorry, young man, but you won't be cheating on my watch."

He picked up the mirror from the table and shuffled across the floor to the back of the room. Neither of his feet lifted off the dirty wooden floor when he stepped, they just slid back and forth like cross country skis. Once he shuffled to the back, he threw the shutters open on a window facing the Coxswain Inn. He held the mirror out the window and into the sunlight. He titled it back and forth with his wrist to signal the hotel. The desk clerk inside, the one who had greeted Michael and stowed his bag, saw the flashes of light in the distance. He rushed to his window and used a mirror of his own to signal back. The signal back indicated he was watching, and was ready to receive a message. He grabbed a pencil and paper from his desk and took notes, one letter after another. When he received the "full stop" signal, he looked down at his paper. *Reggie McHedgie is flying the channel.*

The clerk turned in his chair to face his desk, and tapped out a message on his telegraph machine. On hearing the tones come across the wire, a man sitting at a wooden desk in Paris set down his morning tea and grabbed a pencil. He leaned forward in his chair to transcribe the incoming message. Once he had jotted down the message on a piece of paper, he read it and added his own portal address, 31985, at the end. He placed the slip of paper into a wood and brass pneumatic tube, and twisted the cap shut with a click. He punched in the numbers of a five digit portal address on the end of the tube, and walked to his pneumatic portal. He shoved the tube into the portal and sent the tube on its way. Two minutes later, the tube dropped into its destination portal. Cyril Hastings sat in his office as he heard it fall in. He stood up from behind his desk, and stepped away from his picturesque view overlooking the town center, to check the portal. He opened the tube, withdrew the slip and read the note. With a disappointed sigh, he scribbled a simple response.

"*Disqualified. Let the others know.*"

He put the note back in the tube, punched in the destination address, 31985, and sent the tube back from whence it came.

30

WHAT DO YOU SAY ABOUT FATE?

Michael and his newly-formed crew had loaded their bags and chests onto his boat, and they were well on their way out to sea. Measuring thirty-five feet, stem-to-stern, the vessel was neither the largest nor the smallest in the race. Capable of traveling at twenty-five knots in good conditions, and up to twenty-eight with a strong tailwind, it was also among the fastest. Kamal manned the helm and steered them on a course to Ring Island, and the pointed bow bobbed as it cut through the swells.

The boat was pure white, with a thick blue stripe painted down the side. The ship's name, *SS Soairse*, shown on the port side, painted in thick black letters. The lettering was painted freehand, without the benefit of a stencil or a template. In his living days, Seamus was a man more richly possessed of mechanical aptitude and heart-felt sentiment than he was of any artistic talent. In the case of the lettering, the writing was actually legible, which was better than some of his other work. That showed the special care he took when applying it.

The only other color on the hull of the boat came from large semi-spherical copper balls attached around the outside, each a foot across. The copper balls studded the hull every three feet, forming a ring all the way around the steamer. The cabin of the boat had a fan blade mounted on top, facing forward, like a miniature windmill. The back of the fan had a pulley wheel, and looped around the pulley wheel was a long fan belt that extended down into the hull, turning round and round as the fan blade spun. The sky was clear, with just a few wispy clouds overhead. Darker clouds were forming on the horizon, but a helpful breeze was at their backs.

Inside the cabin, John paced back and forth. He looked bothered, and uncharacteristically anxious about something. The map, which they tore into six separate pieces, lay re-assembled on the table inside. Scarlet stood over the it, studying it. Copper sat in a chair, with his feet propped up across another. His hands were wrapped behind his head, and he was napping.

It was mostly quiet inside, but Michael and Vixen were talking.

"About that boat shed," Vixen asked. "Did you build it yourself?"

"No, my father converted it long ago. In fact, he used it the year he beat the Baron. I remember him talking about it, he was quite proud. So, it was a fortunate turn that we launched out of Gillingham again this year. That doesn't happen every year, you know. The course changes."

"Yes, I'm well aware," she said. "And especially fortunate now, given what happened to so many of our boats last night."

"Maybe we're finally starting a run of good luck," he said. "I could certainly use it."

"Hard to say," Vixen said. "I don't really believe in luck."

"What do you mean you don't believe in luck?"

"What I mean is that I believe in facts and proof. I believe in making conscious choices, based on available information, as adjusted for statistical probabilities. I'm a scientist. I don't think luck has much to do with anything."

"Fascinating. Well, let me ask you this. What if you were just standing next to a tree in the middle of the forest, minding your own business. And out of nowhere, a stray arrow suddenly lodged into the tree, just one inch from your head. The arrow just narrowly missed you. A mere inch away. An inch! That's pretty good luck, wouldn't you say?"

She grinned, welcoming his invitation to debate.

"No. What I would actually say is that the world is quite large, and your hypothetical stray arrow could have landed anywhere within it. The space I take up, relative to the rest of this world, is but a grain of sand in all the vast oceans. The statistical probability of me being hit by this random arrow of questionable origin are so extraordinarily low that I would not chalk it up to luck that it missed me at all. In fact, of all the places in the world for a hypothetical arrow to land, I would say that the odds of it missing me are almost a statistical certainty. One inch, one foot or one mile, it's all the same to me. They are all misses of equal probability and, of the highest possible likelihood."

Michael stared back at her for a second, blinking. He closed his eyes, bowed his head, touched his chin to his chest, and pretended to snore.

"How rude!" she exclaimed.

She furrowed her brow and crossed her arms. She tried to make an angry face, but she smirked right through it. They enjoyed a good laugh at the banter, but then his tone turned more serious.

"If you don't believe in luck, then what do you say about fate?" he asked.

She pondered her answer as Scarlet interrupted the conversation. She was addressing John, but spoke loud enough to grab both their attention.

"John, is everything alright?" Scarlet asked. "You seem agitated."

"Yes, I'm just fine. Don't you worry your pretty little head about me, young lady."

"I agree," Michael said. "You seem out of sorts. Are you ok?"

"I'm fine. I just… I had a plan," he said. "Plans change and I need to adjust. So let me work through it, boy. I'll be fine, I just need to think through some things. On my own."

"Relax John, we're in this together," Michael said. "I know you want to win, and I know you want to beat the Baron in particular. I know you had grand plans to do it all on your own. But we have a solid team here. We can do this. Together."

John didn't say anything. He just stared at Michael's feet and nodded slowly, stroking his beard. He was still distracted by something.

Kamal called out from the bow.

"There are two craft in the waters ahead of us, a half mile ahead."

Vixen looked out at Kamal, then back to Michael.

"I have to say, I'm a little surprised that you turned control of your boat over to Kamal. You don't even know him. Doesn't that make you uneasy? The boat your father built? Staking your success in the race on him driving? You're awfully trusting."

Michael wiped his nose with the back of his wrist and shrugged.

"I don't have any reason not to trust him. He's doing a fine job."

That remark roused Copper from his nap.

"Well I don't trust him quite like you do," Copper said.

"What do you mean?" Michael asked.

"I don't know, it's just a feeling, lad. Something about him. I can't say for sure what it is, but he makes me right uneasy. I have a good sense about these things. Trust me on this. I know people. I read people. I'll be sleeping with one eye open."

"Starting when?" Vixen joked. "They both looked pretty well shut just a moment ago."

"You go ahead and joke about it," Copper said. "I'm not taking any chances."

Michael checked his pocket watch.

"I need to load the firebox, I'll be back."

Michael walked to the rear of the cabin, and lifted a hatch. Through the hatch, he went down into the dark hull where the engine compartment was, and over to the firebox, where the coal fuel burned to heat the steam. It was loud and clanging below deck, the whirring of the engine was all he could hear. He knelt down in front of the firebox and opened its heavy pot-metal door.

"Fuel is low," he mumbled.

What embers remained burned with an intense orange glow from below, casting long dark shadows upward against the inside of the compartment. He tossed a shovel full of coal into the firebox and watched for a moment. He turned to load another shovel full, but as he did, he slammed into John. John's burly frame barely moved. Michael gasped, but John stood still, saying nothing. His skin glowed orange from the cast of the firebox, and his whiskers glistened where the light caught them just right. Dark shadows made for dramatic highlights on the contours of his face, while firelight danced off beads of sweat on his forehead. He just stood there, holding a heavy wrench at his side, staring at Michael.

THE RINGMASTER, PHILLIPPE, AND BELLADONNA ALL STOOD ON the deck of their ship, the *Bearded Lady*. Her sails were full of wind, and they were advancing at a good clip toward Ring Island. The ship was built in the style of the old Spanish galleons, with hand-carved rails, delicate accents and red paint with gold leaf details all around. It was among the largest craft in the race, nearly a hundred feet from stem to stern. Its heavy timbers creaked against each other as the boat rocked through the water and the sails whipped in the wind. The figurehead, the carving on the bow, bore the head and torso of a woman with her arms outstretched. The woman, however, had a full beard, an homage to a circus performer the Ringmaster had tried to recruit, but could never secure. She was the one that got away.

Phillippe looked out over the bow.

"This looks like a terrible place," he said. "It is just a pile of black jagged rocks. Are you sure this is right?"

"This is it," the Ringmaster said.

He held up his map and inspected it closely.

"But I don't understand," Phillippe said. It is just a pile of rock. In the ocean."

"Just do your job, and man the jib. We'll find out soon enough."

Phillippe looked backward, off stern.

"Yes, well, if we are going to find out, then we should do the finding out very quickly. There is a boat right behind us, and a paddle wheel coming fast. Let us not lose much time, yes?"

"Stand down, Phillippe. We just need to circle around a little further to the right, and we should see Cragtooth Tunnel. Everything else will become clear from there."

"The island is big," Phillippe said. "It could take a half-day to walk around it."

"At least," The Ringmaster said.

"That's Ring Island?" Belladonna said. "It's a bloody barren wasteland."

"Yes, that's right."

"There's nothing there. No plants, no people, no signs of life. It looks utterly inhospitable. I love it."

Cragtooth Tunnel started to show from around the side. The first feature they saw was just a large circular pit in the rocks, some sixty feet above the water, and as they continued to round, the tunnel's entrance at the water's edge emerged. As they rounded further, they could see that the ceiling of the tunnel had jagged rocks hanging down at the entrance. Before long, the entire tunnel became visible, a large arched passage into pure darkness. Another large pit in the rocks sat over the opposite side of the tunnel, up and to the right.

"Those big pits look like hollowed out eye sockets, and the tunnel looks like a mouth," Belladonna said. "It's like a giant skull."

"A skull with really bad teeth, perhaps" Phillippe said. "I have decided now, and I know it for sure. I do not like this place."

"Phillippe, ease the sails," the Ringmaster said. "let's gather our bearing and figure out a plan."

With sails eased, they came to standstill. They gently bobbed in the water as waves lapped against the hull, and gulls squawked in the distance.

"Look at all that broken timber and all that rubbish outside the tunnel," Belladonna said. "Do you think it's the remnants of other ships that tried to pass?"

The Ringmaster didn't answer. The shore around the tunnel was, in fact, littered with debris. Shattered timbers, broken masts, and ripped up sails were scattered across the rough and unforgiving rocks. The Ringmaster studied his map quietly.

"This is definitely Cragtooth Tunnel," he said, "the gateway of Ring Island."

"And you want to sail into that tunnel?" Phillippe asked.

"Yes, that's right."

"You mean, like, on purpose?"

The Ringmaster grumbled again as he pondered the notion, but he didn't say anything. He squinted toward the tunnel and rubbed the back of his neck before letting out a sigh.

"Maybe it would be wise to let someone else go first," he said. "We can float here for a while and they'll pass us by. We are close enough that we wouldn't lose much time if we did."

~

Below the deck of the *S.S. Soarise*, Michael stared back at John.

"Sorry John, I didn't see you there. You gave me quite a start, what are you doing down here?"

Just as Michael asked the question, Scarlet shouted down through the hatch from above.

"Michael, you need to come up here and see this right now."

Michael looked at John, expecting a response. He took a moment to say anything.

"I- I just came down to see if you needed any help. Your father used to talk about the steam fittings on this old rig, you know, coming loose. Leaking."

John held up the wrench.

"I just wanted to see if anything needed tightening."

"I don't see any leaks," Michael said. "But tighten away. I need to go see what Scarlet is shouting about. I'll see you up there."

John stared blankly.

"Are you sure everything is alright John? You're really not acting like yourself."

"I'm fine, boy. Go about your business and head on up. I'll take care of things down here."

31

SHE DOES NOT HESITATE, AND SHE KNOWS NO REMORSE

Michael rushed up to the deck, where Scarlet and Vixen stood with Kamal.

"What is all the shouting about?"

"Look at all the wreckage out there," Scarlet said. "This is not good."

Kamal nodded and smiled an unexpected smile.

"It is the challenging journey that is the one worth taking," he said. "It is only the difficult journey that will allow us to grow and learn."

"Well, sure," Vixen said, "as long as you don't die along the way. Apparently, Michael, we are meant to go through that tunnel."

She pointed toward the island. Michael seemed confused.

"What's that scattered across the shore…"

They let the question linger, so he could figure it out on his own.

"Oh," Michael said.

"Yes. Exactly." Scarlet said.

Kamal raised a telescope to his eye. The tooth-like rocks didn't just hang down from the ceiling. As the currents ebbed and flowed through the mouth of the tunnel, jagged rocks appeared through the ebbs, showing above the water's surface. The waves briefly swelled up again to cover the teeth then receded, allowing the jagged rocks to poke through again. Scarlet grabbed the telescope.

"How are we supposed pass through without bottoming out on the rocks?" Scarlet asked. "This is a fool's errand."

"We just need more water," Michael said with a shrug. "That's all."

His joke fell flat, and nobody appreciated it.

"Oh for crying out loud, we're in the ocean for God's sake," Copper said. "How much more water can there possibly be?"

Kamal unclipped his astrolabe, the circular bronze device, from his belt. The round outer frame of the astrolabe held an inner circular plate. The plate was etched with lines that looked like latitudinal and longitudinal markers, like the lines on a globe, and some well-known constellations.

"What are you going to do with that?" Michael asked.

Kamal struck a confident smile.

"I am going to see if we can get you some more water, as you requested," Kamal said.

"With that? How?"

"The astrolabe is an astrological tool, with many uses. I can calculate the current time of day, for example, based on the position of the sun or a star. I can measure the height of a building. I can use it to ascertain our current latitude and longitude, if needed. Importantly, I can even predict celestial events, such as what time the sun will rise, or when a particular star will crest over the horizon. Most important of all, I can predict when the moon will reach a certain position in its orbit of the earth."

"I'm sorry, but I'm still not following. How does that help us get through the tunnel?"

"With patience, of course," Kamal said.

A veteran of the seas, he peered down at his astrolabe and rotated the inner plate, so that one of the lines etched across its face aligned with the actual horizon etched on the plate beneath it.

Eyeballing one of the indictors on the face of the astrolabe, he made sure that it also was even with the horizon. Finally, he turned one of the pointed indicators on the astrolabe's face directly at the sun in the sky and checked the numbers at the edge. With his measurements complete, he glided inside the cabin and pulled a book and pencil from his bag. He leaned over the table, and reviewed the map for a moment. He opened his book, and thumbed through its pages. When he found what he was looking for, he used his pencil to scribble some mathematical calculations on the back of a ripped section of the map. When he finished his calculations, he returned to the bow and reported back to the others.

"Can you tell me what time it is?" Kamal asked.

"It's about 12:30 p.m.," Michael said.

"Your answer is imprecise. It is precisely 12:32, sun time." Kamal said. "Can you tell me the top speed of this boat?"

"Somewhere between twenty and thirty knots," Michael said, "Depending on whether the wind is with us or against us."

"Can you be more precise, without taking the wind into account?"

"Twenty-five knots at the high end, with no wind either way."

Kamal eyed the distance to the tunnel. He stared quietly, his face strained as he worked through some final calculations in his head.

"We should wait here for exactly thirty-eight minutes. Then we'll proceed straight toward the tunnel at the highest possible speed, twenty-five knots. No more, no less."

"No way, man, you've gone mad," Copper shouted. "Nobody ever won a race sitting still for forty minutes."

"Thirty-eight minutes," Kamal said. "And today, we could become the first."

"No offense," Michael said. "But why would we sit and wait so long? That's the opposite of what we should be doing."

"Do you see the rocks at the base of the tunnel?" Kamal asked.

"Yes."

"The tunnel is not passable right now. We could try, but we would most certainly fail. Conditions are improving, though. In precisely forty minutes, the moon will arrive directly at the opposite side of the earth from us, a perfectly opposite orientation. Allowing us the time needed to get up to top speed, we are two minutes from the tunnel."

"I'm sorry, but I'm still not following you."

"When the moon is at its furthest point from us, at exactly the opposite side of the earth, we will experience the apex of a high tide here. High tide is our best and only chance to pass over the rocks and into the tunnel. With the rise in the tide, and the lift from our high speed, we should make it through.

"Should make it, or will make it?"

"*Should* make it. But if the timing is not just right, we'll accomplish nothing. Just a generous contribution to the debris pile."

Michael shuddered.

"Ok, fine. But even if that's right, then how do we get back out?"

Vixen interrupted.

"At the next high tide, of course. There are two per day."

"Precisely," Kamal said.

He gave her a graceful nod, impressed with her knowledge.

"But we're allowing too much time for everyone behind us to catch up," Michael said.

"I am sorry to make you aware of this, but…"

Kamal turned and pointed toward the Ringmaster's boat.

"We have absolutely no choice in this matter. Just like they had no choice but to wait for us. She is a mighty ocean, and her strength is to be respected. She does not hesitate, and she knows no remorse. Just look at the beach, if you seek to dispel any doubts."

"If we go through forty minutes from now…"

"Thirty-eight now."

"If we go through thirty-eight minutes from now, when is the next high tide?" Michael asked.

"Twelve hours, ten minutes. We would be wise not to miss our chance. That would set us a half-day behind anyone who exits ahead of us. That would be a most unfortunate turn of events, and likely insurmountable."

"Oh my god, are we really going to do this?" Vixen asked.

BELLADONNA STARED OFF THE BOW OF THEIR GALLEON, TOWARD Michael's boat. Her thin braids fluttered in the wind against her cheek, as she brushed them back and tucked them behind her ear.

"What do you think they're waiting for?" she asked the Ringmaster.

"I don't know," he said. "Maybe they're waiting for us to go in first."

"And we're waiting for them? Interesting strategy, cupcake. But I think you're doing it wrong. Should I give you a refresher on how races actually work? I can lay it out for you, nice and easy. It will only take a moment."

He waved her off, and turned his attention to his map, looking it over one more time for any indication of another way, an alternate route, anything he might be missing. There were none. He turned his telescope toward the steamer and saw Kamal using the astrolabe, double-checking his measurements one last time.

"It looks like they've found a talented navigator in Kamal. My guess is that he has a good read on the tides. We'll follow him in, closely."

BACK ON THE STEAMER, THEY SAT PATIENTLY WAITING FOR THEIR opportunity. Vixen struck up a conversation.

"So," she said. "What's the background with you and John, anyway?"

"John? We go way back, he and my father were close. After my father passed, John was around a lot, for a while anyway. He helped my mother, looked after her. He also helped look after me. They spent a lot of time together, he and my mother. That is, until they didn't anymore. He eventually moved to Paris to work at the university. He came back a few times to visit, to check on us, and we went and visited him in Paris for a while. Eventually, the visits grew less frequent. And then they stopped."

"Did that bother you?"

"I didn't think much about it at the time. But as you get older, you reflect back and wonder what changed. In your youth, it's difficult to appreciate adult priorities, but then you look back and I guess you kind of wonder why you weren't one. That's all water under the bridge now, I suppose."

"You seemed relieved to have him join us."

"I was. I am. He's been at this a long time, he knows what he's doing. Far better than I do."

"And he always acts this way?"

"What way?"

"Distracted, anxious, befuddled. Like he needs to say something, but he can't get the words out."

"Say something about what?"

"That's my point, I don't know. It just seems like something is troubling him."

"He's fine. He's just a bit of an odd chap. I'm used to him being more boisterous; louder and much more full of himself than he has been. He's probably just upset about losing his boat, and about not being able to control everything around him. That's the way he prefers it, it's kind of his thing. He likes to be in charge."

"Not that anyone asked me," Copper said. "But I'd be a lot more concerned about you-know-who, if I were you."

He gestured his thumb in Kamal's direction.

"Like I said before, I have a good sense about these things," he whispered. "I'm telling you, something ain't right with that bloke."

"I think he's fine," Vixen said.

"And I'm telling you, I don't."

John returned from below deck to join them in the cabin.

"Why are we just sitting here?" John said. "I thought we were trying to win a race. Are we not doing that anymore?"

"We are," Michael said. "But we have to wait for the tides to rise so we can get over the rocks at the base of the tunnel. Kamal has it all figured out."

"Kamal? Hmph," John said.

He looked around the cabin, distracted and anxious.

"Don't be upset, we sorted it all out while you were below deck. We'll be moving in a few minutes."

"Now who's this coming up on our rear? Time is wasting, boy. We need to move."

"We have a plan, just relax," Michael said.

"We're letting the whole field catch up?" John said. "I never would have allowed this."

Two more boats arrived to join the growing collection of sea craft sitting, waiting, bobbing in the water. The first was a cutter captained by Dorado, the other was a single-masted sloop piloted by William Wilfork. They eased their sails and settled into place, trying to figure out what the others were doing, and why they weren't bothering to advance. Dorado smacked on his toothpick while he riffled through his papers and pulled a pocket watch from his vest to check the time. Will leaned over the wheel, and stared out impatiently. Dorado knew there had to be a good reason that nobody was moving, so he waited. And even with as confident and daring as Will was, he thought better of it than to go in alone.

"Is the firebox full of fuel?" Kamal said. "It is almost time for us to go."

He didn't look at Michael, but just stared toward the tunnel, eyes locked.

"We're ready to go," Michael said. "How much more time do we have?"

"None."

Kamal jammed the throttle forward, to full power. Thick clouds of black smoke poured from the smokestacks, the steam pistons whirred and the paddle wheel slapped the water at an ever-increasing rate. The rear of the boat bore down in the water, as the angular bow lifted upward to cut a path straight through the water toward Cragtooth Tunnel.

"They're going!" Belladonna shouted.

"Full sail," the Ringmaster demanded of Phillippe.

"Are you sure?"

"Full sail! Now!"

Phillippe trimmed the sails and they snapped tight, filling with wind. One participant after another gave chase, first Dorado, then Will and then others, falling into line, rushing toward the tunnel. Kamal gradually pulled away, fast and aggressive. As they approached, the waves became more choppy, and the bow bounced more violently.

"Wait a minute," Scarlet said, shouting, over the noise of the wind and paddle wheel.

"The tunnel is completely black."

"Yes," Kamal shouted back.

"We're going really fast. You can't see the path through the tunnel."

"Yes. That is correct."

"So the tunnel may turn left or right. But you can't see it."

"You are correct once again. The tunnel may turn, or it may not."

Scarlet gripped the rail, knuckles white, as the boat chopped along the water toward a blacked-out tunnel. She looked at the others.

"I'm not comfortable with this at all," she yelled. "Anyone else?"

Michael and Vixen looked at each other and back to Scarlet, and they both nodded sheepishly.

"Don't you think we should know for certain before we plow through the entrance at full speed?" Vixen shouted.

"Consider this," Kamal yelled. "We have to pass through this tunnel, and the only way to clear the rocks at the base is to enter the tunnel during the highest tide, moving at the highest speed."

Vixen interrupted him.

"So, you think the tunnel has to be straight, otherwise it would be impossible to navigate?" she shouted.

"Can it be any other way?"

"Well, yes. Of course it can."

"I think it will not."

Vixen gripped the rail with both hands.

"I hope to god you're right about this."

32

INTO CRAGTOOTH TUNNEL

They raced ahead at top speed, and the tunnel entrance was just seventy yards away. Then sixty, and fast-approaching. Kamal heard a steam whistle, just two quick toots. He looked around, and so did Michael. Neither could tell where the sound was coming from. The boats began to converge into a single file line as they approached the tunnel.

Fifty yards.

The Ringmaster was still close, but he was losing ground to Kamal. Will fell back further, unable to keep the pace.

"We need more sail!" the Ringmaster yelled at Phillippe.

Phillippe adjusted some ropes, but he couldn't do much more. The sails were trimmed the best they could be.

"That is all we have," Phillippe yelled back.

Forty-five yards.

Dorado's cutter was surprisingly swift and agile. He passed Will, then a few others. He eventually overtook the Ringmaster, tipping his cap as he sailed by. He was closing in on Michael.

Forty yards to go.

With the most intense focus, Vixen eyed the base of the tunnel as the waves ebbed and flowed. She hoped with the greatest of hope that she wouldn't see any rocks cresting through the water's surface. With teeth clenched, she was powerless to do anything, reliant upon Kamal's calculations being correct. John and Copper stood with eyes fixed on the entrance, holding on with iron grips. Both were worried, but neither spoke.

Thirty yards.

Will stomped his foot on the deck of his sloop, as if spurring a horse, to make it run faster. He looked up angrily at his sails, and stomped again. He was losing ground.

Twenty yards.

Kamal glanced down at his astrolabe. He placed his hand on it in a comforting way. He looked at peace. His measurements were true and his timing was correct. They had to be.

Fifteen yards.

The fan blade on the cabin spun round, as the steamer raced on, and the belt turned laps around the pulley.

Ten yards.

The shrill sound of a steam whistle sounded again. Four quick toots this time, louder than before. As the last one sounded, a fast-moving boat shot out from the dark tunnel, on a collision course with the steamer. As the boat emerged from the tunnel, it turned and banked hard left to avoid a collision, spraying water in the air and across the steamer's deck. Kamal flinched, and steered the steamer hard left to avoid a collision, then back to the right to center himself in the tunnel.

"That was the Baron!" John shouted, pointing at the boat that just came out.

One yard.

Kamal leaned into the steering wheel, pushing hard right. He reduced the throttle and steered the best he could. But it was too little, and too late. Though the *SS Soairse* was fast in a straight line, she had poor maneuverability. They cleared the rocks at base of the entrance, but the left side of the steamer clipped the tunnel wall as they entered. There was a loud bang and a grinding sound. Sparks sprayed in every direction lighting the dark tunnel, and the copper spheres on the outside of the hull grated against the stone walls with a shrill scraping sound. The steamer drifted back off the wall and the sparks dissipated, leaving them cruising full speed ahead through the dark tunnel. As it drifted back, the paddle drew closer to the wall on the other side.

"Don't let it hit," John screamed. "If it does, the paddle will be dashed to bits."

Kamal steered left again. The boat rocked violently. Vixen, Scarlet and John were all thrown down amid the turbulence. John screamed in pain as he fell, and crashed to the deck. Kamal righted the steamer, and got its bow pointed directly at the now-visible light at the end of the tunnel.

"Is everyone alright?" Michael shouted.

One by one, they sounded off to let him know they were. Then Michael heard John's voice.

"I don't think I am," John groaned, "It's my ankle!"

They emerged from the end of the tunnel, back into the sunlight as Michael assessed the situation. The chest was still well-secured to the boat. Vixen lay crumpled on the deck, looking vulnerable and clinging to a rail. He rushed over to help her up.

"Are you hurt?" he asked, as he offered a hand.

"I'm fine I think, just a bit rattled. I'll need a moment," she said.

He knelt beside her and smiled.

"I'm glad you're ok."

Scarlet huffed at the exchange.

"Yes, I'm also just fine. Thank you for asking."

She pulled herself up, and dusted herself off, shooting Michael a cross eye.

"Such a gentleman you are!"

"Sorry, Scarlet, I just," he said.

"No explanation needed, Michael. Your actions speak for themselves."

"I…um."

Michael looked around to find John.

"John!" he shouted.

John called out from behind the cabin.

"I'm back here."

He was leaning against the cabin wall. He was sitting upright, but writhing in pain when they arrived.

"I think it may be broken," he said.

He nodded to his ankle.

"Oh my god," Scarlet said when she saw it. "It's broken alright."

"You all go ahead without me, and do what needs to be done here. There isn't much time with the others so close. I don't even think I can walk, much less keep up."

"Are you sure?" Michael asked.

"I'm sure," he said.

He winced and groaned in pain.

"Go on, boy."

The tunnel had let them out into a magnificent lagoon, with serene blue waters within. Ring island provided a wave-break that settled the otherwise choppy sea water surrounding it. Across the lagoon, there was another island, nestled within the island interior.

"Now I see why it's called Ring Island," Scarlet said, "The black outer rock forms a protective ring, and guards this stunning oasis in the middle."

"It's gorgeous," Michael said.

He stood on the deck in awe.

"It's so lush. And look at all the plants and flowers. So many colors!"

Kamal ran the boat up onto the soft sand on the beach. Dorado ran his cutter up as well, just a few yards away.

The galleon, followed by Will's sloop, beached shortly after.

Nigel and some others anchored further down. A gangplank dropped from the Ringmaster's galleon. The Ringmaster, Belladonna, Mechanicules and Phillippe trotted down, and to the right, with Mechanicules carrying his large case. They dashed across the sand, never looking back, and disappeared into the lush greenery. Dorado and Will went left, into the distance, through some shrubs and out of sight. Two more boats were approaching fast, others were beginning to disembark.

With the boat secured, Kamal rushed to John's side. He crouched next to him and put his hand on John's shoulder.

"Please accept my apology, and my profound sorrow, for your injury, John. Are you able to walk?"

"No. No chance. "

"The maneuver was unavoidable, I was afraid we would collide with the other boat if I didn't move."

John waved him off.

"It's unfortunate, but I place no blame upon you. We're fine, you and I."

Then Kamal turned to Michael.

"Please accept my apology for the damage I have caused your vessel. I am deeply indebted to you, and to John, for the harm I have caused, and I am honor-bound to make this right. The opportunity may not present itself today or even tomorrow. But during our lifetimes, my debt will be repaid to you both, in full."

He folded his hands in front of his chest, bent at the waist, and bowed deeply to John. John nodded. Then he turned and bowed deeply to Michael.

"You all should go," John said. "Really, go on."

"I will stay and tend to John," Kamal said. "It is my duty."

Michael grabbed some papers from the table in the cabin and slung his satchel over his shoulder. He unlocked his chest and sorted through it quickly. He tossed a few items into his satchel.

"We should really go," Scarlet said.

"I'm coming," Michael said.

He double-checked the lock. Satisfied it was secure, he led Vixen, Scarlet and Copper off the boat, dashing across the sandy beach toward the lush overgrowth, in the same direction the Ringmaster went.

33

FAERIE WOOD

The Ringmaster, Belladonna, Phillippe and Mech all forged ahead through the greenery toward the center of the island. The lush leafy plants thickened to shrubs, and before long they found themselves engulfed in a wooded area full of vivacious foliage, vines and flowering plants that played host to the squawking sounds of loud, but unfamiliar, birds. The canopy above filtered the light to a soft illumination that barely reached the ground, other than a few streaks of light. The ground under their feet was soft and moist, and a musty, earthy smell permeated the air. They'd marched for almost four hours before they came to an opening.

"Is this it?" Belladonna asked.

The Ringmaster flipped through some papers.

"This is it."

They stood in front of a monolithic stone building with no windows and only a short stairway leading up to an open doorway. The exterior walls and the stairway were covered in thick green moss and a few vines. It appeared to be completely dark on the inside. A thick sheet of spider webs covered the doorway.

"Mech, we're going to need some light," the Ringmaster said.

Mechanicules knelt down on one knee and placed his case on the ground. He unlatched the lid and opened it to reveal several attachments for his mechanical arm. He brought the piston hammer, a piston spear and an attachment with a pressurized gas cylinder, a pilot light and a wide barrel. With a click and a twist, he removed his mechanical hand, placed it in the case and snapped the gas cylinder into place. As he turned a knob on the cylinder, the attachment made a hissing sound, and he lit it with a sparker from the case. The small flame of the pilot, with the intensity of three or four candles, burned continuously at the tip in front of the larger barrel. The Ringmaster nodded toward the spider webs in the doorway.

"We're going to need more light than that," he said with a smirk.

Mech stood up and pointed his arm at the doorway. *Whoosh.* An enormous fireball shot out of the barrel, through the doorway, burning out most of the spider webs, leaving just a few smoldering bits at the edges.

"I hate spiders," the Ringmaster said.

"Let's get in there and move quickly. If anyone else is coming this way, they won't be far behind."

He flicked a pointed finger in the direction of the doorway. Taking his cue, Mechanicules walked up the stairs first to lead the way in, with this mechanical arm held in the air, like a torch. Surrounded by a halo of light, he stepped through the darkness inside. Belladonna and Phillippe approached the doorway together. Phillippe stepped back with his hand outstretched toward the door.

"Please. Ladies first," he said. "I insist."

Belladonna strutted in, and Phillippe followed, three or four steps behind. The Ringmaster entered last, at a safe distance behind the rest, just in case.

~

MICHAEL LOOKED DOWN AT HIS MAP AGAIN, AS THEY WALKED down the soft, moist path. He stopped in front of a cluster of fungus growing in the center of the path.

"That's odd," Michael said.

"What's so odd about it?" Vixen asked.

"Look at the all mushrooms on the ground, their pattern. They're growing in a perfect circle."

He pointed to the ground. There were hundreds upon hundreds of delicate, pale grey mushrooms, each the height of a pinky finger, densely clustered and arranged in a near perfect circle, a ring ten feet across.

"It's a faerie ring," Copper said.

"*Fff*-what?" Michael said.

"A faerie ring. That's what they say. You know, *Wherever the faerie doth dance in the night, a round ring of mushrooms greets morning's light.*"

He bobbed his head and wagged his fingers in rhythm during his recitation. But his rhyme was met with silence, and dubious stares.

"Oh come on. Faerie rings," he said. "You've never heard of them?"

Vixen snorted at the idea.

"Rubbish."

"Don't blame me," Copper said. "I'm just telling you what they say. Take it as you will. It makes but a pebble's difference to me."

"Let's move along," Michael said. "Shall we?"

"Fine by me," Copper said. "As you wish, lad."

"Well," Scarlet warned. "If there *are* any faeries nearby, then we should definitely watch out for *Bardwogs*. Ferocious, mischievous little creatures. And they pack a nasty bite."

Michael and Vixen giggled at the suggestion. The group walked deeper into the thick vegetation, passing several more of the fabled faerie rings along the way.

"Bardwogs," Vixen said with a chuckle.

"I don't care to be mocked," Copper said.

Back on the other side of the beach, Will and Dorado burst through the greenery, and out onto the sand, running as fast as their legs would carry them back to their boats.

"I told you not to touch it," Dorado said in a scolding tone.

He ran toward his boat, one hand holding his hat atop his head.

"You didn't say *not* to touch it," Will said. "You said '*I wouldn't do that, if I was you*'. It's totally different!"

Both had jagged arc-shaped marks on their arms, faces, ears and necks. Dozens of them, wherever their skin was exposed.

"At least I got my token," Will said. "Did you get yours?"

"Of course I did, but no thanks to you! When we get to the boats, you just keep your distance, young man. You've caused me enough trouble as it is."

"Are they still behind us?" Will asked.

"I don't think so."

"I'm going to keep running anyway."

"Yeah. Me too. Get to the water. They hate being wet."

It had already been a long day, and they were feeling fatigued. Michael and his crew trudged down the path with determination. They came to an open space where the trees thinned out, and reached the steps of another moss-covered building.

Scarlet pointed to the furry, moss-covered steps, where the moss' soft tendrils sat, delicate and undisturbed.

"We're the first to arrive" she said. "Nobody's been up the steps yet."

Michael took two candles from his satchel and lit them with a match from his pocket.

"I learned my lesson at the Citadel," he said with a grin. "I brought these from my chest. Vixen, you should take one."

He handed her the candle. Copper and Scarlet raised eyebrows.

"You didn't bring enough for everyone?" Scarlet said.

"I was in a hurry," Michael said defensively. "No offense intended."

They walked up the steps, and into the dank building, lit only by the light of two candles. The room inside was virtually empty, its rough walls and floor were moist, and the mineral smell of wet rock and mildew hung heavy in the air. There was a square hole in one wall, just a few inches across, ten feet up from the floor. The hole permitted a beam of light to enter from the outside. The beam spread out as it projected across the room, over to the opposite wall, and lit up a mural of the earth that stretched from floor to ceiling, nearly fifteen feet tall. The mural was beautiful, and the continents, oceans, and topography were all rendered with masterful detail. Apart from a pile of cogwheels on the floor in one corner, and some poles rising out of heavy stone bases scattered about, the room was otherwise empty.

"This is strange," Vixen said. "It looked so much larger from the outside. But it's not very large at all."

Michael looked down at the stone block floor. It was inset with cast bronze medallions, each medallion slightly recessed. They varied in shape and each one was imprinted with intricate designs of indiscernible meaning. Some of the medallions were square, some were triangular and others were pentagonal. He studied their random distribution. There was no order to be found in their arrangement.

"Michael, did you hear what I said?" Copper asked.

"Sorry, no. What did you say?"

"I said what now? What are we supposed to do here?"

"Fascinating question," Michael said. "I'm starting to wonder if we're in the right place."

He looked down at the papers again. This is where Copper's map said to go, but why?

Scarlet walked around the room, inspecting the heavy bases, and their protruding poles. She picked one up and carried it toward him, laboring under its weight as she walked. She set it down in front of Michael with a dull thud. The base was a square pillar the size of a milk container, and the pole was topped with a brass eyepiece.

"What do you think we are supposed to do with this?" she asked.

He surveyed the room. Other bases were spread around the room, each with a pole extending upward. Each pole had a different topper. Some had large convex lenses secured with brass rings, as big around as his head. They looked like tall magnifying glasses. Some were topped with simple mirrors, others with large concave lenses, and two others were topped with mirrored triangular prisms, each standing on end. He studied the room, rubbing the back of his neck. Then he looked at the mural.

"I think I have an idea of what we are meant to do here."

"You do?" Vixen asked.

"I do. There was something on my invitation."

He pulled it out from his satchel and read it out loud.

"*View the world through another man's lens. You can learn a lot if you study it closely.*"

"Well, that's right interesting," Copper said. "But it's my map that brought us here, as you may recall, and none of my papers say anything about that."

"It's like I told you before, I think we were all meant to come together. Fate. Remember?"

Copper shrugged.

"So what are you suggesting, lad?" he said.

Michael pointed to the mural of the earth.

"That mural. I think that's the *world* it references."

He walked over to one of the stone bases and peeked through the back of a convex lens, which made his eyeball look gigantic.

"And we need to *view* that world through these *lenses*. So we can learn something," he said. "Maybe it will tell us our next step."

"Then what are we waiting for?" Scarlet said.

"Oh, right. That," Michael said.

He picked up the square-based pole with the eyepiece on top, and set it on one of the square medallion insets, the one furthest from the mural, at the opposite end of the room.

"I think we are supposed to arrange these mirrors and lenses in some useful order, to build a makeshift telescope of some kind."

"A telescope to look at what?" Copper asked

Michael pointed to the mural.

"The *world*. Weren't you listening?"

"But what is that going to do?" Scarlet asked.

"I don't know. But once everything is in place, I think we'll find out. Unless, of course, you have a better suggestion."

She paused.

"I don't. Let's try it."

"Great. So let's get the square pedestals placed on the square medallions, the triangles on the triangles and the pentagons on pentagons, and we'll see what we have."

They arranged the bases on medallions of corresponding shapes. Michael stood behind the eyepiece, watching. He could see it coming together. He placed his fingertip on the eyepiece, ran his finger down its length, off the end, and extended his finger out toward the lens in front of him. Then he traced the line through the lens to a mirror that was set at a 45-degree angle. He continued tracing the line, as if it had reflected off the mirror, through another lens. From that lens, he traced the line through to a triangular prism. The line reflected off the triangular prism, through another lens, then onto a mirror. One last mirror set at a 45-degree angle redirected the line through a final lens aimed directly at the mural. But as he traced the path though, he realized not all the mirrors and lenses were being used. Some were left out. He sighed.

"I don't think we have the right arrangement," he said.

He leaned over to look through the eyepiece.

"No. It's definitely not right. Some of the mirrors and lenses aren't set properly. It's totally out of focus. I just see two blurry squares, set on diagonals to each other.

He pointed.

"Copper, can you switch those two square pedestals?"

Copper switched them, and Michael retraced the line. There were still pieces not being used. He looked through the eyepiece again.

"We're getting closer, but it's not right. I can see some writing. But it's as if someone wrote a letter on a sheet of paper and tore the paper in half. I only see the right half of the paper. There are words and other symbols, but I can't make out the message. It's nonsense right now. Scarlet, turn the triangular prism one click left"

She rotated the prism one turn left on its base. Then he turned to Vixen.

"The triangular prism beside you. Can you turn it two positions on its base, so the apex of the triangle points directly back at the lens in front of it it? I think that will split the view. Half to the left, and half to the right."

Vixen rotated the base two positions. Michael traced the lines out again, on both sides of the prism, and all the pieces were being used.

"Yes! I think that's it."

He leaned down to look through the eyepiece. Then he stood upright, with a big, silly grin.

"What is it?" Scarlet demanded.

"We've got it! It's all come together. All four quadrants and they're all in focus."

"Well? What does it say?" she yelled.

"It says a lot. There is an illustration of a cluster of gears.

There is another cryptogram, like the one we saw in the Citadel, and there are some instructions. Very clever, too. Everything is arranged in a way to be broken up across the borders of four separate quadrants. They all need to be in proper focus make any sense of it at all."

Scarlet stamped her foot loudly.

"So what do the instructions actually say? Honestly, Michael!"

"Well, it basically says that once we open the door, there is a lever in the back. Flip the lever to open the door."

"That makes no sense. Why do you need to open the door if the door is already open?" she asked. "That sounds ridiculous."

"I'm just telling you what it says," he replied.

Copper walked to the mural and ran his hand across it.

"Where is all this coming from? I don't see anything like that. I'm looking right at it. It's all right here in front of me, but I don't see it at all."

"It must be written in supremely small text," Vixen said.

"And broken up into four different pieces," Scarlet added, "and the pieces could be spread out anywhere on the mural."

"That's exactly right," Michael said. "The mirrors and lenses magnify the text and drawings hidden within the mural, wherever they might be and the mirrors bring them all together in one place, right here in the eyepiece. We would never find them otherwise, especially without knowing what to look for."

Copper leaned in closer to the mural, trying but failing, to find something.

"Well I'll be," he mumbled to himself, slow and smooth. "That's right clever."

"Copper," Michael said. "What's the marking on the head of your key?"

"Three triangular clusters of three stars each. Nine stars in total, all arranged to form the outline of a larger triangle. Why?"

Michael looked through the eyepiece again.

"According to the cryptogram, your nine stars translate to a clock face. You should open the lock with a clock face. I think."

"Aye, but this room is empty, laddie. So what do you propose I do with that wee little tidbit? I don't see any clocks or locks or anything else that rhymes, for that matter."

"I don't know. Just remember it for now."

Scarlet called out from the corner.

"Michael, what did you say about the gears?"

"In the mural, there's a picture of a cluster of gears."

She looked down at the ground, at the pile of cogwheels laying on the floor. She also noticed some small square holes in the wall. She knelt down and put her eye to one of the holes. She could see into another room through the hole, but just barely, it was nearly dark.

"That explains why it looks so small in here. There's another hidden room past this wall I think. It's dark though. How are we doing on candles?"

"Half burnt," Vixen said.

"Same here," Michael said. "A few more minutes probably. Then they're done."

She glanced back to the cogwheels on the ground.

"The cluster of gears you mentioned, from the mural. Do they have any particular arrangement?"

"Yes. Why?"

"Can you describe it?"

He peered back through the eyepiece.

"There is a small gear with a crank handle, it's at the lower left position, relative to all the others. It's the smallest one."

She grabbed the smallest cogwheel in the pile, with a square hub protruding from the back. She held the square hub up to the square hole in the wall, at the lowest, leftmost position. She placed the square hub of the cogwheel into the hole on the wall and pushed it all the way in. It went in smooth and tight.

"What's next?"

"A medium-sized one, straight above."

"Ok, what next?"

"Another medium-sized one, directly to the right of the last."

"Ok. And then?"

"Another medium-sized one set on a diagonal, up and to the right. It looks like it has a smaller gear stuck to its face, both rotate on the same hub."

"Got it. And after that?"

"A large one straight above. It's the largest of the set. The teeth of the largest gear mesh with the teeth of the small gear mounted to the face of the medium gear just before it. Does that make sense?"

"It does, but are you sure that's right?"

"Yes."

She pressed the last cogwheel into its mount on the wall.

"It doesn't look right."

"That's what I see. That's what it says."

"But the teeth don't all mesh together. Are you absolutely certain?"

"Yes. Absolutely."

She bent down and picked up the last piece available from the pile, the crank arm. She placed the square hub of the crank into the smallest cogwheel, and turned it. The small cogwheel's teeth turned the second cogwheel, which in turn rotated the third. But the teeth of the third cogwheel didn't connect with the fourth. The first three gears turned, but the last two did not.

"See? It just spins. But there's a gap. The cogs come close, but they just don't meet. There's one more hole. I think we're missing one."

Scarlet spoke with a frustrated tone and gestured at the gap between the third and fourth gears. She stood with one hand on her hip, turning the handle a with the other, just to illustrate.

"See? Nothing."

"Maybe I can help," Vixen said.

Copper rolled his eyes, as Vixen walked over to help Scarlet.

"Oh, lordy," he said. "This ought to be good."

Vixen pointed between the third and fourth cogwheels.

"Yes. See there? There's one more hole that's not being used."

"But look around. We're fresh out of cogs," Scarlet said. "This is a hopeless endeavor."

Vixen placed her bag on the ground and rummaged through it.

"What are you going to do now, lass," Copper said with a chuckle. "Are you going to make it glow?"

She stopped, and shot daggers from her eyes.

"I'm solving the problem. What exactly are you doing?"

"Hmph," he snorted.

"Just as I expected," she said. "Here. Try this."

She reached into her bag and pulled out a sprocket. It was the one from her box at the Citadel, and she handed it to Scarlet.

Scarlet slid the small sprocket into the last square hole. Its teeth meshed perfectly with the cogwheels on either side, and it bridged the small gap where the teeth failed to meet.

Vixen gave Michael a sideways glance and a wink.

"Fate," she said, smiling sweetly. "Or, you know. Something."

With the gear in its place, Scarlet turned the crank again.

"It's really heavy now, with the gears all engaged."

Copper pushed his way in and grabbed the crank with his brawny arm. With some effort, he was able to turn it. One cogwheel turned the next, until all five spun around. As he turned the crank, a portion of the wall slowly rose up, revealing a hidden passage. For every ten turns of the crank, the door rose a half an inch. While he worked the crank, Scarlet rearranged the poles and bases. It took a while to raise the door, but when it was up, Copper pulled a small silver coin from his pocket and wedged it between the gears of two cogwheels, to block their movement and hold the door up.

"What are you doing?" Michael asked of Scarlet.

"This is a competition," she said. "I'm moving these bases off-order. There's no sense in making it easy if anyone comes behind us," she said.

"Fair point," he said. "Cover your tracks. Spy technique, I understand."

"You know," Copper said, "We *could* just snap the eyepiece off the pole. Take it with us."

"Copper!" Vixen exclaimed. "I'll have nothing to do with it."

"Absolutely not," Michael added.

He didn't hesitate.

"I agree with Vixen. It's not in the spirit of the competition. It's cheating."

Copper shrugged.

"Fine, have it your way, lad. It was just a suggestion."

Copper looked at Scarlet. She seemed less offended by the idea. They both considered it, but neither followed through. Pole by pole, they worked as a team to move all the bases off their medallions and back to the perimeter of the room. Michael walked up to the newly raised door. He peeked around the corner and looked in.

"It looks clear, let's go in," Michael said.

Vixen followed him through the doorway by the light of a dwindling candle, and Scarlet nodded for Copper to go next.

"Oh no, you go ahead, lass. I'm right behind you," he said. "Ladies first. I insist."

Scarlet walked through and Copper put his hand on the crank. He turned it just enough to let loose the coin he wedged into the gears, and removed the coin. When he let go of the crank, the handle whirred around rapidly, and the raised door crept back toward the floor. Copper backed away from the door as it was coming down.

"Copper, what are you doing?" Michael yelled.

"He's sabotaged us!" Vixen said.

Copper backed up further from the door as it descended. Then he ran straight toward it. As it eased downward, he dropped down and slid underneath. The door touched back down to the floor behind him. He barely made it through.

"Like she was saying," Copper said, wagging his thumb in Scarlet's direction, "let's not make it too easy for anyone behind us. Now let me see that candle. And by the way, I've sabotaged nothing, thank you very much."

He took Vixen's candle and walked to the wall where the door had just come down, and he held the candle close to it. He could see the backs of the square hubs from the gears that had been inserted into the wall. He poked them with his finger to push them out. As they fell back to the floor on the other side of the wall, he squinted one eye and peeked through a hole.

"Nobody behind us," he said. "Not yet, anyway."

When he turned around he could see Scarlet, Vixen and Michael standing together, staring at him with eager anticipation. The wall behind them was covered with wrought iron lock-boxes. The boxes were arranged side by side and stacked on top of each other like a wall of post office boxes, each emblazoned with a different symbol. Scarabs, frogs, dragons and more, just like at the Citadel.

"There's a box with a clock face," Michael said. "It's your key, Copper. Would you like to do the honors?"

"Aye. That I would, lad."

He grinned as he spoke.

Vixen handed him his key. He placed the key in the lock and glanced up for reassurance. They nodded, and he turned the key a half turn. The door clicked and released. He reached inside and pulled out its contents, a large gold-rimmed token. Its polished silver face, emblazoned with nine raised stars arranged in triangular clusters of three, glimmered in the candle light. He held it up for them to see and they cheered and patted him heartily on the back.

"Now let's get out of here," he said.

"Um, you dropped the door down behind us," Scarlet said. "How do you suppose we get out."

"Now that you mention it, I hadn't really considered that. Bugger. I may have sabotaged us, after all."

He turned back to the door, but Michael put his hand on Copper's chest to stop him.

"Hang on," Michael said. "Did you check to see if there was anything else inside the box?"

Copper sighed his annoyance, but he went back anyway. He reached in deeper and felt around inside the box.

"Hey, there is something."

He removed a thin rectangular metal container, the length and width of a sheet of paper, thick as a notepad. The box was made of hammered silver, with rounded corners and dimpled patterns creating various swirls and other shapes in the face of the box. Its outer decor was unremarkable, just a basic compass-face design, some simple swirling patterns, and a button on the front face at the bottom center. Intrigued, Copper moved his thumb over the button to press it.

"No, not yet," Scarlet shouted.

"Oh, now what is it?" he said.

His shoulders dropped, and he spoke in his most exasperated tone.

"You're always interrupting things. Just let me be, would you?"

"May I see it, please?" Scarlet demanded.

She held her hand out, expecting to receive it, and he handed it over grudgingly. She turned it front to back, inspecting its bottom edge. There was a seam along its length, and a small hole in it.

"Do you know what this is?" she said.

"Aye, lass," he said, smooth and easy. "It's a metal box."

"Clever. But, there's more to it than that. If I'm right, it's actually an ash tablet. We, agents and spies that is, use these for dead drops, a secure means to pass sensitive information and guard against its discovery by unauthorized persons."

"An ash tablet you say?" Copper asked. "Never heard of it."

"Yes, they're used for covert communications. You can write a message on a piece of parchment using a ferrous ink. The metallic ink sets on the parchment. The parchment is then placed in the ash tablet tray, and the tray is slid into the box, locking it in place inside the silver tablet. Then you place the tablet in a fire or a kiln, and the intense heat cooks the parchment into ash, without melting the metal box."

"Well that just doesn't seem useful at all," Copper said, "Burning a letter into ash. How is anyone supposed to read it after that?"

"That's the beauty of it," she replied." The ferrous ink, it's metallic. It holds its form in the ash, even after the paper burns. You can still read it as long as you don't disturb the delicate ash."

"Why not just leave the paper note then? You don't even need the metal box. I mean, if you can read it anyway, what's the point of all that?

He laughed.

"What a waste, you and your fancy-pants way of passing notes. Just pass the paper! Honestly. People make things so difficult."

"It's a security precaution," she said, "you can't just open the tray and read it as easy as that."

Copper grew frustrated.

"Oh yeah? Watch me."

He reached for the tablet to take it back, ready to show her just how wrong she was. She moved it with a smooth and gingerly motion, careful not to shake it or upset its ashen contents. She placed her other hand on his chest to keep him separated from the tablet.

"Be careful, you'll ruin it," she said. "The tablet has a spring-loaded arm inside. It engages when you slide the tray in. If you press the button to release the tray without securing the arm, it will sweep through the ashen message and break it up, rendering it totally unreadable. And it's not like tearing up paper that you can piece back together. It's more like erasing a chalkboard. Once it's gone, it's really gone."

"What are you suggesting?" Michael asked.

"What do you think is in here?" Scarlet replied. "If this ash tablet contains the map or instructions for the next leg of the race, and we open it incorrectly, then we're finished. Only the person with the means to lock the arm in place can release the inner tray and keep the message intact. That's by design."

"Then let's open it the right way. What more do we need?" Copper demanded.

Scarlet gently turned it all around again, looking at the side edges.

"It's a four-rod design, one on each side. Is there anything left inside the cubby?"

He held the candle close and peeked inside.

"No, just a lever in the back."

He reached into the box and pulled the lever as his candle snuffed out. A hidden door leading to the outside released and cracked open slightly in the back corner. By now, it was dusk and the sunlight was fading.

"Ah, now I get it. So that's what that meant," Copper said with a look of wonder. "When the door is open, pull the lever to open the door."

Then he looked back inside the box and swept his hand around one last time.

"There's nothing else in here."

Scarlet thought for a moment, then looked at Vixen.

"You. You had the sprocket we needed to finish the gear wall. Do you also have the rods?"

"No, I don't believe so," Vixen said.

"What do these rods look like?" Michael asked.

Scarlet turned the ash tablet carefully and studied the thin outside edges one last time. Thin metal rods, probably an inch or so long I would imagine, all different shapes. If you look at the ends of the rods, they'll be shaped like a star, a circle, a square and a triangle, respectively. If they're not the right shape, they won't fit and they won't work."

Michael's face lit up.

"Brilliant! I think I might have what you need back at the steamer. When we were at the Citadel, I found a glass vial that contained some metal pins, or rods, as you call them. Maybe they're the keys we need for the ash tablet?

"Let's get back to the boat and see," Scarlet said. "But let's do it carefully, please, without jostling the tablet, shall we?"

34

THE MOTHER STONE

Having retrieved their token, the Ringmaster led his team on the long hike back to their boat. Mechanicules walked quietly, carrying his case, and Phillippe kept a nervous eye on the plants, wary of an ambush. The Ringmaster held up his token to admire it.

"The tokens are quite stunning aren't they? Treasures in their own right, I would say. Two down, one to go."

"As far as we know, anyway," Belladonna said.

"I have to be honest about something," he said. "I'm more than just a little bit bothered that McGillicuddy is still a factor. I thought we were clear with Ramshorn. McGillicuddy was to be taken out."

"We were clear, love. But perhaps he got cold feet. He has a soft spot for the boy. You know that."

"When we reach the continent, I want you to find Ramshorn, and I want you to send a very strong message. Am I being clear?"

"Yes, love. Crystal."

~

"How long before the tide reaches its high point again?" Vixen asked as they stepped outside.

Michael checked his pocket watch.

"Just under five hours."

"Then we better move quickly, it was nearly four hours to get here from the beach, and that was when we had better light."

"Agreed, we should move quickly," he said. "Speaking of light, do you see that?"

The sun had set, but a soft, ambient light danced all around them. A dim but rolling light washed across the trees and the ground, soft but vibrant streaks of green, blue, and purple.

"Where is that coming from?" Michael asked.

"Could it be the *Aurora Borealis*?" Copper asked.

"Not likely," Scarlet said. "Given our southerly latitude and the time of year, that would be an exceptionally rare occurrence. Besides, the northern lights light up the sky, not the ground underneath a canopy of trees. It has to be something else, something already down here with us."

The swirling lights grew brighter and rolled toward them, lighting the leaves and branches above. A droning hum got louder as the band of light continued forth, growing in intensity.

"It's getting closer," Scarlet said.

A swarm emerged over the top of some bushes and circled overhead. Like large fireflies, they swirled above, in a docile and hypnotic rotation. Glowing green, blue or purple, the iridescent creatures swirled above. The blue ones seemed to outnumber the green by a factor of two-to-one, and the purple composed a distinct minority, just a few here and there, but they glowed the brightest. The small creatures descended smoothly from their swirling pattern, into a large hole in a tree. The tree was massive, its gnarly, twisting branches among the thickest and strongest on the island, and glowing streaks of color gushed from the hole as the creatures entered its massive trunk.

"Fascinating," Michael said, "They're utterly mesmerizing."

As he spoke, one of the creatures broke from the swirling pattern and fluttered down toward him, slowly and softly. He held out his hand, inviting it to land in his palm.

"Um, Michael…" Scarlet said.

It landed softly in his palm and stilled its wings. He leaned in close to get a better look. A soft blue glow lit his palm as it stood there, and the light washed over his face and glimmered off the gloss of his eyes.

"It's beautiful" he whispered. "I've never seen anything like it."

"Michael," Scarlet said again.

Transfixed on the creature standing in his hand, he ignored her, though. He leaned in closer, entranced by this tiny glowing creature, the likes of which he had never seen, or even heard about. It stood prone in his palm, wings tucked behind. Five inches tall at best, its miniature, androgynous body was gaunt and lanky, with scrawny arms and legs and broad shoulders where its wings attached. It looked back at him with its large, elliptical head, four sizes too big for its body, and droopy, pointy ears protruding from either side. Its mouth, although closed, was wide. Michael imagined this creature would have inspired the term *smiling from ear to ear*.

"You have to see this," he said. But as he turned to show the others, he jostled it in his hand. Alarmed by the shaking, the diminutive creature opened its oversized mouth, and sunk its oversized teeth into the meaty part of his palm, just below his thumb.

He yelled out in painful surprise, and he waved his hand frantically in an effort to shake it loose. It held on for several shakes, before it released its bite and fluttered away.

"I told you to be careful," Scarlet said.

"What? When?"

"Back at the very first faerie ring!" she said. "I told you to watch out for the Bardwogs. Ferocious creatures? Nasty bite? Does any of this sound familiar? Ninety percent teeth, and ten percent bad attitude. Lucky for you, the blue ones are the least dangerous."

"I thought you were joking about that. And by the way, don't you think you could have told me what they look like?"

She shrugged.

"I thought everybody knew."

He shook the pain from his hand again, as the creature flew away, quickly seeking refuge in the hole in the tree. The others, still circling above, sensed that one of their own may be in trouble, and they broke from their smooth and hypnotic flow. Their tenor grew agitated, and the collective hum of their wings increased in fervor and volume. Their motion turned from smooth and flowing to darting and aggressive, like a swarm of angry hornets.

"Oh no," Scarlet said. "Look at what you've done now."

With a collective hum of beating wings loud enough to make one's ears ring, the Bardwogs descended on the group, fearless, biting ferociously, over and over.

"We need to get out of here," Scarlet said. "And quickly."

Desperate to hold the ash tablet steady, she tried to maneuver her shoulders in a way that would scrape the Bardwogs from her ears and neck, without shaking the tablet. It took every ounce of discipline she had to not drop the tablet and run, or to use the tablet to swat them away. Michael, Copper and Vixen waved their arms and slapped themselves where bitten, but even a dozen hands would be insufficient to shoo so many away. Vixen screamed out in uncharacteristic pain after a deep bite on the back of her neck.

"Everybody run!" Michael shouted.

And run they did. In all different directions. Scarlet took off as fast as she could. She held the tablet straight out in front of her at arm's length, focusing on her strides. She tried, with the greatest of effort, not to bounce, fearful she might break up the fragile ash inside. Vixen and Copper ran in the same basic direction, but Michael went the opposite way. The further they got from the hive, the less aggressive the Bardwogs acted, until they finally relented and returned to their hive. Comfortable that he was out of reach, Michael stopped to gather his bearing.

"Vixen? Copper? Scarlet?"

Nobody responded. Michael was alone. Anxious to get back to the boat, he tried to find the best way back. As he stamped through the bushes looking for footprints, or something leading back to the path, he noticed something laying under the leaves of a fern. It was an injured wood sylph, a young female fae. She was laying on the ground, barely conscious, almost completely hidden by the foliage. He knelt and scooped her off the ground.

"What happened to you?" he said out loud, not really expecting a response. "I nearly crushed you under my boot, are you alright?"

He cradled her in his cupped hands and she slowly sat upright. She was weak and despondent. One of her opalescent wings was broken and flopped over. She was gagged with a cloth over her tiny mouth and her hands were tied behind her back.

"Who would have done this to you?" he asked.

He rolled her delicately into the palm of one hand. With a finger, he moved the gag down from her mouth. Once she was free of the gag, she let out a piercing wail, an apparent call for help. But when she let out her siren-shriek, the sound didn't originate just from her mouth. It came from everywhere. All across the wood, and all at once. In front of him, behind him, from every direction he could hear her call, the sound of thousands of sylphs seemingly yelling together in a choral unison. The familiar glow of the Bardwogs moved toward him, and his shoulders dropped.

"Oh no, not again."

The din of their wings grew closer, louder than before, their numbers had certainly grown. There was no sense in running, they were moving too fast, and coming right at him. As they came closer, he instinctively put his arms up, in an attempt to block the coming assault. He still held the wood sylph, cupped in his hand.

"Stop!"

The voice of an elder fae echoed through the wooded area. It was an unfamiliar voice, and like the sylph's scream, it didn't come from just one place. The voice came from everywhere, all at once.

"Patriella is with him," the voice said.

The Bardwogs stopped, hovering momentarily, then settling into a calm swirl.

"Do not harm him," the voice bellowed. "Not yet, anyway."

From behind the front lines of the Bardwog ranks, an elderly fae emerged, fluttering slowly forward until he hovered right in front of Michael's face, just out of arm's reach. The flutter of his wings sounded like a hummingbird. He had the wise look of a tribal elder, with dark sullen eyes devoid of colored irises. He was twice the size of the sylph Michael held in his hands and, at nearly a foot tall, he was a giant among fae.

Haunting, echoing and deep, his voice reverberated as he spoke.

"I trust you meant my daughter no harm. Release her to my care so that we may tend to her injuries."

Michael was conflicted. As near as he could tell, she had already been taken once. Was she taken by this fae, or by someone else? He looked down at the sylph. She looked back up him, her eyes expecting to be released, and her face showed no signs of an unwillingness to go. She looked calm, her posture was relaxed. He held his hand out, cradling the Sylph in his palm. The elderly fae fluttered forward and plucked her from Michael's hand. He whisked her over to a cluster of Bardwogs so that they could tend to her.

"Take Patriella to the Home Tree, and see to it that she is properly cared for."

The Bardwogs shuttled the sylph away, and the elderly fae returned to address Michael.

"I don't know what you did," he began.

Michael shook his head.

"I didn't do anything to harm her," Michael said. "I swear. I just found her laying here under the fern. I had nothing to do with any of this."

The elderly fae raised his hand to interrupt.

"As I was saying. I don't know what you did to free my daughter from her captors, but I am eternally grateful that we found her safely. She was abducted by a small group of our own kind, a rogue faction that chose to break ranks with the rest of us, an attempted coup. We know who they are, and they will be dealt with in due course. With that said, whether you intended to or not, you have secured her safe return."

"I, like I said, I didn't really do anything," Michael said.

"Not so much as you are aware. But she has been returned to us and for that, I wish to compensate you. Our laws demand nothing less."

The elderly fae fluttered past Michael, floating effortlessly toward a tall outcrop of rocks jutting up from the soil. A detachment of purple Bardwogs flanked him as he went, five on either side.

"If you could please follow me," the elderly fae said as he fluttered into the distance.

Michael followed behind him, walking toward the rocky outcrop, wondering where they were going; and whether he should be going at all.

VIXEN, SCARLET AND COPPER EVENTUALLY FOUND EACH OTHER. They searched in vain, however, to find Michael.

"Do you think he is safe?" Vixen asked. "I hope he's not badly hurt. Or worse."

Scarlet scowled, resentful of her concern.

"I think he'll be just fine," Scarlet said.

Each one of them had suffered numerous bites, with red arc-shaped marks and visible welts raised on their skin from the creatures' wide curved jaws. Vixen touched her fingers to the back of her neck to check a particularly painful bite. When she looked at her fingers, they were wet with blood. Her voice trembled, and her knees wobbled at the sight.

"Oh my, that's a bad one," she said.

Scarlet walked behind Vixen.

"Let me see," she said.

Scarlet tipped Vixen's head down and brushed her hair aside.

"It looks like a purple one got to you. And he took a good chunk with him. The purple are the worst. They represent the third level of metamorphosis, blue being the first and green being the second. Not many make it to the third stage. But the ones that do are particularly vicious."

She leaned down to the ground to scrape up some of the moist soil from the path and dabbed it on Vixen's wound, like a mud poultice.

"This will help dull the pain and stem the bleeding. Don't touch it, just leave it alone and you'll be fine. Now let's go find Michael."

DORADO AND WILL HAD REACHED THEIR BOATS. EACH MAN HAD boarded his craft, and pushed off from the beach. Floating in the lagoon, they bobbed in its calm waters, and waited for the time to pass, while swells of water gently lapped at their hulls. There was no place to go until the tide allowed it. So they sat patiently, watching the other participants, waiting for their next chance to pass back out from Cragtooth Tunnel.

"COME IN HERE, PLEASE."

The elderly fae led Michael inside the rocky outcrop, and

through a narrow crevice in the rock formation. It was a tight squeeze for Michael to get through, given his size, but the fae and his Bardwogs fluttered through with ease. Feeling claustrophobic, he managed to squeeze past the last, and most narrow part of the crevice, which opened up to a cavern within the center of the outcrop. Bardwogs swirled above, casting a glow on the cavern walls and lighting its interior. The walls of the cavern were studded with veins of beautifully colored crystals growing from fissures in the otherwise dull, grey stone.

"What is this place?" Michael asked.

"We call this place the Mother Stone. She is the center, and the lifeblood, of Faerie Wood. Her crystalline gifts provide for us in many ways."

He fluttered over and plucked out a crystal from an emerald-green vein, and fluttered back to Michael to drop it into his palm.

"You may never see us, even now, when you know to look for us," he said. "But we are everywhere, connected together through the Mother Stone. If you are ever in need our help, just rub this crystal. We will be there for you. Take this as my gift to you, a reward for your assistance in helping us to find Patriella. I hope someday that we can return the favor to you."

"I don't know what to say, other than thank you," Michael said.

He looked at the green crystal.

"I appreciate this very much," he said, and he put it in his pocket.

"Just rub the crystal and say my name," the fae said.

"What is your name?"

"My name is how others refer to me."

"Yes I understand that. But what do the others call you?"

"They call me by saying my name. I've already told you everything you need to know."

Michael was frustrated by the circular conversation. But he didn't want to come across as ungrateful, so he changed the subject.

"What about Patriella? Will she be ok? Can you fix her wing?"

The elderly fae fluttered to a different vein and plucked out an orange-colored crystal.

"A few strokes of this crystal across her wing," he said in his echoing voice, "and Patriella will be just fine."

As the fae fluttered back toward the entrance, Michael stared for a second, thinking.

"Wait!" Michael said. "I certainly don't mean to sound greedy. But is there any chance I could take one of those orange crystals with me? For a dear friend. He is on our boat at the beach now. He injured his ankle pretty badly, and it's probably broken. Do you think it could help him?"

"On one condition and one condition only. You must never speak of this place," the elderly fae said.

Michael nodded.

"Absolutely. You have my word on that. Thank you."

Michael walked over to the vein of orange crystals to pluck one out. He tried one after the other, but none came loose. He looked at the elderly fae, feeling confused. He had just watched the far pull them out with ease, but Michael struggled.

"I can't get any loose," he said.

"Of course not, young man. You can't just take it. It has to be given to you."

"And who might be the one to give it to me?"

The elderly fae fluttered over next to Michael, his wings humming. The fae plucked an orange crystal from the vein, as easily as he might have picked a pencil from a table.

"The Mother Stone. She gives to me, and I, in turn, give to you."

He handed Michael the orange crystal.

"Like I said, you must never speak of this place, or tell anyone where this came from. We've been here for thousands of years, and our secret must stay with you. If not, it could be the end of us."

"Why would you take such a risk to help me? You don't even know me."

"You have honest eyes, young man, and you appear to be in genuine need. I have a good sense about these things and I trust you."

"You have my word," Michael said.

The elderly fae fluttered out through the crevice, with the Bardwogs flanking him. Michael squeezed through behind him. As they left the Mother Stone, the elderly fae fluttered up into the canopy and disappeared among the leaves. The Bardwogs followed close behind, and disappeared into the foliage also. Their glow dissipated, and he found himself standing alone in the darkness, among a cluster of unremarkable trees, cold and alone.

"That was simply incredible," he mumbled to himself. "Did that really just happen?"

He checked his pocket watch, and when he saw the time, he realized he had precious little of it left to get back to the beach. Deep in the heart of the island, a sinking feeling set in and he started to panic. He had lost touch with his team and had no idea where he was. It was a long way back and time was running out to make it through the tunnel.

35

AND THAT'S WHAT'S IMPORTANT, RIGHT?

Uncertain, and feeling lost, Michael followed his gut in the direction he thought gave him the best chance of leading back to the beach. He checked his pocket watch again, concerned about the time. There was little room for error, and little time to backtrack. His mind wandered wildly, from his encounter with the fae, to John's ankle, to the tides and the tunnel. From the tunnel to the remainder of the race, and from there to the spoils of victory. The spoils of victory would mark the accomplishment of a lifelong dream and would allow him to save his mother's homestead. It would be an achievement to make his father proud, if only he could be there to see it. Thoughts of his father, of course, led to thoughts of his mother. He hoped she was getting by in his absence, staying safe, not feeling lonely, not doing anything too strenuous. Before he left, he had asked Colin to stop by after work once in a while, to check on her. Colin said he would, but deep down Michael knew he probably wouldn't.

That was when Michael realized how long it had been since he had even thought about his mother. His stomach sank with a knot of mixed emotion. Of course he missed her, but there was more to it than just that. He felt a pang of guilt. He felt awful about forgetting to think of her; for leaving her alone to care for herself the way he had. Guilty for being gone, for getting so wrapped up in his own self-interest, for not being there for her if she needed something, the way he had been his entire life. The feelings stirred his soul, and fixed in him a certain determination. Failure was not an option. He had to get back to the boat. He hastened his stride just as he heard someone calling out in the distance. It was a woman's voice.

"Michael," he thought he heard. But it was just a faded shout in the distance.

"Scarlet?" he yelled back.

"Yes, where are you?"

"Over this way," he yelled through the foliage.

He marched toward her voice. Soon, he heard the welcome sounds of Copper and Vixen's voices. When they finally came together in a small clearing, he saw Vixen. He smiled wide, and walked toward her with open arms. Their eyes met, her face lit up as bright as the summer sun. He was just about to wrap his arms around her, when Scarlet stepped into his path. She threw herself into his arms and wrapped her hands behind his head. She held him in a long, warm embrace, before slowly loosening her grip.

"Oh thank God you're safe," Scarlet said. "I was, um, *we* were so worried about you. It's such a relief to see you're alright. You gave us such a scare, where did you run off to?"

He looked over Scarlet's shoulder at Vixen. He was uncomfortable and unsure how to react. He appreciated the attention, but he was also reluctant to offend anyone, Scarlet included. Reluctant to say or do the wrong thing, to display the wrong reaction, he stuck with what he knew best. He chose not to react at all. Deep inside, he regretted it immediately. He stood with Scarlet in his arms, watching as Vixen processed the meaning of his silence. The brightness in her eyes faded. The curve of her smile went straight. The pits of her dimples filled in gradually, until they were gone.

Michael stepped back from Scarlet's arms, trying to ignore what had just happened.

"Yes, well, anyway," he said. "It's complicated, but when the Bardwogs attacked us, I had to get away. I didn't really think about where I was going, I just ran off, as you all did. But here I am now."

He looked at Vixen, but her eyes would not meet with his.

"We're all back together now. And that's what is important, right?"

Vixen nodded politely, but didn't say a word. She stared at the ground, sullen.

"We can talk more along the way, but we should really get back to the beach," Michael said.

"Aye, that we should, so let's get to it, lad." Copper held up the ash tablet. "We've still got a mess of work to be done."

36

FIRST NORTH, THEN EAST, THE WIND DOTH BLOW

After an exhausting day that extended into the night, and what felt like a never-ending hike back to the beach, Michael and this team arrived at the *SS Soairse*. The Ringmaster's galleon had already pushed back, waiting in the lagoon for a chance to exit Cragtooth Tunnel. He approached his steamer, and inspected the damage caused by the tunnel wall. Most of the copper balls mounted on the left side had been destroyed, and the painted wood was badly scuffed and splintered in spots. The damage was otherwise superficial. The hull was intact, and there was no sign of a breach, so he boarded the steamer and joined the others inside. Kamal had prepared some food while they were away.

"Please eat," Kamal said. "I gathered some fruits from nearby trees, and I managed to catch some fish, which I roasted over a small fire on the beach. The waters of this lagoon are both rich and generous. There is plenty for everyone."

"Oh, thank the heavens," Copper said. "I'm so hungry, I could eat my own head."

"I am not even sure how that is possible," Kamal said, "but I hope you will find this to be a worthy substitute."

"Where is John?" Michael asked.

Kamal nodded toward the back of the cabin. John sat in a bench, lengthwise, with his ankle splinted and his foot elevated.

"How are you doing? Can you walk?"

"Nah, no chance."

John looked like a caged animal, angry and agitated.

"I have something that might help," Michael said. "Hold still."

Michael raised John's pant leg to expose his ankle. It was bruised and badly swollen. He pulled the orange crystal from his pocket and rubbed it across the exposed ankle. As he rubbed it back and forth, the crystal glowed and sparkled.

"It feels warm," John said. "And the pain is going away. What the hell is that thing?"

"It's just something I found. I thought it might help."

Michael rubbed the crystal across John's ankle a few more times.

"Hand it up here, boy. Let me see it," John said.

"I can't," Michael said, holding up an empty hand.

"It's dissolved, or whatever you want to call it. But it's gone now."

He turned his hand side to side. There was nothing in it.

"That's amazing. I feel no pain at all. I feel perfect. We should go back and get a bucket full of those crystals. They could fetch a king's ransom at home. We could make an absolute fortune."

Michael hadn't considered the idea on his own and it made him think. It would certainly solve his financial woes, and then some. But he shook his head. He'd given his word.

"No, it's a waste of time, and we have more pressing things to deal with. It was just laying on the beach and it caught my eye for some reason, I'm not sure why. But in any event, I didn't see any others like it."

"On this beach?" John pressed.

Michael's voice faltered, and his eyes darted around. He'd said too much. To lie made him uncomfortable. To lie to someone like

John, whom he respected so greatly, was doubly difficult. But he had given his word to the elderly fae. This little lie was required, and John would be no worse off for it. Honor ranked above all, superior to money and even friendship. Even this friendship.

"No, not this beach," Michael said. "The beach near the stone mill, at Gillingham."

John stood up from the bench, gradually testing the ankle. It held up fine.

"Well that's a damn shame, boy, because it feels superb! It's as good as new! I'll have go check the beach at Gillingham after all this is finished, to see if there's any more."

John untied the splint and threw it aside, and motioned toward the food.

"Let's eat."

"It's good to see you feeling better," Scarlet said.

"It's good to *be* feeling better," John replied. "How did it go out there? Did you get the token?"

"We did."

"That's good, that's very good indeed."

He looked at Scarlet curiously.

"What the hell happened to your face?" he asked.

Scarlet was taken aback, but then she remembered the bardwog encounter.

"To all your faces," John said. "And Jesus, your arms as well. You all look a bloody mess. No offense."

"Bardwogs," Scarlet said.

"Bar-who?"

"Bardwogs. They travel with fae. Seriously, how does nobody know about these things? They are fierce, protective and loyal to a fault. We passed so many faerie rings on our hike, by the way, that I completely lost count. This island must be very densely populated."

"Faerie rings?" John asked.

"Yes. Rings of mushrooms, indicating the presence of fae."

"Right," he said.

He looked around at the others. Then he turned his attention back to Scarlet.

"And did you happen to eat some of these mushrooms, while you were out there?"

His tone was condescending.

"Because it sounds like you might be hallucinating."

Michael interrupted.

"She's exactly right," he said, as he opened his pocket watch.

He didn't elaborate any further.

"Time is short. We should get back to work."

He snapped the watch shut and put it back in his pocket.

"Well. Look at you, trying to be on time and all. Where is this coming from?" John asked.

"Like I said before, I plan to win this. I have to win. So let's not take any chances."

Copper placed the ash tablet onto the table next to the food.

"Let's get to it," he said.

Michael glanced at at the ash tablet, and walked out of the cabin door.

"I'll be right back," he said. "I need to grab the pins."

He went to his chest, pulled the key from his pocket, unlocked the lid and opened it. He reached in and pulled out the glass vial of pins, and the parchment note that accompanied it. He started back to the cabin, but stopped to look at the contents of the chest. It was mostly filled with old tools; they were scuffed, tarnished and well-worn from years of use. The tools were all arranged neatly inside in little wooden trays, like with like, screws, bolts and whatnot all sorted in jars. It was neat and orderly with everything in its place, just the way Michael liked it. He sighed as he inspected them. For every tool he looked at, he could remember a project that he and his father had worked on together. In some cases, he could even remember a specific conversation that occurred while he held the tool in his hand.

A hinged bi-folding picture frame sat on top of the box of wrenches, and in the frame there were two sepia-tone photographs. One was a picture of Michael and Seamus, the other was a picture Seamus and Soairse. Michael smiled fondly at seeing them. It had been a long time. The way Seamus looked at Soairse, he had so much love in his eyes. And Seamus holding Michael in the air, hands cradling the curves of Michael's armpits, looking up, bursting with pride. Even in still photographs, Seamus seemed so full of life.

He pulled out the top tray from the chest to reveal a lower compartment. The lower compartment held more tools, spare parts, pipe, gears and the like, even an oil lamp and a torch. It also held several automatons that he and Seamus had built together in his youth. Some showed signs of damage suffered during live play. There was also an old envelope, smudged with the grime of having been opened many times by dirty hands. The paper had long ago surrendered its stiffness; it was pliable, worn and creased, having been opened and closed so many times before. Michael opened the envelope one more time, and pulled out a letter. He could hear Seamus' voice speaking to him as he read it.

My dear son Michael:

On this, your eleventh birthday, I wanted to give you a special gift, as my father did for me on mine. In truth, I actually have two gifts to give. Both are of very little cost, but it is my sincere hope that you will attach to each a tremendous amount of value.

The first is this chest. It's the chest that my father gave me on my eleventh birthday. It belongs to you now, my son. I hope you come to treasure it the same way I have, and that one day you will have the chance to share it with a son of your own. Not just the chest, but the all memories and experiences that go along with it.

The second is just some simple advice, in which I hope you find some inspiration: Branch out, and explore life. Live your life in such a way that when you are aged, and reflecting back on the life you lived, you have no regrets; neither for the choices you made, nor the things you left unsaid. Rather, I hope that you will have lived your life in a manner that enabled you, as you look back, to take tremendous pride in the paths you chose, and to marvel in your many accomplishments. Push fear and self-doubt aside, live with honor, and allow your ambitions, colored by wisdom and common sense, to guide you to the full achievement of all your life's desires. I believe in you. And you should never settle for anything less.

With Love,

Poppa.

MICHAEL PONDERED THE WORDS HE HAD READ SO MANY TIMES before. They were especially meaningful today.

"I'm trying, Poppa," he whispered to himself, "but we were supposed to do this together."

He put the note back in the envelope and carefully tucked in the flap. He wiped his nose with the back of his wrist with a sniff, and carefully set the note back into the lower compartment before placing the upper tray back on top. After putting everything back and locking up the chest, careful to double-check, he rattled the pins in the vial and started back to the cabin.

"Here are the pins," Michael said.

"Well, it's about time," Copper said.

"Sorry."

He set the vial on the table.

Scarlet unwound the fine copper wire, pulled the cork and poured the pins into the palm of her hand. She inspected them before she set them on the table.

"Well, open the blasted tablet then," Copper said.

"Not just yet."

"Come on, what now?"

"Just one last thing worth mentioning," Scarlet said. "There is probably a fixed order to follow, when we insert the pins. Sometimes, if you insert the pins in the wrong sequence, it can set the arm off anyway. Same as if you had no pins at all."

Michael realized he was still holding the sheet of parchment.

"This note was with the pins when I found them," he said. "Maybe it will help."

Scarlet read the note out loud.

First north, then east, the wind doth blow
South, then west, will let it go
Box in building, shape of a block
Pins like wind can crack the lock

"Oh, well isn't that just right helpful?" Copper said. "Maybe Vixen can pour some of her glowing goo on top. That, plus your note, and we're still no better off."

"Not true," Scarlet said. "The place where we found the ash tablet, it was in a simple block-shaped building. So, we found a box, in a building *shaped like a block*. So north, east, south, west. That should be the sequence of the pins. To crack the lock."

"That's not a sequence," John said. "How is that a sequence?"

She pointed to the front of the ash tablet, with its dimpled design of a compass face and the arrow pointing up at a capital letter N.

"This is north," she said. She ran her finger from the compass face up to the top of the ash tablet. She tapped her finger on the hole in the top edge.

"And if that's north, then this is east, this is south, and this is west."

"Brilliant," Vixen said. "Then let's open it. Stick the first pin in the top."

"Not so fast," she said.

"Oh, bloody hell. Of course not," Copper said, throwing his hands in the air. "You again, with interrupting things. What is it this time?"

"Shouldn't we start at the bottom?" Scarlet said. "Pins like wind can crack the lock. The first direction listed is north. If a wind blows north, doesn't it originate from the south, and blow northward? I think we should put the first pin in at the bottom, running from south to north, like the wind blowing in a northerly direction."

"If I may," Kamal said, holding up a finger.

"Yes, please do," Scarlet said.

"I must respectfully disagree with you. A northerly wind actually blows from the north. We speak of wind in terms of it's origin. A northerly wind actually comes from the relative north, and blows southward."

"That sounds totally backwards," Copper said. "I think you're dead wrong on this. And my gut don't lie."

"I think Kamal may actually be right," John said.

Kamal sounded certain, but the room was split. They stared at each other waiting for someone to make a decision. Vixen picked up the pins and rolled them around in her palm as she walked around the table.

"So Michael," she said as she approached him slowly. "You're going to have to make a choice here. Scarlet would start at the bottom, south to north. Some here agree with that choice. I, for one, think it's best to start at the top, from north to south. Like Kamal said. What do you think?"

She stepped closer and looked him in the eye. She grabbed his hand, cupped it and dropped the pins into his palm.

"This is in your hands now, Michael. The decision is all yours to make. It's totally up to you."

She closed his fingers around the pins and held his hand between hers, looking him in the eye still, never breaking contact.

"So what's it going to be, Michael? Are you with Scarlet on this? Or are you with me? Do you want the top? Or the bottom?"

John, Copper and Kamal watched, discomfort on their faces. Michael stood silent, painfully self-aware. He hated being put on the spot like that. It was bad enough that she had asked him to make a decision that would affect the whole team, something so important as the opening of the ash tablet which could be their entire key to the next leg of the race; but he also knew she was asking for a decision on something else. As oblivious as Michael could be at times, notorious for missing subtle cues and casual innuendo more times than not, he was crystal clear on this. He knew the weight of his words, and the meaning they would carry. Feeling cornered and uneasy, he chose the words with care and he spoke them with hesitation.

"I have a great deal of faith in Kamal's capabilities, as a sailor and as a navigator. He has proven himself to be extremely competent so far. If Kamal says northerly winds blow from the north to the south, and that we should start at the top of the tablet, then I think that's what we should do."

"Jesus, lad," Copper muttered under his breath. "You are unbelievable."

He shook his head and wiped his hand from his forehead down across his face and off his chin.

"How can you be so smart, and so bloody stupid at the same damn time?"

37

THE ASH TABLET

Michael inspected the hole in the top of the ash tablet. It was shaped like a star, so he pinched the star-shaped pin between his thumb and forefinger.

"It's do or die time, my friends. Fingers crossed everyone."

He held the pin near the hole in the top of the ash tablet. He could see the shape and size matched perfectly, so he pressed the pin into place. At first, it slid in freely. But then it met some resistance, like it was pressing against something on the inside. He pressed a little harder and he could feel something give. The pin snapped into place with a satisfying click, flush with the outer edge of the tablet. He pressed the remaining pins into their respective holes in the agreed upon order. Each pin snapped into place securely. There was no indication anything inside had let loose and destroyed the ash.

He looked up at Scarlet.

"Is that it?"

"That should be it. You should be able to press the button to release the inner tray. Go slowly and be careful with it."

Michael pressed the button and the inner tray released,

protruding slightly from the bottom. He slid the tray out carefully, and as he drew it out, he saw a flat, solid ashen sheet nestled within. A corner had broken off, but it was otherwise intact.

"Careful, lad!" Copper yelled. "Don't break it."

Michael flinched, then glared at Copper. If looks could kill, Copper might have suffered a moderate injury. He turned his focus back to the tray, pulled it completely out of the tablet casing and set it on the table. Like Scarlet had predicted, the tray held a thin sheet of ash. In the sheet of ash, there was some darker ash, colored by metallic ink, bearing a hand-written message.

Congratulations on making it this far. If you are reading this, you have already proven yourself quite worthy. That alone is a feat unto itself, but you're not finished yet. The last leg of the race, the air leg, still lies ahead, beginning in Rouen. On this leg, you are to navigate your airship through two aerial gates. You will find the first gate in the gardens at the Champs de Mars in Paris. Pass your craft through this gate, land in the gardens and proceed to the shop of J. Andouille, Clockmaker, in the downtown. If you keep a sharp eye, and you know what to say, you may receive further instructions from there.

"How much time do we have before the tide reaches its peak?" Michael asked.

"It's nearly 1:00 am. So we only have about twenty minutes," Kamal said. "We should go. Now."

"Right."

"It's several more hours to Rouen once we leave the tunnel," Kamal said. "May I suggest that we rotate and share the shifts piloting the ship? I'm sure we could all use some rest."

"Yes, agreed," John said. "Off you go. I can take it from here."

John walked out to the deck, to man the wheel.

The fatigue on Michael's face spoke for itself, it had been a grueling day. His teammates had already settled into any half-comfortable spot they could find to get some much-needed rest.

"If it is not too inconvenient," Kamal said, "I could benefit from a good slumber myself. And no offense to you or anybody else, but I would prefer the privacy of closed quarters, if I may."

"There's not much privacy here," Michael said, "but you're welcome to go down to the engine compartment. That's really all there is."

Kamal bowed and thanked Michael. He walked over to his bag, pulled out his cloth roll-up case and ventured down to the engine compartment. It was time to observe his evening ritual. Copper stretched out on a bench seat and kicked his feet up. With his feet up, and his hand tucked behind his head, he was snoring before Kamal could even make it below deck. Scarlet, exhausted in her own right, curled up in a chair with a wrap from her bag. Vixen stood outside, on the deck, leaning on a rail and gazing over the water. She was focused and contemplative. Michael joined her on deck as John backed the steamer off the beach and turned the bow toward the tunnel.

DORADO AND WILL EACH SAT BOBBING IN THE WATERS NEAR THE tunnel, just yards from the Ringmaster's galleon. While they waited, the moonlight danced off the shimmering waters like sequins spilled across the floor. On board the galleon, Belladonna, Phillippe and Mechanicules stood at the ready.

"So what's the plan, love? Are we going to just sit here all night?" Belladonna asked.

The Ringmaster breathed in deeply and sighed through his nose. He liked to maintain an air of control, but he found himself relying on the expertise of his competition. That made him uneasy.

"We will go when Kamal goes," the Ringmaster said.

"Do you see the steamer?"

"Not from here, it's too dark, and they're too far. We'll see them soon enough though."

"You're going to just follow them through the tunnel again?"

"Not this time," he said.

He turned away from Belladonna.

"Phillippe. On my mark, you hoist the sails. I want to move in front of them as they approach. We should be the first ones through the tunnel. I want this boat to be the first boat out the other side, do you understand me?"

"Yes, I can do it," Phillippe said with a nod. "You just say the word to me."

"I think I hear them coming now, get ready. As they get closer, we'll pull right in front of them and pass through the tunnel, just as they would have."

The slapping of the paddle wheel grew louder as it got closer to the galleon.

"Now!" the Ringmaster shouted. "Go!"

Phillippe hoisted the sails. The sails filled with wind and snapped taut. The Ringmaster steered the ship toward the tunnel, directly into their path. John slowed to veer out of the way, but righted his course to get on track. He was headed straight for the entrance. Dorado and Will raised sails and followed the pack out. Nigel, for his part, kept close.

"Careful, love," Belladonna said.

Her tone was condescending.

"Just leave the sailing to me, will you?"

Phillippe hunkered down and held on tight in case of a collision. Belladonna, on the other hand, was aware of the risk, and she relished in it. She stood fully upright, with her arms stretched out at her sides. She tipped her head back, and closed her eyes, standing completely prone against the rail. She gulped in a deep breath of the wet, salty air, closed her eyes and let the thin braids of her hair whip against her cheek. The mouth of Cragtooth Tunnel, and its rocky base, were fast approaching. Despite the danger, she felt at ease, accepting of it; welcoming in fact. She dared the fates to try and touch her. And if they did, she thought, nothing worse than sweet release would follow. There was no downside.

"Brace yourselves," the Ringmaster shouted.

Mech and Phillippe did as he said. Belladonna didn't react, except to lean harder on the rail. She stayed standing upright with her arms outstretched, waiting with her eyes closed. If the sea would have her, she was ready. In the end though, Kamal's calculations proved correct, and the galleon sailed through the mouth of Cragtooth Tunnel without incident, into the open waters of the English channel. Feeling suddenly drained by a strange mix of invigoration and disappointment, Belladonna retired below the deck for the evening.

"That's enough fun for today," she said, and headed down below.

"Toodles, gentlemen."

"I'm right behind you," the Ringmaster said. "Mech, you take the helm from here. You know the way. Any questions, you know where the map is."

Mechanicules nodded and took the wheel.

"Phillippe, get some sleep. There's still a lot to do."

He walked down the stairs, below deck, to find an empty bed.

John steered the steamer toward Rouen. At the rear, Michael approached Vixen and tried to start a conversation.

As he stood beside her, he pointed up into the sky.

"Hey, look. A dead bird."

"What?"

"I don't know. It's just something funny my father used to say, as a tension breaker. A distraction from less pleasant thoughts."

"Dead birds are funny to you?"

"Well, no. I mean. It's just funny, because why would a dead bird be up in the air? Nevermind. Forget I said anything."

She grinned, but only slightly, and reluctantly. He could see her lips tense up, she was stubbornly holding back a smile.

"Did it work?" he asked.

"Maybe a little."

"What are you doing out here? It's cold. And late. You should go inside and rest."

"I appreciate your concern," she said. "I'm quite capable to care for myself. But thank you all the same."

"The choice you were asking me to make in there, it wasn't just about the tablet. Was it?"

"I said what I said. You can read into it what you will."

"Why are you so upset?"

"Oh, you think this is upset? It's nothing of the sort, Mr. McGillicuddy. You haven't seen upset."

He paused.

"Look. That evening in Gillingham. After the game parlor. We had a moment, didn't we?"

"Yes, and it was an amazing moment," she said. "But the moment has since passed, I'm afraid. I may have gotten ahead of myself, swept up in the excitement of it all. But I never should have been so forward. I've just been feeling very confused. So if it's all the same to you, let's just say it never happened."

"But it did happen, so I can't really say that. Can you? Honestly?"

"Honestly?"

"Yes. Honestly."

She paused.

"If I'm being honest, the fatigue of the day has really set in, and I need to get some sleep. I'll see you tomorrow, Mr. McGillicuddy. Goodnight."

She walked back to the cabin, leaving him on the deck by himself.

"Sleep well, Ms. Van Buren," he said.

He sighed, watching the moonlight glisten over the water's surface.

38

MECH'S BACKGROUND

Belladonna returned to her cabin below deck. She entered to find Beatrix already there, unannounced and uninvited. She looked happy to see Belladonna, and greeted her with a grin. Their last encounter hadn't ended well, but it was in Beatrix' nature to keep trying.

"There you are!" Beatrix said.

"What are you doing here?"

"Are you always this rude, or just to me?"

"No. It's pretty much always. Is there something you need?"

"I just wanted to visit. All this action has me feeling energized, there's no way I could sleep right now!"

"Sorry, cupcake. I don't *visit*."

"That's fine, I'll start."

"What's the history with you and Phillippe? There's something there. There is right?"

"It hardly bears repeating."

An awkward silence hung in the air, like the stench of spoiled meat. But Beatrix was undeterred.

"What about Mech? He's so dark and brooding. And quiet. What happened with his arm?"

Beatrix' energy was disarming. Contagious. Intoxicating, even to the likes of Belladonna.

"Not that I owe you any sort of explanation," Belladonna said, "but he hurt himself during a performance. It was a long time ago. He was doing one of his one-armed heavy lifts when he faltered and dislocated his shoulder."

"That's it?"

"No, that's not even close to being it. The dislocation was bad enough. But it was nothing compared to the ordeal he endured after."

"What happened?"

"Protective of his assets, as he always is, the Ringmaster took Mech for medical attention. But he didn't visit just any doctor. He went to see Dr. Christian Blackheart. He does things different from most, and has a penchant for experimental procedures. Mech's injury was mild, and his shoulder could have been reset and left to heal in a sling. It would have been an easy recovery if only given the time. But that wasn't good enough for the Ringmaster. He didn't trust the injured shoulder, and feared it would only fail again later. That would be inconvenient for him. He wanted something better, something stronger. And I don't mean better for Mech. I mean better for himself, better for his show. Dr. Blackheart made a proposal, which the Ringmaster happily accepted. Right in front of the young boy, already suffering from the shock of his own injury, the two men reached an agreement amongst themselves. Mech's arm would be surgically removed and replaced with that mechanical monstrosity in its place. He was aged fourteen at the time."

"Oh my god."

"Right, as if one actually exists to allow such treatment. Nobody asked Mech what he wanted, not that it would have mattered anyway. He was immediately restrained, sedated and surgically altered."

"That's terrible."

"Like you have any idea at all. The trauma of it all affected him deeply. So deeply, in fact, he hasn't spoken a single word since."

"That's why he never talks?"

"It is."

"And how do you know all of this?"

Belladonna paused.

"I was there. I wouldn't let them go without me."

"Aw crackers, I can't even imagine," Beatrix said. "You're very close, yes? I suppose you always have been."

"We certainly should be, cupcake. He is my little brother, after all."

Beatrix sat staring, mouth hanging open, struggling to understand what a young Mech must have gone through against his will. What life the two of them must have lived here.

"The Ringmaster, of course, convinced Mech that it was all his fault to begin with, for allowing himself to get hurt in the first place. He told him he could have avoided the procedure if only he had been more careful, but now he had no choice. It's always somebody' else's fault. Mech's physical recovery was long, but he got through it. He eventually accepted his circumstance and adapted as well as he could. But emotionally? That's a different story."

Beatrix shook her head in disbelief.

"We've both been part of this sham circus since childhood, it's the only home we've ever known. Our parents brought us here when we were young. They died in an accident, and the Ringmaster took us in. He's looked after us from a young age and we've been here since."

"So why stay? You never seem very happy to be here, so why don't you just leave?"

Belladonna stared silently. After a long pause, she responded.

"Too many questions. You know where the door is."

She turned her back to Beatrix and readied herself for bed.

39

THE VERUDITE ENCOUNTER

Michael and his crew had long since fallen asleep. With the space afforded by the open waters and the steamer's superior speed, John took a lead over the other boats. As he steered through the channel waters on the way to Rouen, John looked back over his shoulder. The Ringmaster's galleon was close behind, helped by a strong tailwind. He could see the silhouettes of the other vessels, backlit by a moon set low in the sky, as he reflected on his youth, and prior races. This was definitely the most challenging of all of them. Of this, he had no doubt. In some ways, the cards seemed stacked against him. Every participant always had a particular path to victory. But some paths seemed more difficult than others. Certain participants had been favored over others, seemingly by design, and right from the very beginning. Some, he thought, were just never meant to win at all. At least not without overcoming substantial odds.

Things hadn't gone the way he expected, not by any stretch. John liked things to go his own way, by his rules, on his decisions. But he was part of a talented and well-rounded team now. They were all good people. Tragically good. He pondered the difficult decisions he would face in the coming hours and days. They were decisions he didn't take lightly, decisions he didn't look forward to making at all.

The steamer cut deftly through the channel waters, and if John had somehow become lost in his own thoughts, that all changed with a loud and sudden bang. The noise reverberated through the water and echoed through the hull of the boat. The steamer lurched, as if it had run aground in the open waters; the bow dipped down and the back end raised up, before settling back on an even keel. John nearly fell again, but held the wheel tight to save himself. The turbulence woke Michael, Vixen and Scarlet. Copper stirred, but he didn't awaken. The women sat upright, and wiped the sleep from their eyes, as Michael rose and rushed out to the deck.

"Are you alright?" he asked.

"I'm fine," John said, "but I have no idea what that was. We're in the middle of deep channel waters. It can't be rock or land, and it most certainly isn't ice."

"I have a guess what it was," Michael said.

He raised his eyebrows and paused dramatically.

"Well, what is it boy? Spit it out."

"Verudites."

"Oh, bloody hell. It is that time of year, now, isn't it? This is not good. Not good at all."

The channel waters, between Ring Island and the coast of France, serve as a vast breeding ground for verudites, distant but gigantic cousins of the chambered nautilus. With their large pearl white spiral shells streaked with reddish-orange, they quietly propel themselves backward through the water. Most of the time, nobody even knows they're there.

"If you're right, we've got a problem," John said. "Adult verudites can measure twenty feet across, boy. The distance across the eyeball can be the length of a man's arm. Their tentacles are thin but strong, and too numerous to count. At least forty, probably more. What countermeasures do you have?"

"I've taken precautions, John."

There was another bang, and the boat shook. Michael looked to the fan blade mounted on the cabin. It was spinning at a good rate, the belt looping down into the hull and back up again. Another collision cam, much stronger this time. Even Copper woke up. Vixen and Scarlet came out to the deck.

"What it the world is going on?" Vixen asked.

"It's spawning season," Michael said. "Verudites are particularly aggressive when they spawn."

"Verudites?" she said.

"That they are," John said. "And their tentacles can reach fifteen or even twenty feet long. And unlike an octopus, the tentacles don't have suckers. Just a hook-shaped bone at the end, sharp like a cat's claw, to hold its prey. And nestled inside the thicket of tentacles, just inside the shell, is a thick, beak-like mouth. You'll want to stay out of this water at any cost. Trust me on this."

"Are they predatory?" Vixen asked. "I mean, to us?"

"Less predatory, more territorial," Michael said. "Around this time every year they migrate through this channel to lay their eggs in the rocky coastal waters. They prefer to be left alone, and they defend their spawning grounds aggressively."

"Did you bring any barrel bombs," John asked. "I had a dozen on my boat, but they've since been lost."

"No, I didn't bring any."

"Well, why the hell not?"

"I prepared with other measures. Like I said in Gillingham, we're well equipped."

"What types of measures?"

Michael pointed upward.

"That fan atop the cabin."

"That's your defense? Oh good lord, boy, I thought you were smarter than that."

John waved his hand.

"That fan will do nothing against verudites."

"You didn't let me finish. The fan turns a belt on a pulley wheel. The belt, in turn, extends down to the belly of the ship and drives a number of other shafts and pulleys below. Those, in turn, drive a series of electrostatic Faraday discs. The Faraday discs spin against fine brushes, creating a tremendous amount of static electricity. The electricity is captured and stored in the belly of the boat using an array of Leyden jars, like capacitors or batteries, if you will."

"Oh. Ok, that sounds a little better, but then what?"

"Are you familiar with the work of Nikola Tesla?"

"I've heard of him," John said.

Vixen's ears perked up at the mention though, and she interrupted John.

"Are you talking about his Tesla coils?" she said. "With the metal spheres on top? Large bolts of electricity jump between them, like lightning?"

"That's exactly what I'm talking about," Michael said. "The copper balls on the outside of the steamer, they function like Tesla coils. When I close the blade switches at the back of the cabin, the electricity stored below discharges through the spheres. They're mounted around the perimeter of the boat, in case a verudite tries to overtake us in the channel."

"Barrel bombs would have been fine," John said.

" I don't know anything about explosives, John. Electricity and clockwork automation are more my medium. Besides, barrel bombs are just a deterrent. What if you run out, and a verudite latches on to the boat anyway? Then what?"

"I wouldn't let that happen. No chance."

The unmistakable sound of the cracking wood echoed across the water. In the distance, they could see a silhouette of one of the smaller boats. It was in distress. Then more cracking sounds. The mast of the boat tilted to forty-five degrees and waved back and forth. The vessel was being tossed like a child's toy, a verudite was having its way.

"Oh my god, is that Will's boat?" Vixen asked.

"I can't tell," Michael said. "It's either him, or Nigel. Maybe one of the others."

The steamer bumped and lurched again, but the clang was followed by a new sound. A whipping sound, whooshing and cutting through the air, one after another. Tentacles whipped over the port side of the steamer. It's bony claw slammed down, lodging into the wooden deck. Another whoosh and another thud. A second claw sunk deep in the wooden deck.

"Get back inside!" John yelled. "Those hooks will tear through you like a hot knife through butter."

Vixen and Scarlet scurried inside, but Michael went around the side.

"I have to get to the switch," Michael said.

Another one whipped past and set deep into the deck, right in front of him. With several hooks set, the verudite pulled its tentacles tight. Their tension broke the side rail in two spots. Another hook flung over the side. The verudite pulled down toward the water. The hook hadn't completely set, and when the tentacle pulled back, it came loose and ripped another portion of the side rail clean off.

"Throw that switch!" John yelled. "We're in serious trouble! They'll rip this boat to splinters."

Michael studied the brass gauges on the wall at the rear of the cabin, next to a series of blade switches.

"It's not fully charged, we need more power."

Michael looked up at the fan. It was still spinning at a good rate, charging the capacitors. The needles on the gauges were approaching their maximum. But slower than he would have liked.

"Just throw the bloody switch!" John yelled.

"It's not ready. There may have been a partial discharge when we hit the tunnel wall. If I throw it now, I might not be strong enough. It might not work at all."

Two more tentacles whipped through the air and set in the roof of the cabin. As the tentacles retracted, the boat rolled, pulling the roof of the cabin down toward the water's surface. The boat leaned hard to the left.

"Michael, throw that damn switch! Come on, boy, just do it!"

Vixen watched through the window as another tentacle lashed out of the water and set in the deck next to Michael's chest. The hook ripped right through the tethers that held the chest in place. With the tethers cut and the boat leaning as badly as it was, the chest slid downward across the deck, toward the edge where the rail had ripped off. He checked the gauges. None showed a full charge. It would have to be good enough. He reached for the switch, then looked at the damage to the side of the boat. In the distance, Vixen could see the smaller boat's mast dragged under the water. She gasped out loud as she considered its pilot's fate. The verudite pulled and Michael's boat lurched down into the water. The wooden hull creaked under the pressure. The craft rolled further left.

Vixen pounded on the window waving her hand, and shouting as loudly as she could.

"Michael! Your chest is loose! It's going to slide off."

The sound of John's voice drowned her out.

"Are you going to throw that switch or not?" he yelled. "What are you waiting for?"

"The spheres on this side, they're broken from the collision in the tunnel," Michael yelled back. "I don't know if it will work. I'm not even sure it's touching any of them. We need it to move toward the front of the boat, between two spheres that are still intact."

"How are we supposed to do that?" John shouted back.

"I don't know!"

The paddle on the right side of the boat was still turning, free of any tentacles. But the boat listed so far to the left, it barely touched the water. There was no propulsion to drive them out of the swarm. Another tentacle whipped over the side and the boat jerked downward again. A board in the deck gave way. As the verudite pulled, the board ripped out of the deck, with the hook still set in it. The board flew across the bow. It whizzed past Michael and slammed into his sea chest as it flew by, knocking it closer to the open edge. The chest slid further toward the open rail, and abruptly stopped when one of its corners hooked on an uneven surface in the deck.

"Michael!" Vixen shouted, banging her fist on the window from inside the cabin. "You're chest is going overboard!"

This time he heard her. When he looked up, it was right at the edge. Reactively, he dove toward it. He got his hand on the handle just as the verudite gave the boat another jerk. The boat creaked and leaned further left and the chest slid further, dangling precariously over the side, just inches from tipping into the water. Michael clung to the handle, but it was heavy; far too heavy for him to carry alone, or even pull in with one hand. The chest inched further out, while Michael clenched his teeth and held on with all his might. His muscles burned. He could feel himself losing strength. He was caving to unavoidable fatigue.

"Copper!" he yelled. "I need your help! Please!"

STANDING ON THE DECK OF THE RINGMASTER'S GALLEON, Phillippe stuffed a length of fuse into a small wooden powder keg, a barrel bomb. The galleon was large enough that the verudites didn't pose any real threat of sinking it, but several hooked tentacles had caught portions of the sails and sheared large tears into them, affecting the boat's propulsion. Mechanicules pulled out his case, and mounted a gatling gun onto his right arm. Belladonna held a bullet belt up for him and he loaded the ammunition into the gatling mechanism. More hooked tentacles whipped through the air and sunk deep in the galleon's wooden sides.

"Light it up," the Ringmaster said to Phillippe.

Phillippe struggled to light a match in the wind. On his third attempt, he lit the fuse and tossed the powder keg over the side. The barrel bomb landed with a splash, and exploded with a sharp crack and a bright flash of light. Mechanicules pointed his gatling gun down at the water and unloaded one whole belt, a hundred rounds. The verudites released their grips and retreated below the water's surface. Upon recognizing a newly created circle of calm as the verudites ducked to deeper waters, Dorado, Will and Nigel maneuvered their boats in close, just behind the galleon. Some of the verudites had retreated. But for now, there was one less boat among them.

MICHAEL CLUNG DESPERATELY TO HIS CHEST. HIS OWN BOAT WAS still under siege. Another tentacle whipped overhead and slammed into the deck. But the claw did not set. As it retracted, the hook dragged across the deck, ripping a splintery groove the whole way back, and passed dangerously close to Michael's thigh before it dropped back into the water.

"Copper I really need your help! I'm serious."

"Forget the chest and just throw the bloody switch!" John yelled.

"I can't do that, John, I can't let go!"

"Throw it!"

"No. I can't!"

Copper rushed out to help Michael.

"I've got you, laddie. Just hang on a wee bit longer."

Michael sat, sprawled on the deck, totally prone, hanging on desperately. Copper reached around from behind and dragged both Michael and his chest backward, to the center of the deck. The boat was still leaning under the strength of the verudite's grip, but they managed to drag the chest inside the cabin together. With his chest safely stowed, Michael rushed to the switch panel. The hull creaked louder, and more timbers cracked.

"It's not ready," Michael shouted.

"We're out of time!" John yelled.

"Fine, here goes nothing."

Michael took a deep breath, and closed a blade switch. Vibrant electrical arcs sizzled and jumped from one copper sphere to the next, around the outer perimeter of the boat. It looked like a partial ring of lightning surrounding most of the hull. But the chain was broken on the left side. The spheres damaged in the tunnel weren't working. Michael heard a dull hum of electrical resonance, where a verudite tentacle was latched and smoldering. Some electricity was discharging through the damaged spheres, but it lacked the intensity seen on the other side. The depleted current was too weak drive the verudite off. In fact, it only seemed to anger it. Two more tentacles lashed up over the bow, as it pulled even harder. The bow dipped, and water splashed up on deck. Another board cracked.

"We cant' take much more of this, it's going to give!" John said.

Michael saw that the two most recent tentacles that wrapped over the bow had came to rest between a pair of working spheres. This was his only chance. He closed a second blade switch. The chain of electrical arcs lit up bright blue again, as a second set of capacitors discharged. The verudite tentacles quivered and smoked. The verudite wailed, letting out a loud gurgle noise. It withdrew its hooks, and propelled itself down into the safety of the deep channel waters. Others followed it down, as if on cue, and the entire verudite swarm disappeared into the depths. The shaking settled, and the steamer leveled on the water's surface, as a surreal kind of quiet settled in. The sounds of creaking wood and thrashing water gave way to the soft sound of the wind, and the paddle wheel slapping through the water.

"Thank our lucky stars the paddle wasn't damaged," Michael said.

"It's a good thing, too," John said. "I'd hate to have to swim to Rouen. It's a long way out."

"Are you hurt?" Michael asked.

"I'm fine boy, but it took you long enough."

"Do you have it from here, John?"

"I've got it under control. Go ahead inside and check on the rest of them. We'll keep it steady past Le Havre and Honfleur, into the mouth of the Seine. From there we'll take an easy cruise up the river to Rouen. Assuming no more issues."

"Yes. Well, let's hope for no more issues indeed," Michael said.

John looked at Michael with a somber look.

"One can only hope. Now go ahead inside, boy. I've got this."

"Wake me if you need a break."

John turned away.

"Aye," he said.

Inside the cabin, the others were unharmed. Michael shook Copper's hand and gave him a friendly pat on the back.

"Thank you. For the help out there. I couldn't have kept it on board otherwise. It would have been at the bottom of the channel by now."

"Don't even mention it," Copper said.

He spoke with his breezy tone, and a wave of his hand.

"You'd have done the same for me, I'm sure of that. If I know anything at all, I know people. And I know you're a good man. So I'm glad to have helped."

"Well, I appreciate it. You all appear to be fine, but has anyone seen Kamal?"

"No, none. He's still below deck," Copper said. "He never came up."

Through all the tossing and noise, Kamal never woke. The energy consumed by his evening ritual drained him severely. Vixen and Scarlet were shaken by the ordeal, Vixen much more so than

Scarlet. As he stepped toward them, he saw the ash tablet on the floor of the cabin. It was open, and broken ashes were scattered all around.

"It slid off the table when the boat tilted," Vixen said. "I tried to save it, but I was too slow. I'm so sorry."

"We should be ok," he said. Then he tapped his temple.

40

LAST CALL

John drove the steamer to the west coast of France as the others slept. He steered the craft into the mouth of the Seine, and all the way upstream to the port town of Rouen. It was where the next leg would begin. He tethered the boat at water's edge and woke his teammates. It was still the middle of the night, but they dragged their bleary-eyed selves to an inn at the river's bank, taking only the essentials from the boat - maps, papers, tokens and keys. Everything else stayed. Michael tried to wake Kamal, but he wouldn't budge. He slept so deeply, in fact, that Michael placed his hand on Kamal's back, just to make sure he was breathing. He left a note, to let Kamal know where he could find them if he woke before they returned, otherwise they would be back in the morning.

"Can we just leave it?" Vixen asked. "Should we be worried about the boat, given what's already happened?"

Michael was exhausted, far too tired to care about material possessions.

"I'm not worried," he said. "It served its purpose, and sabotaging it at this point would provide little gain for anyone who bothered. I think the boat, and Kamal as well, should both be safe."

They checked in and retired to their individual rooms. Still shaken by the encounter with the verudites, Vixen tossed and turned for another hour before she fell asleep. Once she did, she slept like a rock. Michael and Scarlet, too. Copper never had any trouble sleeping anywhere, so he had no problems on this night either. And once he had settled into his room, John slept as sound as a baby, until he was roused by a sharp, poking sensation on his cheek. Half awake, groggy and confused, he felt another sharp poke.

"Wake. Up," he heard the woman say.

He opened his eyes. When the blurriness cleared, he laid there just long enough to recognize Belladonna standing over him. He drew a breath in to speak. But before he could say a word, Mechanicules ripped him from his bed and dragged him to a side chair near the window. Mech flung John like a rag doll, forcing him into a seated position. Surprised, and barely awake enough to think, John collapsed in the chair in a heap. Mech shoved the chair backward into a corner, and pressed his heavy boot into John's chest to make sure he stayed seated.

"Good morning, handsome," Belladonna said ironically. "Well, aren't you something."

"What the hell is going on?" John asked.

He looked at Mechanicules and instantly recognized him.

"You're the one who ransacked my flat! I saw you leaving!"

Angry, John tried to stand. But he only spent a second on the effort. Feeling the force of Mech's boot on his chest, looking into the coldness of his eyes, and seeing the piston spear mounted on his arm, John decided it was wiser to sit for now.

"He was at your flat to collect your debt," Belladonna said. "You're long, long overdue, and patience with your tardiness has run out. Mech, show him."

Mechanicules raised the piston spear near John's face, and started its reciprocating motion. The tip of the spear thrust back and forth. Mech angled the tip at John's eye. John looked back at him. Mech's face was stone cold, his eyes devoid of any feeling. He inched the thrusting tip closer, just an inch from John's eye. John could hear the sound of metal sliding on metal as it pulsed in and out. He squirmed in his chair, and his face grimaced with fear. His hands clenched the chair tightly; his legs flexed with the uneasy anticipation of the coming pain. The back of his head was pinned in the corner. There was nowhere to go. He whimpered in fear as Mech pushed the tip closer.

"That's enough," Belladonna said. "I think he finally appreciates the gravity of his situation."

Mech looked up, surprised, and disappointed. He was tempted to disobey, but heeded anyway.

"Your debt is due and payable," she said. "You have until sunset tomorrow to repay it, in cash or in services rendered. Have the Ringmaster's money, with all interest owed, tomorrow. If you can't pay in cash, then you know what you need to do. This will be our last call, and your final warning. Next time, Mech will come alone and I won't be here to restrain him."

"Just give me a little more time," John begged. "I can pay it back with the prize money."

"Rubbish," she said. "You're on McGillicuddy's team now, so I think you're missing the point with that line of reasoning. If you win, he wins."

"I can change that. I don't have to stay on his team. I just don't want to do anything brash," he pleaded. "Please, I don't want to do anything to hurt Michael. There has to be another way."

"How you handle your business, cupcake, that's up to you. You know what you need to do. You have until sunset tomorrow."

No one in the room actually believed John could raise the money in time, and he knew his own limits better than any of them. A flurry of emotions ran through his head; anger, anxiety, resignation, despair, sorrow, regret. He knew deep down that it was his own actions, his own decisions, that put him in this position.

He knew his anger was misplaced, but he decided to take a final parting shot.

"If it's so important to you to be rid of him," John said, in a cold and frustrated tone, "then why don't you just do it yourself."

The question delighted Belladonna, and she was eager to answer. She leaned in close with her icy blue-tinged eyes, and stared directly into his.

"You're my tool, John. I own you. And that's doubly pleasing, because not only do I get to have you do my bidding for me, but I also get to watch you torture yourself in the process. Rest assured that, one way or another, we will get to the right place, love. Let there be no doubt about that. And if you won't take care of your business, then I will. It's just a question of what you're willing to sacrifice along the way."

She flipped her glasses down, and stared silently from behind the dark lenses, still as could be. John could see his own reflection, and he hated what he saw. Once a larger than life character, a man on top of the world, he had been reduced a sad, broken heap. Once feeling as though he was in charge of everything, he was now in control of nothing. It was a dramatic transformation, brought about by well-intended but ill-advised, choices he had made. He shook his head in disgust and looked away from his own reflection.

"Let's go, Mech. Leave him to think about his responsibilities. Sunset, John. Don't be late."

Her manner of speaking was sweet, yet unsettling, like she had just invited him to afternoon tea. Mech withdrew his boot from John's chest and they left quietly. John felt weary from a lack of sleep, and overwhelmed by a flood of emotion. He hated the position he now found himself in. He leaned forward in his chair, put his face in his hands and sobbed.

41

BEGINNING THE AIR LEG

It was nearly morning, and the Ringmaster roused his team before sunrise for their communal breakfast. The cold of night still lingered as he paced around the cluster of small sleeping tents pitched at the edge of town. Today was his day, the final leg of the race, and there was no time to waste. Victory was within reach, and his anxiousness was palpable.

"Come alive everyone. Ready yourselves quickly, and get moving at once. No time for errors, no room for delay."

He walked past each of the tents, slapping his hands on the sides, waking anybody still sleeping.

"Breakfast is ready in the meal tent. Everyone up. Pack your things. Step quickly."

He grew more impatient by the second.

"Mechanicules and Belladonna, get some food now and head to the airship. Have it ready to lift off when I get there. Phillippe go help them. *Immediately*."

Having just awakened, they were slow to move. But Mech and Phillippe both rose and did as they were told. He pointed at Chevalier, the mime, and Beatrix next.

"Chevalier, take Beatrix with you. Move ahead to the next point. You know what needs to be done."

Chevalier snapped off a pantomimed salute, to show he understood.

"And you over there. I need you clowns to get these tents taken down, leave no sign we were here. You know the routine. Go, go, go."

Four clowns, actual performers, began to tear down the temporary camp. The Ringmaster had an excellent command of what he wanted, a vision of how things should work, and a well-trained team to carry out his plans. Everything was going according to plan.

As they had agreed the night before, Michael, Vixen, Scarlet and Copper all met in front of the hotel at sunrise. They stood on a cobblestone path, near the water's edge looking out to sea, flanked by tall brick buildings rising up behind them. A cool breeze blew over the water and the morning sun was warm on their faces. John was late, so they talked as they waited.

"We need to decide whose airship to use for the last leg. I assume we'll all fly together, right?" Michael said.

"We can't use mine, it won't hold us all," Scarlet said. "Two at the most. It's built for light, fast travel."

"Aye, same here," Copper said. "My craft will carry my squat little arse, and maybe a cup of tea, but not much more."

"My dirigible is hidden nearby," Michael said. "It can hold us all, and our belongings too. There is plenty of space."

"There's plenty of space in mine as well, it's sleek and fast," Vixen said. "Bigger than what I needed to compete here solo, but when your work is subsidized by your government..."

Michael interrupted.

"There's John now," he said. "John, you're late."

He was late indeed. If Kamal had been there, he would have noted that John was precisely eleven minutes late. John approached them with a slow step, visibly reluctant, marching his slovenly frame toward them. He was donning ill-fitting clothes, his hair mussed, his beard wily.

"I'm glad you're here," Michael said. "We were just trying to figure out which airship to use. Do you have any thoughts?"

John stroked his beard slowly.

"I do have one thought, boy. I wonder if I haven't imposed myself on you all, you know, where I'm not needed. I showed up uninvited here and just pushed myself right in, as I know I have a habit of doing. Maybe you should just go on without me, I would understand if you did."

"Nonsense," Michael replied. "We need you."

"I don't know, I think you might just be better off without me here. I'm probably more trouble than I'm worth at this point."

"What's going on with you?" Michael asked.

He pulled John aside to talk privately. He couldn't understand the reluctance. John was a fierce and eager competitor, a wily adventurer, a seasoned man of the world. John showed none of those qualities in the moment. After talking with Michael, John grudgingly agreed to stay. But despite his pledge, Michael still felt uncomfortable. He felt that John might still disappear at the drop of a hat, but they rejoined their teammates to share the news.

"John is staying on, so we are set," Michael said. "We need to get moving, nobody is going to wait for us. The Baron had a half-day lead on us at Ring Island. We have no way of knowing where he is now. You probably already recognize it, but that lead could prove to be too much for us to overcome. I, for one, don't care about that. I refuse to quit in the face of adversity. I hope you're all with me on this. I'm sure there are others who started out ahead of us this morning. So let's get Kamal and collect the rest of our things and give it our best effort. That's all anyone can ask. We can take a tram to my dirigible. Copper, you should…"

Dorado interrupted with a sudden appearance, as if from out of nowhere.

"You'd better hope your dirigible is still intact," Dorado said in his raspy voice. "Have you seen it today?"

His lip curled into a half-smile. It was the most he was capable of.

"What are you trying to say?" Michael asked.

"I'm not trying to say anything, but you saw the damage done at Gillingham. Do you have any idea who might be so despicable, who would go so low as to burn down a man's buggy, and steal from his personal belongings, just to win a damn race?"

Michael thought twice before responding, but he said it anyway.

"You seem to know an awful lot. Some people said it was you."

Dorado glared at him. He smacked his toothpick, but didn't respond right away. Vixen and Scarlet cringed as the words left Michael's mouth. There was no taking them back, they were already out. Copper put his forehead in his hand, and shook his head in disbelief. Dorado seemed to take it all in stride though.

"Oh, I am aware of what some people had to say," Dorado said. "Others said it was your friend Kamal. So what do you think about that?"

Michael opened his mouth to say something, but nothing came.

"Point is," Dorado said, "it doesn't matter what people say. I sat in my window watching, listening, as people said those things about me. I watched them and heard them accuse me. And him, too."

He pointed at Copper.

"I also watched as the Hellfire Troupe passed by, and set your monocycle on fire."

Then he pointed at Scarlet.

"The other vehicles, too. Your boat was burned."

Then he pointed to Michael and Vixen.

"Your rooms were broken into, and burgled. By the magician, and the tightrope walker, two of the Ringmaster's minions."

He looked back at Scarlet.

"You, young lady. You should know that I saw everything that happened that night. Everything."

Scarlet averted her eyes and stared into the distance, pretending to think about something else. John squirmed uncomfortably, hoping Dorado was unaware, and hoping dearly that he had nothing more to say.

"Why are you sharing this now?" Michael asked.

"Mostly because I don't like my name being dragged through the mud, or being accused of something I didn't do," he said. "But also because I thought you'd like to know. You should feel free to spread the word, if you're so inclined. I don't like the way they operate, they give the event a bad name. This isn't what it was ever meant to be."

He smacked on his toothpick, then tipped his hat with a nod and turned to walk away. Vixen eyed the rifle slung across his back.

"Why do you feel the need to carry such a big gun everywhere. This is meant to be an intellectual exercise, after all. A friendly competition."

"This is no ordinary gun, young lady. It's a work of art, so accurate I can light a match at a thousand yards. Blow the head right off a May fly."

"Is that so?"

"It is. Wedge a match in a knothole of a tree or the boards of a fence. I can shoot a bullet and graze the match tip. Just enough friction to light it, and no more. It's a beautiful piece. But as far as size goes, well, this is not my big gun. Not by any stretch. Good luck to you all with the Ringmaster."

Copper reacted first.

"Son of a-"

"Not now," Michael said. "Worry about it later, right now we have to go."

"But I loved that monocycle," he said. "I loved that thing. And my boat, my lovely *Lady Davina Daracha*. I'll take it straight out of their hides."

"You'll have your chance, but for now let's focus on winning."

Michael held a finger in the air to hail a passing tram.

"We'll need to be wary of the Ringmaster's team. If you see them, don't take your eye off of them. They are not to be trusted."

THE RINGMASTER AND HIS CREW LIFTED OFF IN THEIR AIRSHIP, A large lighter-than-air craft, gradually rising above the city of Rouen. The craft had a long, slender balloon, with a wooden undercarriage that hung down below the balloon, suspended from thick cables. The undercarriage was shaped like his galleon, but on a smaller scale. It had a full deck, like the galleon did, with interior sleeping quarters, storage space, and supplies below the deck. The balloon had turbine engines mounted on either side, like large fans to propel it forward. The craft was built for speed.

The Ringmaster took a second to enjoy the view of the city. He had line of sight all the way to the horizon as they rose, but was soon distracted by two other airships, also rising in the distance, their silhouettes set against the backdrop of blue sky and wispy clouds. He stood on deck, steadfast, flanked on either side by Belladonna and Mechanicules, piloting the airship forward. He turned the wheel and set a course for Paris as more of his competitors rose into the sky to give chase.

KAMAL WAS AWAKE WHEN HIS TEAM ARRIVED. HE HAD FOUND Michael's note, and was packed and ready to leave upon their arrival. Nobody asked why he slept so hard. It wasn't their business, and he didn't feel the need to explain. Once they gathered their remaining belongings, Michael's chest included, they rode the tram a short distance to an old warehouse where Michael's dirigible was hidden. When they arrived, Michael walked them inside.

"Oh no. Absolutely not," Scarlet said without pause. "We don't stand a chance in that thing."

"It must be more than thirty years old," Vixen added.

"You don't understand," Michael said. "The frame, the bones, they're old. But it's a winner, she's won other races. My father used this airship to fantastic result. I put a lot of time in to it. It may not be pretty or new, but it's awfully fast."

"But the propellers are so small. How fast can it go?" Vixen asked.

"At least ten miles per hour, maybe twelve" he said, beaming with pride.

Vixen guffawed.

"Michael, that's less than half the speed of my airship. I'm sure you worked very hard, but let's be practical here. We won't win in this. We can't win in this. All in favor of switching to my airship?"

Everyone raised their hands.

"But…" he said.

"No buts, Michael," she said. "Do you want to win, or do you want to be stubborn?"

He resisted at first, but realized it was only his own stubbornness that stood in the way. The answer was beyond debate. Faster was better.

"Fine," he said. "But we don't have any time to waste. The Ringmaster already lifted off, others too."

He said it was fine. But in truth it was not. He was offended by the slight, even a little embarrassed. It was perfectly capable. There was no need to be so blunt.

"So if that's what everyone wants to do," he said, "then that's what we'll do. We'll make the switch. How far is your airship from here?"

"It's not far. Let's catch the tram driver before he leaves, it will only take us a minute to get back to the docks."

"Back to the docks?" Michael said. "I don't understand."

NIGEL ROSE ABOVE THE ROOFTOPS AND TURNED ON A COURSE FOR Paris. His craft was medium sized and modest. Average-looking and shaped like a cigar, it was mounted with a single, but exceedingly large, propeller at the rear of the gas bag. It hummed louder as he pressed the throttle forward. The air was smooth. Nigel was feeling good about his chances.

MICHAEL AND TEAM ARRIVED BACK AT THE DOCKS. VIXEN POINTED to a craft nestled among a bevy of boats.

"There it is."

"This is a boat," Michael said.

"It certainly looks that way, doesn't it? I should have been more clever with docking my boat at Gillingham, but I wasn't. You saw how that came out. Thankfully, I did better here."

She walked onto the deck of the boat. It was about thirty feet long, with a wide and open deck. Newly constructed, the boards were all smooth and straight with no gaps or chips and a glossy varnish, recently sealed and oiled. The deck was surrounded by a sturdy metal rail, clean and crisp with a polished nickel-silver sheen. There was a large hatch in the center of the deck, and a raised platform at the rear. Stairs on either side of the raised deck led up to a pilot's platform, equipped with a wheel and an assortment of levers and gauges, all mounted on a crowded control panel. No expense had been spared on any of it, she had the best of everything.

As she prepared for launch, she was surprised by the blaring sound of an air horn. In the distance they could see a small airship. It was a one-man dirigible, slowly approaching from over the water.

"Is that who I think it is?" Vixen asked.

"Yep. Good old Ratface Reggie," Scarlet said. "It has to be him. I can't believe he actually made it."

They watched him pedal his tiny airship safely over the water and above the beach. Scarlet marveled at his perseverance.

"He must be exhausted. I mean, honestly," Vixen said. "Imagine pedaling all the way across the channel like that."

"No small effort," Scarlet said, shaking her head. "Such a shame to waste the energy."

"What is that supposed to mean?" Vixen asked.

Reginald McHedgie gradually descended as the air horn blared again.

Rapid reports of a gatling gun rang out from a nearby tower, several shots cracked off in rapid succession. The air bag of his dirigible went limp, and the airship plummeted to the ground with a crash.

"Can't say I didn't see it coming," Scarlet said, speaking with cold indifference.

"What just happened?" Vixen asked.

"Oh. Yes, of course. You're new at this," Scarlet said. "Our friend, Mr. Ratface. He's been disqualified. I tried to warn him at Gillingham, but he wouldn't listen. Some people refuse to be helped."

"Disqualified? That's what disqualification looks like?"

Scarlet nodded.

"*Mmm Hmm*. I'm afraid so."

Scarlet wagged a finger.

"Word to the wise, heed the rules. They're few, but important.

Anyway, we should be going, now. Can we finish loading, please? Stand back Michael, watch yourself."

Vixen walked up to the control panel and pulled a lever. A hatch in the deck opened up. She pulled another lever and a giant air bag rose up out of the hull and inflated to full size. It hung floating above the ship, secured by cables.

"Let's load up," she said. "Get your things on board."

"Genius," Michael said. "This is amazing."

Any feelings of hurt he had were swept aside by admiration of her craft.

"Like I was trying to say earlier, if you can stand the meddling associated with government sponsorship of your work, there are substantial benefits that come along with it."

When the boat was loaded, Vixen pulled a third lever to release the anchors. Free from their weight, the craft rose out of the water. Vixen took the wheel and fired up the boilers. Standing on the raised rear deck, with two large steam engines behind her, she commanded her ship with confidence. As they lifted out of the water, two large propeller-like fan blades mounted at the bottom rear of the hull became visible. She pulled a fourth lever to increase the fan speed and start an accelerated climb out of the city.

"Next stop, Paris."

42

TOUCH DOWN IN PARIS

Vixen's ship glided through the air. It was nearly 70 miles in a straight line from Rouen to Paris, and they were getting close. As they neared the city, she could see the Eiffel Tower rising in the distance. The weather was still favorable, but the cloud cover had thickened, and it hung lower in the sky. Rain was a possibility.

"I do have to say, I'm glad we chose to use your airship," Michael said. "It is incredibly fast, much more so than mine."

Vixen beamed, with her dimples fully pronounced. She gave a playful curtsey.

"So kind of you to say so, Mr. McGillicuddy."

"We passed several craft so far, but I'm afraid I've lost track. Can you tell who is ahead of us?"

"It's hard to say, I really can't."

She was focused on managing her flight and reaching her destination. Michael watched, stricken by her unwavering focus. She stood firm and strong, with perfect posture, calmly checking gauges, adjusting levers and trimming her course. Her flowing dress wavered in the breeze, and loose wisps of soft brown hair fluttered against her cheeks. She stared a thousand yards out, toward the edge of the city. She looked determined and unshakeable, yet delicate, and pleasing to the eye at the same time. The mix of beauty, intellect and strength was an intoxicating combination, and he couldn't look away.

"It's nice to see those dimples back," he said with a smirk. "I must say, you are quite a striking beauty, even when you're angry. And even more so when you're not."

She shot him a glance, lips pressed together, squinting as she tried to fight back the smile.

"No, don't put it away!" he teased. "Leave it. It looks good on you."

Charmed by his words, her smile brightened. Whenever she was around him, she tried to put up a facade of disinterest. But the simple truth was that she fancied Michael. She fancied him a great deal, in fact. And as hard as she tried to fight it, sometimes the truth just presented itself without permission.

"There she is," he said. "It's been a while."

His tone was playful.

"It's good to see you, Ms. Van Buren. Welcome back."

"Terribly sorry to interrupt you two," John said as he walked up slowly, "but we should prepare to land. We're only about ten minutes out."

The vast gardens of the *Champs de Mars* were coming into view, a sprawling park-like grassy area, set in front of the Eiffel Tower, and flanked on either side by tall, perfectly manicured hedges. The area was open and spacious enough to do such things as hold a carnival, or to land a small fleet of airships.

"There's the first gate," Michael said. "You should set a course to pass through it."

In the distance, there was a large floating air-gate tethered by cables staked into the ground. The gate was a large, ring-shaped gas bag that looked like a giant floating doughnut. It hung nearly a hundred feet in the air, in front of the Eiffel Tower just above the gardens of the *Champs de Mars*. The hole through the center was large enough for even the largest airship in the race to pass through. Vixen looked back over her shoulder and saw her competitors closing in. Her lead was shrinking, and the Ringmaster's craft was the closest. Her vessel was fast, and she had cut a tighter line from Rouen, overtaking him along the way.

Vixen adjusted her course, taking a line directly toward the center of the gate. Michael saw what she was doing.

"Are you sure that's how you want to make your approach?" he asked.

"Yes, I'm sure. The goal is to go through the gate, is it not?"

"It is, but just through the back side of the gate is the Eiffel Tower. As you pass through the gate, you'll be headed right at it. There's not much space to avoid a collision."

"Well, what do you propose then?"

"Cut wide around the side and come through the back side of the gate, out to the front, on a smoother course to land on the grass. Much more efficient that way."

She pondered the idea.

"Fair point, Mr. McGillicuddy."

He tipped his cap and she adjusted course.

"Remind me again, where are we going after we land?" she asked.

"The ash tablet said something about a clockmaker," Scarlet said. "If only the message hadn't been shattered."

She glared at Vixen with a cross eye, suggesting blame.

"It said we would find the first gate in the gardens at *Champs de Mars*," Michael said. "We should pass our craft through this gate, land in the gardens and proceed to the shop of *J. Andouille, Clockmaker*. If we keep a sharp eye, and we know what to say, we may receive further instructions from there. Or, you know, something to that effect."

"I know the way to *Andouille*," John said. "It's not far."

"Copper, when we get down to the lawn, tether the bow,"

Michael said. "Everyone grab what you need now, so we can make a quick exit."

Vixen guided the airship around the gate and on a course to pass through the back.

"You need to get down lower, lass," Copper shouted. "You're too high, your balloon will hit the top of the gate!"

She adjusted her course.

"There you go, straighten her out. You're looking much better now."

She evened the glide path, and after a clean pass through the gate, she brought the airship down to the ground. They quickly disembarked from the airship and they headed into Paris.

As his air-galleon landed in the *Champs de Mars* and his crew prepared to disembark, the Ringmaster called out his orders.

"Mech and Belladonna, you come with me. Chevallier, you too. Beatrix and Phillippe, you know where to go. The rest of you keep our craft safe and pitch in where needed. Make yourselves useful and help us all out. We're getting close."

Once he was off, he dashed toward the heart of the city, with Mech and Belladonna at his side, leaving the remaining crew to carry out their orders and make proper preparations.

"It's further down this way," John said, as they walked through a crowded section of Paris' second arrondissement. They were in a busy commercial district, right in the heart of Paris proper, packed with banks, merchants, hotels, and a host of culinary establishments. The cobblestone roads were lined on either side by sidewalks and studded with tall gas lamps. Michael walked with haste, and his satchel slung over his shoulder. Copper walked beside him, smithing hammer in hand, with John on his other side. Vixen, Scarlet and Kamal followed just a few steps behind. They entered the race individually, and had come together purely out of necessity, a collection of competitors begrudgingly working together for lack any better option. But by now they had grown into a team, and Michael had himself a crew. He grinned at the thought, pleased at how things were going. His father would be proud, he thought.

"That's Nico's Patisserie on the corner," John said. "From there it's just around the corner. Down and to the left. That's where we'll find *J. Andouille*."

They turned left and scurried down the *Rue di Rivoli*, around the corner in search of the legendary clockmaker.

43

J. ANDOUILLE, CLOCKMAKER

They entered the shop of *J. Andouille* and were immediately struck by the sheer number and variety of timepieces inside. The ubiquitous ticking of hundreds of clocks was abruptly interrupted by a cuckoo clock, coincidentally timed to announce their entry.

"*Cuckoo-cuckoo-cuckoo.*"

The cuckoo bird retreated back inside the clock, and before long the only sound they could hear again was the din of the ticking timepieces, all ticking in perfect disharmony, one tick filling the gaps between the others, creating a hum that Michael found soothing. It was an impressive display, with wrist watches in cases, and pocket watches abound, all neatly arranged under shiny glass countertops. Densely arranged shelves made of dark, heavy wood stood all around the shop, some five and six levels high, all cluttered with wind-up clocks, table clocks and alarm clocks with bells. The walls were covered with wall clocks, and there was virtually no space on the floor that went unused. Just about any empty space not occupied by shelving, apart from a few narrow paths to walk through the shop, was covered. Floor standing clocks, grandmother clocks, grandfather clocks, water clocks and even sundials. Some of the timepieces were simple, their clockwork gears and springs fully housed inside their tiny enclosures. Others had their inner machinations exposed by design, adding to the beauty of the piece. The intricacy of their shiny inner workings was presented in proud, even boastful, display. The shop was modestly lit by candles and the smell of burned wax permeated the room. A translucent yellow film tinted the insides of the windows.

An elderly man, short in stature, sat on a stool behind the counter reading a book, not even noticing that they had entered. He was none other than J. Andouille himself, Europe's finest clockmaker, purveyor of the most complicated timepieces known to man. He was aged mid-seventies and slightly hunched in the back. His gaunt arms were covered with liver spots, and his pale bony hands ended in long slender fingers, with fingernails in desperate need of a trim. As old as he was, he looked smart and lucid, dressed in black trousers and a starched white shirt, neatly tucked. His sleeves were rolled up to the elbow, and a stiff collar was spread open. Over his shirt, he wore a dark work apron with several pockets in the front to hold pliers, tweezers and some of the thinnest screwdrivers Michael had ever seen. As they walked further in, a wooden floorboard squeaked, drawing his attention away from his book. When he looked up, his bushy white mustache reminded Michael of an old uncle he hadn't seen since he was a young boy, and his glasses were so thick they distorted the size of his eyes to ridiculous effect.

"Welcome to J. Andouille, Clockmaker. I, of course, am J. Andouille. How can I help you?" he said with a warm smile.

He sounded fifty years younger than he looked. Judging by his appearance, Michael had expected a slow-talking, decrepit old man with a wavering, crackly voice, but what he got was a shopkeeper who was spry, alert and energized. The man hopped down off of his stool with remarkable fluidity, and as he did, he nearly disappeared behind the counter. Mr. Andouille was barely five feet tall. As he plopped down from the stool, his thick, heavy lenses slid down his nose. He pushed them back up with his index finger while he looked up at them waiting for a response. He blinked a few times as he waited. Michael didn't normally notice the blinking of a person's eyes, but the magnification of the lenses made the blinks so pronounced, it was noteworthy, and even distracting. Michael was stuck staring at him, at something of a loss.

"So how can I help you?" he repeated.

"I'm not entirely sure, if I'm being honest," Michael said.

He looked at Vixen, then Copper, then John, then Kamal. They all looked back at him with blank looks. Michael looked at Scarlet, but she just shrugged and shook her head.

"Um," Michael continued. "We're participating in a race, and we were told to come here."

"Oh, that's wonderful," Mr. Andouille said. "I enjoyed a good foot race when I was younger. That sounds like great fun, and I wish you the best of luck on your race, young man. But is there anything here I can help you with?"

Michael swallowed uncomfortably. He wasn't sure what to say. Scarlet looked around the shop, searching for something. Anything.

"Think," she whispered to herself. "You know it's here, you just have to find it. *Keep a sharp eye*."

Michael felt flustered. He had come so far, and done exactly as the directions said. But despite that, he felt lost. By now, Copper had lost interest, and stood fiddling with a sundial. Kamal stood patiently waiting, ready to help when called upon. Scarlet, Vixen and John wandered around the shop trying to figure out why they had been directed there in the first place. Michael looked around at all the clocks, hoping for a clue, an idea, anything familiar. He noticed one clock, a table clock, beautifully crafted, with smooth flowing gears all exposed, and the entire piece was housed under a glass bell jar. He studied the gears, turning so smoothly, working in such harmony. It reminded him of the insides of the automatons he used to build as a child. A sinking feeling set in.

"Could we be in the wrong place?" Michael asked out loud to nobody in particular.

Vixen was standing near him. She whispered back.

"I don't think we are. It just feels right to me."

Copper pulled out a sheet of parchment and read it carefully, checking whether he had missed something, some important detail about the ash tablet or otherwise. Michael stared at the clock, expressionless.

"I don't mean to be rude," Mr. Andouille asked, "but would you like to buy that clock, young man?"

"I'm sorry, what?" Michael replied.

"Would you like to buy that clock?"

"No, I'm not really shopping. But thank you."

"Very strange behavior, don't you think, to come to a clock-maker's shop, stare at a clock and then say you're not shopping for a clock."

"Yes, but I'm supposed to be here."

"So you say. Yet you don't know why. That's quite a conundrum now, isn't it, young man?"

As Mr. Andouille spoke, his sharp tone drew Scarlet's attention. She turned and looked at him, then just past him. On the back counter, just behind Mr. Andouille, set apart from all the clocks, there was a wooden carving standing on a shelf. It stood out to her, less for its craftsmanship, or gaudy lack thereof, and more for its single most striking quality: it was not a timepiece. She scanned every inch of the shop with her eyes. Everything inside was either a timepiece, or a fixture to hold one.

"Pardon me," Scarlet said. "that wooden sculpture on the back counter, the carved ostrich. Does it tell time somehow?"

He turned and looked at it.

"That? Sorry no, that's not an ostrich. It's actually an emu," Mr. Andouille replied. "Funny thing about the emu. I'm not sure if you know this. They have wings, they have feathers, they're a bird like any other. But an emu cannot fly. What do you think about that?"

Michael's ears perked up, and his eyes opened wide. He recalled the text from his invitation. He knew what to do now. He walked back to the counter with an exaggerated swagger, and leaned to one side with his elbow on the counter. A cocky look washed across his face, and he began to speak in a preposterously confident tone.

"Well, as a matter of fact my good man, yes. I did know that an emu cannot fly. And by the way; did you know that an ostrich has four toes?"

His tone was smug, and he held up four fingers, waving them side to side. He winked at Mr. Andouille knowingly. Then he pointed at Mr. Andouille's chest, and repeated himself while he nodded.

"Four. Toes."

Mr. Andouille stared back blankly. His glasses looked like windows opening and closing with each blink.

"Intriguing," Mr. Andouille said.

Then he just kept staring.

"Bloody hell, lad, what are you doing?" Copper said.

Copper crumpled up his parchment and tucked it away and shoved Michael aside.

"You'll have to forgive my friend here. I think what he meant to say was penguins don't fly either."

"I see," Mr. Andouille said.

He looked at Michael again and shrugged.

"Why didn't you just say that in the first place, young man?"

Mr. Andouille chuckled to himself.

"For a moment I thought you might actually be in the wrong place. Just one moment please."

Mr. Andouille walked over to the carved wooden emu on the back counter. He stood on the tips of his toes to reach up to the carved bird, and tilted it backward, like a lever. They were startled by a grinding noise behind them. When they turned around the wall had opened up to reveal a hidden room. Mr. Andouille stepped around from behind the counter, and brought a candle with him.

"Follow me," he said.

He led them through the doorway into the room.

"Where are we going?" Michael asked.

"We're going in here," came the answer.

"Yes, but why are we going in there? As I may have mentioned, we are in a race, and therefore in a bit of a hurry."

"Oh. Well if you don't want to come, young man, you don't have to. You're free to go back to your race anytime you like."

Vixen chimed in.

"We'd really just like to understand where we're going."

"It's like I already told you, we're going in here."

He pointed inside.

Vixen mumbled. She didn't like the ambiguity, but she recognized they had no choice.

"Fine," she said.

Despite their shared apprehension, they followed him in. Mr. Andouille set the candle on a small table inside. The candle provided all the light available. As they walked inside and their eyes adjusted, a bank of lockboxes attached to the back wall became visible, arranged in stacks like the ones at Ring Island. Each box was adorned with unique designations on each of the locks, familiar markings they had now become used to.

"Copper," Vixen said, "come in here with your key."

Copper came in and reached into his pocket to pull out the key. He ran his thumb across the shiny nine-star pattern on its head, and searched the room for a match.

"Yes. Well. I'll just wait over there, while you all take care of your business," Mr. Andouille said before he scurried out. "Over there. Behind that counter."

Copper swallowed a tense swallow. He studied the boxes, trying to find one marked with nine stars. Then he had a troubling thought.

"So should I open the box marked with the nine stars? Or am I supposed to open a different one? You know, the cryptogram business?"

They all turned back and called out to him at the same time.

"Mr. Andouille?"

"Sorry folks. I just open the door," he shouted from behind the counter.

He was crouching down, as if taking cover.

"You're on your own from here. Don't you involve me in this."

Through the hazy wax-glazed window, Michael saw a familiar face run out of the Candlemaker's shop across the street, toward the *Rue di Rivoli.*

"That's Nigel! And he's moving quickly. We can't let anyone get too far ahead of us," he said. "Copper, just make a decision so we can go."

"Oh, that's right easy for you to say, laddie. Meanwhile, Mr. Andouille is hunkered down back there, out of harm's way!"

Copper scanned the room and found the box marked with nine shiny stars arranged in three separate triangles around its keyhole. He pushed his key in, and it slid in smoothly. It was a good start, he told himself. He held it in place between his thumb and forefinger, as still as could be.

"But what if it's the wrong one?" he said.

He looked back over his shoulder again, concerned.

"No more time to dilly-dally," Scarlet said. "Now open the box and let's go."

Fresh out of patience, she shoved her way into the room and brushed Copper's hand aside. She turned the key without pause, and the box unlocked with a click. As it released, the small door unlatched.

Copper swung the small square door open and reached inside

to pull out another gorgeous specimen of a token, a stunning, glimmering match to the others with its polished gold outer rim and shiny sliver face.

He smiled.

"Is that all there is?" Vixen asked.

Copper took a moment to appreciate the token's craftsmanship before he swept the inside of the box with his hand and pulled out a note on a slip of parchment. As he read it aloud, its message was remarkably simple.

"*Go to Rousseau's Apothecary to obtain your final token.*"

"That's it?" Vixen said. Her words bore the weight of hearty skepticism.

"Rousseau's. That's near my flat," John said.

He paused before continuing, sheepishly.

"I know exactly where it is."

"I remember it," Michael said. "I saw it on the tram ride, when I came to visit you."

Kamal chimed in.

"Pardon me, but it seems to me that the race is still very close. I still have my advantage token, which we could use if only we knew where to redeem it."

Scarlet scurried across the shop to speak with Mr. Andouille who had just stood up from behind the counter.

"Do you have a portal?" she asked. "I need to use your pneumatic portal to send a message. Immediately."

44

SCARLET MESSAGES BUG

"My portal?" Mr. Andouille said. "Sure. You can use it. But it will cost you."

"Cost me? Of all the nerve. What are you asking for?" Scarlet asked.

"How about that ring you're wearing? I could use the gems to encrust the face of a timepiece I'm working on. It's for a certain unnamed, but very high-ranking, member of the monarchy. I couldn't possibly say who, though."

She was relieved at the request, the ring was worth nothing to her. In truth, it was cheap piece of costume jewelry. But she couldn't give in too easily. If she did, he might ask for more. She had to make it seem unreasonable.

"Forget it," she said. "Apart from its material worth, this ring has sentimental value. I couldn't possibly part with it."

"Have it your way. No ring, no portal. You can go find another one. If you're able. Good luck to you all."

Scarlet looked over at Michael. She was playing coy, feigning conflict. He was nervous, and unaware of her ruse.

Michael looked desperate, and nodded insistently.

"Come on, just do it," he said. "We're going to need it."

She bit her lip and flushed a shade of light red. She hated being taken advantage of, and Mr. Andouille was taking full advantage. It wasn't about the ring, it was the principle of it all.

"Fine," she said with clenched teeth.

She slipped the ring off and placed it on the counter.

"Now, what is your portal address?"

"Well, I'm glad we could finally do some business today," he said with a chuckle. "The portal address is 36963."

He handed her an empty pneumatic tube as he spoke. Scarlet grabbed a piece of paper and scribbled a note on it as Michael looked over her shoulder.

Bug,

It's Scarlet. pp-9iw. I need your help. I'm at J. Andouille, Clockmaker, in Paris, en route to Rousseau's Apothecary. Need to redeem advantage token on the way. Check the maps, work your contacts, and let me know if it's possible. Respond to portal address 36963. Immediately. I owe you one.

-S

She rolled up the note and shoved it into a pneumatic tube. She clamped the tube shut and punched in the five digit address for Bug's portal and thrust the tube into the outbound pipe. The portal was neatly hidden, concealed between two clocks behind the counter.

Shoomp!

The tube was sucked into the portal and out into the network of pipes. They stood impatiently waiting for a response.

Michael leaned in and whispered to Scarlet.

"What is that number you used? Not the portal address, but the other one, pp-9iw?"

"It's a pass phrase," she whispered back. "A secret code, so Bug knows it is really me and not somebody else pretending to be me. We have a few that we use to protect ourselves, in case one of us becomes compromised."

She looked up at Mr. Andouille.

"This could take a minute," she said.

She walked over to the window to peek out to see if anyone was coming, or going. Michael paced the room nervously.

He looked at the portal, then at Scarlet, then back at the portal. Nothing.

"What's taking him so long?" Michael said. "We have to go."

"It'll take a few minutes. The tube needs to get there, Bug needs to read it, act on it, respond and we need to allow travel time back. Just be patient, it's taken care of. Trust me on this."

They continued pacing, waiting for Bug's response, growing more anxious with each moment that passed. Mr. Andouille looked amused.

"Are you sure he's going to get it?" Michael asked.

"I'm pretty sure. We have an understanding. Bug's job is to stand at the ready, just in case I need to reach out for help. We had it all arranged ahead of time."

"Arranged?"

"You know we're allowed to work in teams," she said. "Well, I happen to have a teammate of my own."

Michael looked around confused.

"You do?"

"Of course I do, it's totally within the rules. Nobody said the teammates needed to be here with us."

She smiled and winked.

"I suppose that's right," he said. "Fascinating."

Michael heard footsteps outside. Somebody was running. He peeked out the window and saw the Ringmaster, Belladonna and Mechanicules all run by, toward the *Rue di Rivoli.*

"The Ringmaster's on his way out, too. We're losing valuable time!" he said. "Send another note and tell Bug to hurry!"

"Relax," Scarlet said. "We should hear back any minute now."

"We should just go," he said. "We're down to collecting our last token, then it's over, there's not much more to do."

Scarlet smirked at him.

"You want me to just leave? Not after I gave up my ring. Sorry darling, not for nothing."

"The lad is right," Copper said. "Forget about it, we should…"

Before Copper could say the word 'go,' a pneumatic tube dropped into the portal.

"Bug came through," Scarlet shouted.

She opened it, pulled out a note and read it.

"pp-x13. Fontainebleau's Haberdashery. That's where we can redeem the advantage token."

"Best hats and suits in Paris," John said. "Not that I shop there, obviously. But I know the spot. It's directly on the way to Rousseau's Apothecary."

45

SORRY FOLKS, CHANGE IN PLANS

They thanked Mr. Andouille and rushed out of his shop, jogging toward John's flat in the seventh arrondissement of Paris. They were anxious to redeem Kamal's advantage token. On the way, they reflected on the extraordinary journey that had brought them this far, and about what might lie ahead.

"We must be nearly finished with the race," Michael said.

"Feels right," Copper said. "Redeem for our advantage, collect the final token from Rousseau and then off to the finish line. It'll be tight, but I think we have a right good chance."

"We're nearly there," John said. "Of course, there's no way to tell what fruit the advantage token will yield. But let's handle it quickly and be on our way to Rousseau's as fast as we can."

"No argument here," Copper said.

"The haberdashery is just around the corner now," John said.

John had become more lively, emerged from his cloudy mood, and his competitive side was starting to show through again. Scarlet studied John's appearance. One of his shoes was untied. The lace had broken and was too short to form a bow, so he hadn't bothered. With each step, the long loose lace whipped against his other shoe as it passed. Scarlet pulled on the sleeve of John's shirt. His sleeves were too short, and the middle was wrapped tight around his belly, forcing gaps to open between the buttons.

"Since we're going anyway," she said, "maybe we could get you fitted."

"No time for that," John said. "Besides, it would be a waste. Look at me, after all. Anyway, the shop is just around this corner, here. Kamal, you still have the advantage token, right?"

Kamal patted his pocket and nodded his assurance.

"Good."

They turned the corner. The haberdashery shop was just across the street. But John stopped dead in his tracks.

"Sorry folks. Change in plans."

"What do you mean by change in plans?" Scarlet said. "We need to redeem the advantage."

"What are you doing, John?" Michael said.

Michael peeked over. Mechanicules, Belladonna and Chevalier stood outside the haberdashery. The Ringmaster was likely inside. Could he be redeeming an advantage also? John had little appetite to find out. He ducked back behind the corner.

"We need to go the other direction, down that way, and we need to go quickly. Don't draw attention, just be casual, and try to blend in with everyone else."

"What is this about?" Michael asked.

"Just do as I say, boy, and don't ask any questions. Follow me."

He turned the corner again, only this time he walked away from the shop, not toward it. When he was comfortable that they were far enough down, and out of line of sight, John gave one simple instruction.

"Run."

Michael and the others instinctively followed, but they didn't know why they were running.

"Down that alley on the left," John said.

Their change of direction, however, did not go unnoticed. They had caught Belladonna's eye when they stopped and backtracked, and she watched as they re-emerged.

"Was that Ramshorn?" she said.

She was indignant.

"He's still with Michael. He's still helping him!"

Mech nodded, as Belladonna turned to Chevalier.

"When the Ringmaster comes out, tell him we had to take care of something. Everything is under control, and we'll catch up shortly," she said. "Mech, let's go, we need to have a word with John."

After leading his teammates down the alley, John stopped and leaned against the wall. The alley ran between the backs of several shops. There were a few doors, several garbage cans and a gas light mounted on the wall. The ground was wet with seepage, and garbage was scattered all about. They didn't see any rats, but it was easy to imagine they were close by.

John put his hands on his knees and leaned over, panting heavily. Never terribly athletic, he was out of breath and gasping from the short run. But fatigue was not his only issue. Michael could see John was troubled. He just stared at the opposite wall, lost, mussing his hair excessively. He wheezed, and his eyes darted around. He had a big decision to make, and it weighed heavily on him.

"Why are we running from them, John? And what are you planning to do from here? We have to get to Rousseau's," Michael said.

"I'm thinking," John said. "Just give me a second."

He stared at the wall.

"It's the only way. Follow me. We're going into the catacombs."

"Rubbish," Vixen said. "We're going to Rousseau's and winning this race. Why are you talking about catacombs?"

"The Paris Catacombs will save us, it's a complex network of underground tunnels, they underpin a large portion the city. We can lose them in there, then we'll be on our way to Rousseau's just fine. Just trust me on this."

"Oh, I understand the complexity," she said. "And I know of the catacombs. Men have been lost in there, only to have their corpses lay undiscovered for years. You already know where Rousseau's is, let's just go straight there. Never mind the catacombs."

"I'm afraid we can't do that. While this is usually a friendly competition, I have reason to believe that Belladonna and Mechanicules mean to do us harm. Real and serious harm. We should avoid them at all cost. Now let's go."

"What makes you so sure?" Michael asked.

"You'll have to trust me on this. I know their motives, much better than you might imagine. You're free to do what you want, but I'm going down here."

"You're going inside this shop?" Michael asked.

"Not exactly, no."

John stood upright, and reached toward the gas lamp next to one of the doors. He turned the lamp forty-five degrees and the door clicked and released. Michael expected to see the inside of the shop, but when John pulled the door open, there was no shop interior, just a brick enclosure the size of a closet, or a large chimney. There was no floor, just a ladder leading down below ground.

"Get going," John said.

He nodded downward.

"No time to waste."

Vixen and Scarlet went first, the others shimmied down close behind. John went last. From the inside, with his feet firmly on the ladder he pulled the door shut to close himself inside, and he made his way down to the others. It was dark at the bottom.

"Ok, now what?" Scarlet asked.

She sounded irritated.

They heard a rustling noise in the darkness, then they saw the soft glow of Vixen's illumination orb. The light didn't reach far beyond her hands, but she uncapped the orb and poured a dab onto the ground. As the mixture reacted with the air, its glow grew more intense. Happy with the result, Vixen looked up, then let out a shriek. With one hand over her mouth and the other pointing at the wall, she stared with a look of horror.

"Relax, they've been dead for centuries," John said. "They won't bother you tonight."

Michael and Scarlet both flinched as their eyes adjusted, and they saw what Vixen saw. They were standing in a long tunnel. The walls of the tunnel were lined with hundreds of thousands of human bones. Bones stacked neatly on bones, like one might stack firewood, perpendicular to the wall, perfectly aligned and mostly equal in length. The neatly stacked bones were interspersed with the occasional human skull. Bones, upon bones, as far as the eye could see down the entire length of the tunnel.

"Hundreds of years ago," John said, "to help with over-crowding in cemeteries, old remains, bones, were excavated and relocated down here. To make room for new occupants, if you will. It's been like this for hundreds of years. You've no need to worry."

John reached over and pulled a bone from the stack. He held it out toward Vixen. She backed away uncomfortably.

"Put some of that glowing goop on the end here, we'll use it as a torch to get us where we're going. And stay close to me."

BACK UP AT STREET LEVEL, BELLADONNA STRUTTED DOWN THE street with her classic swagger, one foot directly in front of the other, hips wagging, showing no sense of urgency. Mechanicules marched, just two steps back. They arrived at the alley to find it was empty. There was nobody there. Nobody.

"Down here," she said.

Mech looked skeptical.

"Don't look at me like that," she said. "I know exactly what I'm doing. And I know exactly where John is going. Just follow me."

46

ALLE ALLE AUCH SIND FREI

John led the way, deep into the catacombs. They weaved their way around corner after twisting corner before finding themselves in a straightaway nearly a hundred yards long. Other corridors branched to the left and to the right, but John kept straight the whole way down, with no hesitation. The end of the straightaway was a dead end, nothing but an iron ladder mounted to the wall leading back up to street level.

"Here we are," John said. "Just up this ladder now, I'll go first."

John started his ascent.

"It looks like a dead end," Michael said. "Where are you going?"

"Don't you worry about that, I know what I'm doing. We'll be out of here in no time."

"The ladder just goes to the ceiling, where do you think you're going?"

He reached the top and squinted closely at the ceiling, feeling around with his hand.

"Ah, there it is."

With a metallic grind and a clicking noise, John unlocked a hatch in the ceiling. As he flipped the hatch open, a soft light poured down from above. John climbed out, and disappeared from sight. Michael went up next.

"Hurry, Michael," Scarlet said. "I hear someone coming."

"I'm trying," he said. "It's slippery."

"I definitely hear something."

"I said I'm trying!"

When Michael reached the top, he poked his head up through the hatch, expecting to pop up through the sidewalk, or into another back alley. But he couldn't have been more wrong. John stood just a couple feet in front of him, in a room that looked far too familiar, with his back to Michael. It only took him a second to realize where he was. He was in the middle of John's living room, in the bottom floor of his Paris flat. The hatch in the ceiling John had opened was actually the lid to his chest. The chest was a secret passage. John stood still, in the safety of his own front room.

Michael stood on the ladder, his upper body protruding from inside the chest. It was the chest Michael had admired so fondly when he visited, wondering what secrets it held. It held secrets to be sure, but not the kind he expected.

"John, what is going on here?" Michael asked. "Wait a minute. Is that how Belladonna got into your flat the night I was here? The front door was shut and locked, I remember it. It's bothered me ever since."

"Aye," John said.

His tone was somber.

"So, have you been cooperating with with them this whole time?"

"I wouldn't call it cooperating, no."

Michael shook his head.

"Then what do you call it?"

"Something more akin to extortion."

"They're coming here now, aren't they?"

"That's very possible, yes."

"I can't believe this John. I trusted you. I trusted you with everything."

"Do you remember what I told you when you came to visit, boy? Be careful who you trust. I stood right here, right in this very room and I said it to you. I said it as clear as day, didn't I?"

The words hit Michael like a punch to the gut. He stood on the ladder, stunned, numb.

"What are you saying?" Michael asked.

John turned around to face Michael, his face was sullen. He held a small pistol, pointed back at Michael.

"What I'm saying is I have a big problem. I'm in deep with the Ringmaster, I owe him an awful lot of money."

"For what?"

"It's complicated, boy, and I'm not going to get into that with you right now. You think one year's taxes on your homestead are something? They're nothing, I can assure you of that. I have a large and long-standing debt that he has lost all patience on, boy, and I'm in very serious trouble."

"Debt for what? What kind of trouble?"

"Don't concern yourself with any of that. I've made my own choices, I've done what I've done and that's it. And Mechanicules, if you don't already know, is far more a menace than your bloody tax collector. The Ringmaster doesn't want you to finish this race. He has a long-running grudge against your father, he hated losing to him and he's carried that grudge over to you. He wants you out and he wants me to take care of it. I didn't want it to come to this. I saw you trying to get my attention all those times, I saw you trying to catch up with me. But I tried to avoid crossing paths with you, I really did. All because I didn't want to have this conversation."

"What conversation? Forget all that, John. Let's just finish the race," Michael pleaded.

"I don't think you understand. I mean you no harm, boy, I really don't. But I'm stuck."

"If you were avoiding me, then why did you join up with us? You came to us."

"I did so on a whim, and against my better judgment. I didn't have my key stolen in Gillingham, or anything else for that matter. The only thing I lost was my boat, those bastards burned it down. I needed to get across the channel, and you had a boat. I had my map and everything with me, I could have gotten my own token on Ring Island and parted ways again when we got to the other side. I had it all worked out, I would have moved well away from you and kept my distance. But when I hurt my ankle, that changed everything."

Copper was growing impatient.

"Hey! What are you doing up there?" he shouted. "Move it along, so we can come up, too!"

Michael ignored him, focusing instead on John.

"You used me?" Michael said. "You used us?"

"In a manner of speaking, yes. I suppose I did."

"And after all that, I helped you with your ankle."

"Yes. All water under the bridge, as it is. Here's the bottom line. I have a deal for you this time, and it's really quite simple. If you climb out of that hole, Michael, I'll have no choice but to do something horrible, and I really don't want to do that. So please don't force me. I'll give you the choice to climb back down, and take your chances with whatever is down there, but you better decide quickly. At least you'll stand a chance that way."

"Why are you doing this, John?"

"If I knew another way, I'd take it, but I don't. I'm sorry, Michael, but I did warn you. This all could have been avoided if you had just listened to me from the start. You should have stayed home. If you remember, I did try to tell you that."

John cocked the hammer on the pistol and thrust his hand out to show he was serious.

"Now get out of here, boy! Go on!"

Michael knew there was no other choice. Saddened by John's betrayal, Michael stared back in disbelief.

"You were like a second father to me."

His eyes glossed, and he shook his head, before stepping down the ladder. John flipped the chest shut, without so much as a second thought. It slammed shut and the tunnel plunged back to darkness. Michael heard the chest lock above him. He climbed back down to the floor with the others.

"Michael?" Vixen said. "What's going on? Are we going up, or what?"

"No. We're not going up," he said. "John has betrayed me. He's betrayed us all. We're on our own now."

"I never trusted that bloke!" Copper said. "I told you that, I've been saying it all along. I know people."

He swiped his hammer through the air to show his frustration.

"They're getting closer," Vixen said. "I hear them."

Belladonna's and Mech's footsteps grew more audible, from one of the offshoot tunnels. Belladonna strutted with hard, confident steps. She held her index finger outward, scraping the sharp tip of the talon loudly down the stone wall as she walked. She wasn't sneaking up on anybody. Her dulcet voice filled the tunnels, but with no sense of direction as to where it was coming from.

"Alle Alle Auch Sind Frei," she said.

As was so often the case, her voice was sweet, but haunting.

"You can't hide, pumpkin. I know where you're going, So just come back here, and take it like a man."

Vixen shuddered at the words. Belladonna was getting close.

"We need to get out of here," Michael said.

"The only choice we have is to go right back toward them. There's no way to know which one they are in, they could pop out at any moment."

Michael recalled Vixen's alchemy orbs. In a nervous attempt at humor, he spoke.

"Vixen," Michael said, "your alchemy orbs, they change things. Can you, um, change this wall into a door?"

She thought about it for a second and responded.

"As a matter of fact, I can."

47

HOW TO TURN A WALL INTO A DOOR

Vixen dug through her bag and retrieved an alchemy orb filled with a pink, swirling liquid inside.

"This should do the trick. It transforms stone into air. Where should we use it?"

"Scarlet," Michael said. "Your looking glass. Can you see through these tunnel walls?

She placed her looking glass against the wall to look through it.

"The wall is too thick. I can't see anything, it must be solid bedrock."

"What about the other side? Try the other side," Copper said.

"Yes, there's a tunnel on the other side, it runs parallel to this one. And there is a ladder leading upward. It's right there, I can see it!"

"Vixen, can you get us to the other side?" Michael asked.

"I think I can. If I smash the whole orb against the wall, it should open a hole large enough for us to pass through. I should warn you though, the elixir is unstable, and highly unpredictable. It might only last a few seconds, so we need to go quickly, or one of two things will happen."

"What are they?"

"One is that the hole will close up before you make it through, in which case you'll be stuck here all the same."

"What's the other?"

"The hole will close up while you're inside. You'll end up part of the wall. Like, permanently. That would be very unpleasant."

Copper made a face.

"It's going to be loud," Vixen continued. "The transformation occurs at the molecular level. That's a lot of angry, vibrating molecules that make it work. Are you ready?"

She threw the glass orb at the wall and it shattered. The thick pink elixir splashed across the wall. The liquid oozed down to the floor, and a deep, rumbling sound, like the approaching shockwaves of earthquake, filled the tunnel. It was painfully loud, they could feel it in their chests. They covered their ears waiting for something to happen. A hole opened in the wall.

"Go now! We only have a few seconds!"

Vixen dashed right through, wasting no time. Michael went through just behind her. He turned and looked back through the hole. Copper took a deep breath, closed his eyes and dove through as fast as he could, landing on his belly on the ground on the other side. Kamal calmly glided through, just behind him.

"Come on, Scarlet! You have to get through!" Michael shouted.

Scarlet looked hesitant.

"How much more time?" Scarlet yelled.

"I don't know," Vixen said.

"How much?"

"Go now!" Vixen yelled. "It won't last much longer!"

Scarlet started toward the hole, then held herself back.

"I feel like it's too late. Are you sure it's ok?" she yelled. "I don't want to be closed inside."

They screamed to coax her through. Scarlet looked down the tunnel. Belladonna and Mechanicules had rounded the corner, and they were coming for her. Belladonna fixed her gaze and strode toward Scarlet. Scarlet looked back at her team with a look of desperation. She took a deep breath, preparing to dive through, just as the loud rumbling sound started again.

"Come on!"

Scarlet sighed and stepped back. Her shoulders fell.

"It's too late," she said. "I'll be fine. Go win this."

As soon as the words left her lips the hole closed, sealing her in on the other side.

"Oh my god," Vixen said with a gasp. "This is all my fault."

"Bloody hell," Copper said. "She's stuck inside with them."

"She did say she would be fine," Michael said. "She's very crafty, I'm sure she has a plan, and she'll find a way out. She has to."

"I hope to god you're right," Vixen said.

"This is a most unfortunate turn of events," Kamal said, "And I do not wish to appear insensitive. But it would seem at this point that there is very little we can do for her. It is a solid stone wall, after all."

"We can't just leave her in there!" Vixen said.

"I don't like it any more than you do," Michael said. "But what else can we do? Do you have another one of those orbs? Just open the wall back up."

"No. I only brought two."

"Where is the other one?

"It was stolen in Gillingham. From my hotel room."

"We need to keep going," Michael said. "Scarlet knows we're going to Rousseau's. Perhaps she'll find us there."

"We can't just abandon her," Vixen said.

"As I said, I don't like it, but If you have a better idea, I'm all ears."

Copper agreed.

"The lad's right. There's nothing we can do for her from here. All we can do is hope she gets out of there safely, and take care of ourselves in the meantime."

~

The Ringmaster walked out the door of Fontainbleau's Haberdashery, expecting to find Mechanicules, Belladonna and Chevalier keeping watch out front, but he only found Chevalier standing there.

"Where the hell are Mech and Belladonna?" he asked.

A sheepish Chevalier just shrugged and held his hands out, to pantomime he didn't know.

The Ringmaster kicked at the ground in frustration and stomped his foot.

"My instructions were very simple! Stay here and keep a watch."

Spit flew from his lips as he talked.

"One simple thing I ask. Nothing could be simpler! Just stand here and do nothing. How bloody hard is that?"

48

THE LUNA SQUARE

The decision to leave Scarlet was difficult, and not one the team took lightly. But they also came to realize there was nothing they could do. From the quiet tunnel floor, they climbed up to street level.

"Keep an eye out for John, his flat is just around the corner," Michael said.

"John had better watch out for me," Copper said. "Let him show his face, and I'll smash it in."

As they walked, Vixen looked bothered.

"What's wrong," Michael asked.

"Don't you think that was a little too easy?" Vixen asked. "Getting the token, I mean."

"What's wrong with easy?" Copper asked. "I prefer easy. You won't hear me complain. Not a wee bit."

"There's nothing wrong, really. But given how difficult everything else has been, getting the token from Mr. Andouille was astonishingly simple. It just makes me uneasy, like we could have missed something."

"Like what?" Michael asked. "We got the token."

"I don't know. What if we left something behind?"

"What could we have left behind?"

"Another token, perhaps? A clue or further instructions? Something. We're just going to Rousseau's with no idea why. Just go to Rousseau's? That's it?"

"Yes, that's correct. That's what it said. We did the same with Mr. Andouille."

"Then what?" she said.

"I don't know," Michael said. "We'll find out when we get there."

"I like to have a plan, to know what to expect," she said. "Not knowing bothers me to no end."

Michael didn't respond, he just walked with the urgency of a desperate man, uncharacteristically focused, his determination unyielding. The streets were busy with horse-drawn trams and steam buggies. It was near the end of the workday, and sidewalks were crowded with pedestrians. Michael led the way, pushing his way between people without regard for who he bumped, or shoved past. Then he stopped. After a few more blocks, they had arrived.

"Here it is," Michael said. "Rousseau's Apothecary."

He stood staring in. The window was filled with medicine bottles and elixirs, jars of herbs and a vast assortment of other remedies, just like he remembered. Clear glass bottles affixed with yellowed parchment labels, hundreds of them, filled the window. The labels were written by hand in fountain pen, the penmanship was near perfect. Liniments, balms, salves, elixirs and tonics filled the shelves inside. As he stood staring through the window, he was filled with a new sense of hope.

"This is it," he said. "Our final token is through this door, then we're done."

The furrow in his brow eased, his pursed lips relaxed. A calm came over him and he smiled, something he hadn't done in a while. Vixen smiled back, feeling a weight lifted from her chest.

"We did it," Michael said. "Let's go."

They walked inside. If the window display was crowded with

bottles, then the inside defied description. Shelves upon shelves filled with thousands upon thousands of clear glass bottles, jars and flasks. Some were filled with clear liquid, some with colored liquids. There were dried herbs, powders, aromatics, leaves and roots, even bottles of pills including *Blue Mass* and *Nostradamus' Rose Petal Pills*. Quartz, amethyst and citrine healing crystals were all neatly displayed in square wooden boxes. Michael read the labels as he walked by some of the offerings: *Satchel B. Oleander's Miracle Hair Tonic*, guaranteed to grow hair on anything, *Thaddeus Mumblebeek's Invigorating Elixir*, a sure-fire cure for fatigue, and of course *Jean Valnet's Aromatic Oils*: Eucalyptus to calm fussy children, lavender for anxiety and demonic possession, menthol for achy joints and leprosy, and bergamot to treat sore feet, small pox and the dreaded pig fever.

"He has *Four Thieves Vinegar*," Vixen said. "To ward off the Plague and other contagions."

"The Plague? Why is it called *Four Thieves Vinegar*?" Michael asked.

"During the outbreak of the Plague in the seventeenth century, a group of four thieves marauded through badly infected areas. They went into the homes of the ill, or the dead, and stole anything of value they could carry. Despicable, to say the least. They were eventually caught, convicted and sentenced to be burned at the stake. The authorities, however, were intrigued by their ability to enter Plague infested homes without catching it themselves. Any normal person would have fallen ill and died, but these four men were somehow immune. So the magistrate offered them a deal. If they would tell their secret of how they avoided catching the Plague, they would not be burned."

"So they revealed their secret?"

"Of course they did. It was a solution of vinegar infused with extracts of tree barks, plant roots, garlic, herbs, and flower petals. They rubbed the solution on their face, neck, hands and chest, and carried a small jar with them, for inhaling. At least that's how the story goes, anyway."

"And they were spared from being burned at the stake?"

"As promised, none of the four thieves was burned at the stake. Once they had revealed their secret, they were immediately shot."

"Holy hell," Michael said. "That's awful, but I do suppose they had it coming. Does the vinegar work?"

A voice called out from behind the counter as the man emerged from the back room.

"Of course it works," he said. "It works like a charm. And not just on the Plague, but pox and measles, too. It's two francs if you want it, or four bottles for eight, special price, today only. And by the way, the four thieves weren't actually shot."

"They weren't?" Vixen asked.

"No, not at all. They were hanged shoulder to shoulder. Just in case you want to get your story straight."

The man came out from behind the counter and walked over to Copper. Copper was staring at a glass jar on the counter, filled with water and a dozen leeches swimming inside.

"Do you need a fever leeched?" he asked.

"Me?" Copper asked. "No, definitely not."

Mr. Rousseau spoke quickly, pushing hard to peddle his wares.

"Bloodletting is among the most effective medical treatments known in modern medicine. The leeches will cure anything, and I'm quite good with my application. You see, you just have to master proper placement to provide the most effective treatment. And ideal placement varies, depending on what ails you. For ten francs and I can leech out all your ills, what do you say?"

"Sorry old timer, but I've got the Scots blood in me. Strong as an ox, healthy as a horse, and stubborn as a mule. So you can keep your bloody leeches right there in that jar. Pun intended."

"So you don't want to be leeched, and you don't seem too interested in the Four Thieves Vinegar. So what brings you all here?"

"We've just come from the clockmaker, Mr. Andouille," Michael said. "He sent us here in search of a token."

Mr. Rousseau realized these were no ordinary customers.

"Andouille? A token you say."

Rousseau switched from eager salesman to skeptical gate-keeper. He puffed his chest and crossed his arms.

"Yes, I may have what you're looking for. But first, you'll have to play a little game. If you can find something in this shop that treats not only fever, rheumatism and gout, but also treats scabies, pox and nausea, then I will show you where to get the token you're after. But it has to treat all six, no shortcuts.

Vixen looked panicked.

"There's quite literally thousands of remedies in here," she said.

"I saw something for anxiety," Michael said. "But it could take us hours to read all these labels!"

Copper looked left, then right and scratched his head. He was trying to look interested. But in reality he was just passing the time, hoping someone else would figure it out. He watched as Michael and Vixen frantically moved from bottle to bottle, scanning labels and moving from one to the next. Kamal walked over to him.

"I believe we already know the answer," Kamal whispered.

He pointed to the leeches. Then he called out to Mr. Rousseau.

"The treatment you speak of, it's right here. It's the leeches. You said the leeches can cure you of anything that ails you. So this must be the answer to your question. If it cures anything, it most certainly cures the six ailments you mentioned."

"Brilliant," Michael said.

"Too easy," Vixen said.

"No. He's actually correct," Mr. Rousseau said.

He chuckled to himself and gestured toward Copper.

"Had I realized your friend here was not shopping, I may not have sold them so hard. That was my mistake, and I should have realized why you were here from the outset."

"That's it?" Vixen asked.

She was incredulous.

"You came here looking for a token, miss. You're about to get what you came here for. Why so upset?" he asked with a friendly snicker.

"I'm not complaining, it's just that after all we've done to get here, it just seems too easy. Forgive my skepticism, but I feel like we're missing something."

"Well, whatever it is you're missing, I wish you luck in finding it. Right this way now."

Mr. Rousseau led them to the back of the shop, a storeroom of sorts. He slid a heavy wooden crate across the floor to uncover a trap door. He lifted a trap door in the floor, to reveal a passage back down.

"Another ladder?" Vixen asked. "Not the catacombs again."

"That's up to you," he said. "But the token you're after, it's down this ladder. When you get to the bottom, walk to the end, fifty yards or so, to the door. The token is just on the other side of the door."

"Let's go then," Michael said.

He set his hand gently on the small of her back, to nudge her along. She took notice.

"I believe I know the way, Mr. McGillicuddy. I've used a ladder before."

Despite her strong and stubborn front, she actually appreciated the contact. In fact she welcomed it, even secretly wished for it. In truth, over the course of just a few days, she had become quite smitten with Michael. More so than any other time she could recall. She knew it from the moment they pulled to the side of the road not far from the starting line, and he helped her find her way. But she held back, too stubborn to let on. In her own mind, she had good reasons for doing so. First, she welcomed a challenge of any kind, and she took the race seriously. She wanted to win it as badly as anybody. Losing was something she had never grown accustomed to, and it wouldn't be acceptable here. She was first in her class in school, top of her class at university, and won every tournament she entered. Every endeavor undertaken in her lab eventually proved successful. She desired nothing less here. She was strong, intelligent and respected for her ability by anyone who knew her. She wanted to be seen as such here - capable, valuable and victorious. The idea of allowing herself to feel vulnerable, to be accessible to someone as handsome as Michael, made her uneasy, to say the least.

This was not the right time to let her guard down. She learned that much about herself in Michael's room at Gillingham, and she had kept up a cold front ever since. It was not for lack of interest, but borne solely of a desire to stay in complete control of herself. From time to time, her true feelings, her softer side, peeked out through her prickly facade. A sweet look, an extended stare, a giggle and a hand placed softly on his arm while he spoke. Michael had noticed each time, and she knew he noticed, even if he never mentioned it. Every time she slipped, she caught herself and buried the feelings away, deep inside. This was especially true on Ring Island. When Scarlet embraced Michael the way she did, and Michael acquiesced in her embrace, Vixen's stomach burned with jealousy. But she refused to acknowledge it. As they now stood in the storeroom of the Apothecary shop, with Micheal's warm hand resting gently on her back, Vixen recalled more of the fleeting moments they had shared, including that very first glimpse she caught of him at the starting line in Gatling Meadows. She was inexplicably smitten beyond words.

Maybe she was giving in to the fatigue of their journey, or getting caught up in the euphoria of being so close to another victory. But regardless of the reason, she had tired of maintaining her emotional distance. She tired of forcing herself to be unavailable. She looked him up and down, with his strong build, and innocent good looks. He was a fine, respectable person, genuinely looking out for the best interests of everyone around him, while chasing after what he wanted for himself. Brilliant, but eccentric. He was awkward, but honest and genuine; selfless and fair throughout. He was even silly and bumbling at times, but completely charming through all of it. She nodded to herself, taking it all in.

"Shall we?" Michael said.

She turned to face him. Her lips curled into a sultry smile and her dimples grew more pronounced. She looked up into his eyes and spoke in a confident tone.

"Oh. We shall, Michael."

Then she covered her mouth and giggled. She was positively giddy, and she let it show.

Michael nodded and held his other hand out toward the ladder to invite her down.

"Ladies first," he said.

Vixen scaled down the ladder and Copper stepped forward to go next. He stopped and leaned in to Michael and whispered.

"Do you need me to explain what just happened, lad, or did you get it this time? I don't mind explaining it to you if you didn't understand it. You just let me know, ok?"

Michael waved him off, and motioned for him to go down the ladder.

When they reached the floor below, oil lamps provided a dim glow, and they could see to the end of the tunnel. It ended at a heavy stone door. They walked to the end of the hall and stood at the door, only to find that there was no doorknob or other obvious way to open it. Just a stone carving on the wall, to the right of the door. The carving was several feet square, composed of a raised grid, nine squares by nine squares, with each square bearing an engraved number. The numbers appeared scrambled, in no particular order.

37	78	29	70	21	62	13	54	5
6	38	79	30	71	22	63	14	46
47	7	39	80	31	72	23	55	15
16	48	8	40	81	32	64	24	56
57	17	49	9	41	73	33	65	25
26	58	18	50	1	42	74	34	66
67	27	59	10	51	2	43	75	35
36	68	19	60	11	52	3	44	76
77	28	69	20	61	12	53	4	45

Michael ran his hand over the door. It was cold, heavy stone. He banged on it with the bottom of his fist and tried to move it, but there was no budging it. It may as well have been a wall. Recalling John's trick the alleyway, he tried turning the lamps mounted on the wall, in hopes that one might open the door. But none did.

"Mr. Rousseau said the token would be here, at the end of this hall, so where is it?" Copper said.

"Actually," Vixen said, "he said it was on the other side of this door. We just need to figure out how to open it."

"Step aside," Copper said.

He smashed the heavy head of his smithing hammer into the door with all his might. A loud clang rang out from the impact, but other than a small chip in the stone, the blow did nothing.

"It will take you a week at this pace," Michael said. "Does anyone have a better idea?"

All eyes turned to Kamal, who was standing with his arms crossed, studying the carved squares on the wall.

"Do you think it's a math problem?" Michael asked. "Or a puzzle?"

"I can tell you what this is," Kamal said, " but I don't have any idea how it will help us."

"What is it?" Michael asked.

"This is a Luna Square."

Michael stared at it for a second.

"Fascinating."

"What is?" Kamal asked.

It only took Michael a second to figure it out.

"The rows and columns all add up to the same number."

"What are you talking about?" Vixen asked.

"Look," Michael said. "Pick any row, any column or any diagonal. Add up all the numbers. They sum 369 every single time. What are the odds of that?"

Vixen was far too anxious to bother with the math.

"How could you possibly see that?"

"I don't know. It's just there. Waiting to be seen."

"This is by design," Kamal said. "The Luna Square is a magic square on the order of nine. There are numerous possible configurations."

He paused, taking a moment to add up the numbers of the first column in his head.

"Yes, I agree, the magic constant of this particular configuration is 369," he said.

"What did you just say?" Michael asked.

"The magic constant is 369. As you said, all the rows and columns sum to 369. That makes 369 the constant."

"Magic square? Constant?" Michael said. "Hold that thought for one moment."

He reached into his satchel and pulled out his invitation.

"Yes, it's just as I thought."

He read a section from the invitation out loud.

"Listen to this. Find the Magic Square. 9 steps right, 40 steps up, 8 steps left, and 49 steps down. The constant is your key."

He looked up from the parchment.

"So this constant, as you say, 369. That must be the key to open the door."

"But what about the steps?" Copper asked.

"Fair question," Michael said.

He rubbed the back of his neck, as he looked around.

"I'm not sure. And this tunnel is pretty narrow. Maybe the steps up and down refer to steps up and down the tunnel, or the ladder. But that doesn't really make sense. And there's no way to take nine steps right or eight steps left. The hall is far too narrow."

"And how do we use this so-called *key*?" Vixen said.

"I don't know," Michael said.

He leaned against the wall, frustrated, staring at the ground with his hands wrapped together around the back of his neck. Kamal walked up to the sculpture to inspect it more closely. He ran his thumbnail along the lines forming the squares. He tried several, and became particularly focused on the 8 and the 9.

"Can you repeat the steps you just mentioned, one at a time?"

"9 steps right," Michael said.

Kamal wiped the dust from the numbers and blew on them, then he unsheathed the small dagger on his belt. He wedged the thin blade between the 9 and the 49 on the sculpture.

"I have an idea," he said.

He twisted the blade and a whole block of squares, the 9 and everything to the right of it, slid to the side. He pulled it further right with his hand. The whole block went one step right, and the block marked 25 now formed a jagged edge.

Vixen and Copper looked on, as impressed as ever.

"Well I'll be," Copper said. "I never would have thought of that."

"And the next one?" Kamal asked.

"40 steps up."

With both thumbs, Kamal lifted the square marked 40 and everything above it. The block slid one step up, with the square marked 70 now forming a jagged edge in the top.

"And the next?"

"8 steps left."

Kamal pushed the 8 and everything to the left of it one square left.

"And the last?"

"49 steps down."

Kamal moved the square marked 49 and everything below it down one step. The original magic square now had a two-by-two hole in its face, where the squares marked 8, 40, 49 and 9 used to be.

"Nothing happened," Copper said. "It didn't work."

"Look into the hole," Kamal said.

Michael, Copper and Vixen peered into the square opening. Inside, set behind the larger magic square, was a smaller one. It was a magic square on the order of three.

8	1	6
3	5	7
4	9	2

Kamal ran his fingernail once again between the 8 and the 1, then the 1 and the 5. There was no gap. He checked the crack between the 3 and the 5, and when he pressed his fingernail in, the square marked with a 3 pressed in slightly. With an extended finger, he pressed it in all the way, one cube deep.

"This is it. This is where we use the key," he said.

He pressed in the square marked 6, then the square marked 9.

He had entered them in sequence: 3-6-9. The heavy stone door rose up to reveal an opening into a small room. The room, however, was the same width as the tunnel; and only ten feet deep.

"Great," Michael said. "For all that trouble, we get to move forward another ten feet?"

The room was empty, apart from a small inset in the wall. If the inset had been a recessed bookshelf, it might have held five or six books. But here, there were no books. Just a shiny token, marked with nine stars, sitting in plain sight in the cubby, ready to be taken.

"Copper! It's your last token!" Michael exclaimed.

Copper stepped forward and picked up the token and flicked it into the air with his thumb. It made a metallic ringing sound as it spun through the air. He caught it and placed it into his pocket with the others. It settled in with a solid jingle.

When he removed the token, however, a small stone column, the size of the token, rose up an inch from the otherwise flat surface of the inset. The token had concealed it and held it down, like a pressed button. But with the token removed, it rose back up. As it rose, the heavy stone door slammed down behind them, from where they had just come in.

"We're trapped!" Vixen screamed.

But as the door behind them closed, the door in front of them opened, to reveal another long stretch of hallway.

Copper chuckled at Vixen's panic. She looked sheepish, even a little embarrassed.

"Oh," she said. "My mistake, never mind. Look down there, on the right. There's a doorway."

Down the hall, they saw Nigel running toward them from the other end. He was in a hurry. He sprinted down the hall and turned the corner to go through the doorway.

"Let's go!" Michael said. "Nigel's ahead of us, and there may be others."

As they ran to catch Nigel, they saw Dorado coming from the

other end as well. He too rounded the corner before they could get there. As they got closer to the doorway, they could see the Ringmaster and a group of his underlings, including Belladonna and Mechanicules, storming toward them.

"What is happening?" Vixen shouted. "Where are they all coming from, and why are they all here?"

"I'm really not sure," Michael said. "But let us not be last!"

49

WHO'S UP FOR A GAME OF CUBETTA?

They rushed down the hall and through the doorway on the right. But as they turned the corner, they realized it wasn't an exit at all. In fact, it was an entrance to another cavernous underground room, with stone walls on every side, thirty feet tall. High above the floor, on the left and the right sides of the room, large red velvet panels hung on the wall like giant curtains, three separate panels on each side. Apart from lamps and velvet panels, the room was barren and quiet. The floor was smooth stone, forty feet by forty feet, covered with giant five-foot by five-foot stone tiles. Their footsteps resonated, echoing through the room.

Nigel stood near Dorado and two other new arrivals. Copper and Nigel stood eye-to-eye.

"Copper, nice to see you," Nigel said, with a tip of his cap.

"Nigel, I can see you standing there," Copper replied. "And there's still nothing nice about it."

"Good grief, Copper, let it go."

"Oh, come now. I should think you would know me better than that, laddie."

"Yes, of course. I was just being polite. A true gentleman,

gentle in the most literal sense of the word. Worldly, educated, sophisticated, well-traveled and of a certain refined taste. Not that you would know anything about that. Stay as angry as you like, jealous if you will, but I…"

"Shut your beak, Nigel, before I whack it clean off," Copper said.

He held his smithing hammer out in a threatening way.

"Classic Copper, always the brute, resorting to threats of physical violence. You haven't changed one bit. You know what they say, once a…"

He was interrupted by the Ringmaster's entry into the room. He was followed by Belladonna, Mechanicules and Phillippe. Close behind them came Chevalier and Beatrix. The whole lot of them stared with wonder in their eyes, as they spread out across the back edge of the room, assessing what the next steps might be.

"Looking at this place, I'd be inclined to think I'm in the wrong spot," the Ringmaster said, "but you all are here as well, so there must be some purpose behind us coming together."

Belladonna strutted toward Michael. Kamal stepped in between them to block her approach.

"Not now, Belladonna," the Ringmaster said. "I believe we have more important things to deal with here. I suspect this will require our fullest attention. Save your energy."

They continued to spread out across the back of the room. William Wilfork ran in.

"Good god," he said as he entered the room.

"What is going on here? Why are you all just standing here? Where's the exit?"

"If we knew, do you think we'd just be standing here?" Michael asked.

Michael barely finished his sentence when Baron Kamper von Braun entered. He had all the airs of a man in complete control, confident and bold. He studied the room, looking his competitors up and down, nodding his head knowingly.

"It's the Baron," Michael gasped.

Michael was more than just slightly awestruck. The man was a legend, after all. With his chest out, nose in the air and thumbs tucked into his belt, his commanding presence overtook the room as he chose his spot among them. A heavy stone door dropped down behind him and sealed off the entrance, the sound shook the floor and reverberated off the walls. The participants spread further out, looking at each other distrustfully, unsure what was next. At the other end of the room, they could hear stone sliding against stone. Two doors rose open in the back corner. A series of automatons, each the size of an adult man, marched out in two perfect rows across the other end of the room, their metal clad feet marking time, their steps perfectly synchronized. *Clunk, clunk, clunk.* Perfectly aligned across the opposite end of the room, they stood still, facing the participants.

"Michael, what is going on here?" Vixen asked.

"I'm not entirely sure, but I have my suspicions. Those automatons look positively terrifying. I've heard of people using them for work in warehouses, heavy lifting and the like. But those are clad in battle gear. Piston spears, hammer dashers, flamethrowers. I've never seen anything like it, not that size anyway. And over there. Rotary blades, long blades, crusher claws, even scissor claws."

"Scissor claw?"

"Yes, like giant scissors, but with curved blades that can cleave a man right in half. I hope we're not meant to try and pass them."

"You and me both," she said. "What should we do?"

"I'm thinking."

Once the automatons had settled into position, the red velvet panels above pulled back to reveal an audience looking down at them from raised balcony seating. As the curtains swept open, the crowd above let out blood-thirsty cheers, and money began changing hands between audience members and bookmakers. Wagers were being placed on what was to come.

An automaton stepped forward and the crowd cheered anew, excited that the game had finally begun. A rumbling sound filled the room and the floor started to vibrate.

"Oh no," Michael said. "I was afraid of this."

"What is it?" Vixen asked.

Michael turned to his teammates.

"Listen, I need you all to follow my instructions, just trust me and do what I tell you. Will you all do that?"

They nodded in general agreement.

"Fine, but seriously, what is going on?" Vixen insisted.

The floor under their feet began to rise, some faster than others.

"Vixen, do you remember back in Gillingham, you said you wanted to learn how to play Cubetta someday?"

"Yes, we discussed it at the game parlor. Why?"

"Today's your lucky day, we're about to play a game right now. But it's a life-size game. A game in which we are the game pieces, and the stakes are life and death. Do you have any alchemy orbs with you?"

"I have a few in my bag, yes."

"Good, keep them handy, we're going to need them. Kamal and Copper, stay close, we can maintain a position of collective strength if we stay together in well-coordinated formation, a four-piece detachment, if you will. It will be best for all of us if we work together as a single unit, rather than spreading apart on the board. Are you with me?"

"Aye," Copper said.

Kamal nodded a knowing look. He removed his shirt, revealing his tattoos, and sat down on his square with his legs crossed. He closed his eyes and mumbled some indiscernible incantations to himself.

"Is he… Is he meditating?" Vixen asked. "Of all the times to take a bloody break, this is not one of them!"

She watched him nonetheless, mesmerized, enchanted by the rhythm of his incantations. She looked closer at his tattoos, the three eyes on his upper arm, in particular. In one moment, they were just ink on skin. But in the next, they came to life. Their gaze turned toward her and blinked. She gasped out loud when she saw it.

"Oh my god! His tattoos are staring at me!"

"What do you mean they're staring at you?"

"The eyes tattooed on his arm. They were looking over there. And now they're looking up at me. And they just blinked! How can that be?"

Standing on the opposite side, Michael saw the snake tattoo slither around Kamal's upper arm.

"Aw, bloody hell," Copper said, looking down at Kamal. "I told you there was something I didn't like about that bloke, I told you I had a bad feeling. And now look at him! You shouldn't have brought him here."

The floor rose under their feet. What was once a flat surface across the entirety of the arena gained a new-found topography. Like the Cubetta board in the game parlor, with it's wooden columns shifting up and down at the turn of a crank, each of the squares on the floor rose to find new levels. When the motion stopped, Dorado stepped confidently forward onto the empty space directly in front of him. Once Dorado had moved, the floor reset. A shiny hammerdasher moved one square forward from the other side, and the audience applauded.

The game was in progress. Moves and level sets continued for several more rounds. Each side moved toward the other in succession, as they prepared to do battle near the middle.

Michael studied the variations carefully. With each reset of the board, he watched for patterns in the way the sixty-four blocks reset to their respective levels. After just eleven turns, he felt he had the pattern cracked. Recognizing the pattern within any given Cubetta board could never win a game on its own. But being able to predict the next level set with accuracy had always informed his strategy. Pattern recognition, prediction, visualization and memorization; these were skills only the rarest of players could master with any level of consistency, and most players had no choice but to leave the game to chance. But Michael was exceptional in his ability to see these patterns.

In the same way chess players step through scenarios in their heads before making a move, Michael did the same in Cubetta. It was no easy exercise. Chess boards stay flat, while Cubetta boards do not. Not only was he able to step through branches of possible moves in his head, but to do so effectively, he had to predict not only the lateral moves by pieces, but the vertical moves by the board's varying level sets. After all, a game piece is only allowed to move to an adjacent space at its same level. Successfully predicting the possible moves a piece might make in any given sequence requires a player to predict each square's level relative to the others at any given time during play. Being able to read the board and predict sequences in this fashion, however, had always allowed Michael to align his pieces together in the strongest possible arrangement, and avoid the most overwhelming matchups.

The opening sequence continued, one move after another. Kamal eventually rose to his feet, with all of his tattoos now animated. When the situation called for it, Michael guided his teammates where to move, reminding them to stay close, and grouped in a position of strength. Before long, the participants neared the middle, uncomfortably close to their mechanical opponents. Will and Nigel found themselves isolated, but close in proximity to Michael's group. Dorado and the Baron roamed confidently, each a lone wolf on the board, and the Ringmaster's crew stayed together in a tight cluster. The Ringmaster kept Mechanicules in front of him, as a defensive buffer against oncoming threats. The Baron, for his part, stayed near the back row. He moved with confidence, and had the look of a man who knew he had already won the game. He was just waiting for everyone else to figure it out.

At the next level set, Copper stood face to face with a hammerdasher. Its weapon was a sledgehammer the size of a garbage bin. It wasted no time loading up to strike. It pulled its hammer high in the air. As the hammer rose, the sound of heavy metal springs stretching to their limit was followed by the sound of a trigger releasing. The hammer came down hard and delivered a powerful, if not clumsy, blow. Copper dodged to the side as the weapon came down, barely avoiding its impact. Sparks and chips of stone flew. He nearly tumbled off his square to the square below, but managed to catch his balance.

"Oh, so it's going to be like that, is it?" Copper growled. "Well, you see, where I come from, we fight fire with fire. And we fight hammers with hammers."

The slow-moving hammerdasher stood prone, with it's heavy weapon still fully extended and set on the ground. Without hesitation, Copper took two strides forward and leaped up into the air. With his heavy smithing hammer gripped in both hands, he pulled it back above his head. As he came back down, he thrust the hammer down and struck the automaton with all his might, smashing the head down into its metal torso. He continued to strike the automaton, blow after crushing blow, and smashed a groove straight down the center of it. Three strikes, then four, he growled with an unfamiliar ferocity at every swing of the hammer. Vixen stood in awe of his aggression, as he showed a relentlessness and anger he had never before revealed. The physical threat of the hammerdasher had drawn out his most ruthless instincts. After a fifth crushing strike of his hammer, the automaton collapsed in a heap, soundly defeated. The crowds in the balcony let out a disappointed sigh as Copper stepped forward and took the square he had just won. He stood panting and wiped his brow with the back of his wrist. Money changed hands as they prepared for the next matchup, and the buzz in the audience rose again while the floor reset.

When the floor settled, Chevalier the mime stood toe-to-toe with a flamethrower automaton. Short and squat, with a wide base and large feet, it was not particularly fast. But with large tanks on its back filled with pressurized gas, and flamethrower barrels for arms, Chevalier would have to be quick. He reached into his pocket and pulled out what appeared to be nothing at all, and began to unfold the nothing in classic mime motion. The sound of whirring fans inside the combustion chambers of the flame throwers grew louder, evacuating any gas already in the chamber, and preparing to ignite the pilot.

"Do you have any idea what he's doing?" Michael asked Copper.

"None. In fact, I think he's gone quite mad," Copper said. "And he's about to get roasted."

"Won't matter much what he does here," Michael said.

Chevalier continued unfolding his invisible item and made a motion like he was throwing a fishing net over the automaton. The fans in the combustion chambers stopped. The pilot lights in the flamethrowers ignited with a pop, and glowed brightly. Chevalier placed his hands in the air in front of the automaton, and he moved them up and down like he was pressing them against a large pane of glass. Then he stopped and stood with his hands on his hips. He held his chin high, in defiant opposition of an automaton ready to unleash its fury on him. The sound of pressurized gas whistled as it rushed toward the pilot lights. The barrels were pointed directly at him, but he stood firm and unafraid. When the gas reached the pilots, it ignited, and glowing orange flames shot out both barrels.

But the flames never reached Chevalier. Instead, they swirled around as if enclosed in a square glass chimney surrounding the automaton, like a fiery tornado. The automaton was completely engulfed in its own flames. The flames swirled around and shot upward out of the invisible chimney, and when the flames subsided, all the remained was a burned out melted mass. Chevalier gestured with his hands, like he was wiping them together to clear off some dust. Then, with all his fingers drawn together, he pressed them to his lips, feigned a kiss and threw the kiss into the air. He clasped both hands together and shook them back and forth on either side of his head, a visual celebration of his own victory.

"Well I'll be buggered," Copper said.

"Did he just beat the automaton using the old mime and invisible box bit?" Michael asked.

"Aye. I believe he did, lad."

"Fascinating," Michael said. "Terrible shame though."

"He won. What shame?" Copper asked.

Chevalier stepped forward to take the square he had just won. The floor reset and he settled into position at Aeryx. His face revealed true panic when he realized his predicament. There was a hammer dasher on his left, a hammer dasher on his right and a piston spear directly in front of him. He was hopelessly outnumbered. Both hammer dashers brought their weapons crashing down on his square in near perfect unison. He narrowly dodged their attack, but all three pieces were perfectly coordinated. To dodge the oafish blows of the hammerdashers, he jumped directly toward the piston spear, but it had already started its delayed follow-up strike. The piston spear found its mark in Chevalier's chest, and after four or five rapid thrusts, through his chest and out his back, he fell to the floor, limp and motionless. The crowd roared its unconditional approval, and the squares reset.

"You see that?" Michael asked. "That's what I was talking about when I said it wouldn't matter. Given his position, challenging and defeating the flame thrower only delayed the inevitable. He was already lost before he even engaged with the flame thrower. I have to say, I did see that coming. I even told you as much."

Michael spun around to find Vixen.

"Are you ok?" he asked.

"No, I'm not ok! Absolutely not. Not even a little bit. Did you not see what just happened?"

"I saw it, yes. It's very unfortunate."

"We could be next, Michael. I could be next. I want to get out of here. Right now."

"I don't think that is going to happen. But I can keep you safe. Just trust in what I say, ok? When the floor resets, move one square forward."

He thought about it for a second and corrected himself.

"Wait, never mind what I just said. Don't go forward. Go one space to the right instead."

"Are you kidding me?" she yelled.

When the floor settled Vixen found herself presented with only two choices. She could go forward or she could go right. She looked at Michael with hysterical eyes.

"Which one is it, Michael?"

"To the right. Just like I said."

"You also said go forward. Are you absolutely certain?"

"Yes, absolutely. One square to the right. Now go."

She moved one square to the right, free from any conflict, and as she did she distanced herself from automatons that were approaching. After a few more rotations, the board reset and Mechanicules' square came to rest at Deuryx. He faced a rotary blade in front of him, and a piston hammer at a diagonal. Phillippe stood to his left, presumably ready to help. Both the rotary blade and piston hammer turned toward Mech and readied their attacks. Phillippe reached into the inside breast pocket of his jacket and pulled out two small spheres, each the size of a grape. He tossed them down at the feet of the automatons and they popped on the ground with a puff of smoke. Stage magic. Smoke balls. Hardly devastating. Mech glared at Phillippe while the spinning of the rotary blade accelerated.

"I am sorry," Phillppe said with his hands spread in front of him. "This is what I 'ave. I try to help you."

Like the sound of a saw blade spinning in a saw mill, the whirring got louder. Hesitant to wait for a first strike, Mech thrust his own piston spear right into the gear work of the opposing automaton. He pierced it several times, sending pieces flying and bouncing across the stone squares. The rotary blade automaton swung its weapon at Mech's mid-section. He swatted the blade with his mechanical arm, and sparks flew as the blade grazed him. The damage was superficial, and his weapon still worked. Having safely evaded the strike, Mech thrust his piston spear through the rotary blade's gearbox, and destroyed it.

One of the newcomers, Terrance Blunt, donning a red shirt, faced another hammerdasher as the board reset. He pulled a long chain from his pocket and swung it in circles over his head. After he delivered a few strikes, the automaton dropped its hammer down on him. The blow left him laying limp, and the automaton moved forward to claim his square.

Through a sequence of level sets, Michael guided Kamal, Vixen and Copper safely through the realignments. Dorado ended up in an unfortunate situation, with a scissor claw in front of him, a crusher claw on a diagonal, a hammerdasher to the left and a piston hammer to the right. The piston hammer struck first, but he dodged its thrusting attack. He pulled a gatling pistol from his holster and emptied six shots into its gearbox. It collapsed in a heap.

"Watch out," Copper shouted.

The hammerdasher smashed it's hammer down at Dorado. He side-stepped the blow, barely dodging it, and center shot the automaton with his other six round gatling pistol. The crusher claw, tall and formidable, advanced toward him. Dorado unholstered his long rifle and emptied one shot into it. He hit the opposing piece, but the shot was ineffective and the automaton kept advancing. It's large mechanical claw swept across and knocked the rifle out of his hand, down to an empty square below him.

"He's out of weapons," Vixen shrieked.

His remaining challengers, a crusher claw and scissor claw, stepped toward Dorado and readied their attacks. Dorado showed no fear. He smacked his toothpick, threw off his trench coat and let it drop to the floor.

"It's time for the big gun," he said. With the trench coat off, a heavy metal wrap-around chest plate, like the torso portion of a suit of armor, became visible. A larger gatling gun was mounted to his back, attached to a swivel arm. He swung the gatling gun around to the front, flipped it upright and opened fire on the two remaining automatons. They were nearly sawed in half by the spray of bullets, and they collapsed into broken, smoking heaps.

When the floor reset, Michael's square found its level at Aeryx. He stood in the shadow of a long sword automaton to his right, and Beatrix on the square to his left. Michael reached into his satchel and withdrew a spherical bronze device. It had a flat base and several short nodes protruding from the sphere. He used a clock key to wind up the device, but as he was winding, the automaton struck first, with several downward whacks with its sword-like weapon. It struck repeatedly, trying to split Michael in half from head to toe. Each strike against the stone base produced a loud clang and a shower of sparks, but Michael dodged each blow successfully. At the first available pause, he reared back to toss the bronze sphere at the automaton. Just as he stepped to make his throw, Beatrix kicked his leg out from under him. He fell and landed on his belly. The wind was knocked out of him, but he tried to compose himself. The automaton struck again, bringing the sword down with a hard blow. He rolled to one side, but not quickly enough. The blade came down hard, slicing through his shirt sleeve, tearing the flesh near his shoulder. He yelped, and winced in pain.

"Oh my god, Michael, are you ok?" Vixen shouted. "We have to help him!"

The sword chopped down and slammed into the stone block, sending more sparks flying, but he rolled out of the way. Roaring erupted from the crowds in the balcony as they recognized the prospect of another kill. Michael rose to a knee and flung the sphere at the automaton. Its flat magnetic base stuck to the automaton's outer frame. Thick blue arcs of electricity discharged from the outer nodes, and into the automaton. The flash only lasted a fraction of a second, but the automaton froze in place. While the floor reset its position, Michael shouted to Vixen.

"I'm fine," he said, slightly short of breath. "It's just a cut, but I'm really fine."

"How did you do that?" she said.

"The automaton runs like a clock, some large gears but also a lot of very small ones. The intensity of the electrical discharge welds the finest teeth of the smallest gears together. When those gears seize, so does everything else. It's completely frozen."

"Brilliant," she said.

Then he turned to Beatrix and pointed an angry finger.

"You are a horrible person," he said. "Do you know that? I could have been killed."

Beatrix shrugged, and smiled sweetly. She didn't care. The floor began to reset. Michael looked up as his level changed. Belladonna was on a diagonal from him, one level up. She stood with her hands on her hips and glasses flipped up, glaring down at him. As the floor continued to move, his square rose while hers came down. She passed him on her way down, and her icy stare never broke. She never even blinked.

Her square found its level at Aeryx, right next to Phillippe's. Mech was nearby, and a piston spear stood on her left diagonal. The piston spear set its reciprocating spear tip in motion as it turned toward Phillippe, ready to thrust at him. As soon as he realized it, he leapt out of the way and shoved past Belladonna, pushing her into the path of its attack, trying only to secure his own escape. Belladonna stood prone. She knew her poisons would have no effect on her mechanical opponent.

"Mech, I need you!"

The automaton lunged at her and she barely ducked its attack. The cheering rose louder. Mech held his arm in the air to test fire his piston spear, but it was fully discharged from the prior battle. He needed to wind it. He pulled the small crank from his pocket and set it into the receiver, on the inside portion of his forearm, to wind the springs. But in his haste, he dropped it. Belladonna barely dodged another thrust. The audience roared even louder.

"C'mon, Mech, I need you here," she said.

There was an uncharacteristic panic in her voice.

"Please hurry."

The automaton lunged and thrust at her midsection again, and she lurched out of the way. Despite her extraordinary quickness, it nearly hit her. Mechanicules finally retrieved the crank. He set it in, and wound the mechanism. The automaton struck at Belladonna one more time and she let out a yelp as she dodged it. It was the closest one yet. With his weapon wound, Mech jammed his spear tip into the automaton's torso and let loose its attack, rendering the automaton defeated.

"Thanks," she said. "What took you so long?"

She turned her attention to Phillippe as the board reset. He stood with a sheepish look, fully aware of his own cowardice. He was ashamed of himself on the inside, but showed no outward sign of guilt. He held his hands out to the side and spoke unapologetically.

"You should know what you get with me. And if you do not, then shame on you for your ignorance."

"You're dead to me," she said.

She spit on the ground and turned her back to him.

The floor reset. Vixen was immediately attacked by a hammerdasher. It's heavy hammer smashed down on her square, barely missing.

"Vixen," Michael yelled. "Use one of your orbs! And be careful!"

She pulled an orb from her bag. Like a person startled by a loud noise, lacking even the most basic physical coordination, she flung it awkwardly at the automaton in front of her.

"Is she left-handed?" Copper asked.

He shook his head.

"She must be left-handed. She looks like a left-handed person trying to throw with her right hand."

Michael looked at him cross.

"What?" Copper said. "It's a fair question. I mean, did you see her?"

In a stroke of pure luck, and free of any intervening skill, the orb shattered at the automaton's feet and the elixir it contained washed across the stone surface it stood on. A loud, but familiar, rumbling noise, caused by the transformation of the stone, boomed through the room and reverberated off the walls with stunning effect. Michael could feel the vibrations under his feet and in his chest. He even felt it in his teeth. The stone underneath the automaton's feet transformed to liquid and the automaton fell in. It sank inside the watery column. Vixen shrieked with excitement, and clapped her hands closely in front of her face, bouncing excitedly. She looked at Michael.

"It worked!" she said with happy surprise. "Did you see that? It bloody worked."

The rumbling noise returned, and the liquid turned back to stone, with the automaton sealed inside.

"It worked," she said again in a giddy tone. "I can't believe it worked. Did you see what I did? I kicked its arse!"

Six automatons remained. The floor reset again. Vixen finished her happy claps, and when the floor settled, Mech was challenged by a scissor claw. It was no match, and he quickly dispatched it.

The ensuing reset produced a most unfortunate circumstance. A low probability event, as Vixen would call it. Kamal was surrounded on five sides by the only remaining automatons on the board, all at the same level. The audience went wild. Bets were placed and massive amounts of money changed hands in the balcony. Kamal sized up his situation. There was a crusher claw to his left and a piston hammer to his right. The scissor claw on the left diagonal, opened and closed its enormous metal shear, as it readied its attack, but the sound of the shears scraping against each other was nowhere near enough to intimidate Kamal. There was a hammerdasher on the front right diagonal. Lastly, a dreaded piston spear, one of the most dangerous pieces in the game, stood directly in front of him.

"Oh my god," Vixen said. "There's no way he's getting out of this alive. It's five-on-one."

Kamal stood confidently, ready to accept all challengers. His eye tattoos moved across his skin. One moved to the back of his neck, and one moved around to his opposite shoulder. He stood facing forward, and with the benefit of being able to see through his tattoos, he could see in four different directions all at once, without even turning his head. Will stood near Kamal. He picked up a scrap of metal from one of the defeated automatons and hurled it. But it was futile.

The flurry of attacks against Kamal came in rapid succession. One attack followed closely after the other, first a piston hammer from the right, then the crusher claw from behind. Kamal rolled, ducked and dodged, relying on his four-directional vision. The fire-ball tattoos on his hips glowed. He moved his hands toward the tattoos and grabbed them. He stood holding a swirling ball of fire in each hand. He flung them at his enemies, one at the scissor claw and one at the hammer dasher. The fire balls landed squarely. Fire and cinders flew, but had no effect on the metal-clad automatons. The automatons, in a coordinated attack, chopped, thrust and lunged toward him. He rolled, dodged and flipped to avoid their strikes. He moved like the wind - fluid, fast and without restraint of any kind. He was not only fast, but flexible, able to drop into a deep back bend to dodge a sweeping blow that would have halved an ordinary person at the waist.

"We have to help him," Vixen yelled.

"I want to help, but what can we do?" Michael said.

The hammer dasher pounded its hammer down. Kamal rolled

to the side and popped back to his feet. The crusher claw lunged and attacked him from behind, but he saw it coming through the eye tattoo on the back of his neck. He ducked just as it snapped its claw shut with a loud clang, barely avoiding decapitation. The voices in the balcony sighed their disappointment. Kamal raised his left arm and held it steady, pointing all five fingertips at the crusher claw. The lightning bolts on his forearm glowed brightly.

"*Defri goun*," Kamal said.

On his word, the most magnificent lighting bolt, an intense luminous blue, shot from his fingertips and obliterated the automaton. If the arcs from Michael's bronze sphere were impressive, this was a hundred times better. A thousand times. Like actual lightning discharging from a storm cloud, massive sizzling, crackling blue arcs of electricity leapt from the fingertips of his left hand into the automaton. It stood charred, smoking and motionless before it fell over. Kamal looked down at his left hand. The lightning tattoo was gone. It was consumed, used up in his attack. He slumped over for a second, tired and drained, but he was forced to push through exhaustion by the threat from another automaton. He raised his right hand toward the oncoming piston hammer, with his fingers fully extended, he spoke once again.

"*Defri goun.*"

He let loose a second lightning strike. It was so bright, onlookers turned and covered their eyes. After his strike, the automaton stood motionless, smoldering, its metal cladding charred and welded in spots from the electrical arcs. Drained even further, Kamal fell to a knee. Visibly weakened by such a significant use of his powers, he knelt on the square with one hand on the floor, hunched over. He breathed deeply, struggling to stand. The lightning tattoo on his right arm faded away.

Three automatons remained. They stood over him, within striking distance: a scissor claw, a hammer dasher and a piston spear. They moved toward him in a coordinated motion. Weak and resigned, he bowed his head to acknowledge his own defeat. As he stared at the ground, he heard the metal feet step closer. In the chaos of the match, Copper, Michael and Vixen had become detached and distant. There was nothing they could do for him. He looked at them and spoke softly.

"It is too much to overcome. I understand my fate now, and I accept it peacefully."

"No!" Michael said. "This is my fault. I should have kept us closer together. Kamal, you have to fight through it. Don't give up now."

"There is too little fight left in me. It is my time."

The cheers of the audience rose, but above it all, Kamal could hear the sound of the piston spear start its motion, the rhythmic thrust of metal sliding against metal, increasing in speed. He closed his eyes, tattoos included, and the next sound anybody heard was that of the piston spear repeatedly piercing, with one rapid strike after another, through the center of the scissor claw. After six or seven thrusts, the scissor claw toppled over on its square. The hammer dasher raised it's heavy hammer to crush Kamal, but the Piston spear swiveled around and pierced the hammerdasher with five more thrusts, before it had a chance to let loose its hammer.

One automaton remained. Gameplay halted. A collective gasp burst out from the balcony, and the room fell instantly silent. Nobody on the game floor spoke or moved. The only automaton that remained, the piston spear, stood still. Its weaponized arms came to rest to its sides, and its reciprocating spears rested. The sound of a single metal clasp being unlatched broke a striking silence, and echoed off the stone walls. The outer helmet of the automaton opened and flipped backward, to reveal a human pilot on the inside.

"Scarlet!" Michael shouted.

Gasps rang out from the balcony. She spread open the chest plate, and opened the fronts of the mechanical legs, giving her the room to step forward out of the autonomous battle shell.

"I can't believe you're alive!" he said, with excitement in his voice. "And I can't believe you're here, doing, whatever you just did."

She chuckled.

"All in a day's work, Michael."

With no functioning automatons left on the board, the game was presumably over. Silence reigned. The judges in the balcony debated the legality of Scarlet's tactics. There was whispering, pointing and nodding. After a long silence, the squares all returned to their original levels, restoring the smooth monolithic floor that was there when they first walked in. The game was over. Onlookers in the balcony were stupefied. Michael, Vixen and Copper rushed over to greet Scarlet, and they shared a group embrace.

"How on earth did you get in there?" Michael asked.

"It's a long story, but when Mech and Belladonna were approaching in the catacomb, just after John betrayed us, I pulled out one of Vixen's orbs. I was about to throw it at them, not knowing what it would do, but I was desperate."

"It was you who stole my orb?" Vixen said.

"In Gillingham, I did. I lifted it from your room, while the two of you went to check on the fires and Michaels' buggy. Terribly sorry about that."

"You stole from me?"

"Indeed. And I've apologized now. Twice."

"Once." Vixen said.

"Yes, well, bygones. So as I was saying," Scarlet continued. "I was about to throw the orb at Mech and Belladonna, but it slipped out of my hand and it crashed to the floor. Just like when you opened the hole in the wall to escape from the tunnel, the elixir created a hole in the floor in front of me. I peered down through the hole and it looked like another tunnel running underneath the tunnel I was standing in."

"I can't believe you stole from me."

"Right. Covered that," Scarlet said, glossing over the issue. "So when the hole opened up, I jumped down through, and the ceiling closed above me. I was walking down the tunnel, and as luck would have it, it led to the room where the automatons were being staged before this match. Just behind that door where we came out over there. I overheard two men talking as they finished their preparations, and when they left, I decided to commandeer one of them. You're all very welcome by the way."

She looked directly at Kamal and winked.

"You especially."

"I am forever in your debt," he said.

"Don't mention it."

They were interrupted by a singular booming voice that called out from the balcony.

"For those of you still able to move on, the final air gate will be found hanging in the air directly above the grounds at Versailles. Good luck and Godspeed."

A door in the center of the side wall opened. Dorado picked up his long rifle and holstered it, while other participants bolted for the door.

"About the mime," Vixen said. "Were you piloting the piston spear that…"

Michael interrupted.

"We should really go," Michael said. "You can explain the rest later, but we need to get to the airship immediately, we're already losing ground."

50

TOWARD THE FINAL AIR GATE

Dorado sprinted toward the exit first and, the rest followed in a mad dash to leave the Cubetta room, squeezing up a long narrow staircase. It was a long climb back to street level and Michael fell short of breath. His lungs hurt and his legs burned worse with every step. Pure grit and adrenaline were all that kept him going. Scarlet and Vixen stayed close. Kamal was still very weak, so Copper slung Kamal's arm over the back of his neck to help him up the steps. The long stairway ended in a doorway, but without hesitation Dorado turned the knob and threw the door open. Daylight poured in, and the doorway let out into a back alley between two buildings. Dorado ran the end of the alley to see he was on *Rue de Grenelle*, just a short distance from the *Champs de Mars*, where the airships were anchored. Dorado looked over his shoulder to see the Baron emerge from the same doorway, followed by Michael and his team. Michael ran out the end of the alley onto the *Rue de Grenelle*. He looked left, and then right, straight down the narrow street where he could see the open grassy area and tree-lined space. The Ringmaster's crew was mere steps behind them. A foot race broke out and, upon reaching the edge of the *Champs de Mars*, they scattered in different directions, fanning out across the gardens, racing to board their airships.

While they were below ground the weather had turned worse. The clouds thickened and the wind increased. The Baron was the first to reach his airship and lift off. A veteran of the competition, the exercise was second nature to him. His ship rose into the air, while Michael and Copper struggled to untether their craft.

"Who tied this bloody knot?" Copper yelled.

The tether holding the airship was tied to a heavy iron rail at the edge of the gardens. The Baron rose in the distance while they fought to untie it. Will had boarded his craft, and the Ringmaster's crew was loading into theirs. Vixen took the helm and fired up the boilers while Michael and Copper worked the ropes.

"I can't get the knot out," Copper yelled.

The Ringmaster's craft lifted off the ground and began to gain altitude.

Michael loosened his rope and ran around to the other side to help Copper, but Copper shoved him back.

"Stand back, lad."

In a fit of anger, he bashed the iron rail with his smithing hammer as mercilessly as he had bashed that automaton. With three strikes, the wrought iron loop gave way and flopped over, letting the rope loose from the iron rail.

"Now git yer arse in the boat," he told Michael.

Copper and Michael boarded, and Vixen set a course to climb out of the gardens. She adjusted the fins and increased the fan speed. She looked up to see the Ringmaster's airship rise into the thick clouds and disappear from view.

By the time Vixen got her craft into the air, three others had already moved ahead of her, in the final stretch of the race. The Baron and Will had sizable leads, but were still within reach. The Ringmaster was almost certainly ahead of them, but there was no way to tell.

"Can you go any faster? Michael asked.

"We're steadily gaining, and we have a fair distance to go. It's maybe a half hour flight from here, not much more, but we have plenty of time to overtake them, and our pace is good."

"Everything we've done so far, Vixen, everything comes down to this."

She nodded knowingly, and pressed the throttle forward.

"It's near it's maximum, but we'll be fine. Look, we're gaining on them, and we have time on our side. My craft is fast, probably the fastest here."

She was correct. Michael could see the slow, but steady, rate at which they were closing the distance to the Baron, but it wasn't fast enough to give him comfort.

"We have to go faster," he said. "Too much depends on this to not make it. Don't let it be close, we should aim to beat them big. Leave no room for doubt."

"There's only so much I can do, Michael, the ship has her limits."

She stared straight ahead into the distance. She was done with the conversation. They were closing distance on the Baron, they were going to overtake him. To the rear, Nigel was the next closest behind them, but only a modest threat. Dorado was near even with him, but way off to the side, a good distance away. The remaining aircraft were further behind, seemingly out of contention. The Baron's craft was fast and maneuverable, but Vixen's was faster. It was really just a matter of time, and a question of whether they had enough left to notch a win.

51

CONFLICT ON THE DECK

It wasn't fast enough. Impatient, Michael pressed.

"If only we had gotten off the ground faster," he said.

He paced around on the deck, impatiently minding the gaps between airships. Vixen had closed the distance to roughly fifty yards, but still not close or fast enough for Michael's liking. Copper and Kamal were ready to help if needed, but there was little they could do. A steady hum of the fans drove the craft forward as they waited. The final gate appeared in the distance, a large floating air ring, set against the backdrop of the sprawling gardens of Versailles.

"There it is," Michael said. "The last gate. Once we overtake the Baron, victory is ours."

He looked back over his shoulder, behind them.

"We've got the rest of them beat. They can't catch us, there's no way."

The Baron's lead shrank to forty yards, then thirty as they cruised toward the gate. The Baron saw them gaining and tried to make any adjustment that he could that would increase his speed. Vixen steered the airship to within twenty yards, just off the Baron's left side. She came even with him, then the nose of her airship edged ahead of his. The Baron, aware of his position, calmly adjusted some levers and dials on his control panel, doing eking out a little more speed. His airship lurched forward, even with Vixen's, nose-to-nose, and threatened to pass.

As they competed for every spare inch they could steal from each other, the Ringmaster's airship abruptly descended from the cover of the clouds, directly above them. Dark grey wisps swirled around craft as it burst through.

"You know your assignments," the Ringmaster shouted out to his crew. "Now go!"

A full complement of members of the Black Steam Circus had boarded the ship during the Cubetta match. The Hellfire Troupe, a gaggle of clowns, the juggler, and the knife thrower joined the Ringmaster, Belladonna, Mechanicules, Phillippe and Beatrix to round out a fulsome crew.

"Toss them over the side," the Ringmaster yelled.

The clowns picked up heavy metal balls, like cannonballs, one in each hand. They dropped them over each side, toward the Baron's and Vixen's craft. Some missed as they fell past, some did not. One of them punched right through the deck on Vixen's airship. With a crash, it went straight through the deck and out through the bottom.

"Is everyone alright?" Michael yelled.

Nobody was hurt. More metal balls whizzed past.

"You have to get out from under them, Vixen!" Michael shouted. "Steer left before we take any more hits."

Vixen guided the craft to the left, out from underneath. The Baron, on the other hand, was less fortunate. Several of the metal balls struck his craft directly. They crashed down hard, with a solid impact. And serious consequences. One of the balls cracked the main steam line powering the rotors that drove his airship forward. While not completely disabled, a steady spew of steam shot from the crack, and the loss of pressure slowed the speed of his airship. His craft slowed as Vixen and the Ringmaster pulled away. The Baron banged his fists on the control panel and screamed out in frustration. From the helm of his flying galleon, the Ringmaster barked out orders for next steps.

"Cue the Hellfire Troupe," he said.

Belladonna signaled them to go.

The members of the Hellfire Troupe bellied up to the rail and lit their torches. They launched several of them at Vixen's craft but she drifted further out of range to evade them. On the other side of the galleon, the knife thrower hurled his throwing knives toward the Baron's balloon. The first one missed, so did the second. But the third had just enough force behind it. It reached the gas bag, and knicked it. The hole that opened was small, but troublesome. As it leaked, the Baron lost altitude and coasted toward the ground. Dorado gradually overtook him, and he was closing distance on Vixen and the Ringmaster. With the Baron safely disposed of, the Ringmaster gave new orders.

"Take it down lower," he ordered. "We're approaching the final gate and we need a set good line to pass through it easily."

He turned his attention back to Vixen's airship.

"Mechanicules, use your mini-cannon. Blow them out of the sky."

Mechanicules hesitated. He shook his head resistantly, but something short of defiant.

"He doesn't want to use it," Belladonna said. "It's too powerful. The recoil is too painful for him. You know that."

"I don't really care what he wants. Do it anyway! That's what it's for. That's what you're for, to do as I tell you. Now blow them out of the sky. If you don't, you know what's coming for you."

Mechanicules reluctantly gave in, but hung his head, resigned. He detached his mechanical hand and and replaced it with the mini-cannon attachment. He loaded a heavy shell into the rear and snapped the chamber shut. The barrel was less than a foot long, and the cannon fired one shell at a time. The shell itself was six inches long, and fired an exploding projectile the size of his fist.

"You're a monster," Belladonna said.

"Perhaps," he said. "And I might reconsider, if your opinion actually mattered."

Mech raised his arm and took his aim. He winced with anticipation and he braced himself for the painful recoil that came with the cannon's discharge. He flipped up a cross-hair site and pointed the barrel right at the rear upper deck, where Vixen stood piloting her airship. He adjusted his aim and placed the crosshairs directly on her.

DORADO PRESSED FORWARD, CRUISING AT A GOOD PACE. HE WAS gaining, and had managed to shorten their lead to just under a thousand yards. From the distance, Dorado had watched the Ringmaster and his crew's tactics. He was far enough back to be spared of their threats, but close enough to appreciate the lengths to which they went. He was willing to let most of it run its course, as part of the competition. But when he saw Mechanicules leaning over the rail, arm extended, taking aim at Vixen's craft, he was compelled to act. In a single motion, as smooth and natural as drawing a breath, he withdrew his rifle from the holster on his back, shouldered it, aimed it, fired one shot and returned the rifle to his holster. The bullet sailed through the air, across the vast expanse. It was nine hundred yards if it was an inch. After a short delay, the bullet found its target and crashed through Mechanicules' mechanical weapon. With a clang and a puff of smoke, the weapon was rendered useless. Mechanicules flinched at the noise and tried to fire the weapon. But it was too late, it had been destroyed by Dorado's bullet. Dorado returned to steering his craft, hoping to close the gap further.

"I despise that guy, I really do," he said to himself. "All of them, really. Every last one of them."

Seeing Mech's cannon disabled, Belladonna became frustrated. The two airships raced toward the gate.

"Enough of this nonsense," Belladonna said to Beatrix." Just get me over there."

She pointed to Vixen's craft.

"I'll do it myself."

Beatrix scurried to a cubby near the cabin and grabbed her tote bag. She removed her crossbow, cocked it and loaded the grappling hook. She knelt on one knee, closed one eye and sized up her shot.

"It is too high," Phillippe said. "Down a little bit."

"Shut it," she said.

She raised the angle just a hair, and pulled the trigger. Her original aim was perfect. The upward adjustment was just to spite Phillippe. The hook sailed through the air on a perfect arc and landed on the upper deck, right where Vixen stood. Beatrix pulled the slack out of the line, to latch the hook firmly on the rail of Vixen's craft. She placed the tensioner over the rail in front of her and began to crank the line tight. Her movement was efficient and well-rehearsed. Belladonna suited up in a leather trolley harness, clipped her trolley onto the cable and gave it a tug. She was ready to go, but not before she dipped her talon into a vial on her belt and snapped the lid shut.

"Michael," Vixen shouted. "They've latched onto us with something. A hook of some sort. What do I do?"

"Just keep going. You have to keep going, at any cost," he said from the lower deck.

He and Copper were busy sizing up the damage to the deck from the metal balls hurled at them. It didn't seem too bad, just a surface wound, nothing structural, and the steam lines were still intact.

When Beatrix finished winding, the line came taut and the pitch was perfect; the cable had a slight downward slant for Belladonna to slide across to Vixen's craft. Confident the trolley was secure,

Belladonna leaped over the side for a smooth ride across the long traverse. She looked down at the ground as she crossed over grass and many ponds, from high in the air. If she fell from that height, death seemed likely. It was a circumstance most would fear, but Belladonna found strange comfort. Risk of death made her feel alive, or near freedom. As she approached the side of Vixen's craft, she kicked her legs out and stopped herself against the hull.

Belladonna climbed over the rail and unclipped herself from the trolley. She stood on the rear deck, face to face with Vixen as Beatrix let loose the cable from the tensioner.

"Michael," Vixen shouted. "She's on board with us, what do I do?"

There was a knowing panic in Vixen's voice. Belladonna leaned in close and breathed deep. Michael was distracted, looking down through the hole in the deck with Copper.

"You haven't figured it out yet, dear?"

Belladonna spoke softly, through a slow exhale, calm and relaxed.

"Figured what out?"

"That there's nothing you *can* do. You're already dead."

Without warning, Belladonna seized upon Vixen. Her movement was deceptively fast. She slipped behind, reached around and covered Vixen's mouth with her hand to muffle her scream. She jammed the other hand into Vixen's back. The talon thrust in deeply between two ribs. Vixen stiffened for a moment, and her back arched as she flinched from the pain of being stabbed. Belladonna pulled the talon loose and let go, pushing Vixen aside. Vixen turned and looked at Belladonna, startled and holding her ribs.

"Why...did you do that?"

A look of surprise washed across her face. Surprise changed to terror. Vixen put her hand to her throat, and she began to wheeze. The wheezing turned to gasping. She fell to the deck panting, and struggling to breathe. She gasped and gulped for air, but a free breath simply wouldn't come.

Belladonna stood calmly over her, watching. Smiling.

"Now, under normal circumstances I would have given you a warning, dear," Belladonna said. "But sometimes rules are meant to be broken. And frankly, these circumstances are anything but normal. Don't be too upset though, because this isn't about you at all. It's about Michael. So just relax, go with it. Don't fight it. Things will be easier for you that way."

Vixen gasped and writhed on the deck, as Belladonna stood over her. Her face burned crimson in her struggle to breathe. Her arms flailed, reaching for something to grab, desperate to get a hold of anything that might help.

"Have it your way, love," Belladonna said. "I can't make you listen."

She flipped her glasses down and watched; grinning, basking in the agony she had inflicted.

Michael turned to check on Vixen and saw her collapsed on the deck, and Belladonna standing over her.

"No! What have you done?" Michael yelled.

Belladonna turned and flipped up her lenses to reveal her piercing blue-silver eyes once again.

"And now for you," she said. "I swear to god, I should have taken care of you when I killed your father. In the ignorance of my youth, in more innocent times, long before I buried any sense of compassion I ever had in the deepest, darkest recesses of my soulless, rancid core, I chose to let you live. I've questioned my judgment in that moment every day since. But here we are once again, love. We've come full circle, haven't we, my little tea-drinking waif? Can you believe it? I remember it like it was yesterday. You never forget your first time. Isn't that what they say? Something like that, I don't know, I can't remember."

She stood smug, smirking, almost proud of what she said, with no indication of regret. She spoke as if they were just two old friends, fondly reminiscing.

"What did you just say about my father?"

In the seconds that followed, Michael recounted in his head the day Seamus died, the guilt he felt, the guilt he carried with him his whole life. The events Seamus missed, the times he needed some fatherly advice but had nobody to turn to. He thought of the things his mother had to do, the responsibilities she had to undertake in Seamus' absence, responsibilities that she never should have had to bear.

"I don't understand," he said. "What do you mean by what you just said about my father?"

Michael reached into his pocket, searching for something.

"Oh, right. You thought it was your fault, I remember now. So naive, so sweet. Do you still blame yourself? Haven't you let that go yet? Tisk, tisk, isn't that adorable?"

"How do you know about that? How could you possibly know?"

"I was in your workshop that night. I was sent there with one very specific purpose. I had never done anything of the sort before, with as young as I was. But when the two of you went out to gather wood for the fire, I dropped some poison in your father's tea. It was deadly nightshade, my namesake, in fact. Belladonna, combined with the extract of some doll's eye berry."

"Who sent you?"

"The Ringmaster, of course. He had always resented your father, he could never beat him. And another race was fast approaching. They were both deep in preparation, and the Ringmaster couldn't stand to lose to your father again. So he sent me to make sure that wouldn't happen. And it didn't. Ironic, isn't it? Since the Ringmaster ended up losing to the Baron anyway, and it was all for naught."

"Michael, are you alright?" Copper shouted. "Vixen needs help. Do you need me to do something?"

Michael didn't respond. He just stared for a moment, emotionless, drifting in his own mind without any direction. Vixen lay on the deck wheezing, but less violently now. Her breath was slowing. She was succumbing to the toxin. Belladonna stepped toward him.

"It's not working," Michael mumbled to himself. "Where are they?"

He fumbled in his pocket again and pulled the emerald green crystal out, the one he received on Ring Island. Then he remembered the instructions he received.

"Rub the crystal and say my name? I don't know your name, what do you want me to do?"

But when he said the words 'my name', the crystal started to glow. Belladonna kept talking.

"I hid in the shadows as he drank his tea, as he bounced you on his shoulder. I watched him collapse. I watched him die. I watched you standing over him, weeping. It changed me forever. I wasn't always like this, but the shame and guilt had to be locked away, deep, deep inside in order to go on. From that day forward, I stopped allowing myself to feel; as well as I could in any event."

She closed her eyes and took a deep breath. As she exhaled, she opened her eyes again, and flipped open a vial on her belt. Without looking, she dipped the talon in. It was second nature.

"Let's get this over with, shall we?"

She strutted fearlessly toward Michael, one foot in front of the other, her eyes locked on his like a lion fixed on its prey. Vixen's panting slowed. Michael backpedaled to keep some distance. He searched for the words to convey what he was feeling, the hurt, the knot in his throat, the pit in his stomach, the anger of being stolen from; but the words wouldn't come. Vixen gulped for air. Her face went pale. She grasped her throat, writhing, with a look of knowing helplessness on her face.

"How can you be so broken?" he said.

She started to answer, but was distracted by the purple glow of a bardwog rising just behind him, hovering above his shoulder.

Then there were two. Before long, there were ten. They had answered the call of the crystal. A detachment of ten purple bardwogs hovered in formation directly behind Michael. Belladonna took another step toward Michael and the bardwogs broke formation. They darted around aggressively, their wings buzzed loudly. With the next step Belladonna took, the bardwogs attacked her. They swarmed around her, biting her face and her arms; her neck and her ears as she shrieked in pain. She waved her arms violently to swat them away, and drifted backward as their onslaught continued.

With each bite, the bardwogs took a chunk of flesh. She cried out in pain as their attack continued. She bled from her face, she bled from her neck. Her chest, her arms and even her ankles. Nothing was safe. The bardwogs were too fast, and too numerous. She waved her arms and jerked her head, trying to shake them off. She took another step back to evade their relentless attack, but she was nearing the rail.

Michael looked at Vixen, then he looked at Belladonna. They were each in serious trouble. Vixen lay on the deck of the airship, incapacitated by Belladonna's poison, dying. He was overwhelmed watching her lay there, helpless. Belladonna, on the other hand, was overwhelmed by the bardwogs. With each bite, she stepped back further, edging ever closer to the rail. Michael looked at Vixen laying prone, and then to Belladonna. She took another step backward, arms waving and swatting. Her heel backed up against the edge of the rail. She leaned precariously. There was nowhere to go but down. Michael looked at Vixen one last time, gasping for air, gulping for an easy breath. Michael dashed toward Belladonna, his hand outstretched toward her. With a look of hope, she reached her arm toward him. As she reached for his hand, he reached for her necklace. He ripped it from her neck, just before she toppled over the rail. The bardwogs followed her.

Michael ran up to where Vixen lay, struggling to breathe. Her gasping was getting weaker and her face more pale. Her arms were no longer rigid and desperate, but rather weak and limp. Scarlet and Copper joined Michael to comfort her in her final moments. The throttle lever was still pressed forward, and the wheel had not moved. The airship had stayed its course, even in Vixen's absence, right toward the air gate in the distance. Michael knelt beside Vixen and placed his hand under her limp neck, raising it to tilt her head back. He unscrewed the lid on one of the vials on Belladonna's necklace.

"What are you doing?" Copper said.

"I'm saving her," he said.

"Sorry, Michael. But she's beyond saving, lad. Just comfort her. That's probably just more poison. Who knows what noxious things that wretched woman carries with her! I'll bet the grass don't even grow where her tears fall."

But Michael wouldn't be dissuaded. He poured the clear liquid from the vial into Vixen's mouth and gently pressed her chin to close it. He caressed her cheek and her hair.

"Just swallow," he said. "Can you hear me, Vixen? Just swallow it."

Her eyes were still open, aware, but accepting and at peace. Her body was weak, and getting weaker. Her lips barely came together, despite her effort. She struggled, wheezing, but managed to swallow the fluid. Her mouth fell back open, and she continued to gulp for air, never quite able to get that deep satisfying breath she so desperately needed. Her wheezing slowed, and became less strained.

"She's slipping away," Copper said.

"No she's not. It's working."

"It's not, Michael. It's not working. You're losing her, lad. You need to accept that."

"I won't give up on her."

Her wheezing became even softer, and her eyes relaxed. The gasping eased and the color slowly returned to her face.

"It's working," Michael said.

Even he was surprised.

"You see that? It's actually working!"

Her skin color returned, from pale grey to her more natural rosy tone. The pink in her lips was restored from the translucent blue they had been just a moment earlier. She relaxed the arch in her back, her shoulders went soft and her breathing eased, as she slowly regained composure. Before long she was able to breathe normally, and she tried to sit up.

"Just stay down and relax, will you?" Michael said. "You've been through quite an ordeal. Kamal, can you take the wheel? We're not done yet."

Kamal took the wheel and turned the airship slightly right, on course for the center of the final air gate. Michael stayed kneeling close to Vixen.

"How did you know?" Vixen asked.

He shrugged.

"It was a calculated risk," he said with a coy smile. "I had no choice but to take a chance and hope it worked out for the best. And I most certainly would have lost you if I hadn't."

"Well played," she whispered.

She was still weak. But she managed something that resembled a smile.

"When I first saw Belladonna at John's flat," he said, "when she addressed me, she put her hand to her chest. It was notable, like she was covering the vials to protect them somehow. She did the same thing in the game parlor at Gillingham, when she was harassing you. When she stood near you, she carefully placed her hand over her chest to cover the vials. I saw her do it from the distance. It's a subtle habit, a pattern in her behavior, but she always acted as if there was something special about them. Like they were her most important possession, something worthy of subconscious and habitual protection."

"That's brilliant," Vixen said softly.

"If you work with poisons the way she does, what's more

important than an antidote? In the event you accidentally poison yourself. It's interesting to think about it, looking back on it now. She protected the vials so carefully, but at the same time she kept them so easily and readily accessible."

Vixen stared at Michael contemplatively.

"I heard what she said about your father, Michael. I'm so sorry."

He leaned in slowly, and kissed her lips softly.

"Don't get too familiar, Mr. McGillicuddy," she said.

She laid her head on his lap, and Michael ran his fingers gently through her hair.

"The Ringmaster," Kamal shouted. "He's pulling away from us."

52

APPROACHING THE FINISH LINE

"We have to beat them," Michael shouted. "Kamal, increase the throttle."

"I believe the craft is traveling at its maximum speed already," Kamal said.

Kamal was calm. He merely spoke facts, without the inconvenience of emotion. He was still weak from the Cubetta match, but he had recovered well enough to stand and move on his own.

"Copper, stay with Vixen," Michael said. "Keep a close eye on her."

He ran up the steps to the rear deck, where the boilers and throttle controls were located. He opened up one of the compartments and poked around inside. They were quickly approaching the final air gate. The Ringmaster's airship had edged ahead, and was pulling away.

"What are you trying to do?" Kamal asked.

"I have an idea," Michael said. "Do you have the throttle pressed completely to its maximum?"

"I do, yes. All the way, but it is not enough."

"If I can just find it, and open it, we'll have a chance."

"Find what?" Kamal said.

"It's something my father taught me, a trick he used to win one of his races. Yes, there it is. Now, if only I can get my hand in the right spot."

Michael rolled up his sleeves and gazed forward, focused. He measured up the Ringmaster's lead, then he estimated the time and distance to the air gate. He scurried down to his chest, grabbed some tools from inside, and rushed back up to the raised deck.

"Almost there," he said. "I can get us more speed but it's going to take its toll on the engine, It may even destroy it, so I can't do it too soon. If it's going to fail, it has to fail right at the finish, and not sooner."

He watched for a few more seconds. The Ringmaster was increasing his lead.

"Now. It's time."

He reached inside the compartment again with a wrench and forced the baffle open, beyond its ordinary limits. The pitch of the steam engine and the fan blades rose, and their speed increased. It increased to a point that it sounded like it was ready to explode, whining and squealing, pressed to its absolute limits.

"Hold on everyone, this is the last push. It's do or die time!"

The speed at which the Ringmaster was extending his lead slowed. Then it stopped growing. Then it began to shrink. They were gaining.

"It's working," Kamal said. "We're catching them. I don't know if we have enough time. It's going to be close."

Michael looked inside the compartment. Pieces of the engine that were once black, like pot metal, started to glow yellow. Some even glowed red.

"We're really pushing it here," Michael said. "But she's holding up ok so far. Just keep a steady course. When we're in a position to do so, drift in front of them so we can beat them through the gate."

Michael checked the engine compartment again. Parts that

once glowed a dull yellow now glowed red, and the parts that had glowed red were now bright red, bordering on translucent. A rivet blew from the pressure, and a geyser of steam spewed from a joint in the steam line.

Michael looked across, as they passed the Ringmaster's ship. Mechanicules stood at the side, with his hands on the rails, a look of bottled vengeance waiting to be uncorked. He had seen the confrontation with Belladonna. Through it all, Kamal held the course steady. He extended their lead to a quarter length, and then a half-length. Another rivet blew with a loud pop, and a second geyser of stream spewed out of the steam line.

"It's not going to last," Kamal said. "We're not going to make it."

"We're almost there," Michael screamed. "Stay with it. Don't give up."

The Ringmaster reached his limits of patience.

"They cannot be allowed through that gate ahead of us," he said.

He stormed up and shoved Phillippe aside, to take command of the wheel. He turned it hard left.

"If I'm not going to finish first, I'm sure as hell not going to let McGillicuddy do it!"

As he careened to the left, the bow of his craft crashed into the back of Vixen's airship, causing it to shake violently. Michael and Kamal were thrown to the ground and the rear portion of the hull crumbled. Two of the cables that fastened the hull to the gas bag snapped in the collision, and the rear of the craft drooped downward. The rotors were undamaged and the craft continued cruising forward until the lead increased to just over a full length, out of the galleon's striking range.

"Now, Kamal," Michael shouted. "Cut in front and set us up on a good line to go through the gate, we can't miss it. We only get one chance here."

The gate was a thousand yards out and they had a good line.

The fans whirred at a fever pitch as geysers of steam spewed from the engine compartment. Another pop, five, then six streams. Another pop, then seven. The whole engine glowed bright red.

"Just keep going," Michael said, "we're almost there. Just a few more seconds."

They were approaching the gate. Victory was theirs, and Michael knew it. They had a perfect line through, and the Ringmaster was behind them, blocked out from passage without a clean line other than straight through them. A few more seconds and Michael and his crew would be victorious. Michael relaxed and the airship glided smoothly through the gate with a whoosh.

"Yes!" Michael yelled, as they passed through.

A raucous cheer burst out from the ground below.

"Yes!" he yelled again with fists raised in the air. "Yes! Yes!"

His cheers were followed by a loud metallic bang, like metal pipes slamming together. The engine seized. The fan blades halted. The steam kettles burst with a giant blast of steam. Within seconds, the only sound Michael could hear was the sound of their craft gliding through the air, the wind passing as they drifted to the ground.

"Set her down on the lawn Kamal," Michael said. "We did it. We actually did it!"

Kamal landed the craft amid the throngs of cheering onlookers who had come to see the big finish. Hundreds, if not thousands of them. As they climbed down off the craft, they were greeted by Cyril Hastings, the emcee from Gatling Meadows and a host of other officials. Cyril held his hand out toward a group of people sitting at a table.

"Lest my congratulations come prematurely," Cyril said, "we will just need to validate your tokens, before officially declaring a winner. Right this way please."

Michael looked at Copper.

"Copper, would you like to do the honors?" he asked.

Copper held out a stubborn hand.

"No lad. Not this time. You're the one who got us here. You deserve it. Now you go on."

He grabbed Michael's hand with one hand, and reached into his pocket with the other. He pulled out the four thick, shiny tokens and placed them into Michael's hand. They fell into his palm with a heavy jangle, their polished finish glimmering in the sunlight.

"This is for you to do."

Kamal placed his hands together in front of his chest and gave a thankful bow.

Scarlet stepped forward.

"Not bad, Michael," she said with a smile. "You did a pretty good job out there. For a newcomer."

"Go on," Vixen said. "This means so much more to you than it does to any of us. You've earned it."

"We did it together," he said. "Thank you all so much."

The officiant at the table accepted his tokens and ran them through the validator. Each token ran its course through the levers and slots, and fell into the proper tin cup at the bottom. Michael knew they would. He never had any doubt.

"We have a winner!" Cyril declared.

He raised Michael's hand in the air. The crowd burst out in cheers, as fireworks exploded overhead. Copper and Kamal hoisted Michael up on their shoulders in excitement, bouncing him up and down in a celebratory dance.

"Let's get out of here," the Ringmaster said, watching what was happening below.

He never bothered to touch down at the finish.

"There's nothing down there for us, and I won't be seen to congratulate someone for taking what was rightfully mine. Rest assured, this isn't over."

Despite the celebrations and post-race festivities, the Ringmaster and what remained of his crew cruised off into the distance and disappeared into the clouds once again.

"Mi-chael! Mi-chael! Mi-chael!" Copper and Kamal started the chant. Vixen and Scarlet joined in, and before long it spread through the entire crowd. Michael sat on their shoulders, bouncing up and down, beaming with pride. Then he sighed. It was almost exactly as he'd always imagined. Almost.

EPILOGUE

Three months later...

A great deal transpired in the short period following the race. Michael, of course, was able to pay the taxes due, and he and Soairse continued working their land, just as they always had. With a new-found confidence, he quit his job with Mr. Wentworth and opened his own shop, *M. McGillicuddy, Gadgeteer*. He plied his talents and stretched his creative wings by taking up a new life, and making, well, whatever he wanted to. Never short of ideas, his business thrived and his reputation grew, as demand for his unique brand of gadgets soared. Cubetta boards and automatons were, of course, a specialty. But his other one-of-a-kind puzzles and games were also met with high demand. From time to time, companies hired him to design new industrial items, and he did some "special project" work for some very wealthy clients who generally wished to remain unnamed. He also hired Colin away from the factory, to help organize his inventory and to get him away from horrible Mr. Wentworth.

As for Vixen: She and Michael shared a deep-rooted affection. But they also recognized, reluctantly, that at least for the near-term it was best for each of them to return to their respective homes, and tend to their lives finishing up the obligations they had undertaken prior to the race. Intently focused on their respective work, they wrote and visited often, sometimes in London, sometimes in Utrecht. As for what would come next? They would figure it out when the time was right. For them, it was good enough for now, and they were happy with their arrangement.

As the bustling downtown was coming to life, the clock struck 9:00 a.m. on a Monday morning, and Michael was ready for the day. He hung the 'Open' sign in his shop window and started sketching some ideas he had for a new game when the bell on the door tinkled. He expected Colin to walk in, late as usual, but he was surprised when he looked up.

"Scarlet," he said. "Well, hello. What brings you here?"

His eyes shifted to the drawer behind the counter as he spoke.

"I've been meaning to speak with you for some time now, but I wanted to let things settle down first," she said.

"What's on your mind?"

"The Order of the Blue Cloak."

"The Order? The race is over. So, what about them?"

"You know they evaluated you from afar, yes? That shouldn't be news to you."

"Of course, that's how I was chosen to participate. So what about it?"

"That's not all there is to it, Michael. The race wasn't the end. The race itself was just one of many tests, part of a larger evaluation. The Order is so much larger than you understand right now. There's so much more to it. It's no accident that I sought you out at the starting line. I always intended to keep you close, because I suspected you would do well. I needed to keep a close eye on you. Whether you're aware of it or not, winning the race doesn't just afford you an elite status within the Order. It also comes with its own burdens."

She looked over her shoulder out the window.

"You'll be hearing from the Messenger soon."

"Cyril?"

"Yes, that's right. But exercise caution. Suffice to say, things are not necessarily as they seem."

She looked over he shoulder again.

"I should go. I'll be in touch again very soon, but in the meantime please take care of yourself."

She pulled a hood up to cover her head. She walked out the door, and the bell tinkled as she disappeared into the foot traffic outside. Michael opened the drawer behind the counter and pulled out a postcard. It was from Cyril Hastings, received just days earlier. It was just a short note, hastily scribbled in Cyril's own handwriting.

Michael,

I need to speak with you soon, to discuss some business pertinent to the Order. I'll visit you at my earliest convenience. I'm troubled by the activities of some of our members. Be wary of Scarlet Sinclair in particular. More when we speak.

Cyril

AFTERWORD

Thank you so much for taking the time to read *Michael McGillicuddy and the Most Amazing Race*. I hope you enjoyed reading it as much as I enjoyed writing it. If you loved the story and want to help others find it, please recommend it to a friend, or leave an online review if you have the time.

And stay tuned for a sequel…

Never miss a beat. You can sign up for my email list at http://www.trevordutcher.com and I'll keep you posted on coming announcements!

Made in the USA
San Bernardino, CA
04 February 2020